DECEPTION by DESIGN

Trish Beaudet

New Friends Publishing, LLC

Deception by Design

This is a work of fiction.
All characters and incidents are a product of the author's imagination.
Any relationship to persons living or dead is purely coincidental.

ISBN-13: 978-1-940354-03-3

Cover photo by Kristen Scott
Cover art by Claudia McKinney
Cover design by Catie Crehan

Published by
New Friends Publishing, LLC
Lake Havasu City, AZ

Visit New Friends Publishing's website at
www.newfriendspublishing.com

Printing history
First edition published in August 2013

Dedication

To those who have brought endless happiness, joy, and friendship into my life, and to those who have brought sadness, heartache, and disappointment, I thank you. It was because I experienced every one of these emotions that I was able to draw on them and bring these characters to life.

Acknowledgements

I owe an amazingly large debt of gratitude to my husband, Jim, for all his love, encouragement, and support. He is the one who has always believed in me, constantly telling me that I can. His unwavering faith in me is the reason this book came to be. To my children, Alyssa, Austin, and Christian, who stood by many times waiting to have my attention while I was writing, I thank you for your patience and understanding. To my cold readers, Dena, Stacey, Isabel, and Teri, your insight and critiques proved invaluable. Thank you for falling in love with the characters, and for feeling the emotions I did. The passion you felt for the story gave me the drive to see it in print. To my mother, who doesn't like to read, yet cried exactly when I expected her to, your tears made me truly believe I was an author. To my friend Jason Merrill, I appreciate the time you took to point me in the right direction. I will be forever grateful for all of your help. To my editor, William, thank you for helping me take my first steps down the literary path, and for recognizing the importance of keeping my voice. To Brad, who helped me find that voice, the journey has been worth traveling. And last, but certainly not least, to my best friend, Shannon, who is my Gia. Thank you for your constant encouragement, your wise words, your shoulder, your ear, your arms, and the occasional bitch slap when I need it. I am forever thankful that fate brought us together, and I feel very blessed to have such a beautiful friend in my life.

Prologue

Isabella closed her eyes and breathed in deeply. *How did I come to be in this place?* she wondered. Exhaling, she opened her eyes and took in all the guests who had gathered to see her. From her position in the back of the dimly lit room, she watched them interact with one another as they milled about. Why did they seem to be moving in slow motion? Was it them, or was it her? She was unsure, but she felt strange.

Then she heard the music. It was only a whisper, but the tune caught her attention. Isabella strained her ears to hear the arrangement and block out the noise of the conversations around her. There was something so familiar about the soft, soothing notes that tugged at her heart. She focused on the words, and it was then that she remembered hearing the same song played at her grandmother's funeral many years ago. A shiver ran up her spine. *How bizarre. Is it a coincidence?* she wondered as she squeezed her eyes shut, feeling the warm tears ready to spill over.

Breathing in deeply again, trying to find the strength, she pushed back her tears and opened her eyes, returning her attention to her friends. Some, she noticed, sat in quiet reflection, while others laughed in a way that she knew helped them to cope. Some just listened and smiled, acting as though they were present but undoubtedly wishing they were anywhere else. Who would want to be here? It was certainly not where Isabella wanted to be, certainly not what she had wanted.

She looked over at Ian, who was still a mystery to her. She could not read what was going through his mind. She knew now that if she had opened up to him, things would have ended differently. The sadness in his eyes made her regret her silence, and she turned away.

Her eyes settled on James, whom she could read like an open book. Her lip quivered as she tried to remember the sparkle that had filled his eyes just a few days earlier. She looked away, knowing she was the reason his sparkle had been extinguished. She wrapped her arms around herself as she walked past the rows of chairs, looking down at the floor to avoid the painful gazes of her friends.

She hadn't always been sad. In fact, like James, there had once been a sparkle in her eyes, back when she was happy. Now all of that was gone. There would be no more sparkle or happiness. There would be no more anything.

Her flowing white dress swept the floor as she made her way to the front of the room. Her mind raced. *I can't believe this is happening. I don't want to be here.* She wanted to run, to scream, to cry. *It wasn't supposed to be like this. It's my fault. It's always my fault—just like when Mom left me. I'm not a good person. I don't deserve their love. Why are they here? Look at them sitting there, supporting me.* She knew she should be grateful, should somehow show them how much she appreciated their presence, but she couldn't. All she could think about was him . . . the one she loved the most.

Isabella stopped at the foot of the bronze casket and placed her hand on top. The coolness of the metal made her shudder. She bowed her head and finally allowed the tears that had been welling up inside her to fall as she remembered . . .

Chapter 1

Grayson Hughes lay in bed, staring up at the steel beams on the ceiling, thinking of the day ahead but cautiously trying not to focus on what it could mean. He had been through this before, but this time it had to be different.

The morning sun streamed through the windows onto his body, which was half covered by a white sheet. He brushed the hair from his eyes. Like his father and his grandfather, he had been blessed with sandy blond hair that fell in careless waves. He had always kept it longer than his mother would have liked, but she felt that there were more pressing issues to nag him about, so she let her dismay go. Though he had his father's hair, Grayson had inherited her creative mind and artistic skill. And it was her eyes, blue as the Caribbean Sea, that he saw each morning when he looked into the mirror—a daily reminder of her now that she was gone.

Thirteen years. Had it really been that long since he had seen his parents? Sometimes it felt like it was just yesterday that he had gotten the call. His mother and father had been in London, celebrating yet another one of his mother's successful contributions to a well-known art gallery, when the brakes had failed in the car they were driving and they had blown through a red light. The crash had killed them both instantly. Grayson was devastated, as he and his father were close. Even though he was already twenty-four years old, being an only child with no other family to speak of, he felt alone and lost. Like Grayson, his father had become another casualty of his mother, Lauren Hughes. *Damn her*, he thought.

Despite his grief over losing his father, Grayson had also felt relief, followed quickly by guilt. He was free. He would no longer have to live in the shadow of his mother's success. He had never quite measured up to her standards, and in some way, she had always made him feel like a failure. There came a point in his life when he was resigned to the notion that he belonged in her shadow, and he had drifted away from her clutches. It wasn't until after her death that he had stepped back out into the light and tried to become as successful in the art community as she had been—not to make her proud, but to prove that he didn't need to ride her coattails to make something of himself.

He squinted as the sun shone through a gap in the curtains and temporarily blinded him. His light hair, light eyes, and olive skin contrasted with the features of his beautiful wife, Isabella, with her deep brown eyes, creamy skin, and silky hair the color of dark chocolate.

"Isabella," Grayson whispered to himself. His thoughts traveled to her as they had so many times recently. Had he failed her as he had failed his mother? *How could I not?* he thought. She would never admit it, though. Isabella didn't have it in her to stir that relationship pot, but he knew when she looked at him that she must share his mother's disappointment.

Grayson returned his attention to the beams on the ceiling, recalling her excitement when the beams were uncovered during the renovation six years earlier. Of course, it was Isabella who had purchased the loft. He had been content in their tiny one-bedroom apartment and didn't understand the need for such an expansive space. But, after much begging and pleading on Isabella's part, he had given in, as he always did. Some things just weren't worth it—like the arguments he'd had with his mother. She had been the one in control, and he knew it was best to just stand there and nod. Unbeknownst to Isabella, he did that quite often with her.

There wasn't one wall, ceiling, or floor in the loft that Isabella had left untouched. With her master plan, she had overseen the demolition, construction, and installation of every detail. Grayson shook his head, remembering the countless hours she had spent picking the right tile, the perfect hardwood, the spectacular furniture pieces—all the while dragging him along when he didn't care and would have preferred to be working on his paintings.

He closed his eyes, letting the warm sun beam on his face again, wishing his anxiety away as he tried to take comfort in the silence. He groaned when he heard her footsteps on the staircase. He was not in the mood for talking and wanted to be left alone with his thoughts.

He opened his eyes as Isabella came bounding into their second-floor master suite, wearing one of his white dress shirts and carrying a breakfast tray. Through the thin fabric he could see the outline of her perfect breasts and tiny waist, which instantly aroused him. Her long hair was tousled and fell loosely over her shoulders. She was a vision of beauty.

"Good morning, my love!" Isabella said, beaming from ear to ear. "Do you know what today is?"

"Yes, Izzie, how could I forget?" He didn't share his wife's enthusiasm.

Isabella set the tray down on the silk-upholstered bench in front of their bed and plopped onto her knees next to him. Grayson noticed her mischievous mood, and he let out a deep sigh. He was not in the mood for games.

Isabella leaned in close to him. The gold flecks in her brown eyes sparkled in the morning light. "Hmmm . . . well, Mr. Grumpypants, I wouldn't expect you to forget about your gallery showing tonight, but our anniversary . . . now that's a different story." She winked. Her face told him that she knew he had forgotten.

Feeling like a total shit, Grayson frowned. "Baby, I'm so sorry. I don't know what to say. With everything that's been going on . . ."

Isabella put her index finger on his lips to silence him. She kissed him softly, then pulled back and met his gaze. "You have nothing to apologize for," she assured him. "I love you, and I know you love me. I also know that this show tonight means a lot to you, as it should. And, Mr. Hughes, considering you have not forgotten the previous nine anniversaries, you're off the hook this time." She planted another kiss on his lips before hopping off the bed.

Ten years. Had it been that long? Feeling more depressed now than when he had woken up, Grayson continued to lie there as his wife bounded off toward their bathroom. At the door Isabella turned, smiling, oblivious to his tainted mood.

"When your artwork is a success," she said, "you can repay me one day, my love. Now eat your breakfast, because you're going to need your energy today. I made your favorite—cinnamon French toast with sausage. I wish I could join you, but I have to get to the office." Isabella blew him a kiss and slid the bathroom door closed.

If she only knew, he thought. If she only knew how much it weighed on him every day, every moment he breathed. The weight had been there for years, just as it had been there with his mother. He closed his eyes and sighed.

"One day . . . one day."

Chapter 2

Isabella raced down the front stairs of her building, juggling her briefcase and a steaming cup of her favorite hazelnut coffee. She looked impeccable as always in a long-sleeved, lavender silk blouse, black pencil skirt, and her signature five-inch stilettos, bringing her vertically challenged five-foot-five-inch frame to a full five-ten. She had gone for a simple, sleek look today, with diamond stud earrings and her long hair pulled back in a high ponytail. Isabella's wardrobe decisions were always based on two things: who she was meeting, and where she was going. In her twelve years of running her interior design business, she knew exactly what impression each of her clients expected of her. She prided herself on personally knowing each client, and she worked on every aspect of their project. Nothing was done without her expertise, her hand, or her creative eye touching it.

Isabella hit the bottom step of her building, and on cue, as he did every morning, Sebastian, her driver, opened the door to her Town Car.

"Good morning, Mrs. Hughes," he greeted her.

Isabella smiled and hurried past him, throwing her briefcase into the car. "Good morning, Sebastian. Could I please ask you a favor?" Not waiting to hear his answer, Isabella slid into the back seat.

Smiling, Sebastian shut her door and slid into the driver's seat, already knowing the favor. "Yes, Mrs. Hughes, I'll step on it."

But despite Sebastian's best intentions, the car crept along through bumper-to-bumper traffic. Isabella used the time to read and return a few emails. *Why is traffic so bad?* she wondered. She kept looking down at her watch, knowing full well she was late.

"Why can't I ever be on time?" she muttered. "I try, I really do. I don't know what the hell happens!" She looked up from her BlackBerry when she heard Sebastian laughing.

"Mrs. Hughes, I have been driving you for six years now. I know and accept the fact that you're always late, and I think it's time that you do too." Isabella started to protest, but Sebastian held up his hand. "Save it, young lady. What is it you always call it, your designer fifteen minutes, right?"

Isabella waved him off with a smile, knowing he was right. "Yeah, whatever, smartass. Just keep driving!"

Finally they pulled up in front of the forty-two-story office building that held Isabella's design firm, Hughes & Associates. The office, located in the middle of downtown Manhattan, occupied the entire top floor. Every day that Isabella arrived, she was reminded of the modest design studio where she had started her business twelve years before. The thought of the tiny one-room design studio packed from floor to ceiling with samples, not to mention the countless files that buried her desk, kept her grounded and thankful for where she had started out and how far she had come.

Isabella had led a simple and quiet life while growing up in a small town in Ohio. She had never known her father. Her mother, unable to cope with being a single parent, had disappeared, leaving Isabella to be raised by her grandparents, whom she adored. She enjoyed being on the farm when she was younger but always knew she wanted to spread her wings and fly far away from that life. Her loving but strict grandparents had taught her what it meant to have a strong work ethic and made her participate in daily farm chores before she headed off to school each morning. Isabella focused her time on her studies and her duties on the farm, and didn't have many friends. Rumors about how her mother had abandoned her had flown around town faster than a raging forest fire. She became known as the girl whose mother didn't want her. Her classmates thought there was something wrong with her and would tease her until she ran home in tears to the safety of her grandmother's arms. Unfortunately, even though her grandmother insisted differently, Isabella believed the kids at school were right. Despite the many talks she'd had with her grandmother, and despite the reassurance that it was her mother who had the problem and not her, Isabella knew deep inside that there must have been something she had done, or something she was missing, to make her mother leave.

Her grandmother would take her on long walks to the pond at the far end of their property, where she loved to watch the ducks swim and play. After weeks of anxiously awaiting the birth of a new family of baby chicks, Isabella had run to the nest to find that all the eggs had hatched and the chicks were gone. Well, all but one.

"What happened to the babies, Gammy?" Isabella asked, looking adorably innocent in her little red dress and pigtails as she looked up at her grandmother, confused.

"Well, sweetheart, they hatched and went off with the mommy duck to learn to swim and fend for themselves."

Isabella examined the small chick still left in the nest and then looked back at her grandmother. "Why did they leave without this one?"

Her grandmother gazed down at the tiny sleeping chick, knowing it was sick and wouldn't live much longer. She sighed. "Well, it looks like this one is special and the mommy knew she wouldn't be able to take care of it."

Isabella bent down and carefully picked up the chick in her tiny hands, feeling sad for the baby bird. "It's just like me," Isabella whispered as tears filled her eyes. "There's something wrong with it. The mommy didn't want it."

"Bella, you know there is nothing wrong with you. You are perfect."

Isabella shook her head and looked back down at the baby chick. "Gammy, can I bring it back to the barn with us? I promise I'll take care of it, really I will," she begged.

Her grandmother touched Isabella's face. She knew Isabella couldn't bear the thought of the chick being left behind. "You sure can. I know you'll make the chick very happy."

"Thank you, Gammy, you're the best!" She grinned from ear to ear.

The memory made Isabella smile even now. She remembered how surprised her grandmother had been that the chick thrived under her care and stayed around the farm for many years following her around as she did her chores. Dudley, as Isabella called him, became her only friend in the world.

Her grandfather had fallen ill and passed away before she had graduated from high school. It wasn't long after his passing that her grandmother died of what Isabella believed was a broken heart. Although her grandparents had left the farm to her, she knew she couldn't stay. There were too many memories, and the pain was too difficult to bear. She had sold the farm right after her graduation, packed up her few belongings, and left for New York, where she enrolled in NYU. Isabella was determined to make something of herself and make her grandparents proud.

Fresh out of college with her diploma in hand, she had begun her business at the age of twenty-two with a dream of becoming an established, successful interior designer. The first year was hard. There were times when she wanted to give up because she had no support from friends or family. Even though she had the determination and drive she had learned from her grandparents, it wasn't until Grayson had come into her life that she flourished.

She remembered the day like it was yesterday. She was at her friend Brayden's house for a Christmas party. The mood was festive, and everyone was having a good time, even Isabella, despite the fact that she didn't know many people there. She never had problems engaging in conversation with others, even strangers. She thoroughly enjoyed getting to know people, and they gravitated toward her. It was then that she saw him on the balcony, smoking a cigarette and running his hand through his sandy blond hair, his blue eyes sparkling. He was stunningly handsome.

Brayden approached her and noticed her staring through the French doors, mesmerized. "Oh, for the love of God, do I need to get a tissue to catch the drool dripping from your mouth?"

Isabella laughed. "I'm sorry, was I that obvious? Who is that? And why have you been holding out on me?"

Brayden grabbed her by the hand and pulled her outside. "Oh please, honey," he said quietly. "You know I only hold out on the cute ones if I'm not sure which pond they fish in, but this one, I can assure you, fishes in your pond . . . trust me."

Isabella put her arm around him. "Thank gosh. And by the way, have I told you how much I love you?" She kissed his cheek.

"Yeah, yeah. I'm sure that's the alcohol talking. But just in case, do me a favor and remember to make me a bridesmaid. I've always wanted to wear a pretty pink dress."

Isabella laughed and shook her head. "No pink! You are such a princess!"

The man on the balcony turned as Isabella and Brayden approached. Brayden gave her a nudge, pushing her closer to him. "Grayson, I'd like to introduce you to my friend Isabella. Isabella, this is Grayson Hughes."

Isabella extended her hand. "It's a pleasure to meet you." She smiled up at him through her lashes.

He drew her hand to his lips and kissed it. "The pleasure is all mine, I can assure you." Grayson's blue eyes danced as he smiled back at her.

Butterflies fluttered in her stomach, and her cheeks burned. His soothing voice and mesmerizing eyes made Isabella weak in the knees.

Brayden watched the two of them for a moment and rolled his eyes. "Now both of you play nice with one another while I go fix myself another martini. My work here is done." Brayden turned on his heels and pranced away.

Isabella and Grayson laughed as they watched him hurry back to the bar.

The next month was a whirlwind for the two of them. They were constantly together. She would later tell him that it was during that month she had fallen in love with him. The chemistry between them was intense. She had never wanted anyone as much as she wanted him, and he felt the same about her. They shared so much with each other, talking for hours about their feelings, their innermost thoughts, their hopes and dreams, their deepest fears. They made love over and over. The touch of his hand, the way he kissed her, sent warmth through her like she had never felt before. The more she had of him, the more she wanted. The more he had of her, the more he wanted. She would never forget the way he took her face in his hands when they were in bed, looked deep into her eyes, and never broke eye contact as he kissed her. It was so sensual, so intimate. It made her melt. Grayson touched a place in her that she had never known, and she never wanted the feeling to end. This was true love, she was sure of it.

Grayson had exposed Isabella to his world. She loved sitting on the floor of his cramped apartment, watching him paint. She was mesmerized by the ease with which his creations came to life. He took her to galleries throughout the city and explained the paintings and the meaning behind them. Grayson ignited a creative passion within her that excited her senses, helping her thrive in the design world.

Things with Grayson were simple and easy. Isabella enjoyed their laid-back dates spent lounging on a blanket in Central Park. They looked up at the cloud formations for hours as Grayson told the story of each cloud as he saw it. It was there in the park, on a blanket, that Grayson had proposed to her, telling her the most romantic cloud story.

Six months to the day after they had met, Isabella and Grayson had eloped, marrying on a beach in the Caribbean. It was the happiest moment of her life and everything she had dreamed it to be. Brayden pouted for weeks about not being a bridesmaid, but in time he forgave her.

With Grayson in her life, Isabella flourished, as did her business. As an artist, Grayson brought out new creativity in her. He seemed to know how to motivate her when she doubted her abilities and wanted to give up. He was always by her side, encouraging her to push through the difficult times and achieve her goals. She was thankful he had come into her life and that fate had brought them together.

Isabella smiled at the memory as she hurried inside her building. She ran and caught the elevator door just before it closed, sighing with relief. When the elevator opened on her floor, her flamboyant assistant, James, was standing there, tapping his Burberry loafer and looking at his watch. Isabella rolled her eyes as she rushed from the elevator and flew past him like a bolt of lightning, trying to avoid the inquisition.

James turned and was on her heels, handing her the papers she had requested for her meeting. "These are the final estimates from the contractors. I've already added them to the proposal binder and—"

"Thank you, James," she said curtly and took the papers from him, never missing a beat in her step.

James was almost at a run, wondering how the hell she managed to move so fast in her damn stilettos. "So you're all set for the meeting, which I might add you're late for." James stopped his speed walk as Isabella continued down the hallway. Out of breath and convinced he really needed to hit the gym, James yelled out to her, "Conference Room Two!"

Isabella turned at the end of the hall and entered the conference room through a large mahogany door. The room was situated in a corner of the building and offered a spectacular view of the city on three sides. The June sun streamed in through the windows, casting a glow through the room that enhanced the warm, modern decor. Isabella had selected a soft crème brûlée silk covering for the wainscotted walls, and white silk drapery panels were strategically placed on the windows so as to not obscure the impressive downtown view. Three large crystal chandeliers hung over the ebony-stained custom conference table. Comfortable, high-back cream velvet chairs embellished with nail heads sat around the table.

Her client Richard Lafayette sat at the table, along with his business partner, Jonathan, and Isabella's design assistant and best friend, Gia. Richard was shrewd and arrogant—a pompous ass, really—but Isabella had learned how to appease him when she worked on his projects. Privately, she believed he had a soft spot for her, so, like any woman would, she used that to her advantage.

Richard and Jonathan looked irritated. Isabella glanced around the room and noticed that Gia had displayed all four design boards of the project as she requested and had placed the project binders properly before them.

Isabella smiled warmly, trying to melt the ice she felt as she walked into the room. "Gentleman, my apologies for running behind this morning." She didn't offer any excuse for her tardiness, as she knew Richard couldn't care less about excuses. "I take it that Gia has gone through the design boards and concepts of the project with you?"

"Yes, very thoroughly, I might add." Richard pursed his lips.

Isabella shot a questioning look at Gia, but Gia shrugged and looked back down at her papers. *What the hell has she done this time?* Isabella wondered.

"Bottom line, Isabella, your designs are amazing, as always," Richard said in his usual icy tone, "but we have discussed our budget restrictions with you in detail. I'm not willing to exceed that."

Isabella had known this was coming. She smirked and reached for the two binders, handing one to him and the other to Jonathan. "Then I take it you haven't read over the budget breakdown. Why don't you open that binder and let me know what you think?"

Richard and Jonathan flipped through the binders, searching for the breakdown.

"Last page, gentlemen." Isabella smiled confidently as she waited.

"Well, well, Isabella, I believe you have outdone yourself here. All of these contractors are available and ready to go?"

Isabella knew she had Richard right where she wanted him. "Yes, Richard. Just say the word."

Jonathan leaned forward, staring Isabella down. "And you will personally oversee the entire project start to finish?"

Isabella leaned toward him and smiled sweetly, although she had never cared for him. "As I always do."

Richard closed his binder and stood up, prompting Jonathan to stand as well. Gia tried to hide her smirk as she got up and moved to the door.

Richard extended his hand to Isabella. "You will have the signed contracts on your desk by the end of business today. Well done."

She shook his hand. "Thank you, Richard. It's always a pleasure doing business with you." She looked at Jonathan and extended her hand to him as well. "Jonathan, nice to see you again."

Her skin crawled as his limp, clammy hand took hers. "Likewise. I look forward to working with you again." He winked at her, causing bile to rise in her throat.

Gia opened the door for Richard and Jonathan. As she left to escort the men out of the office, she turned back and looked at Isabella. The two friends smiled at each other triumphantly.

~~~

Isabella's office sat on the opposite end of the floor from the conference room. It was identical in size and shared the same fabulous view. Her warm, modern, glam taste in design was exemplified by her office. She had chosen stunning Italian white marble flooring, laced with flecks of sparkling silver. When she had first seen it, she had literally gasped in awe. Every time she walked into her office, it looked as if she were walking on thousands of tiny diamonds. Her desk had been custom made to her specifications, with a massive, high-gloss white desktop and crystal legs. The drawers were large enough to hide everything that usually covered the desktop in case she needed to clear it off in a hurry. The drawer pulls were vintage crystal doorknobs, each
~~~

with a small white diamond in the center.

Her desk chair was large compared to her tiny frame. She had lost count of the times Gia or James had thought she was out of her office when the chair was turned out to face the windows. That worked well, as there were moments when she needed time to herself. The tufted chair matched those in the conference room, with a straight back and large, comfortable arms, but with larger nail heads and white velvet instead of cream.

On the wall opposite her desk stood a twelve-foot-tall bookcase made of glass, with gold leaf on the interior surfaces. Isabella had the glass cut to create curves on top. In the center of the bookcase hung an impressive sixty-inch flat-panel plasma TV, which had come in handy for private presentations in her office. But Isabella preferred to have music playing when she worked. She found that it helped her to focus and stay calm.

To the left of the bookcase, Isabella had created a comfortable sitting area where she could host casual conversations or relax while working. The sofa had a neo-baroque frame with an intricate, hand-carved scrolling design. It was sprayed with an impeccable white, high-gloss finish. She had chosen vibrant hot pink velvet upholstery and had the back tufted with rhinestones. Sitting low in front of the sofa was a large, square cocktail table made of clear acrylic. Isabella liked to keep the top clean, with just a few of her favorite magazines and a white coral sculpture that sat on a crystal base. Flanking the sofa on either side were two robust round end tables done in gold crocodile leather. The curve of their legs replicated the curved legs on her desk. On top of the end tables sat two massive lamps with sheer silk shades. Thousands of crystals varying in size dangled from within the lampshades so that they resembled crystal chandeliers.

Adjacent to the sofa were two Barcelona chairs covered in the highest quality Italian navy blue leather. In between the chairs sat a petrified tree trunk with a gnarly wood finish. Grounding the furniture was a white, fluffy fur rug that Isabella loved to feel on her bare feet after she kicked off her stilettos for the day.

She was standing behind her desk, looking over some contracts, when Gia strutted into the office. “Thanks for keeping me hanging this morning,” Gia said. “I was ready to take off my shoes and show them what a great pedicure I got the other day.” Her long, curly red hair bounced over her shoulders as she plopped down in one of the chairs in front of Isabella’s desk. Isabella wondered if she ever even attempted to run a comb through it.

"I'm sorry, I know, but I wanted to make sure Grayson started his day off well this morning."

Gia smirked and raised an eyebrow. "I bet you did. Did someone get their freak on before coming to work?"

"Get your mind out of the gutter where it always seems to be. Breakfast, hello! Remember, it's our anniversary today." Isabella rolled her eyes and smiled, remembering just why she loved Gia so much. She was the yin to Isabella's yang.

The two had met at a flea market one morning shortly after Isabella had met Grayson. They were looking at the same vintage dresser when they struck up a conversation. Two weeks later, Isabella ran into Gia again at a coffee shop near her design studio, and the two had been inseparable ever since. Gia, having a background in design as well, had come to work for Isabella one month later. She had been a valuable asset, not only as a talented associate, but as Isabella's confidante and most trusted friend. Everything there was to know about Isabella she kept safely tucked away in her mind, occasionally using this as a bargaining tool to get something she wanted, proclaiming she was the "keeper of all secrets."

Gia's style was the opposite of Isabella's. A little loud and sometimes off the wall, Gia wore things Isabella wouldn't dare, but somehow she always managed to pull off the outfits.

"You wear fishnet thigh-highs and look adorable," Isabella complained. "I wear them and feel like I should have a corner in Chinatown."

Gia laughed Isabella's insecurities away, telling her, "It's not the clothes you wear, it's the confidence you exude while wearing them."

The two friends had developed a favorite pastime of flea-marketing together, heading out bright and early on the weekends to look for vintage furniture pieces for clients and, of course, vintage couture prize finds for themselves. Grayson didn't mind. In fact, he had happily given up schlepping around with Isabella, looking at what he called "old junk." It gave him more time to paint, knowing too well that the flea market outings took up a large portion of the day and always ended with lunch and plenty of wine to soothe aching feet.

"Excuse me, but what's wrong with the gutter option?" Gia said, laughing. "Happy anniversary, by the way." She threw a pen at Isabella.

"Nice, Gia. Thank you . . . I think." Isabella returned her attention to her paperwork.

Isabella was startled when Gia popped up straight in her chair and exclaimed, "Hey, by the way, good work in there today playing poker with Richard. Nice touch!"

Isabella smiled and leaned back in her chair. "Yes, well, handling Richard has become an art of mine. This is what, the fifth project of his we've taken on? And with each one he makes me jump through all these hoops, only in the end to award us the design. Typical Richard."

"And you're going to oversee every aspect of the project on your own, hmmm?" Gia raised an eyebrow, knowing the answer, but she always liked goading Isabella.

Isabella picked up the pen that Gia had thrown and tossed it back at her. "No, my sweet Gia, *we* are."

Acting deflated, Gia fell back into her chair. "I knew it. By the way, what was up with Jonathan? He gives me the creeps."

"You and me both. Thank goodness we won't have much contact with him during the renovations. Speaking of which, I would like to get in touch with Tyler this morning and let him know we are a go on this project. I want to make sure he starts rallying the troops so they're ready to go."

"I agree," Gia said, picking at her chipped nail polish.

"Great. I'm glad you do." Isabella watched Gia pick away. "So why don't you make yourself useful and get on that?"

"Oh, I'm supposed to call?" Gia asked, looking up.

"Unless you would rather sit here and braid each other's hair all day."

"As tempting as that sounds . . . all right, point made. I'm going. Is there anything else I can do for you, Princess?"

"As a matter of fact, can you grab the files we left in the project room last night?"

"As you wish." Gia hopped up and bowed before heading out of the office.

"Oh, and Gia . . . it's Queen Bitch, not Princess."

Isabella laughed as Gia flipped her the finger before disappearing down the hall.

Isabella couldn't believe how fast the day flew by. Between the meetings and the countless phone calls, she couldn't remember if she had even eaten anything. Standing behind her desk while on the phone with one of her suppliers, Isabella stared out the window and watched the sun sinking in the distance. Seeing the beautiful, serene sunset, she could only imagine how gorgeous the day had been outside the walls of her office.

She was hanging up when James pranced into her office with a large envelope and garment bag in hand. "The contracts Madame signed and sent over from Richard's office," James announced as he handed her the envelope. Then he held out the garment bag, balancing the hanger on his finger. "And your dress for the gallery showing, which I picked up because I knew you would be running late."

Isabella looked down at her Rolex and jumped straight out of her chair. "Oh shit! I'm running late. Seriously, Grayson is going to kill me." She ran around the desk, grabbed the garment bag from James's finger, and planted a kiss on his cheek. "You are a lifesaver, James. What in the world would I ever do without you?"

Isabella hung the garment bag on a hook and unzipped it, revealing a beaded, champagne-colored cocktail dress.

James shook his head. "I can't even fathom the thought. You would be a hot mess, sister."

Isabella smiled as she pulled the dress from the bag. "Did you grab my . . ." She turned to see her crystal-encrusted Christian Louboutin shoes dangling from his finger. ". . . shoes?"

James handed her the shoes and leaned in to hug her. "Hot mess!" he said, looking at her over the black frames of his glasses.

Chapter 3

Isabella checked the time again as the black Town Car pulled up to the Stratton Gallery on West 29th Street. She was an hour late, more than her usual designer fifteen, and Grayson would not be happy with her. She hurried inside, noticing that a large crowd had already gathered and were milling around, looking at Grayson's art pieces.

The guests seemed to be in a festive mood. Waiters strolled through the crowd with trays of appetizers and champagne. Even Isabella had to admit that she looked stunning in her beaded cocktail dress, which she had recently purchased from one of her favorite boutiques in Manhattan. Not having much time to dilly-dally with her hair, she had simply taken her high ponytail and brought it low on her neck into a loose but elegant chignon.

As she searched the crowd for Grayson, she grabbed a glass of champagne from a passing tray. Finally she found him standing amongst a group of his friends, laughing and smiling. That was good, she thought. Maybe he wouldn't be pissed at her after all. She wandered over and came up behind him, putting her arms around his waist and kissing him on the cheek.

Grayson turned his head slightly, still engaged in conversation with his friends. "Why am I not surprised that you're late?" he whispered.

"I'm sorry, baby," Isabella whispered back.

Grayson's friend Aidan was the first to notice her. "Isabella, it's so nice of you to join us!" he exclaimed, causing the entire group to turn toward Isabella.

Isabella shot him an annoyed look.

"Stuck at the office again with a big design emergency?" he continued. "Tell us, was the shantung you ordered the wrong color?"

Isabella rolled her eyes and smirked back at him. "You're very funny, Aidan. Always the comedian. By the way, it concerns me that a man like you knows what shantung is." Isabella tilted her head and raised an eyebrow.

The others burst into laughter.

Isabella turned her attention to them. "Hi, guys. Sorry I'm late. How are things going? What does everyone think of Grayson's new pieces?"

"I personally think this man here has out done himself this time," Grayson's friend Andre chimed in. He walked through the group to give Isabella a hug. "It's so great to see you," he said, kissing her cheek. "You're looking beautiful as always. You didn't miss much, honestly. We were just discussing which piece is our favorite. What's yours?"

Isabella returned his squeeze. "Actually, I haven't seen anything yet." Isabella jabbed her elbow into Grayson's side. "This one here has been very secretive, locked away in his studio, not willing to allow his wife a look."

Grayson looked down at her and cracked a small smile.

"I was thinking of buying this one to hang on the wall in front of my toilet," Aidan said as he walked to a nearby painting.

Isabella shook her head in disgust. "You're such a shit, Aidan—pun intended."

The love/hate relationship between Aidan and Isabella provided plenty of entertainment for the group of friends. The sarcasm they threw back and forth at each other added a comical dynamic to their circle. It was always in good fun, though.

Just then, the gallery owner walked up to the group and touched Grayson on the arm. Grayson turned to her and announced, "Everyone, I would like to introduce Elise Stratton, the owner of the gallery."

Isabella was the first to extend a hand to Elise. "It's an absolute pleasure to meet you Elise, Isabella Hughes. I've heard so many good things about you."

Elise smiled and reciprocated the handshake. "Likewise, Isabella. Grayson, can I steal you away for a moment? I have someone important that I would like to introduce you to."

"If you would excuse me," Grayson said to his friends as Elise escorted him away.

Isabella wandered through the gallery, taking in the art that Grayson had created. She soon realized why he had been so secretive about it. The pieces were quite different from anything Grayson had done before. His previous work had always calmed her. Her favorite piece hung in the dining area of their loft over an antique mirrored buffet. A distressed gold and silver frame set off the painting's beautiful descending colors of blue, cream, and gold. It reminded Isabella of the beach where she and Grayson had been married. The depth of the color palette, how each color transitioned into the next, left her breathless every time she looked at it.

No, these new pieces certainly did not evoke those same feelings. Moody and dark, scattered and chaotic—these were the words that came to her mind as she stood before each one. His characteristic soft color palettes were replaced with bold, harsh shades layered on the canvas with hard strokes. Isabella was reminded of a storm at sea, engulfing everything in its path. These pieces did take her breath away, but not in a warm sense. Instead, she felt a sense of shock. Her heart pumped violently, and blood rushed to her face.

Not sure if it was the champagne on an empty stomach, or the sudden realization that something was disturbingly off with Grayson, Isabella started to feel flushed and woozy. She snatched a few sushi rolls off a passing tray, hoping the rice would help settle her stomach. She sat down on a bench in front of the final piece and devoured the rolls.

Feeling a little better, she scanned the gallery for Grayson and saw him engaged in conversation with a tall, distinguished-looking gentleman. Isabella stood, steadying herself to make sure she was, in fact, feeling better before she wandered over to join the conversation. When Grayson noticed her approaching, he looked at her with questioning eyes, but Isabella winked back to assure him she was okay.

"Mr. Vanderbeck, I'd like to introduce you to my wife, Isabella. Isabella, this is Charles Vanderbeck."

Vanderbeck smiled, flashing perfectly white veneers. "It's a pleasure to meet you, Isabella."

"The pleasure is mine, Mr. Vanderbeck. Are you enjoying the show?"

"Very much so. You have a talented husband. His work intrigues me. The intensity speaks volumes. It's quite surprising."

Isabella looked at Grayson, and their eyes met. "Yes, very surprising."

"Do you share your husband's passion for creating?" Vanderbeck asked, not noticing the look they were exchanging.

Isabella nodded. "I do, sir. I am a designer by trade."

"Interiors or clothing?"

Isabella smiled, wishing she could design her own clothing. God knew she bought enough of it. "Interior. I specialize in commercial design."

Vanderbeck put his hand to his chin in thought. "Hughes . . . Hughes . . . Hughes & Associates, right?"

"Very good, sir. Yes, guilty as charged."

Grayson, who had been quietly watching the interaction between Isabella and Vanderbeck, stepped back as if to remove himself from the conversation.

"The Lafayette building over on Fifth, was that your handiwork?"

Vanderbeck was asking.

Isabella was surprised and impressed that he had recognized her work. "Yes, Richard Lafayette has been a client of mine for years. In fact, my firm was just awarded his new project this morning."

Vanderbeck shook his head. "How many more buildings does that man need?" He laughed. "I've had the unfortunate pleasure of meeting him. My sympathies go out to you, young lady."

Isabella laughed with him. "Thank you, but honestly, Richard is all bark. After working with him over the years, I know how he ticks and what keeps him happy: on time and under budget."

Feeling Grayson's stare, Isabella glanced in his direction. She sensed something was not quite right with him, but minded her manners and returned her attention to Vanderbeck.

"Ah yes, he has quite a reputation for being a penny pincher, and that is as kind as I can be in describing that man." Vanderbeck looked at Isabella as though something had triggered a thought. "You know, I just acquired a large space myself and was looking for a designer. To be honest, I've had it with the overpriced drama queen I'm currently using. I could use someone like you, with your obvious sense of style and what seems to me savvy business sense. Interested?"

"I would absolutely be interested and honored to work for you."

He reached into the inside pocket of his tailored Calvin Klein suit and produced a business card, which he handed to Isabella. "Call me tomorrow and we'll schedule a meeting."

Isabella took the card from him, noticing the expensive cardstock. "I'm looking forward to it. I'll call you first thing tomorrow."

After they had said their goodbyes, Isabella turned to find that Grayson had left. She began searching the gallery for him, sensing that something was very wrong.

~~~

Isabella and Grayson arrived back at their loft in Soho around midnight after a long, silent, uncomfortable ride home. Isabella had tracked him down at the gallery but had barely gotten two words out of him. He had spent the drive back staring out the window, not willing to accept her attempts at conversation. When the Town Car pulled up in front of their building, Grayson hopped out before it could come to a complete stop. Isabella wished Sebastian a good night and hurried in after her husband.

Five stories up, Grayson pulled open the large metal door to their loft and walked inside. Isabella shut the heavy door behind them, pushing the bolt through the metal latch, then watched Grayson as he went to the
~~~

kitchen.

"You haven't said a word since we left the gallery," she called out after him. "Is everything okay?"

"I'm fine," he mumbled.

She found him in the kitchen, pouring a glass of scotch. He kept his attention conspicuously on the glass as she leaned on the counter and watched, taking note that the amount of scotch was higher than usual.

"I think the turnout was good, don't you?" Isabella asked.

"It was fine," he said before taking a long gulp of the scotch.

"There seemed to be a good amount of interest in the pieces, don't you think?"

He avoided eye contact with her. She could tell that he was starting to get annoyed. "Yeah, I guess."

Tired of the guessing game, Isabella grabbed the glass from his hand. "Grayson, what is wrong? I've gotten three short answers from you. It's obvious that something is bothering you. Talk to me, damn it!"

He ripped the glass out of her hand and downed the last of the remaining scotch, then poured another glass. He took a swig, set the glass on the counter, and stared at it before finally looking up at Isabella's pleading eyes. "Please tell me why you came to the gallery tonight, Isabella."

Although relieved that he was finally talking, she was confused by the question. "I don't understand. Why wouldn't I be there? You're my husband, this was a big night for you, and I wanted to be there to show you my love and support."

Grayson shook his head and took another drink. "You're right. It *was* a big night for me, and it was going well until you decided to step in."

"I'm not following you."

Grayson grew more irritated. "Vanderbeck!" he spat. "Christ, Isabella, do you have any idea who he is and the influence he has in the community?"

Isabella was stunned by his anger. "I'm sorry, Grayson. I didn't realize—"

Grayson cut her off. "Where have you been for the last six months? My gosh, Isabella, are you so wrapped up in your own world that you don't even hear what I say to you? Do you listen when I speak, or do I just waste my breath? Vanderbeck came there tonight to see my pieces and discuss the possibility of commissioning me to do some work for him on a larger scale!" Grayson was shouting now. "Do you have any idea what that meant for me? Do you?"

"And that can't happen now just because I spoke with him?" Isabella shouted back.

"As soon as you walked over, the man completely lost interest in me and my work."

"Now you're being ridiculous."

More agitated, Grayson felt the pressure inside, the pressure he had kept hidden from her, ready to explode. "Am I? Am I really, Isabella? Let me ask you this, then. Did he purchase any of the pieces tonight? Let me answer that for you: no, he did not! And please tell me which one of us walked out of there tonight with his card? Yes, that would be you now, wouldn't it?"

Isabella was horrified. She had never seen him like this. Sure, he got angry from time to time, but this rage was disturbing. "What the hell has gotten into you? Where is all this anger coming from? I love you, and I would never sabotage your night or get in the way of your dreams of being a successful artist. You know I totally support you!"

"That's right, Izzie, *you* support *me*. Don't you get it? For once in my life I would like to have something of my own, buy something on my own, buy something for you, feel like I have value, feel like I am something more than Isabella's husband. But I can't. It's always about you! Your career, your dreams, your goals. I'm tired of it!" Veins protruded on his forehead as he shouted at her.

Tears filled her eyes. His words stung. "You're wrong," she protested. "What we have isn't just because of me, it's because of *us*. How quickly you've forgotten the times I was struggling in my design studio, and there you were right beside me, pushing me, encouraging me to go on and succeed. I couldn't have gotten to where I am today without you. Not a moment has gone by that I'm not grateful for your support. So to answer your question, no, I *don't* get it, and no, I *don't* see it that way!"

"When is it my turn?" he responded. "When can I contribute or feel good knowing that I could support you and the family that you're always talking about having? Please tell me when? And you wonder why I keep putting you off. Well, wake up—that's why!"

Isabella's mouth hung open. "How many times have I wanted to use your artwork on one of my projects? How many times have you refused?"

Grayson began to pace back and forth in the kitchen. "I don't want a handout. And please, don't think for one moment that I would ever allow you to use one of my pieces for Vanderbeck now!"

Isabella stepped in front of him, trying to take his hand, but Grayson pulled his arm clear of her reach and backed away. His eyes were filled with resentment and disdain.

"That's insane!" she said. "It's not a handout. Your artwork moves me, Grayson. That's why I want to use it in my projects. How does anyone get anywhere in life without the help of the people around them? Things like that open doors—doors which may not have been possible to open otherwise!"

Grayson stared coldly at her. When he spoke, she felt the hatred in his voice. It was something she had never felt in their ten years of marriage, and it frightened her.

"I want people to want my artwork because they connect with it, not because my wife likes the colors and thinks it fits within her design plan."

Isabella couldn't believe what she was hearing. She was flabbergasted. "Is that what you think? That's wrong on so many levels. I'm not the one sabotaging your career—you are!"

Grayson hurled his glass across the loft. The sound of the glass shattering against the wall startled Isabella. Grayson stormed out from behind the kitchen island and headed for the door. He paused in the living room and turned back to see her still standing in the kitchen.

"That's right, Isabella. It's my fault—always my fault!" He turned and continued to the door, which he unlocked and threw open.

Isabella raced after him in a panic. "Where are you going?" she cried out.

Grayson ignored her as he stormed into the hallway and stepped into the freight elevator. He pulled down the grate with a harsh slam as Isabella arrived in the hallway. She rushed to the elevator and grabbed the bars as the elevator started to descend.

"Grayson, don't leave! Please come back inside and talk to me! Grayson!" Isabella pleaded with him, but he looked up at her silently and then looked away. She leaned her head on the bars, sobbing. "Grayson, please come back!"

He was gone.

Chapter 4

The next morning, Isabella stepped out of the Town Car in front of her office building, moving slowly, showing signs of exhaustion from lack of sleep. Her red, swollen eyes were hidden behind the darkest oversized sunglasses she could find. Having no desire to make any effort in getting ready, she had chosen a simple black shift dress and a single strand of pearls. Her unwashed hair was pulled back in a loose ponytail low on her neck.

Still reeling from her fight with Grayson, she walked to the entrance, lost in thought. The words he had spoken cut her heart. Her worst fear had been realized. Memories of her childhood flooded her mind. *No, it is not the same*, she kept telling herself.

As she reached the door, she looked up in time to avoid bumping into a group of businessmen making their way past her. They were obviously in a big hurry to get to wherever they were going. She noticed Gia standing at the door, holding two cups of coffee.

"I thought you could use this"—Gia handed her one of the coffee cups—"and some fresh air. Come on, missy, let's go for a little walk."

Isabella took the coffee from Gia and sighed deeply, not really wanting to walk, let alone talk, but she knew that protesting would be futile.

Gia and Isabella proceeded down the street. The weather was perfect for a June day, not too hot or humid, which made Gia's hair frizz out, causing it to look like a rat's nest, as Isabella had pointed out many times. Instead, it was warm and breezy, with ample sunshine and few clouds. Despite the early hour, the sidewalks were crowded with pedestrians. Isabella's eye caught on a mother pushing her baby in a stroller across the street. As she watched, a fuzzy yellow bear toppled out of the stroller, and the baby began to scream. The mother stopped and picked up the bear, and the baby squealed with delight when the toy was returned. The happy scene only upset Isabella further, and she struggled to blink back tears.

Gia finally broke the silence. "So, I take it that after we spoke, Grayson didn't come back home last night?" Gia pointed to an empty bench near the entrance to Central Park, and Isabella nodded in agreement, glad to stop walking.

She let out a sigh as she sat down on the warm bench that had been baking in the sun. “No, he didn’t. I assume he stayed at his studio last night. I tried calling him several times, but he didn’t pick up. At some point my calling must have annoyed him and he turned his phone off completely, because it started to go straight to voicemail.”

“What do you think has gotten into him? I’ve known Grayson forever, and when you called me last night, I couldn’t help thinking, what the hell is going on with him? You don’t think he’s doing drugs, do you?”

Isabella shot Gia a look and shook her head. “No, no drugs. Grayson would never do that. His best friend in high school died of an overdose after he and Grayson had been partying one night. That was a sobering moment for him, and he hasn’t touched anything drug-related since. No, this is different. I have no idea. It’s all very strange and so out of character.” Isabella took a sip of her coffee and stared off into the distance. “I should have known something wasn’t right when I saw his artwork last night. His pieces were so . . . tortured and moody, which is unusual. His pieces are generally so beautiful and peaceful. They make you feel good. These were different from anything I’ve ever seen him do.” Isabella looked down at her cup and began picking at the top of the plastic lid.

As Gia watched her, a thought crossed her mind. Unsure if she should voice her concern given Isabella’s state, she reminded herself that neither of them had ever held back their thoughts with each other. “Would you suspect, um . . . I mean, would you think that, um, Grayson, could be, you know, having . . .” Gia paused and took a deep breath. “That Grayson could be involved with someone else?” she sputtered.

Isabella stopped demolishing the lid of her cup and pulled her sunglasses off, exposing the tears that had been filling her eyes. “I don’t know, Gia. I never thought of that. I guess anything is possible, but surely I would have sensed something before this. We’ve been fine. He’s been fine. Our sex life has been more than fine . . .” Her voice trailed off. The tears were falling harder now, and she felt like she couldn’t breathe. “I don’t know! I don’t know what to think or say or feel. I’m numb. It’s like seeing a side of someone that you never thought existed, and boom, there it is, out of nowhere . . . this dagger plunging into your chest that you never saw coming.” Isabella buried her face in her hands and began to sob, her shoulders shaking violently.

Gia pulled her closer until Isabella’s head fell onto her shoulder. “I’m sorry, Izzie. I didn't mean to upset you further. I'm probably wrong. I just didn't know if that was something you considered." Gia leaned her head on Isabella's and kissed her forehead.

"It's not what you said that upset me," Isabella murmured. "It's just everything. I can't deal with it right now. He walked out. He actually left."

Gia put her arms around Isabella and squeezed her tightly. "Go home, take some time for yourself today, time to figure things out with Grayson. I can handle everything at the office." Isabella started to protest, but Gia held up her hand. "You will be of no use to me, to yourself, or anyone else, for that matter. I'm sorry, girlfriend, but you are a wreck right now, and you need to take care of yourself. Screw everyone else. They can wait."

"Richard . . . we have to get Richard's contractors moving, and I was supposed to call Mr. Vanderbeck to set up a meeting." Isabella sighed. "I'm not even sure I should now, knowing how Grayson feels, and—"

Gia silenced her blabbering by putting a finger to her lips. "And nothing! I have it—really, I do. After all these years of working with you, I believe I am quite capable of walking around in those crazy high-ass shoes of yours for a day."

Isabella glanced down at Gia's Nike sneakers and shook her head.

Gia laughed. "What? We were walking. I didn't know how far we might be going."

Isabella smiled despite herself and reached for her friend's hand. "Thank you, baby girl. I don't know what I would do without you."

Gia stood up and pulled Isabella to her feet. "To quote James"—Gia did her best James impression, pulling down her sunglasses and looking over the top of them at Isabella—"you'd be a hot mess, my darling."

They burst into laughter.

Gia put her arm around Isabella's shoulders as they started to walk back. "Come on, kiddo. Let's get Sebastian to take you home."

~~~

"Grayson," Isabella called out as she walked through the door of their loft. "Grayson, are you here?"

She stopped just inside the door and listened carefully. She hoped to hear some sort of noise, any noise or movement that would let her know Grayson was there, but she was greeted only with silence. She closed the door, set her keys and Gucci sunglasses down on the small console in the entryway, and dug through her purse in search of her BlackBerry. *How many compartments can one purse have?* she wondered. *And why do I never put my phone back in the same place?* Just as she was about
~~~

to dump the contents out on the floor, she felt the phone at the bottom of the center compartment and yanked it out, looking at the screen. No call from Grayson; only the little yellow envelope on the display, alerting her to the twenty-five emails she had already missed. Disappointed, she tossed the phone on the console. The emails could wait.

As she passed through the living room, she heard a crunch under the heel of her Jimmy Choo slingback. She moved her foot, exposing a chunk of clear glass. She gingerly picked up the jagged shard, remembering the ferocious way that Grayson had hurled the glass of scotch across the loft, causing it to shatter into what must have been a thousand pieces.

In the kitchen, she threw away the shard and retrieved the small handheld broom, dustpan, and towel her housekeeper kept under the sink. She noticed the half-full bottle of scotch sitting open on the counter and tipped it into the sink, spilling its contents down the drain.

From the kitchen, she scanned the loft, trying to remember just where it was that Grayson's glass had hit. Looking to her pricey white French silk sofa, she breathed a sigh of relief, knowing the glass had easily cleared the top, saving her a costly cleaning bill. With the dustpan and broom in hand, she made her way through the great room toward the expansive wall of windows, sweeping up a few shards here and there. Isabella let her gaze wander to the antique mirrored buffet and the painting she treasured that hung above it. Tears welled up in her eyes, and she looked away to continue her mission.

Just past the buffet sat an exposed brick wall they had uncovered during the renovation. Isabella loved the natural element that the brick brought to the room. Grayson had wanted to paint it white, but Isabella argued over and over with him that the brick had the most beautiful red and cocoa tones. She knew it would add interest to the space and would look amazing with the furniture pieces she had chosen. It had taken a lot of battling back and forth, but Isabella won in the end. She was sure that by now he had come to love the natural brick, although he would never admit it.

She stopped in front of the brick wall, where the stench of stale liquor permeated the air. There, piled on the planked ebony hardwood, was the shattered glass she had been searching for. Isabella swept the pieces into the dustpan and wiped up the scotch still puddled on the floor.

After she had thrown out the glass and returned everything to the cabinet, she headed upstairs. On the landing, instead of going to their bedroom, Isabella turned left and proceeded down the only hallway that remained in the loft. At the end was a door, and behind it was an empty room. Grayson had once used it as his art studio, but it was too small and had inadequate lighting, as he put it. He had found a small studio in Greenwich Village that allowed him enough space to paint. This room now sat as a reminder to Isabella, a promise of the nursery she would design for the family that she had so desperately wanted and that Grayson kept putting off.

Isabella reached for the top of the molding around the door and felt for the key hidden there. She had made Grayson install a lock on the door, thinking that if she kept it locked, she wouldn't freely wander in and torture herself with her desire for a baby. She unlocked the door and opened it, exposing the barren room. This was exactly how she felt inside: empty.

The room was a perfect rectangle, with a large bank of warehouse windows on the front wall, still covered in dust. The metal framing around the windows was rusted, showing the age of the building. Isabella turned in a circle, imagining the nursery she longed to have and the baby that belonged there. She recalled Grayson's words last night, and the realization set in that she might never know the joys of motherhood.

Unable to bear it any longer, Isabella left the room and locked the door behind her, replacing the key on the molding. Tears fell again as she found her way into the master bedroom. She took off her strand of pearls, tossed them on the dresser, kicked off her heels, and fell onto the bed. She curled up in a ball and buried her face in her pillow, sobbing uncontrollably. Her heart must be broken, she mused. She couldn't imagine anything feeling worse than this did. Actually, she could, but that had happened a very long time ago. She lay there for hours, replaying the events from the previous night. Where had she gone wrong? Self-doubt filled her. She blamed herself for what had happened. Had she unknowingly tried to sabotage Grayson? She knew in her heart of hearts that was absurd. She loved him. Why wouldn't she want him to succeed? No, she was tired—delusional, in fact, and needed to sleep. Eventually she passed out from sheer emotional exhaustion.

Isabella opened her eyes to a warm, soft glow coming through the windows. She knew from the quality of the light that the sun would be setting soon. The clock on her bedside table said it was almost 7:30, and still no word from Grayson. Isabella rolled onto her back and stared up at the metal beams on the ceiling.

A creak on the top step of the staircase broke her focus, and she turned her head. Grayson stood in the doorway.

He wore the same dress pants and white button-down dress shirt he had worn the previous night. Never taking her eyes from his, Isabella sat up on their bed and pulled her knees to her chest.

"Where have you been?" she asked, her voice hoarse. "I've been worried sick about you."

Grayson walked to the bed and sat down next to her. Looking tired himself and reeking like a dive bar at closing time, Grayson ran a hand through his thick hair and sighed. "Isabella, I am so sorry for what I did and said last night. It was completely uncalled for, and my behavior was inexcusable. I had no right to treat you that way. Please tell me you'll forgive me."

Isabella hugged her knees more tightly to her chest. "I can't forgive you without an explanation. The way you behaved, and the cruel things you said to me, were completely out of left field. If you want me to move past this, you need to explain what's going on with you."

Grayson lowered his head to avoid the pain he saw in Isabella's eyes. "There is no excuse for my behavior last night. None." He looked back up at her. "I was out of line, period, but I'm truly sorry. You know how long I've waited for that big breakout moment. I think I put too much pressure on myself this time, knowing that it might very well be my last opportunity to shine. I've been feeling so anxious since I began working on my pieces for this show. I think the pressure grew into something I couldn't control." He met her gaze. "Izzie, I've watched you become more and more successful year after year. When I look at where I'm at, I find myself exactly where I was when I met you ten years ago. Honestly, it makes me feel like a failure. I've watched all the dreams and goals I had for myself fade away. At this point in my life, I'd hoped to be somewhere entirely different than where I am now. It weighs on me, baby. I feel like I've accomplished nothing . . . that I am nothing."

Isabella tilted her head, trying to comprehend this. She took his hands in hers. "Grayson, when I first met you, you were so full of passion and fire for your art. Nothing else mattered, and I loved that about you. You never cared if you had to eat rice or leftovers from a friend's fridge for weeks. What made you happy was that you could spend your days doing what you loved, what excited you. That's the person I fell in love with. That's the person I love to this very day. I love that you don't confine yourself to timelines and deadlines or get caught up in the corporate nonsense that I deal with all the time. I love your free spirit, your quest for just being in the moment. You make me feel free, too, in my crazy scheduled world. I think somewhere along the way you lost touch with who you really are. You need to find that again, not just for me, but for yourself."

Grayson was looking down at their intertwined hands and rubbing the back of her hand with his thumb. "You're right. I've been so focused on trying to be successful at what I do that I forgot why I love doing it in the first place. Somewhere along the way I started thinking that I could never measure up to your success, and that began to overwhelm me."

Isabella let go of his hands and scooted to the edge of the bed. "I know you have a hard time believing it, but I meant what I said last night. I would be nothing without you. The success I've had is just as much yours as it is mine. Don't think for one moment that I feel this is mine and that is yours. It's ours. This is our life, our success."

Grayson took a long look at her. "I'm sorry, Izzie. You're right. It's hard at times, though, being a man and all. I want to be able to provide for you, and for our family one day."

Isabella held him tighter. "You do provide for me. You provide me with your love and support every day. You should know how much that means to me. You're the only family I have. It's me and you, baby. Without you I would be lost."

"Do you have any idea what a wonderful woman you are, Isabella Hughes?" He laid her down on the bed and climbed on top of her. "Do you have any idea how much I love you?" Pushing his full weight against her, Grayson smiled and started biting at Isabella's neck.

She giggled. "No, but you could show me, Mr. Hughes."

Grayson took Isabella's face in his hands and looked longingly into her eyes. "With pleasure."

He brought his lips down to meet hers. His mouth was warm and wet, his lips soft. With her face still in his hands, he kissed her slowly. Isabella felt excitement stir within her. Feeling her passion rising, Grayson began to kiss her harder and more feverishly, biting at her neck and rubbing her breasts. Isabella pulled him further down on her body, and as she wrapped her legs around his waist, she felt his erection. He reached under Isabella's dress, which had fallen up near her hip, and caressed her soft skin, teasing as he let his hand slowly graze the inside of her thigh. Isabella arched her head back and let her legs fall open on the bed. Grayson pulled off her dress, exposing her flawless body. Isabella lay there in her lacy black bra and matching thong.

While running one of his hands from her neck to her breasts, Grayson used the other to unbutton his dress shirt and unzip his pants. He slipped them off, and in one quick movement pulled off Isabella's lacy thong. She moaned softly, wanting him, waiting to feel him inside her. She wrapped her legs around his waist again and pulled him back down on top of her, pressing her body against his. Their lips found each other's and they frantically began to kiss, harder and faster. The passion each felt for the other was more intense than it had been before.

Grayson paused, causing Isabella to open her eyes. They stared at each other, his eyes looking at her, through her.

Damn those eyes, she thought. They were intense, yet serene. No one else could make her feel the way he did when he looked at her.

With their gazes locked, he slowly lowered his lips back down to hers, neither breaking eye contact, and very gently he entered her.

~~~

Isabella was thankful that the weekend had come when it did. It allowed her and Grayson the time they needed to reconnect. They spent Saturday in bed, exploring one another and, in Isabella's opinion, having the best makeup sex ever.

When they left their loft on Sunday afternoon, the weather was gorgeous and the streets showed it. The sidewalks were crowded with people enjoying the warm summer day. Isabella and Grayson headed down the street from their loft to a little café they liked. They had gotten to know the owner and the chef and often went there for lunch, or just to sit and people-watch as they enjoyed a bottle of wine.

The café was more crowded than usual, Isabella thought, but she had known it would be with the warm temperature outside. Not everyone was like her and Grayson, coming to the café in the dead of winter or in the heaviest of downpours. They lucked out and scored a table outside.

They ordered their usual meals, which the waitress had memorized. As Grayson took his vibrating cell phone out of his pocket, Isabella turned her attention to the people passing by. It was the typical neighborhood crowd she was used to seeing on the weekends. The usual couples slowly strolling down the street hand in hand. The usual joggers trying to get in their daily runs before indulging in an evening of drinks with their friends. The usual tourists gawking at the skyscrapers and posing for pictures. The usual families returning from the park. One dad was holding a blanket and picnic basket while the mom pushed their sleeping baby in a stroller. Isabella smiled at the baby, whose cute, chubby face was red from the sun—or was it from a sticky red sucker? She wasn't sure, but he looked so adorable with his head propped up by a rolled blanket. Isabella glanced back at Grayson to see if he was watching the stroller as she was, but to her dismay, he was intently clicking away on his phone.

"Anything wrong, Grayson?" Isabella asked as she looked back to
~~~

see where the couple with the baby had gone.

Grayson closed his phone and put it back in his pocket. "Nah, just Aidan giving me grief for ditching him today. He, Andre and Joel are playing a game of basketball at the park with some other guys."

"Why didn't you tell me you had plans this weekend? I wouldn't have minded if you wanted to hang out with your friends. In fact, I would have loved to watch you guys play . . . well, all of you except Aidan." Isabella grinned.

"It's no biggie, believe me." Grayson winked at her. "I had more fun getting exercise with you than I would have had with the guys."

As their food came, Isabella saw Gia and her flavor of the weekend walking toward them, juggling more than a few bags.

Gia spotted Isabella and ran over to their café table, pulling her man along behind her. "Hey, guys! What's up? Can you believe how awesome this weather is?"

"I know, right," Isabella said. "Looks like you guys hit the mother load shopping. Where were you?"

"Flea market," Gia proudly exclaimed. "I found the most amazing thing. You're going to die." Gia dropped her bags to the ground and started digging through them. "Ah-ha, here it is!" she squealed, causing every patron in the café to turn and look. She whipped out a small, black, quilted clutch purse. "Vintage Coco Chanel!"

Wide-eyed, Isabella looked at the clutch dangling from the delicate gold chain on Gia's index finger. "Shut up!" Isabella reached for the purse, but Gia snatched it away.

"Not so fast, sister. This one is mine!"

Isabella crinkled her nose. "Please tell me it was horribly expensive."

"Are you kidding? I practically stole it from the poor, unsuspecting peddler who didn't have a clue what the hell she had."

Deflated, Isabella shot her a nasty look. "I hate you, Gia. I really do!"

Grayson looked over at Gia's guy, who was standing there in awe of the interaction between Gia and Isabella. "That much of a reaction over a purse," Grayson said. "Wouldn't every guy love that type of reaction from his girl when he walked through the door?" He extended his hand. "Grayson Hughes. Nice to meet you."

"Skylar Camden." Skylar shook his hand and leaned into Grayson. "Are they always like this?"

"Always!"

Gia picked up a napkin from the table and threw it at Grayson, then turned back to Isabella. "So are you guys enjoying your weekend?"

Isabella smiled, knowing her friend was checking to make sure that everything was okay with her and Grayson. "Yeah, we've had a fabulous weekend. How about you two? Where are you off to now?"

Gia picked up her bags and locked her arm in Skylar's. "We've had a fierce weekend"—she winked at Isabella—"and now that all this shopping has worn us out, we're going back to my place for a little wine and relaxation."

Skylar looked over at Gia, raising his eyebrow. "Are we now?"

Gia leaned in and kissed him hard on the mouth. "You better believe it, baby."

They said their good-byes, and Skylar's hand was on her ass as Gia led him off down the busy street.

Grayson leaned toward Isabella as he watched them walk away. "How long do you give that one?"

"Please, it will be 'Skylar who' by morning." Isabella rolled her eyes.

Feeling full from lunch, they decided to take a stroll around the neighborhood. The streets were a little clearer now. Half an hour later, as they were waiting for the stoplight in front of their building to change, Isabella noticed a white BMW stopped nearby.

"Is that Andre?" Isabella said, pointing to the BMW. "I thought he was playing basketball this morning."

Grayson turned upon hearing Andre's name. "Um, I'm not sure. Maybe he dropped out early." He looked away, his attention on their building across the street.

"I think it is. Wow, he looks all snazzy in his suit. I think he's got a hot girl in the car, too." Isabella moved forward, trying to get a closer look, but Grayson pulled her back.

"Izzie, he's probably on a date. Don't bother him." Just then, the light changed, and the BMW sped off. Grayson took Isabella by the hand and pulled her across the street. "Come on, nosey Rosie, let's get moving."

"I wasn't being nosey. I just wanted to say hello." Isabella stuck her tongue out at him. "I like Andre."

Grayson laughed at her childish antics. "I have a place you could put that tongue."

She swung around in front of him, causing him to stop on the curb. She got up on her tiptoes, getting nose to nose with him, and gave him a sassy smile. "Care to show me where that would be?"

Grayson scooped her up in his arms and started up the front stairs of their building. "Absolutely. Right this way."

Chapter 5

Isabella arrived at her office early Monday morning. Having missed a full day of work on Friday, she wanted to get caught up and to plan out her week in advance. The office was nice and quiet, just the way she liked it. She sat at her desk, looking over the contracts that Richard Lafayette had signed. As usual, he had made some changes, but overall the contracts were good and signed, which made Isabella happy. She reached for her coffee and turned her chair around to look down at the city that was awakening from its slumber. Isabella had never been a morning person. She always found it difficult to get out of bed and repeatedly hit the snooze button on her alarm clock. However, sitting there in her office, she appreciated the quiet that accompanied each new day as it dawned.

As she drank her coffee, her thoughts turned to Grayson. Although they'd had a great weekend, there were moments when something felt off—maybe not off, but different. As they made love, Grayson's touch had at times become rougher than usual, or she caught him staring at her as if deep in thought. When she questioned him, he had said, "Do you know how beautiful you are right now?"

Isabella shook her head. Why did she always have to question everything? Their relationship was good. Why the doubts?

After their horrific argument, she had never thought she would feel this good again. Grayson was her life, and the only family she had. She hated when there was turmoil between them. The fights were rare, but when they came, Isabella feared that Grayson would up and leave her. It wasn't his fault. She knew that her insecurities were directly related to her mother abandoning her when she was six years old—or so her therapist had once told her.

Hearing James's Burberry loafers clicking on the marble floor, Isabella spun her chair around. The stack of papers he carried flew through the air when he saw her.

"Jesus, Mary, and Joseph!" he exclaimed, his face pale. "You scared the shit outta me, Isabella."

Isabella burst out laughing. "You should see your face. Oh my gosh, it's priceless! I think you may need to check yourself."

James looked annoyed as he bent down to pick up the papers that had scattered across her office floor. “Not nice,” he said. “I swear I am going to install a mirror on the window so I can see you sitting there when I come down the hall. That’s like the millionth time you’ve done that to me.”

Isabella chuckled. “That’s why it’s so funny. You’d think you would be used to it by now.”

James dumped the papers on her desk in a messy pile, then put his hands on his hips and glared at her. “Yes, well, I wasn’t expecting you so early, as I know *someone* is not a morning person. Which brings me to the question, what the heck are you doing here, missy?” He sat in one of the chairs in front of her desk.

“Hmm, that would be working. What else would someone do in their office this early?” Isabella pulled the stack of papers in front of her.

James pursed his lips and stared at her over his glasses. His blonde hair was impeccably spiked, as always, with gosh knows what combination of products. Today he had opted for a cashmere sweater vest over his dress shirt instead of his usual cardigan, paired with his perfectly tailored pants.

“Just remember,” he warned playfully, “payback is a biznatch.” He pulled out his calendar and started going through the appointments he had scheduled for her. “An assistant for a Charles Vanderbeck called, wanting to schedule a meeting between the two of you. She said something about him having to go overseas for a while, so I scheduled him for the beginning of next month.”

Well now, Isabella thought. She didn’t see the harm in meeting with Vanderbeck. Grayson didn’t have to know. If things went well, she could tell him. She added the appointment to her BlackBerry calendar and sent James off with a request for more coffee.

“Yeah, yeah,” he said over his shoulder as he walked out. “I’m still mad at you for scaring the shit out of me, so drink with caution. I may squirt some Visine in there to give you the runs.”

Gia passed him as she swept into the office with an armful of files.

Damn, this is a busy place in the morning, Isabella thought. *No wonder I show up late*.

“Cute outfit, Izzie,” Gia gushed. “LOVE, LOVE the necklace. Oh yeah, that’s because I bought it for you.” She grinned. “You’re looking mighty flirty and fresh today. Someone got laid plenty this weekend, didn’t they?”

Isabella smiled as she looked down at her top. She had worn a hot pink silk babydoll top, which she had embellished with a five-strand beaded necklace dripping with crystals. To tone it down, she had chosen a sleek pair of flared white pants and simple platinum slingbacks. The top was more vibrant than she normally would have worn, and the necklace a little more gaudy, but she was in a fabulous mood and figured what the hell.

"I'm sure you had me beat in that department this weekend," Isabella replied, "but thanks, I do feel fresh and rested. Grayson and I had a good weekend." Isabella wasn't sure if she was trying to convince herself or Gia.

Gia knew her too well. "Izzie, stop worrying," she reprimanded. "You guys are fine."

"I know, I know. I just want things to be perfect."

Gia shook her head. "They are, Debbie Downer. Let it go and be happy."

"Hey, speaking of good things, how is it going with Skylar?"

"Who?" Gia asked, clueless as to who she was referring to.

Isabella rolled her eyes.

"Oh yeah, my date on Sunday. You know how it goes, he kept me company shopping, and I kept him very happy afterward." Gia winked.

"My God, Gia, I hope vintage Coco Chanel is the only thing you picked up this weekend."

Gia's mouth dropped opened as she tried to look offended. "As if! You know I'm a safety girl. No balloon, no party. No glove no love!"

Isabella stifled a laugh and waved her hand in protest. "It's too early for smut talk. Save that for later. Now where is the file for Chantal's Couture? I have to check on the status of the custom shelving we ordered. She emailed me Friday. She needs those this week."

Gia stood. "I'll get it. Just remember, Izzie, all work and no play . . ."

"You play enough for both of us, I swear." Isabella shooed her away to get her file.

A phone call from Richard's contractors a few minutes later ensured that Isabella wouldn't be getting any more done at the office that morning.

"We have to head over to Richard's new building," she told Gia as she grabbed her purse. "There's some confusion with the contractors regarding the entrance and lobby area."

"Seriously, do they not know how to read plans?" Gia rolled her eyes.

"Obviously not."

Gia followed her out of the office. So much for easing into the work week.

~~~

In the Town Car, Gia updated Isabella on Richard's project. "According to the schedule, which is tight, I might add, demo needs to be completed by the end of the month. These contractors need to get their ducks in a row. We can't have confusion about which walls are coming down and which ones are staying. They should have gone over that beforehand."

Isabella looked over the schedule for what she was sure was the hundredth time. "It's very doable. Tyler and his crew should be competent enough to get it done. I'm sure Richard's last-minute changes are the source of the confusion."

"I swear, sometimes I think Richard does things like that just to keep you on your toes. It's as though he knows you're busy and wants to make sure you're paying attention to his project."

Isabella raised her eyebrow. "Possibly. When have you ever known Richard to put his full faith in anyone?"

"From your lips to God's ears."

Sebastian wrangled his way through the throng of traffic and parked near the entrance of the building to drop them off. In the vestibule area they found a group of contractors sitting around as if they were on a coffee break, which irritated Isabella. When they saw her and Gia, the men scrambled to their feet with guilty expressions.

Tyler, the main general contractor, came up to greet them and handed each of them a hard hat. "Ladies, if you please. This is a construction site, after all."

Gia let out a moan. "Really? I was having a great hair day."

"You kill me," said Isabella. "Just put the damn hat on!" Isabella slid the hard hat on over her perfectly coiffed hair and extended her hand to Tyler. "Good morning, Tyler. I hear there has been some confusion with the demo. Let's take a look at the plans and see where the problem lies."

"Right this way." Tyler led them to a large table where the building plans were laid out and explained the confusion over a non-load-bearing wall slated to be removed. On some pages of the plans, the wall was gone, but in others, it remained. "We didn't want to start hacking down the wall if it was your intention that it remain," he concluded.

Isabella studied the plans carefully, trying to recall conversations she'd had with Richard regarding the wall and its relevance. Then it came to her. "Remove it. We're going to have a cascading water feature that will sit in its place. The existing wall will need to be removed so the foundation for the waterfall can be erected."

"You're sure about this? Maybe we should call Mr. Lafayette. Once
~~~

we tear it down, it's gone, you know."

Isabella folded her arms across her chest. She was used to dealing with male contractors who questioned the authority of the women they worked with. "I can assure you I understand what the term 'demolition' means. I am, however, concerned about your ability to follow my directions, seeing as I am the head designer on this project and I'm the one who worked hand in hand with my architect, whom I employ, to come up with the design. Remove the wall!"

Tyler took a step back, as if he expected her to bare her claws. He turned to the group of workers huddled in the far corner of the entrance, listening in on the conversation. "You heard the pretty little lady. Tear it down."

Isabella took a step closer to Tyler. She could smell his cheap aftershave as he turned back to her. "Two things. Since my associate and I drove all the way down here, we are going to walk through this building with the plans floor by floor with you, just to make sure we're all on the same page and demolition isn't halted again."

Tyler shrugged. "Fine by me," he said nonchalantly. "It's your time. What's the second thing?"

Isabella leaned in even closer, smiling viciously. "If you ever call me a pretty little lady again, the head on your shoulders won't be the only head that will need protecting." She pulled back, keeping her eyes glued to his. "Do I make myself clear?"

He straightened up, looking impressed with her feistiness. "Crystal clear, Mrs. Hughes."

With Gia at her side, Isabella turned on her heels and yelled back over her shoulder, "Let's go. Grab the plans. We'll start at the top and work our way down."

"My thoughts exactly," Tyler muttered salaciously.

Isabella turned to see him ogling her from head to toe, but she gritted her teeth and let it go. She just wanted to get this over with.

Chapter 6

Isabella lay in bed with her head resting on Grayson's chest. He stroked her long hair while she listened to his heart beating. She loved quiet mornings like this, when they could sleep in and be close to one another. Her week had been hectic and chaotic. Between meetings, emails, and phone calls on top of too many visits to job sites to check on the progress of ongoing projects, Isabella had been going nonstop. She had put out so many fires, she felt like she was part of the NYFD. She was thankful for the weekend and the opportunity to spend some much-needed cuddle time with Grayson.

He kissed the top of her head. "Baby girl, I got to get up and get moving."

Isabella sat up and groaned. "Why? What do you have to do? I thought we would spend the day together."

Grayson slid out of bed before she could trap him as she often did. Standing there naked, with the sunlight highlighting every muscle, he looked like a god. "No can do, Izzie. I'm meeting up with the guys this morning, and then I was planning on going to my studio to finish up a piece I'm working on for a client."

"Aw, come on, I haven't seen you all week."

Grayson turned to look at her as she kneeled on their bed, naked. She looked adorable with her pouty lip and her head tilted to the side. Her body was irresistible. Her nipples were hard, and her skin glistened in the sunlight. For a moment she almost had him, but he shook his head.

"That's not going to work, Isabella Hughes. You are not going to seduce me back into that bed with that hot little body of yours."

Isabella fell back and groaned again. "Come on, Grayson, I miss you!"

He took her hands and pulled her up, bringing her to her feet. "I miss you too. I missed you all week while you were working like a maniac and I was here waiting for you with dinners that went cold, but I didn't complain."

Isabella started to plead her case, but Grayson put a finger to her lips to silence her. "I'm not complaining, I'm just stating the facts. I'm used to you working like a fiend. I understand that's who you are. I would love to spend time with you today, and we will, later." He headed for the shower. "It's a beautiful day out. Go shopping with Gia. I'm sure you two will have fun and do plenty of damage to our bank account."

Isabella glared at his back as he disappeared into the bathroom. "Fine, go to your studio and leave me here all day by myself. Whatever."

While Grayson was in the shower, Isabella went downstairs to make coffee and wrangle up something to eat. By the time he appeared in the kitchen, she had managed to make his favorite breakfast and had it perfectly displayed on their nook table. Martha Stewart would have been proud. Grayson admired the beautiful presentation, complete with fresh-cut fruit and freshly squeezed orange juice, and shook his head at his wife.

"You are insatiable, Izzie. Do not think for one minute that you can entice me with breakfast so I will stay here. I know you, and your little antics are not going to work this morning."

Standing in the kitchen pouring her second cup of coffee, Isabella pretended to be insulted by her husband's comment. He snatched a piece of French toast off the plate as he walked by and came around the island to kiss her on her cheek. "Nice try, love. You get an A for effort, but I gotta run."

Isabella pulled him into her arms and kissed him passionately. Grayson tried to resist, but quickly fell into her trap. Lost in the moment, he feverishly kissed her back, exploring her warm mouth with his tongue. Feeling his excitement pressing into her, Isabella reached down and rubbed his erection, which was trapped beneath his jeans. Groaning, Grayson grabbed her hand and pulled away.

"Not so fast," he said, breaking free from the sexual web of desire she was attempting to spin. "You almost had me there." He adjusted his erection in his pants. "My God, Izzie, the things you do to me."

Isabella laughed wickedly as she reached back out to him, but he side-stepped her and made a beeline for the door.

"All right, all right," she whined. "I guess it's breakfast for one, then."

Grayson pulled back the loft door and turned around, giving her a smirk. "I'll be back later to finish what you started, I promise."

"You better," she called after him.

After eating and cleaning up the mess she had made while feverishly preparing breakfast, Isabella showered and threw on a pair of denim cut-off shorts and a white tank top, knowing it was going to be a scorcher. She slipped on rattan wedge shoes, tied her hair back, and put on a wide-brimmed straw hat. As soon as she stepped outside, the summer heat hit her. *Eighty-nine my ass*, she thought. *Feels more like one hundred and ten.*

She wandered without a plan, lazily window shopping and people watching. Soon she found herself outside her favorite children's boutique. Although she had never bought anything for herself there, she'd done a fair amount of damage buying gifts for her friends' kids.

As she opened the door of the tiny shop, the cool air flowed over her damp, warm skin, and she sighed. It felt heavenly. The bell rang, and Anastashia Ruton, the owner, looked up and smiled.

"Isabella, darling, how have you been?" she asked in her heavy Russian accent. She rushed over and hugged Isabella tightly. "It's been quite some time, no?"

Grinning, Isabella returned the squeeze. "Yes, it has been too long." The two had developed a fond friendship over the years, and Isabella had missed Anastashia and her delightful accent.

Anastashia pulled away, still holding Isabella's arms, and looked at her questioningly. "Is there something special that brings you in today? Something for you, I'm hoping?"

Isabella's smile faltered. Yet she was touched that Anastashia had always been rooting for her to become pregnant. "Not yet, I'm afraid to report. It's not a good time right now."

Anastashia waved her hands back and forth like she was shooing away a fly. "Pish posh, is there ever a good time? That husband of yours needs to let it go, throw you on the bed, and make you a baby."

Isabella laughed at her friend's not-so-subtle opinion. "One day he will, but for now we're having a lot of fun practicing." She winked.

"Ahhh, that's what I like to hear about," Anastashia purred, "the hot and sexy love-making stuff."

Isabella chuckled. "Of course you do. I always thought you should have owned a sexy lingerie shop instead of a children's boutique."

Anastashia raised an eyebrow teasingly at Isabella and whispered in her ear, "You haven't seen the back room, no?"

They laughed again, and Isabella put her arm around Anastashia. "Oh, how I love you, you little Russian vixen."

"So what brings you in today, darling?" Anastashia returned to the box she was unpacking on the counter.

"Nothing really, I just wanted to stop in and say hello." Isabella sat down on the counter stool in front of the box and pulled out a couple of tiny shirts. She felt Anastashia's eyes on her as she meticulously folded the shirts.

"What is it?" Anastashia asked. "You seem sad."

Isabella looked up into her eyes. "I'm not sad. I'm nothing, really. I've been working a lot, and things are crazy. I haven't seen Grayson all week, and I was hoping to spend the day with him, but he had plans with friends. I get that he needs to see them, but I wish he had asked me or made other arrangements during the week."

Anastashia turned her lipsticked mouth down in a frown of disapproval. She was all too used to hearing this from Isabella. "You and Grayson are like two ships passing in the night. You need to change courses and sail together. Life is too short. You must stop and enjoy it. You work so hard all the time, and for what? Work won't bring you true happiness the way love and a family will. You need to make time for each other. When is the last time you took a vacation, just the two of you, to some exotic destination and simply enjoyed each other?"

Tears welled up in Isabella's eyes. Anastashia was right. It had been so long since she and Grayson had spent that kind of time together. It seemed impossible to get away. She was always in the middle of a large project, or he was in a groove with his paintings, with neither willing to put their passion aside for the other. What did that say about their relationship?

Anastashia tilted Isabella's chin up with her hand. "I don't say this to make you sad, my dear, I say this because you need to hear it and start making changes before it's too late."

Touched, Isabella took Anastashia's hand in her own. "I know. Thank you for being honest with me. We need to work harder to make time for each other, and I promise we will." As if a light bulb had turned on in her head, Isabella jumped off the stool and grabbed her purse from the counter. "In fact, you've inspired me. I'm going to head over to the travel agent's office and see about booking us a trip somewhere."

"That's my girl. Make it somewhere beautiful and quiet, where you can have a lot of passionate lovemaking and hopefully make a baby to wear my adorable clothes."

Isabella laughed and blew her a kiss as she ran out the door.

Excited by the prospect of surprising Grayson with a mini-vacation, Isabella turned the corner without paying attention and collided with someone. The impact knocked her straight on her butt.

"Hey lady, where's the fire?" he said. She looked up from her scraped knee and saw Grayson's friend Andre grinning at her. "Are you okay?" he asked, extending his hand to help her up.

"Andre? Oh my gosh, I'm so sorry! I was distracted, not watching where I was going and . . . hey, why aren't you with the guys today?"

He helped Isabella to her feet and gave her a squeeze. "No worries, Izzie, I think you took the brunt of the impact for sure." He laughed as he patted the dirt off her behind. "Where are the guys? I wasn't aware they had plans."

Isabella found this strange. Andre, Aidan, and Joel usually stuck together like glue. But she shrugged it off. "I don't know what they're doing. Grayson said he had plans with the guys today. I just assumed since you were one of the guys, he meant you as well. Maybe they're mad at you for not showing up at the basketball game the other weekend. But don't worry, Grayson didn't go either. I saw you driving near our loft that day, looking rather sexy in your suit with a hot little thing in your car, I might add."

Andre smiled. "Yeah, she was hot, all right. Good times with that one."

Isabella hit him in the arm. "You are so bad, Andre, but I like it."

Andre flashed a sly smile and took a bow. "But seriously, I'll have to check with the guys. I didn't know about any basketball game either, so that's twice now they left me out. They're all in trouble." Andre was trying to look tough, like he was going to kick some ass, but Isabella knew better.

"All right, doll," she said, "it was great bumping into you, pun intended, but I have to get moving. I still have to make a quick stop before meeting Gia for lunch."

Another lustful smile appeared on his face, and Isabella punched him in the arm again.

"Don't even go there, Andre!" She knew Gia and Andre had hooked up at least once in the past.

Andre shrugged and tried to look innocent as he rubbed his arm. "What? Can't a guy enjoy a hot, steamy memory?" He blocked her next punch and pulled her to him in a brotherly hug.

"Great seeing you too, baby girl. You look amazing as always, and tell that husband of yours he has some explaining to do."

"Will do!" Isabella kissed him on the cheek and took off again down the street, this time watching where she was going.

~~~

Isabella had a productive afternoon. At the travel agent's office, she picked up information on a few vacation hot spots Grayson might be interested in. She was leaning toward a luxurious villa in St. Lucia, tucked away on a secluded part of the island with its own private beach. The house was larger than they would need, but it came complete with a housekeeper, butler, and cook. It intrigued her to think of being waited
~~~

on hand and foot, which would allow them the time they needed to concentrate on each other.

After leaving the travel agent's office, she met Gia for lunch, and the two friends spent the afternoon shopping in all their favorite boutiques. Isabella bought a sexy black number that she was planning to wear that night for Grayson. Not that he cared about sexy lingerie. He always remarked that it would be off her and on the floor in two minutes, but she wanted to put forth more of an effort for a special night with him.

At the end of their shopping tour, Gia was supposed to go with Isabella to the market and help her pick out something special to make for dinner. Grayson complained that she never cooked dinner, so she wanted to surprise him. Unfortunately, she lost Gia to the "hottie with the body" standing outside the shoe store, watching with conspicuous interest as Gia tried on a pair of come-fuck-me pumps.

"He is cute, I will give you that," Isabella said, "but you were supposed to help me."

"Come on, Izzie, look at him and tell me if you were me, you wouldn't ditch the grocery store for him."

Isabella rolled her eyes and waved Gia off. "Go, have your fun. I'll muddle through by myself and find something to make for dinner."

Gia let out a squeal. "You're the best. I will give you all the details Monday morning."

Isabella raised her hand and said, "Please don't." But Gia was already out the door, making her moves on Mr. Shoe Peeper.

At the market, after an agonizing decision-making process not helped by the impatient butcher behind the counter, Isabella picked out stuffed chicken breasts and fixings for a Martha's Vineyard salad, then spent at least ten minutes staring at the extensive wine selection, unsure about the proper pairing for stuffed chicken. Finally she gave up and went with Grayson's favorite, scotch.

By the time she arrived at the loft, it was just after six o'clock. Grayson hadn't said when he would be back, but she assumed it would be soon. She dumped the handfuls of shopping bags on the counter and got to work. An hour later, she was showered and dressed, her hair was tousled just the way Grayson liked it, and the delectable aroma of baked chicken filled the loft.

Grayson still wasn't home, and he hadn't responded to her text. When he was painting, he liked to be left alone, so she tried not to bother him. Nevertheless, she was in a great mood. She danced and sang as she assembled the salad, set the dining table with her grandmother's white china, lit tapered candles in crystal candleholders, and sprinkled red rose petals across the tabletop. She wanted everything to be perfect and intended to surprise him with the trip she was planning for them.

With everything ready, she checked her phone again, but still no word from him. She tried calling, but the call went straight to his voicemail. She made herself a vodka and soda and took her drink out onto the balcony, where she sat down at their café set to enjoy the cool evening breeze.

It was a beautiful night. Isabella watched the pedestrians down below, some returning from outings, looking tired from the heat and glad to be home, and some leaving for the night, all dolled up and ready to hit the town. The sky turned a deep lavender as the sun set over the never-ending sea of rooftops. She glanced at her watch and was surprised to see that it was after eight-thirty already.

Back inside, she checked her phone again. Still nothing from Grayson. Irritated, and knowing that dinner was likely cold, she left a message on his voice mail. She made herself another drink and returned to the balcony. Another half hour went by. Feeling a little tipsy, she decided she'd had enough. She was hungry, so she would eat without him. She blew out the candles on the dining table, made herself a plate of food, and sat on the sofa to eat, staring at the beautiful table she had set up for them. She was hurt that he hadn't come home to spend time with her as he had promised that morning, and hadn't even bothered to call.

Her stomach churned, and she realized she had lost her appetite. She threw her dinner in the trash, arranged Grayson's portion on his plate, and placed it back on the dining table.

Isabella dimmed the lights on the first level of the loft and walked upstairs to the bedroom, where her black nightie still lay on the bed. She marched back downstairs with the nightie in hand and draped it over Grayson's chair. Back in the bedroom, tears filled her eyes as she pulled off her dress and crawled into bed. Anastashia was right: they were like two passing ships never on the same course. How had they gotten that way? Could they fix it before it was too late? Isabella stared up at the ceiling, too emotionally spent to cry, too numb to feel. Eventually, she curled into a ball and fell asleep.

Hours later, she heard the noise of the loft door opening and glanced at the clock on her nightstand. It was one o'clock in the morning.

Chapter 7

Unable to sleep, having tossed and turned most of the night, Isabella finally got out of bed at six—too early for a Sunday, she thought. She was exhausted. She stood at the side of the bed, gazing at her husband, who lay there sleeping peacefully.

When he had arrived home, she had pretended she was asleep, fearing she would say something she'd regret. Watching him now, part of her wanted to wake him because she had plenty to say, but part of her felt guilty because she knew he had worked late at his studio and probably needed the rest. She opted for a run in the park, hoping it would clear her head and dispel her gloomy mood. When she returned home, she would wake him and they could talk and perhaps salvage some part of the weekend together.

The morning was already warm when she stepped outside, but she was grateful for the cool breeze. She threw her headphones on, turned her iPod to *shuffle*, and took off running toward Central Park. The streets were almost deserted, which suited her just fine. She wasn't in the mood for dodging people left and right.

Isabella tried to keep her mind clear as she entered the park, but her iPod was not cooperating. It kept selecting what Gia referred to as "those damn sappy love songs." Isabella hit the forward button over and over to change songs, but after ten hits, gave up, realizing it was useless. *Note to self—change your playlist*, she thought.

Her mind wandered stubbornly back to Grayson. She had thought things were back to normal—even better than normal—after their make-up last Sunday, but now perhaps she'd assumed wrong. If she was honest, she had to admit they had drifted apart in the past few years. She tried to remember just when and where things had gotten off track, but nothing stood out as that "ah-ha" moment. She knew that she worked a lot, but Grayson had always encouraged her to succeed with her business and never complained about her long hours. Well, he had never complained until now.

In her mind, they had the perfect setup. She would go to work in the morning, and he would have his whole day free to work at his studio. They would come home from their day apart and spend the evenings and weekends together. Now and then—well, maybe more days than not—she rolled in later than she would have liked. There were times when it couldn't be helped, and he knew that. Working on commercial projects ranging in the millions of dollars required quite a bit of her attention. Deadlines were a factor, and she liked to run each project like a well-oiled machine. Her clients hired her and kept coming back because of the reputation she had built. Not only was she known for designing amazing spaces, but for her precision in overseeing every detail of a project. Yes, she had her assistants and other junior designers in her firm who were capable of working on the projects, and she allowed them to do much of the legwork, procuring products and keeping the schedules moving. But she knew it was her name and reputation that were on the line, not theirs, so she was always involved.

She could cut back on her hours, she thought, maybe work from home one or two days a week. But she had to admit it would never work. Her phone was constantly beeping at her with emails and phone calls. One design emergency after another would drag her away to a job site. Working from home would only disrupt Grayson. Maybe she could make an effort to be home earlier and keep the weekends clear, allowing them more time together. That was apparently what they needed—time to reconnect and find their way again. Was that what Grayson wanted? Or was he content with how things were? Had they become so accustomed to their lifestyle that this was what worked for them? Was she the one with the problem? He certainly didn't complain much about not spending time with her, except for the occasional jab about her late evenings. In fact, it apparently didn't even bother him not to speak to her all day. Then he showed up at one in the morning after promising her that they would spend the afternoon together.

Isabella felt her chest tighten with anxiety. She had been so wrapped up in her thoughts that she didn't realize that she had been running at a full sprint. She tried to slow herself to catch her breath, but then the tears began streaming down her face, and she ran faster and faster. Spotting a pond in the distance, she left the trail and wove her way through the trees that lined the path, dodging bushes and branches. Just before she reached the pond, she tripped over a log and threw her hands out in front of her to avoid smacking her face into the dirt. Her hands skidded along the ground, and her momentum flipped her over. She rolled and landed flat on her back near the pond's edge.

The dewy grass moistened her already damp shirt as she lay there, her heart racing and her breath coming fast. Above her, a band of clouds slid over the sun. She closed her eyes and began to sob. After a few minutes, she managed to sit up and look down at the damage she had done to her hands. Other than a few minor scrapes, which stung, they were fine. She hugged her knees to her chest and rocked back and forth as the tears silently flowed.

"Boo-boo?"

Isabella lifted her head to see a little blond-haired, blue-eyed boy standing next to her, looking worried. She wiped at her tears and smiled at him. "No, bud, I'm fine."

The boy smiled back and pointed to his elbow. "I'm Bryce. I had a boo-boo. I fell down, and Mommy made it better with a Band-Aid. You need a Band-Aid. Then you'll be all better."

Isabella smiled at the adorable little boy who had trouble pronouncing his *R*'s. She guessed he was about three.

"Thanks, Bryce. I think I do need a Band-Aid." *A really big Band-Aid*, she thought.

Just when she was about to ask him where his mommy was, she heard a woman nearby calling his name. "You better go, bud. I think your mommy is looking for you."

The boy ran off, but paused and turned to blow her a kiss and wave. Isabella waved back at him. She stood, dusted the dirt from her legs and her butt, and returned to the main trail at a walking pace, this time watching where she stepped.

When she arrived back at the loft, Isabella was surprised to see that she had been out running for two hours. The loft was quiet. She washed away the dirt on her hands, poured herself a glass of ice water, and kicked off her tennis shoes before heading upstairs to wake Grayson.

The bed was empty. She set her glass down on the nightstand, and that was when she noticed the note on her pillow.

Izzie,

I'm sorry about last night. I got caught up painting at my studio and lost track of time. The dinner looked amazing. Sorry I missed it. I will be at my studio most of the day finishing up. I figured you left this morning to go flea marketing with Gia.

Catch ya later tonight,
Grayson

Isabella stared at the note until her eyes blurred with anger. Her blood boiled inside her. She crumpled up the note and tossed it in the trash, then picked up her glass of water and hurled it across the room at one of Grayson's pieces.

"Fuck you, Grayson," she screamed at the top of her lungs.

~~~

Isabella spent the day alone, stewing. She could have phoned in a 911 call to Gia, but she didn't have the energy to talk about it. Grayson spent the entire day at his studio again and, like the previous night, rolled in after one in the morning while Isabella lay in bed and fumed. She was relieved when the weekend ended so she could focus on work. She left earlier than usual, without uttering a word to him.

Isabella thrived when she worked. It was where she belonged. Interior design was her comfort zone, the one thing she did extremely well and was passionate about. She was grateful that her grandparents had passed on their strong work ethic. She did nothing half-assed when it came to her work, and it showed. As a formidable businesswoman, she held her own against some pretty tough dogs that she dealt with on a daily basis. But when it came to relationships, she crumbled. Her insecurities made her vulnerable, and the willpower and level-headedness on which she prided herself went right out the window.

By the time her staff arrived, Isabella had outlined the delivery and installation schedules for the week and noted points of concern for existing projects. She was getting ready to head down to the conference room for the Monday morning staff meeting when Gia came into her office, dressed in a rumpled outfit that looked like it had been balled up overnight in a corner of a bedroom that wasn't hers.

Isabella shot her a look of disapproval, but Gia waved her off.

"It's not like you're not used to seeing me like this, Isabella. If you hadn't made the meeting so damn early, I would have had time to go home from Kris's and change."

Isabella looked up from the papers she was gathering on her desk. "Who?"

"Kris, a.k.a. hottie with the body."

Isabella rolled her eyes. "Please spare me the details. I'm not in the mood this morning."

Gia flopped down in a chair in front of her desk. "You think? Geez, who pissed in your Wheaties this morning?"

Ignoring her, Isabella moved for the door, but Gia jumped up and blocked her. "Let me guess. Grayson? Why didn't you call me?"

"Please, I don't want to talk about it right now. This is the one place where I can come and focus on something other than my idiotic husband. Let's just concentrate on work, okay?"

Looking a tad guilty, Gia touched Isabella's hand. "Of course, and you know I'm here for you whenever you need me, right?"
~~~

"Yes, and I appreciate it. I would also appreciate it if you could change into one of those emergency outfits you have in your office to avoid looking like you've been ridden hard and put up wet."

Gia tried acting insulted but burst out laughing, and Isabella couldn't help but join her.

"Well, truth be told . . ."

Isabella held up her hand. "Stop right there! Conference room, five minutes. Some heads are gonna roll this morning."

During the meeting, Isabella reviewed the status of their projects, quickly losing patience with an assistant designer who had let several orders fall through the cracks. "Amber, you need to step up your game," she said, jabbing a finger in the girl's direction. "I'm sick and tired of mistakes being made and work not getting done. Just do your damn job so I don't have to do it for you. After all, isn't that what I pay you for?" She looked around the table. "And that goes for all of you. I want to know that I have competent employees working for me who will go that extra mile. I want you to identify what needs to be done and do it, instead of waiting for direction. I need to know things aren't going to fall apart when I'm not around."

Gia, James, and the others stared at her open-mouthed. She took a long, slow breath and tried to relax. "Thanks, everyone. That's all I have for today." She dismissed them and retreated to her office to calm down.

When she emerged half an hour later to refill her coffee, she found James and Gia in the hallway, whispering about something. They hushed up when they saw her coming their way.

"Everything okay, Izzie?" Gia asked tentatively.

Isabella rubbed her forehead and nodded. "I'm okay. I know I was a little hard on Amber." She cringed when she recalled her words.

"A little? I think the poor girl is still in the bathroom cleaning herself up."

"I'll speak to her this afternoon and apologize for my tone, but I meant what I said. Actually, I shouldn't have been so hard on all of you. Things have been a little . . . stressful."

James put an arm around Isabella's shoulders. "Girl, you know you can always count on us. We won't let anything go down the shitter. Gia may go to the gutter, but that's an entirely different topic."

Gia punched James in the arm.

"Ouch, that hurt, you biznatch." James rubbed his arm.

Gia stepped in front of him and wedged herself between him and Isabella, making James stumble. "We love you, Izzie. Whatever you need, we're here for you. Now let's stop playing around and get to work, people." Her voice boomed through the office, causing most of the staff to turn and look.

Isabella raised her eyebrow. "Wow, Gia. What's gotten into you?"

James pushed himself between the girls, wrapping his arms around their shoulders, and proceeded to walk them down the hall. "Um, don't you mean *who*?"

"Watch it, mister." Gia bumped him with her hip.

Isabella and Gia spent the rest of the morning in their selections room, pulling together items for a new day spa that Isabella's longtime hair stylist, Brit Montgomery, was opening. Isabella had personally wanted to oversee the selections, as she knew Brit well. Truth be told, she knew she would be spending a lot of time there now since the spa would be offering massages and facials, so she wanted it to be spectacular. Better yet, it was located between her office and her loft. It would be the perfect location for a quick pick-me-up after work.

"I want to incorporate some traditional elements, as I know Brit would appreciate that," Isabella said as she thumbed through a catalog of furniture for reception and waiting rooms. "I would also like to mix that with modern lines, and of course a whole lot of glam."

Gia brought over a few rings of fabrics and set them on the large project table. "Ooooh, I like that, and so will Brit. That totally sums her up, you know, traditional girl"—Gia made a face—"but she dresses chic and mod and always has on some form of bling. She's jazzy." Gia shook her jazz hands.

Isabella laughed. "Knock it off. You like her, don't you? Brit's a good person."

"Yeah, I do, except for the traditional part. The thought of being with only one man makes me shudder."

"Um, hello, I'm with one man."

"Yeah, but you're married. That's different. She and Colin have been together, like what, forever? And they're not even married." Gia wrinkled her nose as if smelling something rancid.

"You know," Isabella remarked, "not everyone is a ho like you." She ducked as Gia threw some fabric swatches at her.

"Well, they should be. Gosh damn, I have a lot of fun. Maybe that's what you need, Izzie, a little some-some on the side?"

"Yeah, that's just what I need, another man in my life. No thanks. One is plenty for me."

"I'm not talking about a boyfriend. God knows you don't need that. I'm talking about hot, steamy, booty-call sex."

Isabella only half listened to Gia's rambling as she returned to the catalog. "Booty-call sex?"

Gia hopped up on the table and sat Indian-style like a child would in a show-and-tell circle, eager to tell. "Yeah, someone you can call up just for sex when you're stressed. No strings attached, just a whole lot of fun. Pretty cool, huh?"

Isabella stopped flipping through the catalog. "My poor dead grandmother is rolling over in her grave right now. What the hell is wrong with you?"

Gia smirked. "Where do I begin?"

"You kill me. One day, Gia Hausen, when your heart is ready again, you will love. It's not always bad, you know." Isabella knew she was touching on a taboo subject, but it had slipped out.

Just before the two had met, Gia had fallen in love and married an older man who had promised her the world, only to deliver a year of heartache and pain after Gia found out he already had a wife in another state. Gia was devastated. She felt like such a fool. It was then that she had launched her no-attachments, no-regrets, pure-fun approach to romance.

Gia shrugged it off. "Oh yeah? Which one of us do you think has more fun? That would be me."

"Okay, you keep your booty calls while I live vicariously through you as you share all the sordid details. When I'm stressed out, I'll go to Brit's spa and relax in the meditation room, sitting in this." Isabella turned the catalog around to show her an elegant chaise lounge with a curved, tufted back. "And we can have them upholstered in this." She held up one of the velvet fabrics Gia had pulled out.

Gia took it and rubbed it against her face. "Oh my gosh, it feels like heaven."

"Exactly. It's the perfect theme for a meditation room: heaven." Isabella handed Gia the catalog, with instructions for Amber to copy the pages she'd tabbed for the upholstered items. As Gia started to leave, Isabella stopped her and put her arms around her friend, squeezing her tightly. "I want you to know that I love you and appreciate you trying to help me, even if you are twisted. I couldn't imagine my life without you."

Gia rested her head on Isabella's shoulder. "Aw, you're gonna make me cry. Stop it." Not one for mushy moments, Gia added in a whisper, "I'm telling you, booty-call sex. You're missing out."

Isabella swatted her on her butt and shooed her out of the room. "Go, and when you get back, we're going to Chantal's Couture. The furniture pieces were delivered this morning, as well as the artwork and the silk panels for the dressing rooms. I want to check up on the installation."

"No problem. Do you think we could squeeze some lunch today, too?"

Isabella winked. "Well, hello—there's always time for lunch."

Chapter 8

Isabella sat in the back seat of the Town Car as Sebastian navigated to the curb in front of Rosalini's, a quaint Italian restaurant where she was meeting Charles Vanderbeck for lunch. The past few weeks had flown by. To her relief, her projects were now running smoothly; her staff had obviously received the message loud and clear. Now she was anxious to hear about the project Vanderbeck envisioned for her. Although she had once fretted over what Grayson would think after the incident at the gallery showing, she no longer cared. Things between them had been strained for weeks. They had exchanged a series of hellos, goodbyes, and I'll-be-back-laters, and not much else. Isabella felt that she didn't owe him anything. Business was business; she would be a fool not to meet with Vanderbeck.

Vanderbeck's secretary had requested that Isabella be prompt, as he had a tight schedule that day. He would have only forty-five minutes to meet with her. The secretary had also forwarded Isabella a menu from the restaurant, requesting that she select a meal so that it would already be prepared when she arrived. Isabella thought that perhaps she should have James include that in emails to her clients: *Isabella has a tight appointment schedule today, so please be advised that you may only annoy her with design uncertainties for thirty minutes.*

Isabella chuckled to herself. There were some clients she adored and loved working with. Their design outlook went something like this: *Here is what I need. This is your budget. Work your magic, and don't concern me with the details. I just want to see it completed.* Those were her favorite clients. Then there were those who liked to micro-manage the design process, overanalyzing every detail, fabric, and color. They didn't understand that you couldn't focus on each individual detail; you had to focus on the big picture, the ending design vision. They hindered the process and wasted her time, insisting that she show them option after option, only to go with her original selection in the end. They caused backups in her schedule as she coddled them through each step, each installation, and each delivery. They were the ones who made Isabella want to take off a stiletto and whack them upside the head. Yes, those were the ones who needed that email.

Inside Rosalini's, as the hostess escorted her to Vanderbeck's table, Isabella instinctively scanned the décor, running down a quick list in her head. She had always had a gift for walking into a space and envisioning its potential end design, even as a child. Rosalini's earned an eight out of ten. *Just a few tweaks here and there. Not too bad*, she thought. She appreciated that it boasted modern elements, especially considering that it was a traditional Italian restaurant, including crisp white linens and hundreds of yards of white silk drapes—elegant and classy. Sleek, circular, white leather booths with extra high backs for privacy lined the outer walls. She could see why this served as an excellent location for a business lunch. The large-plank, highly distressed wood floor was finished in a rich ebony with subtle caramel highlights, reminding her of the floor in her loft. Her eyes scanned the crimson Murano glass chandeliers hanging from the ceilings. Although the scale of the fixtures was impressive, she would have liked to see something rustic to compliment the floor and contrast with the modern sophistication of the tables and booths, something like a chunky iron chandelier, vintage-looking but adorned with plenty of crystals.

The hostess stopped at a booth in the left rear corner of the restaurant. "Mr. Vanderbeck, Mrs. Hughes has arrived. Shall I tell Marcus to bring your food out for you?"

Charles Vanderbeck flashed his perfectly veneered teeth at the hostess. "Thank you, Deanna, and please do."

The hostess reciprocated with what Isabella considered a too-friendly smile before walking away.

"Isabella, it is so nice to see you again." Vanderbeck was wearing another expensive navy blue Calvin Klein suit. He stood up from the table and took both of Isabella's hands in his own, then brought her right hand up to his lips and kissed it. "A vision of loveliness, as always."

Isabella smiled, remembering her indecision as she had perused her closet that morning. She had decided on a sleeveless, cream-colored dress with a rounded neckline and a narrow black belt. She had paired it with simple, yet sexy black slingback pumps and pulled back part of her hair with a black vintage hairpin.

"Great to see you again as well, Mr. Vanderbeck."

"Please, call me Charles. I insist."

Charles took a seat across from her as the waiter arrived with their food. The presentation was exquisite, and the aroma rising from the plates made her mouth water. Isabella had ordered the frutti di mare, an Italian stew with calamari, mussels, shrimp, lobster, and assorted vegetables swimming in a wonderfully rich marinara sauce. It was Italian her way, without the carbs. Charles had ordered roasted red pepper chicken with a healthy side of pasta.

Noticing a long poured scotch across the table from her, Isabella requested a glass of the house white wine.

As they dug into their meals, Charles said, "Isabella, I initially wanted to meet with you to discuss a specific space I recently obtained, but that has changed."

With her mouth full, Isabella looked up in surprise.

"My daughter Evette, who is one of my project managers, approached me with the idea. Evette is somewhat of a free spirit. She is artistic, like your husband, and I have been pushing her to get more involved in our family business for years. I would like her to have a more structured career. When she came to me with this idea, I thought it was brilliant, and I believe you would be the perfect person for it."

Isabella dabbed her mouth with her napkin. "You have me intrigued, Charles."

Charles took a long swig of his drink and leaned toward Isabella. He smiled, knowing her curiosity was piqued. "As you know, my company has been successful in acquiring buildings and renovating them into residential spaces. This new building we're looking at is quite large and won't only have condos and penthouse living quarters, but we will also incorporate a full retail area. Residents will be able to shop for everything they need, from household items to gourmet foods and high-end designer clothing. We are also looking to incorporate a high-end restaurant and café, a full-service spa and salon, and a state-of-the-art gym with personal trainers. It's a one-stop concept, if you will. Live, shop, pamper."

Excitement stirred within her. "I think it's a wonderful idea. There aren't many residential developers who have taken the concept to that level. I like it."

"I'm glad to hear that. These are going to be over-the-top shops offering special services for the wealthy and spoiled."

Isabella smiled, but she was secretly trying to wrap her mind around the vast amount of design that would entail. Though excited by the concept, she also knew such an undertaking would require an enormous amount of time. "So, Charles, you want me to design the retail spaces as well as the living quarters and common areas?"

Charles reclined against the high back of the booth and raised his eyebrows, giving her a sly look. "Yes, but there is more."

Isabella couldn't imagine what ideas were floating around in his head. She was literally on the edge of her seat. "So there's more than just designing the space? I'm all ears."

Charles chuckled. "You know, Isabella, I've made a name for myself dealing in real estate for quite some time. I've dabbled in other ventures here and there, but nothing that has really held my interest. What I'm thinking of would take the Vanderbeck name to a whole new level. With this new building, I want the residents to have the complete Vanderbeck lifestyle. That's where you come in. I would like for you to design an entire line of home furnishings that we will brand as Vanderbeck Home. The concept is to have three uniquely designed furniture plans that residents can choose from, with the option to intermix the pieces if they choose."

Isabella's mouth fell open. Never in a million years would she have guessed what he was proposing. "I'm not sure what to say, Charles. I've never designed a furniture line before. I'm not even sure I would know where to begin."

Charles held up his hand. "Please don't give that a second thought. During my trip overseas last week, I was able to procure a manufacturer in Milan to produce all of your designs. I toured three plants personally and selected the very best for you. I have also assembled an excellent team for you to work with, sparing no expense. You will have access to the finest finishes, woods, stones, marbles, and glass, anything your heart desires. All you need to do now is say yes, and it's yours."

"I'm . . . I'm flabbergasted." Her head was reeling. "I don't know what to say. Why me? I'm sure you must know many people who could take on this project, people who have actually designed furniture lines. We just met." Isabella knew she must sound like a blubbering idiot as she broke the first rule in business and revealed to a client that she wasn't confident in her abilities. But she was stunned. Every designer dreamed of developing his or her own furniture line. She had never expected to be given the chance to do so, and with carte blanche.

"Isabella, from the moment I met you I felt that you had that special something I was looking for. I liked your style and your wit. I knew a little of your work, but didn't know much about you. Truth be told, I did some checking around on you, and in doing so, I knew my instincts were right on the money. Small-town girl raised on a farm by her grandparents with no other family to speak of, who wisely used the money from their estate to put herself through college. Started her own design company fresh out of school and turned it into a multi-million-dollar design firm here in Manhattan in a very short time. You are a fighter, Isabella, someone with drive and determination to see things through. That is a quality I need in my designer . . . in you."

Isabella was speechless. She felt extremely flattered, and at the same time a little invaded that he had done a thorough background check into her life. *Thank gosh nothing from my senior spring break trip to Cabo San Lucas came up*, she thought.

"Wow, Charles, you've blown my mind. I would love to say yes, but I need some time to think. This is a major undertaking, and while I would welcome the challenge, there are many factors I need to consider."

"I completely understand. I wouldn't consider you a great businesswoman if you didn't give this careful consideration. I've had my lawyers draw up the contracts and project specifications, and they're being delivered to your office this afternoon. Take some time, read them over, and let me know your thoughts. I would like to hear from you by the end of the week. The train is moving out of the station, and I want you on board." Charles nodded, wearing a knowing expression, like a father speaking to a child whom he was sure would follow his advice despite other options available.

Mesmerized, Isabella felt herself nodding in return. "I'll read over the specifications as soon as I receive them, and you will have my decision by week's end."

With their time quickly running out, they finished their meals, talking with enthusiasm about the project. Finally, Charles rose from the table, causing Isabella to stand as well. Her legs felt unsteady.

He took her hand and again kissed it. "Thank you for meeting me today, my dear. Please stay and finish your lunch. I must head out to my next appointment. It was a pleasure, as always."

As he left, Isabella plopped back into her seat, realizing this man might very well change her life. For the first time that afternoon, her thoughts traveled to Grayson and the million-dollar question: Would the change be good, or disastrous?

"Madam, may I bring you another glass of wine?" the waiter asked.

"No, but I'll take a Stoli on the rocks."

"Very well, madam." As he turned, Isabella laid a hand on his arm. "Make it a double, please."

"Certainly, madam." He smiled knowingly and slipped away.

~~~

"How much?" Gia shouted in disbelief as she reached over Isabella's desk and snatched the contracts out of her hands.

Isabella snatched them back. "Give me those. It says here that he's paying me five hundred thousand to start, and another five hundred
~~~

thousand on completion. It also says that I'll be compensated eight percent of the net revenue from the sales. This is all in addition to the fees for designing the building's interior. Do you have any idea what kind of numbers we're talking about here?"

Gia gave an exaggerated shrug. "Hello! I'm not a numbers girl, remember?"

"Okay, try to follow me here. Let's say there's ten million dollars in net revenue, which I'm assuming would be pretty easy to hit, seeing that this line is going to be very high end. I would get eight hundred thousand just off that revenue."

"Holy shit, Izzie. This man is not joking around. He definitely wants you to design the line and is putting his money where his mouth is."

"But wait, there's more. It says that I will have, at my disposal, a private jet to use for trips back and forth overseas to meet with the manufacturer, and that all my travel expenses will be covered and booked by his company. All that's required is a twenty-four-hour notice before departure."

Gia leaned over the desk, trying to peek at the contract. "Shut up. Does it say you can bring your assistant?"

Isabella bopped her over the head with the contract. "You don't think I could or would do this without you, do you?"

Gia rubbed her head. "Well, I was hoping you wouldn't, but I didn't want to be pushy and all up in your business about it."

"My love, I could never do something like this without you. We're in this together, and if I do decide to do this, I'm going to need all the help I can get from you."

"*If* you decide to do this? Isabella Hughes, what the hell is wrong with you? I will personally whoop you upside the head with your own stiletto if you pass this up."

"There's a lot to consider. If you think we're crazy now, what do you think something like this is going to do? Do you have any idea the vast amount of time it will require? Not only do we have to design the building, but we're also designing an entire line of furniture simultaneously. We'll also need to put together a budget for the building's renovations and our design fee schedule." Isabella dropped the contract on her desk and began to rub her temples.

Gia took a glass off the wet bar, threw in a few ice cubes, and poured a hefty amount of vodka before setting the glass down in front of Isabella. "Drink, bitch."

Grateful, Isabella tipped up the glass and took a long sip.

"Listen, Debbie Downer, we have the resources to do this. Our staff is seasoned enough to handle it. You just have to let them. We will create a plan of attack, then step back and let them do the work, with our watchful eye over them, of course. We'll set up weekly progress meetings and assign one person as the head designer, who will be in charge of the others. While all that is being done, you and I can concentrate on designing the furniture line. See, easy-schmeasy." Gia snapped her fingers and looked victorious, as if she had just solved world hunger.

"Okay, genius, tell me who will be running our current projects in the meantime."

Gia groaned. "Isabella, we have ten designers back there whom you hired, so I'm assuming they're not all stupid. But if you want to up the caliber of talent, then hire someone new."

"As if I want to take on hiring new designers right before all this starts."

"Why don't you just admit where all this doubt is coming from?" Gia tapped her foot, waiting for Isabella to say what she already knew. Isabella glared at her. "Well, Izzie? I'm waiting."

"All right, all right . . . Grayson. There, I said it. Are you happy?"

"Seriously, Izzie? Seriously?"

"You know as well as I do that Grayson is going to blow a nut about this. We had a huge, blow-up fight after I merely took a *business card* from Charles Vanderbeck. Imagine how he'll react when he finds out Vanderbeck has awarded me a project of this magnitude and level of prestige. Not only that, but it'll eat up all my time. We already don't have enough time together. We would never see each other, and considering the way things are right now, my marriage might not survive it."

"That's bullshit. You always make things work, and you will make this work too. Grayson would be stupid to deny you this opportunity, especially since he'll benefit from it. You need to talk to him about this, but you need to be strong in your decision. You can't go in flipping and flopping like a fish. Make your decision and stand by it."

Isabella's head was pounding.

"You want this, don't you?"

"Yes, I do, I really do, but . . ."

Gia held out her hand to stop her. "Shhhh. But nothing. You will do it, and I am going to help you. You talk with Grayson, and I'll start getting everything else organized on this end. If you want me to line up interviews for some new peeps, I can do that as well."

Isabella stared at her for a long moment. "Okay, go ahead, line up some interviews. I'll deal with Grayson tonight."

Gia grinned, looking like a cat that ate a canary. "Congratulations, Isabella Hughes! You are now going to design a furniture line. How does that make you feel?"

"Good, actually. It feels really good." Isabella wasn't sure if she was trying to convince Gia or her own stomach, which was churning with anxiety about the fight she would soon face with Grayson.

Chapter 9

Isabella left the office at a reasonable time, with the hope that not arriving home late would help her cause with Grayson. Traffic was heavy, as usual, so she used the time to organize her thoughts, trying to prepare herself for every possible scenario. The best approach, she thought, was to offer a timeline, make a deal that the project would only occupy her for so long, and then she would take some time off just for them. She could offer to cut back and start a family afterward, show him that she just wanted this last hoorah before stepping back.

Isabella was feeling pretty confident as Sebastian pulled up in front of her building, but as he opened the door and she stepped out, she felt her stomach clench again.

"Have a good night, Mrs. Hughes," Sebastian said, "and good luck."

Confused, Isabella wondered if Gia had mentioned something to him.

"My vision may have gotten worse as I've gotten older," he said, "but my hearing is still spot on. I could hear you mumbling your pros and cons the whole way home."

"Well, since you heard me, did it sound good?"

Sebastian put his arm around her shoulder and pulled her in for a squeeze. "You'll do just fine. From what I know of Mr. Hughes, he is smart and level-headed."

Isabella hoped Sebastian knew her husband as well as he thought he did.

Inside, she heard Grayson fumbling around with some pots in the kitchen. As she pulled the door closed behind her, she was greeted by the smell of homemade bread. She was surprised to see that the dining table had been set with her grandmother's china, and he had replicated what she had done with the rose petals sprinkled across the table. In the center of the table sat a large bouquet of Isabella's favorite flowers, gardenias.

Grayson was feverishly working away in the kitchen, jamming to his iPod, unaware that she had come in. Isabella watched him for a few minutes, observing the obvious change in his mood. It was like night and day with him lately. She never knew which Grayson she would get when she came home: the crabby, moody, I-don't-have-time-for-you

Grayson, or the carefree, upbeat, I-love-you-so-much Grayson. It was just her luck, she thought, that he was in a great mood. While that would work to her advantage with the news she had to deliver, it had been so long since he was like this that she hated to ruin it.

Grayson spun around to grab a bowl from the upper cabinet next to the fridge and saw Isabella standing there, watching him. He pulled his headphones off and grabbed his chest. "Babe, you scared the crap outta me." He approached her and pulled her to him, kissing her full on her lips. "Mmmm. That will be for dessert." He moved back and kissed the top of her nose. "Perfect timing. Dinner is almost done."

Isabella was still suspicious of his behavior, but decided to let it go. "How did you know what time I would be home?"

"A little birdie told me." Grayson winked at her.

"A little birdie with short, spiky blond hair and black-rimmed glasses, I'm guessing."

"Um, yeah, that would be the exact birdie."

Isabella raised her eyebrow and tilted her head in the direction of the dining table. "What's all this about?"

"What, can't a man surprise his wife with a home-cooked meal?"

"A man can most definitely do that, but usually the man is talking to his wife when he does so." Damn it, she couldn't let it go.

Grayson rubbed her arms. "I know, Izzie. I've been kind of a shit to you lately."

"Kind of?"

"I deserved that. Okay, a *real* shit lately, and I'm sorry, baby. You know how I get when I'm creating. I'm in a zone, focused, and everything else around me just causes unnecessary chatter in my head."

Isabella took a step back. "I'm unnecessary chatter?" *Shit. Shut up*, she told herself.

"You know what I mean, and you know that I don't think that about you. I love you. I know we haven't been close lately, and it's my fault. I felt like a shit when I came home and saw the special dinner you had for me. I was wrong, and should have called you, but honestly, I lost track of time. When I saw you were gone the next morning, I thought you were just plain pissed at me, so I left. I didn't want to fight with you. The world isn't right when we fight." He smiled at her, trying to get her to reciprocate.

Isabella whacked him on the shoulder. "You are very lucky, Grayson Hughes, that I still find you irresistibly adorable."

He pulled her close again, bringing her nose-to-nose with him until she felt his warm breath on her face. "I thought it was because you love the fact that I'm packing nine inches." Grayson thrust his hips into her, and she could tell that someone was getting a little turned on.

"Well, that too." Smirking, she grabbed his face and kissed him hard on the mouth. His mouth was warm and wet, and she felt herself getting turned on. Her breath came faster, and she slipped her hand into his jeans.

Grayson pulled her hand out and backed up. "Not so fast. Dinner first, dessert later." He backed up into the kitchen, keeping his eye on her.

"Ugh." Isabella threw herself down on the sofa. "You're killing me here. You did that on purpose, you shit."

Grayson burst into an evil laugh. "No, baby, not me. I would never tease you like that."

Isabella took a pillow from the sofa and threw it at him.

"Oh, is that how you wanna play?" Grayson picked up the pillow and slowly moved toward her, pretending he was going to smother her with it. Isabella sat there laughing at him. This was the Grayson she adored. Just before he reached her, he threw the pillow at her and pounced on her, pinning her to the sofa.

Isabella wrapped her legs around his waist and squeezed them together, trapping him. She seductively pursed her lips. "Whatcha gonna do now, big boy? Looks like I'm the one who has you."

Holding both her wrists with one hand, Grayson caressed her cheek and traced her lips with his finger. As they stared into each other's eyes, he brought his lips down on hers, kissing her sweetly. Isabella felt her pulse quicken. She tried freeing her hands so she could touch him, but he kept his grip tight. He worked his way from her lips to her neck, kissing her while his hand roamed down her leg. Her passion was building, and there was nothing more she wanted than to feel Grayson inside her. She craved his touch, his love—all that he had been denying her, she wanted.

He returned his mouth to her lips as his hand slid beneath her dress and tugged at her silk thong, which was moist with her sweetness. Isabella dropped her legs from his waist, letting them fall open, and Grayson rubbed her sweet spot through her thong. Isabella groaned and pushed against his hand.

He pulled his lips away from hers, and his hand returned to her face and lifted her chin up toward him. Isabella opened her eyes and looked at him, waiting. He grinned.

"Looks like I'm the one who has you," he said, and jumped off of her, chuckling. "Isabella Hughes, you are too easy."

Isabella sat there on the sofa with her mouth hanging open. "That was *so* not nice, Grayson. If my husband wouldn't sexually neglect me, I wouldn't be so easy to get."

"Aw, poor baby. A whole two weeks—you are so deprived." Grayson pulled her up from the sofa. "Come on, dinner is ready. We have all night to play, and I promise you by morning you won't be feeling neglected."

As they moved to the dining table, she suddenly remembered her meeting with Charles, and her stomach sank. She struggled to set aside her anxiety as Grayson served her an impressive meal of baked Chilean sea bass stuffed with lobster and crab, topped with red peppers, artichokes, and scallions. She took a bite, downed her glass of wine, and asked him about his work, knowing that she was merely stalling and delaying the inevitable.

Ten minutes later, Isabella was still pushing the food around her plate. Finally Grayson asked, "Is the meal okay?"

She looked up, forcing a smile. "Yes, it's delicious."

He stared at her as if trying to read her mind. She knew the time had come.

She set down her fork. "Grayson, we have to talk."

"Is there something wrong?"

"No, nothing is wrong. I just have a very big decision to make, and I want to hear your thoughts on it," she said, treading lightly.

"All right then, shoot. I'm all ears." He took her hand in his.

Here we go, she thought.

"I had a meeting today with Charles Vanderbeck." Isabella paused as Grayson removed his hand and leaned back into his chair.

"I see. And?"

Isabella noticed his "I'm all ears" attitude had changed quickly. "And he has obtained a large building that he's turning into upscale condo and penthouse living. The building is also going to have specialty services and high-end shops for the residents. The concept is live, shop, pamper."

"So I take it he wants you to design the entire building for him?"

"Well, yes and no. There's more."

"I'm listening."

Isabella took a deep breath and exhaled. "Charles—"

"Charles?" Grayson snickered. "Wow, you're already on a first-name basis with him. Nice. I'm sorry, please continue."

She stared at him. "Why bother? You're already irritated. Forget it. I shouldn't have bothered you for advice."

"Sorry, but I'm just a little bitter from the night at the gallery. I wasn't prepared for you to bring up his name. Although, I shouldn't be surprised. I knew you would meet with him. Couldn't resist, could you?"

"Stop it," she said, raising her voice. "I understand how you feel, but this is important business. What he is proposing could change our lives for the better. Will you at least let me finish?"

"The floor is all yours." He folded his arms across his chest.

Great, she thought, noticing his body language.

Isabella watched him for a long moment, wondering if this man whom she had been with for years had somehow become bipolar. One minute he was happy, the next minute he was angry and moody. One minute he was all over her, the next minute he wouldn't touch her with a ten-foot pole. It was like living on a roller coaster, and her stomach couldn't take anymore.

"I'm going to cut to the chase," she said. "Charles Vanderbeck would like me to develop a furniture line for him called Vanderbeck Home. He wants to create a Vanderbeck lifestyle, if you will, with this building and its residents. He already has a manufacturer overseas willing to produce all the furniture, and he is looking to have me design them. For doing so, I will be compensated a total of one million dollars and eight percent of the net revenue sales. There will be all the design fees associated with the project as well. We stand to make a lot of money on this, Grayson."

"*You* stand to make a lot of money on this," he fired back.

"I am *not* going down this road again with you about money. We've been there, and I'm not interested in going back." Isabella poured herself another glass of wine.

"So what do you want me to say? Are you asking me if you should do it, or are you telling me you're doing it?"

"I wanted to talk to you about it because this affects both of us. I haven't given Charles my answer and will not do so until you and I talk this through. This is a huge undertaking. I'm not blind to the fact that it will quadruple my workload and will give us less time to spend with each other than we do now. It will only be for a little while, but considering the way things have been, I don't think we'll survive unless you're on board." Isabella was starting to feel like she should bow out of the project, that it wasn't worth it.

"What are we talking about here, Izzie? Six months, ten months, years? What is it?"

"Honestly, I don't know. I'm gonna guess a year at least. Charles wants to move quickly on this. He has the manufacturers ready to go, and they've already sent samples of materials to his office. They're waiting on me. Once I give them the go-ahead, I can start designing the pieces."

"And while you're designing all this furniture, who is working on the building? I know you. There's no way you are going to walk away from that and allow someone else to take over."

"Well, Gia and I discussed that today. We're planning to choose a head designer and assign some assistant designers to the project. Our goal is to get the direction of the project set, then let them roll with it, with weekly check-in meetings, of course. We also thought it wouldn't be a bad time to look for new designers to bring on board. We could use some new talent."

"Sounds like you two girls have this all figured out. I'm glad you discussed this with her first."

Isabella let out a deep breath, remembering Gia's words to stay strong and not waver. He wasn't making it easy.

"We have nothing figured out," she insisted. "We were just talking about how we could make it work. I need to know where you stand on this. Your opinion is what matters here, Grayson."

"I thought you wanted to start lightening up your load. You've been talking about that for almost a year now, and about starting a family. How is any of that going to be possible if you have this going on?"

Isabella reached for his hand, and he reluctantly gave it to her. "I know that's what I said, what I've been saying, but this is a once-in-a-lifetime opportunity. It would be the pinnacle of my career, designing my own furniture line. You know that's always been a dream of mine."

"But the line wouldn't even be yours. It's Vanderbeck's line. His name will get all the recognition."

"In some ways, yes, but I will get the creative credit for the line. It's 'Vanderbeck Home designed by Isabella Hughes.' So my name will be out there, and those will be my creations. I want to create pieces that people will enjoy in their homes; that would mean something to me. You know how good you feel when you see a piece you've created in someone's home or in a restaurant or office building. It feels amazing, you can't deny that. I want to feel that." She was pleading with him now.

"Don't you already do that? You create spaces every day, and those spaces evoke more than just tangible goods. They evoke feelings and set moods. That's something you can and should be proud of."

"Of course I'm proud of what I do. Every day I'm thankful that I'm able to do what I love. I just want this one thing that I've never tried before. I want to challenge myself, and succeed at it." She looked into his eyes. "Not just for me, but for you, for us."

Grayson sighed; it was always just one more thing. He knew her too well. When she got bored with this, she would be out searching for that next "one thing." He sighed again and reached for her hand. "Isabella, I'm already proud of you. You don't need to do this to prove something to me. I just worry about you. This is a lot."

"It is a lot. I know that. I see it as my last big hoorah before I take some time away. I do want to start a family with you. I've always said that, Grayson. I just know that if I do that now and let this pass me by, I may never see an opportunity like this again. I would always regret my decision, and I do not want to live my life regretting. You know me, I have always followed my heart, and my heart is telling me to go for it. With that being said, my heart is also telling me that I need you there with me."

Grayson took a long, hard look at her. He could see her passion for wanting to take on the challenge, but he could also see how torn up she was about it. He knew what he had to do, what he had to say. He knew he could not be the reason she didn't accept the job.

"Okay," he said, "you have my support."

Isabella squealed and jumped out of her chair to hug him.

"Not so fast, missy. I have conditions, so sit down."

Isabella sat back down cautiously. "And they are?"

"First of all, I want your lawyers to look over the contracts thoroughly and make sure everything is on the up-and-up so you're not screwed out of money that is due you."

"Done. I sent them to my lawyer before I left the office."

"Secondly, I want you to promise me that you, your ho, and Tinker Bell"—Isabella laughed, knowing he was referring to Gia and James—"will sit down and come up with a precise plan stating who will be in charge of what. The furniture line and Vanderbeck's building are not your only projects, so you'll need to allow someone else to take over them for you. Your nose can't be everywhere. Got it?"

"I hear you, I do. That will be hard, but I think with all that I'll have going on, I'll be distracted enough not to be bothered." At least, she hoped. "Is there a third request?"

"Yes. I want you to look into hiring a project manager."

Isabella was puzzled. "I don't need a project manager. I have James and Gia."

"That's not the same. Gia will be helping you design and acting as your contact with the other designers. James will be running the office, handling phone calls, emails, deliveries, all that stuff. You need someone who is going to have your best interests in mind and coordinate the business end of it so you can concentrate on the design. If this is truly what you want, I want to make sure you're not wasting your time."

"But I've never hired an outside project manager. I wouldn't know where to find one, and I'm sure I don't have the time to figure it out."

"Let me do it for you, then."

"Why would you want to do that?"

"Well, for starters, I love you, and you're my wife. I don't want to see you overwhelmed. There's more to designing furniture than just picking out pretty materials and drawing up sketches, babe. There's a whole other side to it, one you and I know nothing about."

Isabella shrugged. "If that's what it's going to take for you to be on board, then okay. But I'm not sold on having someone I don't know take care of my business."

"I understand. Let me make a few phone calls and see what I can come up with. I'm sure someone will know somebody who could help."

"Okay then, done. Anything else?"

Grayson grabbed her hands and pulled her around the table and into his lap. "My last request is that even though things will be crazy, we'll make time for each other at least once a week." He kissed the top of her forehead.

"Just once a week? You know I hate to go that long." Grinning, she sat up and stared into his beautiful blue eyes. "I promise I will make time for you. I'll never let this come between us."

Grayson stared backed at her, knowing better but opting not to say anything. He simply kissed her on the lips softly. "I know, baby girl, I know."

Feeling as if a weight had been lifted from her shoulders, she said, "Can we have dessert now?"

He scooped her up from his lap and made a beeline for the staircase. "We sure can, and you, my love, can have seconds."

Isabella giggled. "I'll have my first dessert course in bed, and my second in the shower."

"Mmm, I like the way you think," he said, and nuzzled his face into her neck.

Chapter 10

The next few weeks flew by. Consumed with meetings with her staff of head designers and their assistants, Isabella was quickly thrown into Mr. Vanderbeck's project with full force. Gia and James had put together a huge board showing the status of every project that was currently open, the shipping status of materials, the items still to be selected, and any other pertinent information. At a glance, she could assess where the project was and where it needed to go for completion. The board reminded Isabella of the crime scene board detectives used on television shows. All that was missing was a mug shot of the client.

Isabella was impressed with the way Gia and James had stepped up. James had taken on responsibility for updating the board every morning as nightly progress reports were emailed to him by the designers assigned to each project. Gia, who knew Isabella so well, was in charge of assigning designers to projects. In addition, she interviewed new designers and passed along the ones she deemed worthy for a final meeting with Isabella. In the end, they hired three new designers, all of them men, all gay, and all fabulous, in Isabella's opinion. James was overjoyed—Gia, not so much.

Charles Vanderbeck was elated that Isabella had, in his words, "gotten on board the train." She had been meeting with his staff to go over the building plans and spent hours behind closed doors with the owners of the manufacturing plant that would be producing the furniture line. They wanted her to have a better understanding of the entire process. She also had several meetings with Charles and his daughter Evette to discuss some key points they were interested in seeing in the building and the furniture.

Charles was right: Evette was a free spirit. Isabella could not see her in the corporate setting. What she did see, though, was Evette's father pushing her to be there. Evette had short blond hair cut in a pixie style that suited her face and personality well. The bottom layers of her hair were colored dark brown, signaling a rebellious side. She was a little thing, about five foot two and a hundred pounds soaking wet, and had large brown eyes that reminded Isabella of the Kewpie doll she'd had as a child. She was a talented painter, but unless you were among the crème de la crème, making a living at it in New York wasn't easy—a fact Isabella was well aware of, being married to Grayson. She got a sense, though, that Evette lived quite comfortably off her daddy's money. This seemed to be something, Isabella noticed, that Daddy was getting annoyed about.

Within the new transition, Isabella found that her life had become a whirlwind. At times she wasn't sure if she was coming or going, but she managed to keep her promise to Grayson and spend some special time with him once a week. Sometimes he came to see her at work, and they had lunch in her office behind closed doors. Lunch usually ended with a quickie on her desk. Then there were times when they didn't eat at all, instead they just made use of her plush sofa. Gia and James were well aware that she was not to be bothered when Grayson came for lunch. Although their time together still wasn't enough, she understood it was the best they could do . . . for now.

~~~

Isabella had just returned to her office after a long meeting with Richard Lafayette, who had dropped by as he often did to make sure she was still on top of his project. He wanted to make sure she had kept her word and was solely overseeing the renovations. Of course, little did he know that ten minutes before meeting with him, she had sat down with Gillian, the head designer Gia had assigned to the project, who had given her a quick summary of the project with the aid of the golden dry erase board.

She made her way to her desk with her eyes glued to her BlackBerry, reviewing emails. Four were from Gonzolo, the owner of the manufacturing plant, who was pressing her for furniture sketches.

"I know, I know." Isabella tossed her BlackBerry on her desk and began rubbing her temples. "He can get off my back anytime now," she muttered to herself, something she found herself doing more and more. "I'm well aware of what I need to get done, damn it."

"You know, it's better if you start at the top of your neck and massage your way down to your shoulder. That's where the tension is coming from."

Isabella jumped and opened her eyes to see a handsome man seated in one of the chairs in front of her desk. She hadn't noticed him when she walked in. His piercing green eyes were set off by dark, wavy hair long enough to brush the top of his collar. His face was strong and chiseled, with just the right amount of scruff. Although he was seated, she could tell he was tall. His tailored Armani suit was paired with a large-cuffed white dress shirt unbuttoned at the top. He looked like he
~~~

had stepped off the pages of *GQ* magazine.

Mesmerized, Isabella stuttered, “I’m sorry, can I help you?”

The stranger smiled, and Isabella was glad to be sitting down, as she was certain her knees would have buckled under her.

“No, but I’m sure I can help you.” His voice was deep and smooth.

Detecting a hint of arrogance in his tone, Isabella raised her eyebrows. “Is that right? Well, how about you tell me who you are and what you are doing in my office, and I will be the judge of that.”

He stood and extended his hand to her. “My name is Julian Grossaint. Please call me Julian.”

Holy crap, he is tall, she thought as she reluctantly shook his hand. “Okay, Julian, what is it that you think I need help with?”

He returned to his seat, arranging himself so that he looked confident yet comfortable. “I hear you’re in desperate need of a project manager, so I’m here to save you.” Julian grinned.

Isabella narrowed her eyes. “Well, Julian, *desperate* and needing to be *saved* have never been used to describe me. You must have spoken with my husband, Grayson. This whole thing is his idea, so you’ll have to excuse me if I’m not fully on board with it. Frankly, I don’t see the point.”

“I get that. You’re an independent woman accustomed to handling things on her own. You don’t want a stranger telling you how to run your business. I understand. But I’m only here to help and will focus exclusively on your best interests. For starters, we’re going to have to work on getting you to smile more. Companies prefer working with, and investing in, happy people. I can see that you’re stressed, which means we could probably do a better job of organizing and managing your time.

“Oh, and we definitely need to do something about your partner, Gia. I could have been someone coming in here to harm you, yet she allowed me into your office alone, after only a few minutes of conversation.”

Isabella frowned. *Why does that not surprise me?* she thought.

“It’s my job to work closely with you and ensure that you and your company are receiving the full potential benefits of this venture. There is endless opportunity in this for you, and I will work to create those opportunities, present them to you, and guide you into making the right business decisions with them.”

He was well-spoken and professional. There was something about the way he talked that soothed her and made her want to engage in conversation with him. His smile was warm and inviting.

“So tell me, Julian, how do you know Grayson?”

"I don't. I've never met him, actually. We spoke on the phone last week. I believe he did some work for one of my clients, which is how he came to contact me."

Isabella nodded, feeling less comfortable knowing that Grayson didn't actually know this man. "I see."

He seemed able to read her like a book. "Listen, my resume is on your desk. Call around, check me out. You need to feel comfortable with me, Isabella. I want you to feel you can trust me, or else I can be of no use to you. I have a feeling you and I would work well together, and that we could have some fun in the process."

He stood and handed her his card. "It was a pleasure to meet you, and I look forward to hearing from you soon. Call me anytime." He turned on that megawatt smile again, and she felt a little lightheaded.

She took the card and shook his hand, this time a little more warmly. "It was nice meeting you as well."

Isabella watched him as he walked down the hallway, thinking again, *Damn, is he tall.*

Moments later, Gia bounded into her office, giddy and breathless. "Okay, how yummy was he? Have you ever seen eyes like his before in your life? They were so green, with a hint of blue. It was like looking into the Mediterranean Sea. He *has* to be a model." Gia was rambling so fast, Isabella could barely understand her.

"Whoa, let's turn down those hormones. He's a project manager, not a model. And listen here, missy, I don't care how hot some guy is, you can't let a stranger into my office without me knowing about it. I was blindsided there."

"Yeah, yeah, whatever. Holy crap, this is who Grayson sent over? I love your husband, but is he stupid? He wants you to work side by side with that?" Gia jerked a thumb over her shoulder.

"Grayson has never met him. He found his name from a client or something. I don't even know if I'm going to hire him. I think we're managing just fine around here."

Gia's mouth fell open. "Now that's just crazy talk. Hello, are you the stupid one? Imagine how pleasant your days would be letting that sweet thing manage your projects."

Isabella laughed. "Wow, he really has you fired up. I'm not sure it's such a good idea bringing him on board if you're going to walk around here all day googly-eyed. Nothing would get done for sure."

"Oh, stop it." Gia waved her off. "It's just been a while since we've had a manly man in this office. You keep hiring all these queens."

"Hey, I love my gays. They dress impeccably, they design

fabulously, they're drama free, and they have no problem telling you when something makes your ass look big."

Gia snorted a laugh. "You're certainly right about that."

Isabella handed Julian's resume to Gia. "Here, make some phone calls for me and check him out. I want to know what his previous client thought about him, whether he was a valuable asset or not."

Gia took the resume and grinned. "No problem. My pleasure."

Isabella glared at her suspiciously. "And make sure you ask appropriate questions. I want to ensure that he knows what he's doing. The last thing I need is more headaches right now."

Later, in the selections room, Isabella reviewed the ideas for the furniture line. She and Charles had agreed that she would do layouts for three collections: a Classic Modern Collection, a Warm Modern Collection with vintage glam accents, and a Transitional Collection featuring some antiqued pieces. She had several of the main pieces for each one, but a number still waited to be designed. She decided to concentrate on the Warm Modern Collection first, which was her favorite.

First she sketched out a bed that would be the star of the master bedroom, with an oversized, baroque-style headboard. It stood six feet tall at its center point and featured a large scrolling detail that came up the sides and met in the center. The center of the headboard was upholstered and tufted, with an option of silk or velvet upholstery. The frame of the headboard would be offered in two high-gloss finishes, either white or black. The smaller footboard featured the same scrolling detail and was anchored by large, chunky posts.

She moved on to the nightstands, dresser, and armoire, all with simple, straight lines but sized to compliment the massive headboard. Gonzolo had sent her a sample of antiqued mirror that she wanted to use for the nightstands. The dresser and armoire would be done in a dark, espresso-stained wood, with the antique mirror used on the dresser drawers and on the inset of the armoire doors. She selected large sunburst crystal knobs for the hardware. For the oversized circular handle on the armoire front, she chose an antiqued gold finish.

Gia and James gushed over her choices. As they sat down to fresh salads from the corner café, Gia said, "Oh hey, I called the last lady Julian worked for. She said he did an amazing job, that he was easy to work with and extremely professional and well organized, which kept her on schedule. She highly recommended him."

"What type of business does she have?"

"Something to do with real estate development. She sounded young.

What do you think?"

"I think I can't make a decision yet. He's the first person I've met with, and he showed up unannounced, I might add. I'm sure he's not our only option."

"He's a damn fine option, if you ask me." Gia winked and nudged Isabella with her elbow.

"He's extremely handsome, I will give you that, but I'm not hiring him because of his looks." Isabella paused. "Maybe I need to meet with him again. He threw me off guard today, surprising me in my office."

"Call him up then. Set up a meeting. I just have one small favor to ask of you." Gia smiled.

Isabella rolled her eyes. "Oh God, no, you may not be there."

"Not fair, Izzie. So not fair." She pouted.

"You'll get over it." Isabella stood and threw the uneaten portion of her salad away. "All right, let's see how fast we can bang this out. Time is ticking."

"I'm ready," Gia said as she tossed her wrappers from lunch in the trash. "Let's rock it out and design some furniture."

Chapter 11

Isabella woke up early the next morning, but not by choice. She had tossed and turned all night, her dreams filled with furniture pieces coming to life and attacking her as Gonzolo bound her with yards of fabric. She realized she needed to relieve some stress before she exploded. It had been forever since she'd had time to exercise. Perhaps a run would help relieve some of her tension so she could start off the day with clear thoughts.

Grayson was softly snoring beside her. She lifted the sheet and peeked under it, exposing his perfect, naked body. Maybe she could start off her day exercising in another way, she thought. She moved close to him, curled up against his warm skin, and began kissing his chest and neck with just the right amount of pressure to make him stir. Grayson let out a groan and stretched his arms up. He opened his eyes to see her head on his chest and her big brown eyes staring up at him mischievously. He glanced at the clock on their nightstand.

"Are you kidding me, babe? It's five o'clock in the morning."

"So?" She continued to kiss his chest and let her hand roam down between his legs, trying to get something else to wake up too.

Grayson pulled her hand back up. "Leave him alone, Izzie. Neither of us needs to be up at this hour. You should go back to sleep." He rolled over, causing Isabella to slide off his chest, but she wasn't giving up that easy. She spooned her body against his and kissed his shoulders.

"Isabella, please, I'm tired."

"Come on, I promise we can be quick. I thought I could start my day off with a little mattress aerobics." She slid her hand down his abs, searching for what she really wanted.

Grayson stopped her just shy of his package. "Not now, babe. Why don't you go for a run or something else that doesn't involve disturbing me?"

"Ugh, whatever." Isabella rolled away from him and slid out of bed. She picked up a pillow off the bed and threw it at him.

He laughed. "Yes, you're so sexually deprived. Go run. It'll do you some good."

"I'm going," she snapped, not thrilled that the choice had been made for her.

Fifteen minutes later, Isabella was at the entrance to Central Park. She figured she would run for at least thirty minutes, head back home to shower, and make it in to work by six thirty. She was running at a good pace, listening to her music, and not thinking about anything furniture-related for the first time in a long time. Actually, she wasn't thinking about much of anything—just enjoying the fresh air. She hated to admit it, but Grayson was right. *Damn him.*

After fifteen minutes, Isabella stopped for water. She had worked up a good sweat and could tell that it was going to be another hot summer day. As she was about to take off for her last fifteen-minute segment, a figure running down the path toward her caught her eye. He was bare-chested, and sweat dripped down from his smooth chest to his six-pack abs. She also couldn't help but notice that his loose black sports shorts sat low on his hips, showing off the deepest v-cut she had ever seen, as well as what Gia liked to call the goody trail. His body was amazing.

As they approached each other, her eyes returned to his face and his stunning green eyes. Isabella came to a halt as she realized who it was.

She stood there, mesmerized by his physique and lost in her not-so-pure thoughts, until he was nearly upon her. She began to panic. She hadn't expected to run into anyone, let alone him. Knowing it was already too late, as he must have recognized her, she remained still and sipped her water.

He slowed down and stopped beside her. "Isabella?" he managed between breaths.

She pulled down her sunglasses but quickly pushed them back on, remembering she wasn't wearing any makeup.

"Hello, Julian. How are you?"

"Good, I'm good." He smiled. "Just hot as hell. I've been running for almost an hour now."

"Wow, you're an early riser."

Julian shook his head. "Nah, not always. Just when I have a hard time sleeping. There's something to be said for running outside in the fresh air. It does the mind good. What brings you out here, besides the obvious, of course?"

"Same thing. I couldn't sleep, and it's been weeks since I've gone on a run, with everything going on."

"You have to make time for yourself, Isabella. Being stressed doesn't help anyone. You'll be more efficient when you give yourself time to breathe."

"Yes, well, for me it's a matter of finding the time."

Julian smiled as if he was going to say something, but he held back. Instead, he just took a sip of his water.

"What?" she inquired, wanting to know what it was he wanted to say.

"Nothing." He smiled and took another sip of his water

Isabella looked at him suspiciously. "You were going to say something, but stopped yourself. Please tell me."

Julian gazed at her for a long moment, noticing how cute she looked in her tank shirt, shorts, and running shoes. It was a very different look compared with the sophisticated businesswoman he had met the other day in her tight skirt and heels. Julian realized she was watching him, waiting for him to say something.

"I was just going to say, that's what I'm for. My job is to make this easy for you so you have the time to do things like this. When I sign on with a client, I am theirs completely. I don't take on other clients simultaneously. I want to be able to give my full attention to you and your company. I know my clients appreciate me being there beside them every step of the way." Julian paused. "I know you'll appreciate it too."

Isabella's gaze fell to her shoes, and she absently kicked at the pebbles near her feet. She was conflicted. Naturally, she was unsure about allowing someone new to play such an intimate role in her business. At the same time, she was intrigued by the prospect of having someone there who would personally guide her through the craziness the project would bring her. The prospect of finishing the process without killing herself was appealing.

"What's going through your mind, Isabella? Tell me."

His green eyes took her breath away as she looked up at him. She bit her lip. "I don't know, Julian. What you're proposing to me is like moving in with a roommate after living on your own for years."

"I promise I won't leave the toilet seat up or squeeze the toothpaste from the center of the tube, if that's what you're worried about."

Isabella laughed and felt herself blushing. Her eyes returned to the ground.

"Ah, finally, a smile from you. I knew it was in there somewhere. You should do that more often. It makes you even more beautiful."

She looked back up at him. "Ha ha, very funny. I smile all the time, as a matter of fact."

"I'm sure you do, but do you mean it? Are you really happy?" Julian raised his eyebrow.

He certainly was a charmer and had a way of getting into her head. "Whatever. I'm just stressed right now."

"Let me help you. I know you won't regret it."

"You're not going to give up, are you? Do you always stalk your new clients like this?"

"Only the beautiful ones." He winked and nudged her with his shoulder.

"Lucky me. How about you send me over your retainer contract, along with your monthly fee schedule, or should I say *blackmail fee*, and I'll look it over and give you my decision."

Julian burst out laughing. "Wow, you're a comedian too? Isabella Hughes, I'm learning all sorts of new things about you this morning."

They said their goodbyes, and Isabella returned home. She quickly got ready for work and decided to stop at Richard's new building to check on the progress of the pre-construction so she wouldn't feel as guilty about lying to him. She was pleased to see the progress being made. The project appeared to be on schedule. Just as she was about to leave, she saw the general contractor, Tyler, walking toward her.

"Mrs. Hughes, it's so nice to see you. It's been a while, huh?" He smirked.

Isabella glared at him. "I've been here many times, Tyler, but you're never around," she fibbed. "Have you been sitting in that cushy trailer of yours while your men bust their asses over here?"

"Hardly," he scoffed. "You know me better than that."

"As you know me, so don't imply that I'm not doing my job."

Tyler returned her glare for a moment, then smiled. "You are one tough cookie. I like that."

"Thanks. I'll sleep so much better tonight knowing that." She felt his lecherous eyes on her as she turned and hurried out of the building.

Isabella arrived at her office just before eight and found a large yellow envelope on her desk. On the front of the envelope was a handwritten note.

Isabella,

It was a pleasure running into you this morning. Enclosed is my retainer contract and blackmail fee schedule. Ha ha. I look forward to hearing from you very soon.

Sincerely,
Julian

Isabella couldn't help but smile. He was persistent, but she liked him. She felt comfortable in his presence. She read the retainer and was pleasantly surprised to see that he wasn't that expensive after all. She laughed when she noticed a handwritten line item on his fee schedule:

Extra toothpaste - NO CHARGE. (I lied. I do squeeze from the middle.)

"What's so funny?" Gia asked as she entered the office.

"Nothing, just Julian and his fee schedule. It's an inside joke. I ran into him this morning in the park."

"Oh, do tell." Gia leaned across her desk.

"There's nothing to tell. He was running, I was running, we spotted each other and chatted for a bit, and that was it."

"What was he wearing?"

"Oh, for the love of everything holy, Gia, I didn't take notes. Maybe I shouldn't hire him. I have this feeling you're going to make a mess of that situation, and I'll have to wind up firing him." She sighed as the image of Julian's perfect chest and six-pack abs popped into her mind.

"Take a chill pill, Izzie. I was just . . . wait, so you are going to hire him?" Gia was grinning ear to ear.

Isabella laughed at her. "I think so, but you have to promise you'll leave him alone. He is off limits to you. I don't need things getting messy around here with romantic drama. Got it?"

Gia rolled her eyes. "Fine. But I will tell you this, Mrs. Rule Maker, as soon as this is over, all bets are off."

"Deal. But for now, keep your kitty cat claws to yourself."

"When are you going to tell him?"

"I'll probably make him wait a few days. Make him sweat a little."

"Who has the kitty cat claws now? Meow." Gia scratched at the air.

~~~

Gonzolo called that afternoon to tell her that he had met with his production staff to look over the sketches for the Warm Modern Collection, and everything looked good. He felt confident that Mr. Vanderbeck would be pleased. They would proceed with making prototypes and fly her out to Italy to approve them before they went into mass production. In the meantime, she would continue designing the remaining pieces for this collection and start on the other collections. Although she was relieved, she felt the noose tightening around her neck just a little.

Isabella and Gia spent the remainder of the day working on the rest of the sketches for the Warm Modern Collection. They made progress in completing the living room area furniture, along with some additional accent pieces. When Isabella returned to her office to retrieve an email from Charles regarding specific items he wanted to see, she was
~~~

surprised to learn that it was already after six o'clock. No wonder the office was so quiet; everyone else had left an hour ago. She dismissed Gia, who had a baseball game to attend with Josh, her latest fling.

Alone in the office, she made herself a glass of vodka over ice, kicked off her shoes, and collapsed on the sofa, rubbing her tired feet on the furry rug. *I need a massage*, she thought.

Her phone chimed with a text from Grayson:

> *Hey babe. I know you're probably working still. I'm heading out with the guys for drinks. Catch ya later at home. XOXO*

She returned to carefully looking over the details of her sketches, making sure she was satisfied with each piece before she sent them off to Gonzolo, when a voice startled her.

"By my calculations, you've been going at it for over thirteen hours now."

With her heart pounding, she glared at Julian. "Do you always make it a habit of sneaking up on people?"

"Usually people are more aware of what's happening around them. You're the only one I can sneak up on."

She set the sketches beside her on the sofa and looked past him down the empty hallway. "How did you get in here? It's after hours." A light bulb went on in her head. "Let me guess, Gia?"

Julian pointed his finger at her. "Bingo. She yelled something about being late for a game and that you were still in your office, and since I knew the way, I could find you myself."

Isabella shook her head, exasperated. "As you can see, I have top-of-the-line security here."

"We'll need to work on that. May I?" He gestured to the seat next to her on the sofa.

"Sure." She moved the pile of papers back to the cocktail table. "So what brings you here at this hour?"

He sat down on the sofa next to her. "Actually, I had a meeting with another potential client in your building. I knew you would still be working, so I thought, what the hell, I would come up and see you. Did you have a chance to take a look at the contracts I sent over this morning?"

"I did. Thank you for getting those over to me."

"Did everything seem to be in order?"

"Yes, everything was clear," she said. "Cut and dry, really."

Julian looked at her for a moment, trying to read her further, but Isabella gave nothing away.

"Care to share any thoughts you may have?" he asked.

She crossed her arms and leaned back in her seat. "Why are you so persistent?"

"I have to be. That's my job. Also, this project is different from others I've worked on. I like the variety and the challenge. Anything else?"

"Well, there is one thing."

"Which is?"

"I want to make it clear that I prefer Crest over Colgate." She watched him with a serious expression.

Julian looked confused. "I'm sorry, I'm not following you."

"In your fee schedule, you said that there was no charge for toothpaste. I just want it made known that I prefer Crest."

Julian grinned. "Ah, I have it now. Noted." He looked at her slyly. "So are you granting me the privilege to work with you, Isabella?"

"I am. Privilege granted."

He laughed. "You'd already made your decision before I came here, didn't you?"

"Yep."

"You were just trying to make me sweat a little."

"No, I would never do that." Isabella smiled innocently.

"Okay, I see how this is going to be."

Isabella's smile widened. "Are you scared?"

"No, I can keep up with you and your antics. Are *you* scared?"

"Not in the least. Should I be?"

"Yes, be afraid. Be very, very afraid," he teased. "Your life, as you know it, is about to change."

"Change is good, and I'm ready."

"Well, so am I." Julian stood, grasped her hands, and pulled her up, then picked up her heels and handed them to her. "As your new manager, I say you're done here for tonight. I'm going to take you out for a proper dinner, because I'm sure the last time you ate off an actual plate was a long time ago. Over dinner, you can fill me in on details of the project. I need to have a clear understanding of what is being asked of you, what you've done so far, and what you need to do."

"I can't. I have to work. I need to get these sketches to the owner of the manufacturing plant tonight."

"Well, technically, you will be working at dinner. These are things I'm going to need to know from you, Isabella. I would rather have your undivided attention now than be constantly interrupting you during the day tomorrow. Tell you what, those sketches look like they're completed to me. Knowing what I know of you thus far, I'm going to venture a guess that you're feeling gun-shy about sending them. I'll give you twenty minutes to give them a final once-over, and then you will send them on their way to the owner of the plant. Then you and I are going to dinner."

Isabella narrowed her eyes at him. "Are you always this bossy?"

"Yes, especially when I know I'm right." He smirked.

"I already don't like you," Isabella muttered. But he was right. She was a perfectionist.

Julian laughed. "I'm not worried. You'll love me by the time this is all over."

"Cocky, too? Just peachy."

Julian looked at his watch. "Time is ticking away, Isabella. I would start if I were you."

"Fine." She sat back down on the sofa and grabbed the sketches as Julian wandered to the wet bar to make himself a drink, smiling to himself the whole way.

Chapter 12

The transition of getting Julian on board went seamlessly. He was the perfect addition to the office. The ladies adored him, and the gay men drooled over him. Everyone was thrilled with Isabella for bringing him on board. He had more than proven himself to her as a valuable asset, acting as her liaison with Evette and Charles's project managers, as well as working with Gonzolo to find more cost-effective materials to make the furniture pieces more profitable. She was impressed.

As the weeks passed, Isabella felt more and more comfortable with Julian. She enjoyed having him around and often used him as a sounding board. He became more than just a business manager; he was a friend. He and Isabella were together nearly every day, feverishly working on the project. Even though the hours were insane, she felt less stressed in his presence. He was constantly reminding her to take time out for herself. When she didn't, he set up massage appointments for her or made her meet him in the park for a morning run. She was thankful that she had taken a chance with him. Having a shadow wasn't as bad as she had expected.

Isabella had just arrived back home from one of her morning runs with Julian when she heard a commotion in the bedroom closet. She peeked in and saw Grayson struggling to get a suitcase down from the top shelf.

He turned to see her watching him. "Why do you stack your sweaters on top of the suitcases?" he demanded. "I can never get them down without everything falling on me."

"Because I have no room in there. I need a bigger closet."

"You would have room if you stopped shopping, or got rid of some of the clothes you don't wear."

"Stop shopping? Are you insane? Did you whack your head getting out of bed this morning?" She grinned, still in a great mood from the run.

Irritated, Grayson turned back to the suitcase. "Very funny. Seriously, you have so much shit, why don't you think about donating some of this stuff?"

"As if I have time to organize my closet right now," she snapped. "What do you need the suitcase for, anyway?"

With one final tug, Grayson freed the suitcase from the shelf, and down came a pile of sweaters around him. He threw the suitcase aside and began picking them up.

"Just leave them," Isabella said. "I'll take care of them later. Where are you going?"

Grayson carried the suitcase to the bed and opened it. "I got a call from a gallery owner in London. They've recently acquired a large collection of my mother's paintings from an auction and are creating an exhibit in her honor. They want me to come and say a few words on her behalf."

"Oh wow, that's amazing! You must be so proud."

"Yeah, my mother would have loved it." He sighed and began opening dresser drawers, looking for clothes for the trip.

Isabella watched him for a moment. She was worried about him. Even though it had been thirteen years since his parents' death, Grayson still had a hard time dealing with the fact that they were gone. She also knew that he felt he had let his mother down by not achieving the status she had achieved in the art community.

"Are you okay?" Isabella asked. "When are you leaving?"

"I'm fine. Please don't read too much into this. I'm just mad at your sweaters." Grayson went to the closet for more clothes. "Unfortunately, I have to leave today. They want me there a day before the event to meet with the owners of the gallery."

"Today? Really? When did they call you?" Isabella was shocked.

"A day or so ago. They had a hard time locating me for some reason, but I told them I would be there, so I have to go."

"You're just telling me this now, the day that you're leaving? Don't you think that's a bit rude?" Now Isabella was the one who was irritated.

"I'm sorry, but you've been busy, and truth be told, I just made my decision last night."

Isabella's wheels began to turn. "Okay, then let me go with you. We can make a fun trip out of it," she said excitedly.

"You can't go with me, Isabella," he said as he folded a shirt. "You're right in the middle of designing your furniture lines. You just can't up and leave on such short notice."

"I'm the boss. I can up and leave anytime I want. I want to be there for you. I know it will be hard for you and will bring back a lot of memories. I want to go and be your support." Isabella touched his hand.

"I appreciate that you want to support me, but honestly, I'm fine. Besides, as much as you like to think you're the boss right now, you're not. Vanderbeck is. You going with me to London would just make you crazier trying to play catch-up when you got back. I don't want to put you through that. It's not worth it."

"It's worth it to me to be there for you," Isabella shot back.

He looked up and stared at her. "I'll only be gone for three days," he said with an edge in his voice. "You won't even have time to miss me. But three days for you to be away is three days you will have fallen behind. Everything's going well, so don't mess it up now."

Isabella was surprised that he refused to budge. "I get what you're saying, but I still think it stinks that you don't want me there to support you. That hurts." Isabella retreated to the bathroom and closed the door behind her as tears brimmed in her eyes.

She heard his exasperated voice through the door. "I'm not the one who took on such a big project!"

Without replying, she turned on the shower, letting the sound of the water drown out his words and her troubled thoughts.

~~~

Isabella sat in her office, gazing at the fluffy white clouds beyond the window and trying to hold back tears of disappointment about her conversation with Grayson that morning. What had bothered her the most was that he hadn't even told her about getting the phone call or making the decision to go. It made her wonder just when he was planning to tell her. She felt unwanted and unimportant.

"Good morning," Julian said behind her. "I brought you coffee. I know you must be dying for some right about now."

Isabella turned from the windows to face him. He carried two steaming mugs.

"Thanks," she said. "I could use some right now." *Spiked with a little vodka*, she thought.

He looked concerned as he handed her a mug. "What's this?" he asked, pointing to her face. "This isn't the Isabella I saw at the park this morning. I leave you for an hour and a half, and this happens? What's going on?"

She wrapped her hands around the mug and sipped her coffee. "It's nothing. I'm fine."

"Oh, really? Do you always cry when you look out the window? Is this something I should be aware of? Because if that's the case, I'm going to start closing the blinds."

She sighed. "Stop. Forget it. Where are the sketches I was working
~~~

on last night?"

"Not so fast. I'm fine if you don't want to talk about it, but I'm not fine with whatever is bothering you clogging up your mind today."

Julian walked around the desk and stood behind her chair, placing his hands on her shoulders. "Do me a favor and close your eyes." Isabella looked back at him in protest, but he silenced her with his finger. "Do it." She turned back around and closed her eyes. "Now, I want you to take five slow, deep breaths, exhaling fully between each one."

Isabella did as he said while Julian applied light pressure to her shoulders, squeezing them to release the tension. As she breathed in, all she could smell around her was Julian's cologne. It smelled fresh and clean, yet strong and masculine. She didn't remember noticing it on him before.

As she exhaled her fifth breath, she opened her eyes, and Julian gently spun her chair around to face him.

"Feeling better?" he asked.

She felt a little strange as she realized that she had been thinking about the smell of his cologne the whole time. "Yes, strangely enough, I do feel better."

He smiled. "Good, I'm glad. Five deep breaths gives you time to calm your body and mind. It's something I learned in a drama class I took back in college. It really works. I do it all the time."

She raised her eyebrows. "You took a drama class?"

"Yeah, didn't everyone back in college?"

"Um, no, I never did."

"You're missing the point. I made you feel better, didn't I?"

"Yes. Thank you, and please feel free to massage my tense shoulders anytime you like."

Julian winked. "My pleasure, Isabella. Anything to reduce your stress."

She lowered her voice. "Grayson is leaving for London today. He just told me this morning."

"Why is he going to London?"

"A gallery has obtained a large collection of his mother's artwork, and they're creating an exhibit in her honor. They want him to be there."

Julian sat on the edge of her desk. "Why does this upset you?"

"It doesn't upset me. The fact that he didn't say anything about it until this morning does, along with the fact that he didn't want me to go with him."

"I see." Julian looked at her for a long moment. "I get that you're upset, and you have every right to be."

Isabella's gaze fell to her lap.

"Look, this project has probably been hard on both of you. I'm confident, though, that he was just looking out for you. What man wouldn't want you with him?" Julian lifted her chin with his finger, bringing her eyes up to his. "He knows where you're needed right now, and unfortunately, it's not in London."

"It's not just that. It's a lot of little things that have been happening for a while. It's been hard."

"I'm sorry," he said. "What can I do to help?"

"I appreciate all you've done already. Thank you for listening."

He laid his hand over hers on the desktop. "Anytime, Isabella. So are you ready to get back to work, or do we need to take more breaths?"

She sat up straighter. "I'm ready."

"Good, because I've been working on something for a few weeks now, and I just got confirmation this morning that it's a go." He was beaming from ear to ear. "You're going to love it."

"I'm listening." She placed her elbows on her desk and rested her chin in her hands.

"Well, the other day I was wondering how visible your business name is, so I Googled you. What I noticed was that your name is out there, but more times than not, it's referenced in an article about someone else. You're mentioned as the lead designer in this building or that store, but nothing solely about you and your company. When is the last time you've done an interview?"

"It's been years. I haven't had time."

"Interviews will bring attention to your business. The more your name is out there, the more people will know about you, the more desired you will become, the more furniture you will sell, and so on and so on. We need to create a buzz about you."

"But my business has been strong. Clients hear about me by word of mouth because of my reputation. I haven't felt like I needed to create a buzz."

"You were never designing a furniture line before. Now that you are, you're going to want people to know who you are. We need to create hype about you so they want to buy from your line."

With the picture becoming clear in her head, Isabella moaned. "Julian, what did you do? Did you set up an interview for me? I hate doing interviews."

Julian laughed. "Yes, I did set up an interview for you, you big baby."

"Why? It's not for TV, is it? I'm not good at interviews, especially ones for TV. I get nervous, and my stomach always feels like it has bats in it."

"Calm down, or I'm going to make you take five breaths again. It's just a little interview with *Elle Decor* magazine."

Isabella's eyes nearly bugged out of her head. "*Elle Decor*?" she shouted. "Nothing is just a little anything with *Elle Decor*. Oh my gosh, how in the world did you get that lined up?"

"A friend of a friend. I do have connections in this town, you know."

"I know you probably do, but *Elle Decor* is a big deal. This is insane. What am I going to talk about?" She covered her face with her hands.

"It's not insane, it's brilliant. The article will be read by millions, many of whom live right here in New York. You'll be talking about yourself, your business, and the project with Mr. Vanderbeck. I want you to get people excited about the development. That will help to boost interest and increase sales, which will in turn create more revenue for you on the furniture end. This is a good thing, Isabella. Trust me."

She knew he was right, but she was worried about making a fool of herself. "Will you be there with me?"

"Of course. I wouldn't make you do this on your own. I'll be there for moral support."

"Okay, I'll do it," she said reluctantly. "When is it scheduled for?"

"They'll be at your loft Sunday morning at ten with a writer and a photographer to shoot some portraits and shots of your loft." Julian leaned back in his chair, waiting for the eruption he knew was coming.

Isabella's jaw dropped open. "That's in two days! I'm not going to be ready for that. I have to make sure my loft is cleaned so everything looks perfect for the photos, not to mention getting myself pulled together. Can't we move it to next week?"

"I love how I can predict what your reaction is going to be. It's kind of scary." Julian laughed as Isabella glared at him. "We can't move the interview. This is a favor I'm calling in here. You will have plenty of time to get ready. You have tonight and tomorrow, and you'll have me to help you. I'll be there for you, Isabella, so please calm down." He tried to soothe her, as he had quickly and masterfully learned to do.

Isabella let out a big huff and rolled her eyes. "And Charles? Did you get his approval for this article?" She hoped he hadn't, since that would buy her some more time to prepare.

"Are you seriously asking me that?" He smiled at her. "He was the first person I asked. Have some faith in me. I know what I'm doing here."

"Fine, whatever!" She hit the button on her desk phone. "James, I need you to call my housekeeper and get her over to my loft today or tomorrow. Tell her I want it spotless. I was just informed I'm having some important people over on Sunday." She glared at Julian again. He smiled, amused that he had won this round with her.

"No problem, Izzie," James said. "Who's coming over?"

"*Elle Decor* magazine."

She heard him gasp through the phone.

~~~

Gia was standing in Isabella's bedroom, staring at the outfit options Isabella had pulled out for the interview.

"How about something more colorful?" Gia yelled to Isabella, who was in her closet grabbing more options.

"I really don't do color, you know that. I don't want to be too flashy. I'm going for chic and sophisticated, with maybe a little edge."

"Boring, in other words," Gia mumbled.

Isabella emerged from the closet with two more options. "What? Did you say something?"

Gia shook her head and smiled slyly. "Nope, wasn't me."

Isabella rolled her eyes. "You're not helping me here. I want to pick out my outfit tonight so it's one less thing I have to do tomorrow. Focus, please."

"Well, I definitely don't like the pencil skirt with the white button-down shirt. It's too businesslike. I also don't like the nude-colored dress. With your fair skin, it'll make you looked washed out in the picture. How about going casual, jeans and a cute top? You know, sitting on your sofa with no shoes on, looking comfortable and relaxed. What do you think?"

Isabella groaned. "I think that's been done a million times already. I really didn't want to be that casual. I need something between that and a business look."

Gia looked back down at the clothes lying on the bed. "Hang on. I think I have an idea." She went to the closet and came out with a pair of tall black boots and a long, chunky necklace of gold links.

"I don't want boots. I prefer heels."

"Who cares? It's only for the photo. There." Gia laid the necklace on a black, strapless dress Isabella had on the bed, took away the heels that were there, and put the boots next to it.

Isabella looked down at the outfit. "I don't know. Isn't it a little bar-like?"

"If you wore this to a bar, I would slap you silly. No, it's not. The dress is not short by any means. It comes to your knees and has a little
~~~

flair. There's your sophistication. Pairing it with boots instead of heels makes it not as dressy, giving you the edge you wanted, and the necklace makes it chic. There you go—all three looks wrapped up in one." Gia patted herself on the back. "My work here is done."

Still unsure, Isabella tried on the outfit and stood before her full-length mirror. "What do you think?"

"I think it's fantastic. But you need to wear your hair down, to soften the look." Gia pulled out Isabella's ponytail and fluffed her hair up with her fingers. "There, like that. Perfect. What do you think? Do we have a winner?"

"Yes, I think we do. The contrast will look good against my silk sofa downstairs, too."

As Gia helped her out of the dress, conversation inevitably turned to Julian.

"You're still gaga over him, aren't you?" Isabella teased.

"Who wouldn't be? Tell me you don't think he's insanely sexy." She flopped down on the bed and watched Isabella hang up her clothes.

"I don't think of him that way. I mean, yes, I'll admit, he is easy on the eyes, but we're together all the time, and it's all business."

"All business, huh? You know what I think?"

"God only knows."

"I think he likes you."

Isabella scoffed. "Why on earth would you say that? I'm married, a fact Julian is well aware of."

"Oh, I know, but it's the way I catch him looking at you sometimes. It's like he's watching you, thinking of something other than work. When he notices me watching him, he looks away. I think the project isn't the only thing he'd like to work on, if you get my drift." Gia smirked.

Isabella fell onto the bed next to Gia and slapped her foot. "Stop it. Now you're being just plain delusional. You're going to give me a complex, thinking he's watching me. Yes, we've become friends, but that's it. He has never done or said anything inappropriate."

"Not yet, that is." She winked.

"You are such a troublemaker." Isabella threw a pillow at her while Gia laughed, goading her on. "You are evil. I don't know why you're enjoying this."

"For starters, because I'm not blind. I see the chemistry between the two of you. You've been happier lately, and I like seeing you happy. And I don't think it's the project. It's Julian's presence that has made a difference in you."

Isabella considered what Gia had said. She knew she had felt happier lately, but she didn't attribute it to Julian. Yes, he made her feel more organized and less stressed, and in turn, that made her happy. It was nice to have someone else at work to lean on. There was nothing wrong with that. After all, wasn't that what she had hired him for?

She brushed the thoughts aside. "I'm starving. What do you say we go out for a quick bite and a glass of wine, my treat?"

Gia laughed. "There's that infamous Isabella sidestep. Sure, Isabella. I've worked up quite an appetite talking about you-know-who. And I bet you have, too." She wiggled her eyebrows.

"That is *enough*!" Isabella yelled, and attacked Gia with a pillow while she laughed hysterically.

Chapter 13

When Isabella woke the next morning, her thoughts went to Grayson. He hadn't called her to let her know he had arrived in London. Being cynical, she assumed he had made it, since there wasn't anything on the news about a plane crash. She called him, but got his voicemail. Disappointed, she left a message.

While she was still in bed, she heard the front door open. She was startled at first, but then remembered that Maria was coming to clean. She dragged her butt out of bed and threw on her running clothes. After her run, she would hit a few stores to pick up things for the photo shoot, including candles and fresh flowers.

She met Maria on the stairs. "Buenos días, Maria."

"Buenos días, señora."

"I'm heading out for a while. Can you please make sure everything gets a thorough cleaning? I'm having pictures taken tomorrow for a magazine, and I need the loft to be perfect."

"Sí, señora, I will make sure you are happy."

"Bueno. Gracias." Isabella smiled at her and headed out for her run.

After an energizing run, Isabella popped into the nail salon, opting for a simple French manicure. From there, she stopped at the florist and bought three bouquets: fragrant gardenias for the bedroom; sophisticated calla lilies for the dining table; and for the kitchen, a colorful arrangement of Asiatic lilies, alstroemeria, and birds of paradise, accented with red hypericum and green ti leaves.

At the candle shop, she picked up a dozen of her favorite candles, which had a fresh, clean scent called "Water" so the loft would smell heavenly for the interview. Not that smell mattered, but she wanted everything to be perfect.

Back home, she arranged the flowers in vases and took a shower while Maria finished cleaning downstairs. She took her time getting ready, plucking her eyebrows and applying a facial mask so that her skin looked its best for the photo shoot. She threw her long locks into two pigtails and slipped into a comfy pair of cutoffs and one of Grayson's white dress shirts, which she loved lounging in. By the time she was done, Maria had left.

Isabella spent the next hour rearranging furniture and setting everything in its perfect place. She examined the rooms with a careful eye, knowing something that looked good in everyday life might translate differently in a picture. She staged her accessories rather than keeping them in their usual spots. Lastly, she set the candles strategically throughout the loft. Isabella stepped back and looked over the main floor one last time. Satisfied, she retrieved her briefcase from the front closet, pulled out the last of the sketches she was still working on, and laid them out on her coffee table.

She spent the next few hours relaxing on the sofa, nibbling cucumbers with hummus, and finishing her sketches while music played in the background. It was just after six when her intercom buzzed. She got up and hit the button. "Yes?"

Isabella was surprised to hear Julian's voice. "I figured you've probably been busting your ass all day long and haven't eaten," he said. "I brought dinner. Can I come up?"

"Um, sure. I'll buzz you in."

A minute later, Julian stepped into the loft and caught her in the act of frantically trying to clean up the mess she had made on the sofa with her sketches. She turned to see him watching her and shaking his head.

"How did I know you would be working?" he said.

She blew her breath out and threw the sketches on an armchair. "You know, it's not a crime to work on the weekend."

He set the paper bag he was carrying on the counter. "Then why do you look like you got caught doing something wrong?"

"You just surprised me, that's all. I mean, look at me. I wasn't exactly expecting company." She looked down at her shirt and shorts and remembered that she wasn't wearing a bra. Her cheeks flushed with embarrassment, and she folded her arms across her chest.

"There's nothing wrong with the way you look. You look comfortable and relaxed, which I like to see." He grinned. "And may I say, quite adorable in pigtails." Julian grabbed a pigtail in each of his hands and gave them a little yank.

Isabella shooed him away. "Knock it off. You're just making fun of me."

"Never." He looked down at the plate on the coffee table, scattered with a few desiccated cucumber slices. "So was I right? Have you not eaten yet?"

Isabella wrinkled her nose. "What is it with you? I swear you must have a camera on me twenty-four seven."

Julian laughed and retrieved the bag of take-out from the kitchen. "No, no cameras are on you. I told you, I make it my business to know my clients. I'm very observant. That's what makes me good at my job. Getting to know you allows me to give you exactly what you want and need. And right now, I know you want sushi." He opened the bag and set several containers of sushi rolls on the cocktail table.

Her eyes grew big. "Oh my gosh, you have no idea. I'm starving. There is nothing in the fridge."

"Well, I'm glad I came, then. Dig in."

Isabella retrieved plates and, at Julian's request, a bottle of pinot gris and two wine glasses. As she sat down next to him on the sofa and sipped the refreshing white wine, she had to admit it was a good idea.

"How are the last sketches coming along?" he asked, glancing at the array of them around the room.

"Good. Actually, I think I'm done with the last collection. I should have the final pieces over to Gonzolo on Monday." She smiled proudly.

"Really? Wow, you have been working hard today. I'm impressed."

"Thanks. I can't wait to see them in person."

"I'm sure that will be an exciting moment for you." He seemed genuinely proud of her accomplishment. "May I see the sketches you did tonight?"

Isabella stuffed another California roll into her mouth and retrieved a pile of sketches from the nearby armchair. She explained each one as she passed it to Julian.

"I really like what you've done here," he gushed. "I don't understand how you keep coming up with ideas. There seems to be no end to your creativity. Your mind absolutely amazes me."

Isabella blushed. "Thank you. That is sweet of you to say."

"I mean it, I really do." He leaned back into the sofa and sipped his wine. "Were you always this creative?"

She shrugged. "My grandmother said I had an overactive imagination. I remember as a child constantly changing things around our house. Every time she came into my room, there was something new or something I had rearranged. So, yeah, I guess I've been this way my whole life." She realized she didn't know much about Julian. "What about you? How were you as a child? I can only imagine—probably busy bossing your friends around."

Julian chuckled. "No, not quite. I had a . . . difficult childhood. I grew up in a small suburb of Chicago. My parents both had drinking problems, which led to a lot of fights in our house. I practically raised myself because they were too drunk most of the time to take care of me. When I was eighteen, I left and moved here, and never looked back."

Isabella felt bad for asking. "Oh, Julian, that's awful. I'm sorry to make you bring that up."

Julian patted her knee. "It's okay. I don't feel bad about it. Leaving home at that age did make me grow up fast. I wouldn't be where I am today if I hadn't, so please, don't apologize." Julian reached for the wine bottle and poured some more into his empty glass. "Would you like some more too?"

"Yes, please." Isabella watched him as he poured a generous amount of wine into her glass. She was surprised at how similar their childhoods had been. Both of them had parents who weren't there for them. "I know how you feel, actually. I was raised by my grandparents. My mother abandoned me when I was little, and my grandparents died around the time I graduated from high school. I moved here shortly after."

"I didn't know that. That must have been hard for you. But look at you now. Your grandparents would be proud of what you've become." He looked her in the eye. "*You* should be proud of what you've become."

"I am, but boy has it taken a lot of blood, sweat, and tears, let me tell you." She laughed softly, trying to lighten the mood.

"I'm sure it has. And Grayson has to be proud of you too, huh?"

Isabella looked down at her wine glass and rubbed her finger around the rim of the glass. "I guess he is. It's not like he comes out and says it, especially lately."

"Isabella, I'm sorry. I shouldn't have asked. I wasn't thinking."

Isabella looked up at him. "It's pretty sad, isn't it?" She felt tears filling her eyes. "It's sad that you ask a simple question—if my husband is proud of me—and I can't even answer because I don't know. After all this time, you'd think I would know, but I don't." A tear escaped and slipped down her cheek.

He moved closer to her and wiped away the tear with his thumb. "Isabella, please don't cry. I'm so sorry. I don't want to see you upset."

"It's not you, Julian. You didn't upset me. He did." Isabella returned Julian's gaze for a long moment. She tried to speak, but her voice shook.

"Shh, it's okay," he said as he rubbed her arm. "You don't have to say anything."

Isabella inhaled deeply, trying to compose herself. "You know what really sucks? I chose to take on this project with Vanderbeck, and now I'm sure it will wind up costing me a lot more than I'm receiving."

Julian took her hand in his. "Don't say that. What's happening between you two is not your fault."

Isabella looked down at her glass again. "It's always my fault. Grayson makes that pretty clear," she said bitterly. It had been that way for years. It was always *her* work or *her* friends or *her* problems that caused issues for them, or so he had reminded her time and time again. It was never his fault. She was the one who was made to feel like the bad wife.

Julian lifted her chin with his finger so that she looked at him. "That couldn't be farther from the truth. When you love someone, you stand behind them no matter what. Love is a give and take. You help those you love to succeed in the things they want to succeed in, no matter what the cost." Julian had moved so that he sat right beside her. "You don't deserve to be treated the way he's treating you, and I hope you know that love is not always like this."

Julian touched the side of her face gently with his hand, and their eyes locked. Isabella felt his warm breath on her face and heard his heart beating—or was it hers? She wasn't sure.

Julian began to caress her bare leg. "Isabella," he whispered.

Sensing that they were treading in dangerous waters, Isabella put her hand on his to stop him. "Julian, thank you for your support, but I think you should go now."

He removed his hand from her leg. "I'm sorry. I didn't mean to . . ."

Isabella put a finger up to his lips to silence him. "It's okay. I'm just tired, and we have an important day tomorrow. I need to get some sleep, and so do you."

Julian looked at her for a moment, trying to figure out if she was telling the truth or not. Watching her, though, he could tell she was being sincere. "You're right, I should go." He stood up and held out his hands to help her off the sofa. "Are you okay? I can't leave here without knowing you are. I'll worry about you."

"I'm fine, really I am. Thank you for bringing me dinner. You're a good friend to me."

Julian put his arms around her and hugged her tightly. "I'll see you tomorrow."

At the door, he turned and kissed her on the cheek before leaving.

"Good night, Julian," she said as she closed the door. She remained there for a moment, touching the spot where he had kissed her. Gia's words filled her mind: *I see the chemistry between the two of you. You've been happier lately. It's Julian's presence that has made a difference in you.*

Isabella exhaled loudly and closed her eyes, trying to block out the voice inside telling her that Gia was right. She shook the thought from her head as she extinguished the lights and went to bed.

Chapter 14

Julian showed up at her doorstep again the next morning with two steaming cups of coffee. He stopped in his tracks when he saw her.

"Is something wrong?" she asked worriedly. "Should I change?"

Isabella was wearing the outfit she and Gia had picked out—black dress, tall boots, gold necklace—and had left her hair down as Gia suggested, but added large curls that she ran her hands through, making her hair look soft and sexy.

"No, you shouldn't do anything," Julian said. "You look stunning. From the dress to the boots to your hair . . . my God, you have the most incredible hair. Who knew?" He approached her and gingerly touched one of her curls. "You're a vision of beauty."

She laughed uncomfortably. "Okay, stop it. You're just trying to pump up my confidence before the interview."

"No, I'm not. You're perfect."

"Well, not quite. I need help with my zipper. I think I've gotten it stuck on the fabric." She turned to show him.

"Let me take a look." Julian set the coffees down on the table and turned around to see Isabella standing there with her back to him, holding her hair up out of the way. Her dress was open, exposing her bare back. He could see that she did not have a bra on.

As he came up behind her, Isabella looked back at him. "Can you see what the problem is?"

There is definitely not a problem back here, Julian thought to himself as he gazed at her bare back.

"Anything yet?" she asked. "I think I must have caught the dress in the zipper as I was trying to zip it up."

"Yes, that's exactly what you did. Hold still, and let me see if I can get you unstuck here." Julian played with the zipper for a bit, but it wasn't moving. "You really did a number on this one, Isabella."

"Crap! I don't want to change. I love this outfit. Can you keep trying?"

"Sure, let me try to work it out from the underside." Julian held the zipper on the outside of the dress with one hand and slipped his free hand up the backside of her dress. On his way up to finding the zipper, he felt her lacy silk thong brush against his hand. He instantly became aroused. His mind wandered.

Reaching the fabric that was jammed in the zipper, he gave it one quick tug, and the fabric broke free.

"Got it!" he said triumphantly as he slid the zipper all the way up and patted Isabella's shoulders. "You're all set."

Isabella turned around and kissed him on the cheek. "You are a lifesaver! Thank you, thank you." She smiled at him.

"You're most welcome, Isabella. Anytime." He smiled back.

"So, how about that coffee? I could use it right about now."

Julian picked up her coffee off the table and handed it to her. "Here you go. Drink away."

She accepted the cup and took a gulp. "Thanks again. I really appreciate everything you do for me. It's above and beyond anything you're supposed to do."

Still enthralled with the way she looked at that moment and remembering the electricity that ran through his body when his hand touched her skin, he stood there thinking thoughts of being intimate with her.

"Julian, are you okay?" Isabella asked. "Is something wrong?"

He exhaled deeply. "About last night . . ."

She held up her hand to stop him. "Please, don't worry about that. There was wine, you were comforting me. I get it. I don't want you to think I'm upset. I'm not. I like having you around. You make me feel sane in my crazy world." Isabella took his hands in hers.

Holding back his words, knowing it wasn't time, Julian just smiled at her and said, "Thank you, Isabella. I'm relieved to hear you say that."

She smiled back at him and grabbed his chin. "Good, because I mean it. I want you around for the long haul, so unfortunately you are stuck with me, mister," she teased.

Julian laughed. "The things I will have to endure, I can only imagine."

She pushed him away and laughed. She was relieved that there was no awkwardness between them. "Hey, was that a dig?"

Julian chuckled. "No, not at all."

They spent the next half hour preparing for the interview, and before she knew it, the writer and photographer from *Elle Decor* had arrived. Isabella showed the photographer, Marcus, to the second floor, indicating that the only rooms upstairs to be shot were the master bedroom and bath. While he got to work, Isabella sat down with the writer, Zane Caudwell.

The interview lasted over an hour. Zane asked her about her background, her start in interior design, her company, and her project with Charles Vanderbeck, including the furniture line. Julian gave her reassuring smiles from across the room while Isabella answered Zane's questions with a poise and ease that surprised even her.

Afterward, Marcus asked her to pose on the sofa and in the dining room while he took portraits. Isabella felt Julian's eyes on her as she followed the photographer's instructions, feeling self-conscious.

When Marcus and Zane had gone, Isabella looked at the kitchen clock. It was already close to noon; they had been going at it for almost two hours. No wonder she was exhausted. She collapsed on the sofa, and Julian sat down next to her.

"Whew, I'm exhausted. That was work," she said, massaging her cheeks. "It's hard to smile for that long."

"It was work, but aren't you glad you did it?"

"I am. I have to admit, it was kind of fun." Her stomach growled loudly, and they both laughed.

"How about some lunch?" Julian suggested. "Maybe a picnic in the park?"

"Yes! I love it. I haven't done that in years." She clapped her hands in excitement.

"Perfect. I brought a change of clothes, so why don't you go change, and we can get out of here and feed that beast of yours." He lightly tickled her stomach. She laughed and swatted away his hands.

Julian had his shirt off when she returned downstairs a moment later.

"Did you forget something?" he asked.

Isabella pointed to her back, averting her gaze from his smooth, muscled torso. "Could you help unzip me, please?"

"Come here," he said, smiling at her obvious shyness.

Her pulse was racing as she approached him and turned her back to him. "I'm sorry. I probably should have waited until you were done changing."

Julian moved her hair aside and laid it over her shoulder. "It's fine, Isabella. I'm not shy."

She felt a shiver run down her spine again as he found the zipper, his hand brushing the nape of her neck. Isabella closed her eyes and bit her lip as she felt his breath on her skin and the warmth of his body close to hers. He slowly moved the zipper down, exposing her back. She pressed her hands to her breasts to keep the dress from slipping to the floor. Julian continued until the dress was fully unzipped, and she knew her lacy black thong was exposed.

She turned around, and their eyes met. Her voice was barely a whisper when she spoke. “Thank you, Julian. I’ll be down in a minute.”

He touched her arm. “I’ll be waiting.”

Julian couldn’t take his eyes off her as she headed back up the staircase and disappeared into her bedroom. He knew he had to have her. He could feel that she wanted him too, but she was fighting it. She was strong, at least for the moment, he thought.

He had finished changing when Isabella returned downstairs wearing a pair of jeans, a black sweater, and military-style boots. She had pulled her long hair into a side ponytail.

Julian smiled when he saw her. “Don’t you look cute,” he remarked.

She found herself blushing yet again. “It feels good to get out of that dress and get comfy.” Her hands flew to her head. “Oops, forgot my sunglasses. Will you grab a blanket? They’re in the closet by the front door.”

“No problem.” While Isabella ran back upstairs, Julian went to the closet and opened the door. He pulled a blanket from the top shelf, knocking over a small box in the process and spilling its contents on the floor. He set the blanket down and began to pick up the papers that had fallen out of the box. Among them he noticed two passports. He opened the first one and saw that it was Isabella’s. She looked perfectly made up, as usual. *Who takes a good passport photo?* he thought. He put it back in the box and reached for the second one. It was Grayson’s.

Julian shook his head. *What an idiot*, he thought. *A passport is something you should have if you’re traveling to London.*

As he heard Isabella coming down the stairs, he shoved the passport back in the bottom of the box and returned it to the shelf.

“Is this one okay?” Julian asked as he emerged from the closet, holding up the blanket.

“Perfect,” she said, and opened the loft door.

Julian stepped out into the hallway and reached for her hand. Isabella hesitated for a second with doubt in her eyes, but she put her hand in his with a smile. Hand in hand, they left the building and strolled down the street to the market.

~~~

They found a sunny spot in Central Park and sat on the blanket, eating lunch, drinking wine, and enjoying the beautiful fall day. They laughed and joked with one another as Julian told stories of his first few years spent struggling to survive in New York. He opened up about his childhood and how difficult it was to be raised by parents who had an addiction. Isabella felt she could relate to him in so many ways.
~~~

He was an only child as well, and his stories of how he coped reminded her of things she had done when her mother had up and left her.

In turn, Isabella shared memories of her childhood spent on the farm with her grandparents. She explained how she had ended up in New York and the years she had struggled through college. She recalled how she and Gia had met and all the fun they'd had in the early years at her small studio.

The conversation turned to their tastes in music and movies. "I don't get a chance to see very many movies," Isabella said, "but I like love stories, murder mysteries, comedies, anything, really." She paused. "Well, anything except movies with ghosts and evil spirits and spooky things. That stuff freaks me out."

"Wait, so you have no problem watching a murder mystery, but won't watch anything with ghosts?" Julian smirked. "You know, you have a better chance of being killed by a crazy person breaking into your house than a ghost."

"I know, but those movies scare the crap out of me. Ever since I saw *The Ring* years ago, I still make sure the TV armoire is closed in the bedroom before I go to sleep. Is that crazy or what?"

Julian shook with laughter. "Are you kidding? Silly girl."

She slapped his arm. "I know it's silly, but I do believe in ghosts and spirits. My grandmother told me a story of how she was sleeping one night and woke to see a man wearing a long, black trench coat and a large-brimmed hat standing by her dresser. She thought she was just imagining it, and simply closed her eyes and went back to sleep. The next night, she woke again, and he was standing at the foot of her bed, so when she got up that day, she went to the church to light a candle and say a prayer for him. That night when she woke up, he wasn't there."

"Come on, that didn't happen. You believed her?"

"Of course I did. Why would she lie about something like that?"

He shook his head. "You always hear people telling stories of ghosts secondhand. It's never something they actually experienced themselves."

"Okay then, for three nights after my grandfather passed away, I was having the same dream about a boat. My grandfather liked to fish at our pond on the farm. I can't tell you what the dream was about, but, on the third night of the dream, I do remember trying to help people off the boat. I had a flashlight in my hand and was scanning the cabin to see if there was anyone left, and that's when I saw a hand. When I moved the flashlight up to his face, it was my grandfather. I said to him, 'Give me your hand and let me help you.' But he shook his head and said, 'No,

I'm fine. You need to go.' When I started to protest, he said, 'I'm fine. Go.' It was then that I woke up and opened my eyes to a warm light coming from the hallway. I remember thinking I was still dreaming, so I rubbed my eyes and pushed up on my elbows and looked again. There stood my grandfather, dressed in one of his suits. He was smiling at me, then waved and disappeared."

Julian looked skeptical. "Seriously, that actually happened?"

"Seriously, it did. I figured it was his way of telling me he was okay, and that I didn't need to worry about him." Isabella smiled at the memory.

Julian gazed out across the rolling lawn. He seemed to be trying to decide if he believed her or not. "Well, since you're clearly not a crazy person, I believe you. But I've never had anything like that happen to me."

"I have a few other times, too. I think we all experience signs of some kind from those we love after they die. Sometimes we see them, and sometimes we don't. I think it depends on how much we pay attention."

"Interesting perspective. I'll keep that in mind while I'm searching for ghosts in my armoire," Julian teased, and she whacked him in the arm.

"Are you laughing at me?"

"I would never laugh at you. I'm laughing with you."

Isabella picked up a grape from her plate and threw it at him. "Well, *I'm* not laughing, you big dummy."

"You will be now." Julian pinned her down on the blanket and began to tickle her. Isabella kicked her legs and tried to push him off of her, but he grabbed her hands and pushed them over her head, holding them with one hand. Isabella stopped thrashing and looked up at him. Their noses were almost touching. A smile appeared on Julian's face, and he started tickling her again with his other hand.

Isabella burst out screaming. "You are evil! Get off me before I hurt you."

Julian released her hands and sat up. "See, I told you you were laughing."

Isabella lay on the blanket with her knees bent and her hands over her stomach, which hurt from laughing. She looked over at him as he continued to smile at her.

"I will make you pay for that," she playfully threatened him.

"Promises, promises." He winked at her.

Isabella lay back and gazed up at the sky.

"What are you looking at?" Julian asked as he lay down next to her.

"Nothing, really. Just the clouds. They're so fluffy, like you could fall back into them and float away." She felt so relaxed that she closed her eyes and fell asleep.

Julian lay next to her, watching her sleep. Her breathing was slow and relaxed. He didn't want to disturb her, because he knew that she hadn't been getting much sleep, so he simply let her drift away into a deep sleep. He thought about how close they had become, but not close enough in his mind. He lay there watching her for over an hour before she finally stirred.

She woke to find Julian gazing down at her. "Did I fall asleep?" she asked, sitting up. There was a chill in the air.

"You sure did. You were talking about clouds, and the next thing I knew, you were out."

She noticed the sun already setting behind the city's skyscrapers. "How long have I been asleep?"

Julian looked at his watch. "Over an hour now."

She pulled her knees to her chest and smoothed her hair. "How come you didn't wake me? I'm so sorry, that was rude of me."

"I didn't wake you because you looked so peaceful. I know how hard you've been working lately. I figured you could use the rest." He looked at his watch. "It's almost seven. Do you want to go back?"

"I think we should. Don't laugh, but I'm starting to get hungry again."

"Me too. Why don't we stop and get something on the way back?"

"I need a pizza or a burger. I'm craving carbs."

"You got it."

Julian took Isabella's hand as they left the park and crossed the street. As they rounded the corner, she caught sight of a mass of fiery red hair walking directly toward them. Isabella pulled her hand away from his quickly and muttered, "Oh no."

"Don't you two look cozy?" Gia said, smiling when she noticed the blanket tucked under Julian's arm. "Did we have a picnic in the park?"

Isabella rolled her eyes, knowing Gia was just stirring the pot. "Yes, we did. Julian was nice enough to take me out after the interview."

Gia looked at her watch. "Wow, that interview must have lasted forever. It's after seven now." She smirked.

Isabella glared at her, mouthing, *Knock it off.*

Gia smiled innocently and turned her attention to Julian, who had been standing there observing them.

"So, Julian, how did she do today with the interview?"

"Perfect, as she always is."

Gia raised her eyebrows and turned her gaze back to Isabella. "Perfect, huh? I can't wait to see the article."

"Where are you off to?" Isabella asked, changing the subject.

"A friend's house for dinner."

Isabella knew that translated into a night of drinks and wild sex at some hot guy's apartment. "Just dinner?" she asked with a meaningful look.

Gia fired out a fake laugh. "Do you really want to start that up again? Because you know I'm the master at this."

Isabella knew she was right. Gia was the master of the innuendo. "No, I don't. Go have your fun, and we can catch up tomorrow at the office."

"Absolutely. Can't wait to hear all about your weekend." She leaned in and hugged Isabella. "All business my ass," she whispered in her ear.

Isabella pulled back to see a smug smile on her friend's face.

"See you later, Julian. Have fun." Gia waved and continued down the sidewalk.

"What's up with her?" said Julian. "I can never figure out what the hell you two are talking about. It's like you have a twin code or something."

"Never mind her. She's always trying to cause trouble."

"I guess that's what best friends are for, right?"

"Right." Isabella glared back over her shoulder just in time to see the troublemaker and her fiery hair disappear around the corner.

~~~

Isabella lay in bed that night thinking about Grayson. He had called her that morning during the interview and left a message saying he would be back the following evening. She wondered how, or even if, they would be able to reconnect. Was that something he still wanted? For that matter, did she? Everything had been so disjointed between them lately. The turmoil of their relationship was starting to take a toll on her.

Her thoughts wandered to Julian and the past few days she had spent with him. She smiled, thinking about their time at the park. It felt good getting to know him outside of their everyday routine. She felt so comfortable and relaxed around him. Even though it had been only a few months, it was like they had known each other for years. He seemed to sense exactly what she needed, when she needed it. There were things he knew about her that made her pause and wonder, *Did I tell him that?* He already knew her that well.
~~~

She closed her eyes, trying to focus on Grayson, but the vision of Julian standing in the loft with his shirt off popped into her mind. She remembered the feeling of his breath on her neck and the wave of emotions his touch had sent through her. Even though nothing had happened, she felt guilty; she knew that it easily could have. Her feelings had come out of nowhere and surprised her. She was confused by the fact that someone other than Grayson could affect her like that. She had never thought of Julian as anything other than a business associate. Isabella knew she had no right to feel what she was feeling.

She looked at the picture of her and Grayson on her nightstand as she remembered a happier time not too long ago. She drifted off to sleep, and even though Grayson's face was the last she saw, it was Julian who filled her dreams.

Chapter 15

"Spill it, sister," Gia said as she burst into Isabella's office and closed the door behind her.

"Spill what?" Isabella asked. "There's nothing to spill."

"Oh, please. I run into you and Mr. McSexy walking down the street holding hands, coming from the park where you had a picnic that lasted for hours. Oh yeah, sister, I think there's plenty to spill." Her head bobbed back and forth, accompanied by some serious finger-wagging.

"Gia, it's not what you're thinking. Julian came over for the interview yesterday, and after we were done, we were hungry, so we decided to eat in the park, since it was so nice out. We just sat there talking, and—truth be told, I fell asleep. That's it."

"Really? Nothing else happened?" Gia looked dejected.

"No, nothing else happened." Isabella knew it was best not to mention anything about the zipper incident or what had happened at her loft the night before the interview.

"Why don't I believe you?" Gia narrowed her eyes.

Isabella sighed. "Nothing else happened. After we saw you, we stopped for some pizza, and he walked me home and left."

Gia let out a big huff. "Well, I'm disappointed in you. I was hoping that at the very least, just being around him would make you all tingly. It would be good to know that you're not dead over there."

Isabella couldn't resist a small smile. She looked down at the paperwork on her desk to avoid making eye contact. "Sorry to disappoint you. I guess I'm dead."

"Oh my gosh," Gia said slowly. "He did, didn't he? He got you all tingly. He got to you, I knew it." Gia clapped her hands loudly as she gloated. "Don't even try to deny it. I know you better than the back of my hand, Isabella Hughes, and I can tell that he got to you. Dish, please."

Isabella glared at Gia as she sat down in front of her desk, smiling like the Cheshire cat. "I do not like you right now." She blew her breath out. "Okay, I will admit that there were awkward moments that made me pause and think, but nothing happened."

"But you wanted it to, right?" Gia was sitting on the edge of her seat.

"Just because someone wants something doesn't mean they have the right to take it. Unlike you, I can restrain myself."

Gia rolled her eyes. "Whatever. Just remember that I called it. I knew this was coming."

"Why are you so happy about this? It's so wrong on so many levels. I have Grayson."

"Who has been a complete shit to you for quite some time. Tell me the last time he was there for you, Isabella. I mean, really there for you. Lately all I hear about is him disappointing you or hurting you, or not even wanting you to be there for him. Wake up. Something isn't right."

Isabella cringed. "Ouch. You could have at least spread a little sugar on that. Kick me while I'm down, why don't you?"

Gia sighed. "Izzie, I don't say these things to hurt you. I say them to empower you. You let Grayson walk all over you and your feelings. Now if you want me to go all Freud on you, I will."

"Oh please, wise one, enlighten me with your psychoanalysis."

Gia looked at her for a long moment, as if choosing her words carefully. "Isabella, you put up with the crappy things Grayson does to you because you're afraid if you don't, he'll leave you like your mother did. What you have to realize is that your mother didn't leave because of something you did or didn't do. She left because she was the one who had a problem, not you. Just because you constantly appease Grayson and put up with his moods doesn't mean he'll stay. It just means you'll have put yourself through a lot of unnecessary heartache for someone who may not be worth it in the end."

Isabella let her eyes fall again to the papers on her desk. She drew a breath to speak just as James buzzed in on the office line.

"Isabella, Grayson is on line one."

"Thanks, James," she said, and hit the button on her phone. She stared at the phone for a moment with her hand on the receiver.

"Izzie?" Gia whispered.

Isabella looked up at Gia and shook her head. "Please, not now. I don't want to talk about it anymore."

Gia nodded as Isabella picked up the phone and tried to sound cheerful. "Hey babe, how are you? Are you at the airport yet?" Isabella sat there, nodding and listening to Grayson while Gia watched in silence. "Yep," Isabella said to Grayson. "I get it. It's okay. I'll see you then. Goodbye." Isabella set the phone back down on the base and looked up at Gia. "Grayson is staying a few extra days in London. He ran into some old friends there, and he's going to hang out with them for a few days."

"Are you okay?"

Isabella stood and began gathering papers. "I'm fine, Gia, perfectly fine," she snapped. "We need to stop sitting around wasting time. We have work to do today. I want to check on the status of the building design for Charles. Have Bradley and his assistants meet me in conference room two, please."

"Are you sure you don't want to talk about it? I can tell you're upset."

"Yes, I'm sure. I'm sick of talking. I just need to work." She walked past Gia and left her office.

Isabella spent most of the day in the conference room with the lead designer, Bradley, and his assistants, looking over the schedules and design plans for Charles Vanderbeck's building. She made it clear to everyone in the room that she was not happy with the progress and the way things were being handled.

"I don't get it," she said to Bradley. "I went through all of this with you before you started. Was I not clear about my expectations?"

"You were, Isabella," he said. "We've been working hard on this for the past few months now."

"Well, not hard enough. Where is the pricing on this?" Isabella threw the flooring selections down on the table. "Or this?" She slammed down another selection sheet. "All of this should have been priced out already, approved, and ready to go. This is how we keep projects moving. Has any of this even been ordered?" Isabella felt herself going livid, but couldn't calm down.

"No, it hasn't. We were waiting on—"

She held up her hand to stop him. "Are you kidding me? Unbelievable." Isabella rubbed her forehead. She looked at James, who sat quietly at the other end of the conference table. "Get Gia in here now," she ordered.

He disappeared, and a minute later, Gia slipped into the room alone. As soon as the door closed, Isabella started in on her.

"Have you seen this? What the hell has been going on here? This is exactly what I was worried about. All of these estimates should have been completed by now." Isabella handed her a stack of papers. "These items haven't even been selected yet. Do you have any idea how pissed I am right now?" Isabella looked at the others seated around the table. "Get out, all of you. Just get out, before I start firing people." Within seconds, Bradley and his assistants had cleared the room.

"Calm down, Isabella," Gia said quietly as she began to look through the selections sheets.

"I can't calm down. You promised me that shit like this would not fall through the cracks, yet here we are months into the project, and I'm finding out that this is not done. And this is just one project. What in God's name do the other projects look like? I'm about ready to have a stroke." Isabella raised her hands over her head, looking up to the ceiling. "Why me? Please just shoot me now."

"We can fix this. It won't take us that long to get everything back on track. You and I can devote time where it's needed."

"What the hell have you been smoking? First off, in order to fix just this project, you're looking at a solid week, at least, not to mention all the other screw-ups we're going to find on other projects. Secondly, I finished the sketches on the third collection this weekend, and I wanted to review those with you before sending them off. Thirdly, I'm expecting a call from Gonzolo this week. You and I are supposed to go and view the prototypes he has completed on the first two collections. So please tell me, with all that going on, how the hell do you think all this is getting fixed?"

"I will do it," Gia said calmly, trying to talk her down from the ledge she was ready to jump off of. "I will personally see that this is all corrected, and you can help me until you have to leave. I won't go with you to see the prototypes. I will stay here where you need me."

"Really? You're going to give up the chance to go to the manufacturing plant and see all of our hard work?"

"Yes, in a heartbeat, because I know this is where you need me. You have a camera, you can take pictures, and I'll get to see them that way. Besides, there will be other opportunities to go."

"I don't want to go alone. I want you to be there with me."

"You won't be alone. Julian will be there for you."

Isabella felt unbelievably overwhelmed. This was one of her worst fears with this project. She blamed herself for not taking more of an initiative to stay on top of the design aspect. Instead, she had allowed herself to solely focus her attention on the furniture line. She knew Gia was right; she had to stay behind and fix it. She was the only one Isabella trusted to get it done properly.

"All right then, let's get started," said Isabella. "First I want to go over the sketches with you, and then we can start on this. We need to get Julian in here as well. I know he's been tied up with me on some other aspects of the project, but I need him to start managing these elements as well."

~~~

After reviewing the sketches, Isabella had Julian send them over to
~~~

Gonzolo so she and Gia could start working on the missing items and pricing. They spent the rest of the day trying to clean up the mess made by the other designers.

As they were about to leave for the evening, Isabella received the call from Gonzolo that she had been expecting. He was pleased with the remaining sketches and was ready for her to come and view what he had completed so far on the other two collections. Isabella would contact Mr. Vanderbeck and have his company schedule the trip, as they required twenty-four-hour notice. As Isabella hung up with Gonzolo, Julian came into the selections room.

Isabella told him about the call. "We'll be leaving in a day or so. I have to shoot an email over to Charles's office so they can make the arrangements."

"That's great news. You two must be excited to see it all in person."

"It is great news," Isabella said, "but when I said *we*, I meant you and I. Gia is staying here to keep an eye on the progress with the building. A lot of mistakes have been made lately, and I need her here to get everything back on track. I would prefer not to go by myself. Do you mind going with me?"

"Are you kidding? I would be honored to go and see your creations."

"Perfect, then it's settled. Now let's get the hell out of here. I'm starving and ready for something other than the peanuts I've been snacking on all day."

Gia stood and gathered her things off the table. "You'll have to count me out. I have plans already."

Isabella looked at Julian. "Are you hungry?"

He grinned. "When am I not hungry?"

In the Town Car on the way back to Soho, they agreed to order in at Isabella's place.

"How does a big, juicy cheeseburger and fries sound?" Julian asked.

Isabella's mouth watered. "You know that's my comfort food. Well, that and ice cream. Wait—and anything chocolate."

They laughed.

Julian pulled out his phone. "Okay then, I'll order a burger and fries and chocolate ice cream for dessert."

"Are you insane? I'll be five pounds heavier by morning." She puffed out her cheeks.

"No worries. I'll have your ass out at the park bright and early tomorrow morning, running it off."

Sebastian dropped them off in front of her building, and Isabella went inside to change while Julian walked down to the café nearby to pick up the burgers.

Her head was pounding, so she took out her high ponytail and let her hair fall long on her shoulders, hoping it would release some of the tension in her head and neck. She poured herself a double vodka and soda. *It's definitely a double night*, she thought. As she finished making her drink, Julian arrived with the food.

"Perfect timing. Would you like a drink?" she asked as he came in.

"Sure. I'll have what you're having."

"Are you sure? Mine's a double."

"I figured." He smiled and set their food down on the cocktail table. "That works for me."

She carried their drinks to the living room. "I'm so glad you suggested this," she said as she grabbed her food container and sat down. "I was not in the mood for a crowded restaurant, and this"—she pointed to her hamburger—"smells amazing."

They fell silent as both took big bites from their burgers. Finally Julian said, "I know you had a rough day. Do you want to talk about it?"

"Not really. I'm glad it's over. It was just one thing after another today. I felt like a hamster on a damn wheel."

"Well, you're definitely cuter than any hamster, and you smell better, too."

"You're trying to cheer me up, aren't you? Is that what all this is about?" She gestured to the food.

He smiled. "Is it working?"

She threw a French fry at him. "Maybe."

Julian caught the fry and laughed at her. "I heard that Bradley almost lost a nut in the conference room this morning."

She frowned. "That incompetent ass is lucky he still has a job. He's been working with me forever and knows better. That is exactly why Gia and I assigned him to lead this project."

Julian paused while he took a drink of his cocktail. "Gia told me about Grayson extending his trip. Are you okay?"

Her frown deepened. "Did she now? Gia has a big mouth." Isabella shrugged. "I'm fine. There's nothing I can do or say to change it, so I'm not going to worry about it yet."

"I'm sorry."

"Please don't be sorry. I'm not," she said nonchalantly. "I was angry and now I'm nothing, so there it is."

Julian looked at her carefully and moved closer to her on the sofa. She set her hamburger down and was about to ask him what he was doing, but then he took her chin in his hand. Her heart began to race as she wondered if he was going to kiss her. But he merely wiped the side of her face and sat back on the sofa.

"Ketchup," he said. "You had ketchup on your cheek."

"Seriously, you could have just said, 'Isabella you have ketchup on your cheek.' Your whole act was a bit dramatic, don't you think? I think you've been hanging out with my gays way too long."

This time it was Julian who threw a fry at her. "What, did you think that I was going to kiss you?"

"Please, I would have decked you."

"Is that right, tough girl?"

"Yep, that's right."

Their eyes met for a long moment, and he started to move closer to her again. Isabella pushed her back into the arm of the sofa and moved her knees in front of her, but he kept leaning into her. She thought he was just joking, so she decided to play along with his little game. He put one arm around her waist, resting his hand on the sofa cushion, and brought himself face-to-face with her. Suddenly Isabella wasn't so sure he was joking around. Her heart started to race again. She didn't know if she was panicked or excited—maybe a little of both. She kept thinking that she needed to get up, but she couldn't move—or didn't want to.

With his other hand, Julian moved her hair out of her eyes so he could see them fully, then caressed her cheek. He knew without a fraction of doubt that this was the moment to make his move. Nothing was going to stop him.

"Julian," Isabella whispered, but he put his finger to her lips to silence her.

"Don't talk, don't think. Just be here with me in this moment. Want me like I want you."

His touch sent a wave of excitement through her. As she cautiously watched him, he brought his mouth near hers and softly touched her upper lip with his, causing her lips to part slightly. They kissed slowly at first, their lips barely touching. Julian placed a hand behind her neck and brought her head forward before pressing his lips fully on hers, kissing her passionately. Electricity rushed through her, and she knew in that moment Julian had awakened something deep inside her. He had unleashed a desire that she had been fighting to control.

Isabella pulled her body against his and cupped his face in her hands. His kisses grew deeper and more desperate. His breath was coming fast, and in one quick movement, he pulled her down onto the sofa, pressing his body on top of hers. His hands wandered from her face to her breasts, and he pushed her legs apart with his knee. Isabella felt his erection throbbing against her as he began to grind himself into her. She wrapped her legs around his waist and feverishly unbuttoned his shirt, letting her hands explore his smooth chest. *He's absolutely perfect*, she thought.

Her lips found his neck and slowly made their way down to his chest, his scent arousing her further. Isabella closed her eyes and breathed in his heavenly fragrance. Julian pushed her shirt up and moved down to kiss her stomach. "Your skin is like silk," he murmured. He pushed her shirt up further, exposing her bare breasts, and teased her with his tongue. Isabella arched her back as her nipples hardened with excitement. A feeling of ecstasy overtook her. She grabbed his shirt and pulled him on top of her again. She wanted him. She wanted all of him.

"Oh my God, Bella, I want you so much right now," he said, his breath ragged. "Tell me you want me. Say it."

She touched his face, keeping her hands there as she looked into his beautiful green eyes. "I want you, Julian. I want you so much right now," she whispered, frightened of the words she spoke, but at the same time wanting nothing more than to be with him.

"You can have me. All of me."

With that, Julian scooped her off the sofa and carried her to the stairs, his lips never leaving hers. Just when they had reached the landing, the intercom buzzed. Julian pulled his face from hers and looked at her questioningly.

She sighed. "I should see who that is." She descended the stairs reluctantly and pressed the button on the intercom. "Yes?"

"Izzie, it's me. Can I come in?" Gia sounded like she had been crying.

She certainly had impeccable timing. Isabella looked up at Julian apologetically. "I'm sorry. You know I want this, but I can't turn her away."

He combed his fingers through his disheveled hair. "I wouldn't want you to. She's your friend, I understand."

Isabella pressed the button again. "Sure, baby girl, come on up."

Julian buttoned his shirt and hurried back to the sofa while Isabella ran to the mirror in the dining room, trying to quickly fix her hair and makeup. Just as they sat down on the sofa and grabbed their drinks, Gia pulled back the sliding door.

Chapter 16

Two days later, Sebastian drove Isabella and Julian to the airport together to catch their flight to Italy. Isabella had spent the previous day tied up at the office and preparing for the trip, and to her relief, she had barely seen Julian. Now, as she sat in the back seat with him, she felt awkward. Every time she saw him, a vision of them entangled on her sofa, ripping at each other's clothes, came to mind. She kept thinking that if Gia hadn't shown up when she did, they would have succumbed to temptation. In her head she knew it was wrong, but in her heart she felt something entirely different, and it confused her. The passion between them was off the charts. The simple thought of his touch made her stomach churn with excitement, but was also followed by a wave of guilt.

"I've never been to Italy," Julian was saying. "Have you?"

Isabella turned her gaze from the traffic beyond the window. "No, I've always wanted to go."

He laid a hand on hers across the middle seat. "I can't think of anyone I would rather share it with, Bella."

She smiled. "Ditto, Julian, ditto." She liked the way he called her Bella. Her grandparents had called her that growing up. It was odd to her that he had chosen the nickname—but odd in a good way.

Julian leaned in and kissed her softly on her lips. Her heart fluttered, but it quickly turned to panic as she remembered Sebastian was driving. She nervously checked to make sure the privacy glass was up.

Julian smiled. "You are adorable when you're nervous." He caressed her cheek, causing her to blush. "I put the glass up when I got into the car because I knew I would want to kiss those lips of yours."

Isabella looked down to her lap and smiled as impure thoughts ran through her mind again.

He gently lifted her chin with his finger and gazed longingly into her eyes. "You can expect that and a whole lot more in Milan, too."

She caught her breath and blushed again, now knowing exactly what was going through his mind.

At the airport, they walked onto the tarmac where Charles Vanderbeck's massive Gulfstream IV sat waiting for them, its shiny white finish shimmering in the early morning light. It was immaculate. On board, a friendly flight attendant handed them each a mimosa while Isabella gazed around in awe. The interior was designed in a cream, black, and tan color palette. Several high-back swivel chairs in a soft cream leather were paired with small, round, black tables in between, forming mini conversation settings throughout the plane. Several sofas were intermixed with the chairs, all done in the same soft cream-colored leather. The sofas would be perfect for kicking back during the eight-hour flight. The lavatory, located at the front of the plane, was sleek and modern, with an ebony vanity cabinet and glass vessel sink with a brushed-nickel, wall-mounted faucet. A small private office for Charles occupied the rear of the plane.

"Welcome aboard," Charles greeted them. He took Isabella's hand and pulled her toward him so he could kiss her cheek. He then extended his hand to Julian.

"Thank you for having us," Isabella said. "We are thrilled that Gonzolo is finally ready for us to see the prototypes."

After a few minutes of excited discussion about the project, Charles retreated to his office, and Isabella and Julian sat in two swivel chairs to relax. Julian raised his glass to her.

"Here's to you and me and an amazing time in Italy," he said.

"To Italy," she echoed, and raised her glass to his.

The plane's door closed, and within fifteen minutes they were barreling down the runway. As the plane took off with ease, Isabella stared out the window, watching the city disappear below. She was ready for adventure. It excited her, but at the same time made her wonder just what she would find on the journey.

~~~

"Bella." Julian was sitting on the edge of the sofa, shaking her shoulder to wake her. "Bella, you have to see this. It's incredible." Isabella stirred and opened her eyes. He pointed outside. "Look out the window."

Isabella sat up and gazed out the small window at the beautiful city of Milan below. The architecture was so different from what she was used to in New York. The structures looked old, yet charming, with unique architectural details. Gargoyles perched high atop the roofs of some buildings, as if keeping a watchful eye over the city.

"Oh my goodness, it's so beautiful, Julian. I've never seen anything like it. I've seen pictures and have imagined what it would look like, but seeing it in person is truly amazing."

"I agree, it's spectacular." Julian patted her knee. "Thank you for
~~~

bringing me along with you. We're going to have an amazing time here, I'm sure."

"You are most welcome," she said, well aware of the sensation his touch sent through her body.

Within minutes, the plane was on the ground, and Charles, Isabella, and Julian made their way down the steps and right into a waiting limousine. The ride from the Linate Airport to their hotel was a quick twenty-five minutes. As they drove through the city, Charles spoke of previous trips to Milan and pointed out places he had visited.

"See that little restaurant tucked in the corner over there?" he said, pointing. "They serve the best authentic Italian cuisine I've had. It doesn't look like much from the outside, or the inside for that matter, but the food is outstanding."

"I love those hole-in-the-wall finds," Isabella said. "There's an Italian restaurant I go to in Cabo San Lucas called Salvatore's. It's just like that place, not much to look at, but the food is outstanding."

Charles nodded. "I know the place. It is excellent. The hotel we're staying in, however, is a far cry from a hole in the wall." He laughed. "When I come here, I always stay at the Four Seasons. It's a beautiful hotel that sits on a quiet street, surrounded by historic buildings. Isabella, you will especially like this—the hotel is located in the city's Quadrilatero Della Moda."

Isabella looked at him questioningly. "You'll have to excuse me, Charles, but my Spanish is much better than my Italian, and that isn't saying much."

"The Quadrilatero Della Moda offers the world's finest designer shopping. Valentino, Gucci, Prada, Versace, you name it, and it's there. Believe me—my ex-wives have cost me a pretty penny on these streets." Charles laughed.

Isabella swooned. "I think I just found heaven."

"You're actually right in the middle of heaven. Our hotel sits between Via della Spiga and Via Montenapoleone. These are considered the two best streets for shopping here in Milan."

"Charles, I hate to tell you this," Isabella said, "but I'm not sure how much work is going to get done while we're here. Asking me not to shop is like telling a three-year-old she can't eat the big, fluffy cupcake dripping with frosting and sprinkles that you just set in front of her."

Charles and Julian burst into laughter. "It's true," Julian said. "I've heard her closet has its own zip code."

Isabella whacked his leg.

"Show me a woman who doesn't like to shop," Charles said. "I've been married four times, and between all of them, I could open up a three-story department store. You two will have time to go out and enjoy the city a bit. I have other work to attend to here as well, so there will be plenty of opportunity for eating, drinking, and shopping to your heart's content."

Isabella grinned. "Music to my ears."

Julian raised a finger. "I want it made known now that I didn't come here just to hold your bags for you while you shop."

"If I pay you enough, you will," she teased, nudging him with her leg.

"Ah, here we are, my home away from home," Charles announced as the limo pulled into the circular driveway of the hotel. The beautiful building, constructed out of smooth, tan stone, looked much newer than any of the other buildings they had passed. The first-floor windows were made of gold stained glass with a wrought-iron harlequin pattern, while the two rows of second-story windows had black shutters. Above the hotel entrance sat a balcony with three flags and a black wrought-iron railing overflowing with lush foliage.

A doorman wearing a black suit and white gloves opened the door of the limo and escorted them inside, where they were greeted with a warm reception at the front desk. The hotel had 118 guest rooms and 41 suites surrounding a courtyard. Each room was uniquely designed, allowing the guests a different experience each time they visited. The décor throughout the hotel was Mediterranean, with ornately carved furniture, tapestry fabrics, wrought-iron elements, and rich, cream-colored marble floors. The colors were warm yet vibrant, creating an inviting, exotic ambiance.

The concierge handed Charles the keys to the Royal Suite, which occupied the entire fifth floor and had a private entrance. Isabella and Julian received the keys to the third-floor Visconti Suite, a 2,650-square-foot two-bedroom suite with French windows in the living room that offered a wonderful view of the courtyard.

"I hope you two don't mind sharing the suite," Charles said. "We thought this would give you both more space than if you were in separate rooms."

Julian and Isabella looked at each other with surprise. "We don't mind," said Isabella with a smile. "Thank you."

When they stepped into the foyer of the suite, Isabella's jaw dropped. The floor was a medium, caramel-colored hardwood, except in the bedrooms and bathrooms, which had carpet and marble. Julian's suitcase had been placed in the first bedroom, located immediately to the left of the foyer. The bedroom had its own bathroom and dressing area. As they proceeded down the long hallway, they noticed four doors on the right. The first door led into the master bathroom, and the next three were for the master suite, which would be Isabella's room. The bedroom walls were covered in pale gold wallpaper with a subtle scrolling pattern. On the wall adjacent to the living room sat a king-sized bed. The tufted headboard was upholstered in a pale gold silk fit for a princess. The soft, luxurious bedding included four king-sized bed pillows and six toss pillows in varying shades of eggplant, which matched the silky duvet comforter. In front of the bed sat a long bench covered in a complimentary fabric. Isabella's room also had a cozy sofa, sitting chair with ottoman, and a desk that she could work at if she wanted.

They stood there in awe of the sheer size of the room.

"I think your room is bigger than mine," Julian teased.

"Well, of course it is. Don't you know, women always get the bigger closet and bigger room?"

"Yes, of course. What on earth was I thinking?"

They stepped into the living room. The vaulted ceilings and fireplace wall were wood. The remaining walls were painted cream. The fabrics were rich, warm, and inviting. Isabella counted eight sitting chairs and two plush, oversized sofas covered in a sea of throw pillows, which were perfectly fluffed and lined up across each sofa. In the far right corner of the room sat a sizable dining table with six chairs.

"Who the hell do they think we're expecting?" said Julian.

Isabella chuckled. "Haven't you ever been in a suite before? There's always tons of seating to accommodate any type of gathering. Besides, from a design standpoint, how else would you fill the space in a living room of this size?"

"How stupid of me. I forgot I was traveling with a design expert."

With a recommendation from Anthony, the doorman, they made their way to Bice Ristorante, a quaint Italian restaurant not too far from the hotel. The atmosphere was perfect, not too busy and not too quiet. The food was incredible. Isabella had the sea bass with steamed vegetables, while Julian opted for the Sicilian swordfish with capers and olives. They ordered a bottle of wine and enjoyed their first night out in Italy with plenty of good spirits, amazing food, and lively conversation.

"I think they're ready to kick us out," Isabella whispered to Julian as she looked at the waitress, who was staring back at her while speaking to her manager in Italian.

He leaned toward her across the table, motioning her forward with his finger. "Why are you whispering?" he whispered back. "They don't speak English." He raised his voice. "They can't understand you."

Isabella laughed and pushed his face away, covering his whole face with her tiny hand. "They can understand us. You are a nut, you know that?"

"No, they can't. They're only pretending to." He winked at her. "And yes, I know I'm a nut. It's my job to keep you in stitches, because I've learned that when my Bella isn't happy, no one is."

Isabella rolled her eyes. She laughed at him, then let out a big yawn.

"Oh no, is someone getting sleepy?"

"Just a little. It's been a long day. Would you mind if we headed back?"

"Not at all. I could use some down time myself."

Almost on queue, the waitress came by and set the check down on the table.

Isabella smirked at Julian. "See, I told you she could understand us."

Julian looked at the waitress, who winked at him and walked away.

Back in their suite, they retreated to their rooms and began unpacking. Isabella rolled her suitcase into the large dressing area, which had ample space for hanging all the clothes she had brought. First she changed into a pair of comfortable shorts and a cotton tank. As she tackled her suitcase, her cell phone rang from the bedroom. She made a mad dash for it and answered out of breath. "Hello."

"Isabella, it's me," Grayson said.

Isabella froze. She hadn't spoken to Grayson before she left. She had tried, but had gotten his voicemail, so she had simply left a message explaining the trip. From the tone of his voice, she could tell he wasn't happy.

She tried to sound light and cheerful. "Hey, how are you?"

"Where are you? I came home today to find you gone, and when I called your office asking for you, all they said was that you were out of town."

"I left you a message telling you exactly where I was," Isabella snapped back, throwing her cheerful tone right out the window.

"Think, Isabella. I obviously didn't get it, otherwise I wouldn't be calling you right now."

Isabella let out a loud huff. Now she was the one who was getting annoyed. "Well, I left one explaining that I had to come to Milan to review the prototypes that the manufacturing plant completed. I just got here today."

"Why couldn't you have waited until after I got home to leave?

Don't you think that's a little inconsiderate?"

She pulled the phone away from her ear and looked down at it. Who the hell did he think he was? She felt the anger boil inside her. "I'm sorry, Grayson, but this is a business trip. I'm not frolicking around Europe having a good old time with my friends."

"It's always about business, isn't it?" Grayson was shouting at her now. "You and your business. You're always spending all your time and attention on that instead of on the people that really matter in your life."

Isabella stood there with her mouth hanging open. Her heart was pounding in her chest. "Are you fucking kidding me with this?" she screamed. "I've tried to spend time with you consistently since I started this project, and you're the one who always seems to have better things to do. What those are, I have no clue, but time and time again I've cut you slack. I never ask what you're up to, or what is so important that you can't spend time with me, yet here you are, accusing me of being neglectful to you and your needs. You know, I'm the one who actually has a job that requires my attention." She knew that would cut him, but she didn't care anymore. She let the venom spew from her mouth, directing it right where she knew it would hurt.

For a long moment, there was silence on his end. "You know what, Isabella, fuck off." He hung up on her.

Shaking, Isabella threw her cell phone on the bed and rubbed her forehead. As she turned to go back into the dressing room, the rage inside took over. She picked up a crystal sculpture from the nightstand and hurled it across the room, letting out a scream of frustration. The sculpture hit the wall and shattered into a million pieces. Tears streamed down her face as she fell to her knees and buried her face in her lap.

She felt Julian's arms around her, picking her up off the floor, telling her it was going to be okay. He lifted her onto the bed and sat her up against a pile of pillows. Isabella pulled her legs to her chest and rocked back and forth, crying.

Julian sat down on the bed in front of her. "Shhh, it's okay. You're going to be okay, I promise. I'm here for you."

Still in disbelief, Isabella shook her head, as if to erase Grayson's hurtful words. "What have I done to deserve this?" She looked at Julian, her eyes pleading for an explanation. "Please tell me what I've done. I don't understand." Her voice quivered. "Why does he treat me this way? I don't understand him."

"You haven't done anything. You don't deserve to be treated this way. I don't know what's wrong with him. All I know is that you deserve to be treated much better." He kissed the top of her head. "What did he say?"

She recounted the conversation. "Do you know what else he said to me?" she added between gasps for air. "He told me to fuck off. Who says that to someone they love?" Isabella started sobbing again. "Do you have any idea how hurtful that is?"

Julian stroked her hair and pulled her closer to him until his head rested on hers. "He had no right to say that to you, no right at all. Based on what you've shared with me about his behavior lately, I hope you know that you are not to blame here. It's obvious that he's the one with the problem."

Isabella closed her eyes and listened to the sound of Julian's heartbeat, which calmed her.

Finally, he said, "We need to get you to sleep. It's almost one in the morning. You have a big day tomorrow, and I need you to be on top of your game." In one clean sweep, he knocked half the pillows to the floor and pulled the covers down. "Come on, climb in and try to close your eyes."

Isabella slid between the covers, realizing what a good person Julian was and how much he genuinely cared about her. She reached for his hand. "Will you stay with me? I don't want to be alone."

"Absolutely," he said, touching her face. He climbed into bed behind her and snuggled up close. He put his arm around her waist, rested his head on her pillow, and softly kissed her neck.

"Thank you for staying with me and being here for me," she whispered. "It means a lot."

He kissed her neck again. "I told you that I'm always here for you, Bella, and that will never change."

Soothed by the warmth of his body, she drifted off to sleep.

Chapter 17

Isabella was confused when she opened her eyes, trying to remember exactly where she was. Then she saw the luxurious bedroom around her and remembered. The clock on the nightstand said it was just before six in the morning. She looked over her shoulder at Julian, who slept peacefully beside her, his arm still wrapped around her. She watched him, remembering the first time she had seen him in her office. The memory made her smile. Their relationship had come so far in such a short amount of time. Who would have thought that Julian would be the one who was beside her now, encouraging her when she was doubtful, helping her to focus when she was distracted, and calming her in her chaotic world? He obviously cared about her a great deal. She was extremely thankful he had come into her life.

As Julian slept, she gently touched his face, allowing her fingers to trace his perfect lips. She carefully sat up, as not to disturb his slumber, and leaned over him, bringing her face close to his. She placed her lips on his and kissed them.

Julian stirred slightly, and she paused. When she felt assured that he was still sleeping, Isabella brought her lips back down. With the second kiss, Julian opened his eyes. He took her face in his hands and pulled her mouth back to his, this time with a fiery passion. He pulled her on top of him so that she straddled him and kissed her over and over again, each kiss becoming more passionate than the last.

His hand slipped under her shirt. His touch was so soft, so pure. Isabella shivered as his hand moved to her breasts, caressing them delicately. He sat up, and his mouth found her stomach. He worked his way up her body with only his tongue and pulled off her top. He stopped for a moment to gaze at her perfect breasts, then caressed each nipple before bringing his lips to them. Isabella heard him catch his breath as each one sprang to life in his mouth.

Isabella felt an instant rush of electricity run through her. Her heart was racing, and her breath was fast. She felt an insane desire stir within her, and she knew the moment had come. She would have him. She pushed him down on the bed and feverishly found his lips again. She began to grind her hips into him as he held onto her waist, pushing her down into his body. Isabella felt him growing with each thrust of her hips. She slowly moved his boxers down his hips. Julian breathed heavier as she maneuvered his boxers completely off, exposing just how well endowed he was. In one quick movement, Julian flipped her over, pushing his body on hers. He kissed her hard on the mouth, his tongue finding hers again and again. He pulled off of her slightly, taking her shorts in his hands, and ripped them off, tossing them on the floor. He pushed her legs apart with his. With his hands resting on the bed above her shoulders, he hovered over her and gazed into her eyes, moving his hips slowly into her. She felt his hardness between her legs, teasing her softly. Desire had made her wet, and her sweetness covered his hard cock. The feeling made her quiver, made him ache with the longing to take her.

"I want you so much right now, Bella, you know I do. Tell me that you want me too. I want to hear you tell me."

Isabella gazed into his beautiful green eyes. "I want you, Julian," she whispered. "I don't want to wait any longer. Please make love to me," she begged.

Julian brought his lips down hard on hers again as he lowered his body on hers and entered her slowly. Isabella threw her head back and moaned, feeling his fullness inside her. Julian pushed deeper, taking her fully. He grabbed the back of her head, bringing her eyes to his. They stared at one another, joined by the sheer ecstasy between them. With each thrust, Isabella was filled with a pleasure that sent a fire raging through her entire body.

She grabbed Julian's face and kissed him again, the passion between them reaching a new height. Isabella buried her face into his shoulder as she dug into his back, pushing him further inside her as she wrapped her legs around his waist, squeezing his hardness as it throbbed inside her. Julian began to thrust faster and faster, sensing she was close. Isabella laid her head back down on the bed and touched his face as she gazed into his eyes. It was in that moment that they became one.

Julian kissed her lips and buried his face into her neck, trying to catch his breath. His body was on fire, his senses awakened with desire for her.

"That was a wonderful way to wake up." He smiled and kissed her again. "Truly amazing, and worth the wait."

Isabella smiled contentedly, her body still tingling from the passion he had delivered upon her. "It was, indeed. Why is it that we waited?"

"I don't know, but I will tell you this. Now that we've finally experienced it, I definitely want more . . ." Julian kissed her. "And more . . ." He kissed her again. "And more." He buried his face in her neck, biting her softly, making Isabella giggle.

"Stop! I'm ticklish, remember?" Isabella tried bringing her shoulder to her ear to protect herself, but Julian pushed her hands up and held them over her head, leaving her neck wide open for his lips.

Isabella screamed out in laughter. "Julian, stop! I swear I will hurt you."

Julian stopped and looked into her eyes. With her hands still held over her head, he brought his lips to hers. His kiss was pure, so pure it made Isabella feel warm inside. He released one hand from her wrists and reached down between her legs to caress her swollen clit. Isabella moaned as he explored her with his fingers—at first one, then two, as he masterfully swirled around, hitting her sweet spot. Her legs trembled. She felt consumed by his touch. With her desire quickly building again, she wiggled her arms free and reached down to take him in her hand. She began to move up and down his hard shaft, circling the head with her finger, causing moisture to drip from his tip. She brought her finger up to her lips and licked it as he watched her.

"Oh Bella, that is so hot. Do you have any idea how turned on you have me right now?"

She stroked him again. Julian moaned in pleasure. "I think it's easy to see how much you're turned on right now," she said.

Julian flipped her over, pulling her on top of him. He grabbed her hips and lowered her onto his stiff shaft. Isabella let out a small gasp as he entered her again, filling her completely, causing her wetness to surround him. Julian grabbed her breasts and squeezed her nipples between his fingers, and she screamed in pleasure. He grabbed her by the back of her head and pulled at her hair, bending her back as he sat up. Isabella wrapped her legs around his waist and moved up and down, grinding further onto him.

"Yes!" Julian cried out. "Goddamn, Bella, you are so sexy."

Isabella pushed down into him, taking every last inch of him inside her. She grabbed onto his arms and buried her face into his shoulders as she screamed out, climaxing with an intensity that she never thought possible. Julian grabbed hold of her hips again and quickly pumped inside her, releasing with her.

Breathless, they lay together, unable to speak. Isabella rested her head on his chest as he stroked her hair. Her body felt numb, yet exhilarated.

"We really should get moving. What time is it, anyway?" She yawned.

Julian glanced at the clock. "Almost seven thirty. What time are we meeting Charles?"

"Eight thirty." She was surprised that they had spent the last hour and a half making love. "I need to shower and get ready yet. Would you be so kind as to release me so I can do that?" She laughed.

"Ummm, I don't know about that. I'm rather comfortable right here," he teased.

"Ugh, Julian, you are going to make me late."

"Okay, okay. But, just so you know, I'll have you back in this position tonight." He winked at her.

"I kind of figured that. I don't mind either." She winked back at him.

Isabella made her way to the bathroom, her mind racing. She quickly hopped into the shower, letting the water drown out the voices in her head and the feelings of guilt that ran through her heart.

~~~

Gonzolo met Isabella, Julian, and Charles at the entrance to the manufacturing plant at nine o'clock. The plant was located in an industrial area just outside the city. A tall fence enclosed the entire property, and access was gained only through the front gate, which was secured by a gatehouse. The gate opened immediately when the limo pulled up to the gatehouse.

Behind the gate lay a city within itself. Some of the buildings in the complex looked like traditional office buildings, while others were large enough to house a cruise ship. The limo proceeded to the far end of the property and stopped at one of the larger warehouses. Isabella noticed a man standing near the entrance and assumed that was Gonzolo. She had talked to him several times since the beginning of the project, and from his voice, she had created a mental image of him. *Boy, was I wrong*, she thought. Gonzolo was short for a man, about five foot eight, and had curly, jet-black hair accented with gray. He was also a little on the heavy side.

"Isabella, it is so nice to finally meet you," Gonzolo said as he pulled her to him, kissing both of her cheeks. "What a vision of beauty you are. You are absolutely stunning."

"Thank you, Gonzolo. You are so sweet. It's wonderful to meet you too. I'm anxious to see everything you've done."

He explained that he had designated one warehouse for their review of the pieces and divided it into three areas, one for each of the collections. Today they would review the first collection, the Warm Modern, thoroughly inspecting each of the pieces with an eye for construction flaws and finish imperfections.
~~~

"We want to make sure that these pieces closely represent your vision," Gonzolo explained to Isabella as he led them inside. "If there is anything that is not satisfactory to you, please speak up. Tomorrow we will review collection two and a few of the items completed on collection three. I'm estimating about four to six weeks for the remaining items in the collection. I've been pushing hard to get those completed.

"As you walk through, reviewing the pieces, you will be marking your assessments down on each sheet. If there is anything that you feel needs to be changed, or that is not working for you, please note that, and we will make those changes during production. We have also created a binder containing photographs of each piece. We will need you to create a name for each of the pieces. This, of course, does not have to be done while you are here, but will need to be completed soon."

Isabella nodded. *Great*, she thought, *more work*.

Inside the warehouse, Isabella's mouth fell open in awe when she saw all the furniture pieces lined up. She gasped when she turned her attention to the first piece: the massive, high-gloss white headboard. It was absolutely beautiful. Isabella got goose bumps as the reality of actually having her own furniture line sank in.

"Well, Isabella, what do you think?" Gonzolo asked as they stood in front of the bed.

"I'm speechless. It's more than I imagined. It's stunning. The finish is pristine. I love it."

"We chose a special paint technique. It was sprayed three times to give us a nice coat, and then the finish was baked onto the piece. This will ensure durability throughout its lifetime." Gonzolo pointed to the black version behind it. "The same technique was used on this one as well."

"That shines like new money," Julian said.

"I'm blown away," Isabella said. "I've always been partial to a high-gloss white finish, but the black is equally impressive. I love how you opted to show the velvet tufted center with the white bed, and the silk tufted center with the black. I know they're interchangeable, but I like how this looks from a marketing standpoint."

Gonzolo nodded. "Yes, all the fabrics you selected for the tufted inserts work extremely well with either option. We wanted to show them in both, so we chose our favorites."

Charles was thrilled. Isabella heaved a sigh of relief. Having never created a furniture line before, she had feared that she would design something that would create a production nightmare, causing Charles to lose faith in her abilities. In that moment, though, she was extremely proud of all the effort she had poured into the line so far. She looked over to Julian, who was beaming at her. Isabella knew there would be cause for celebration that night. She blushed, thinking she knew exactly the type of celebration Julian would be looking for.

Over the next five hours, they walked through the warehouse, inspecting the other pieces. Overall, there were only a handful of items that Isabella felt needed changes. The corrections ranged from the final paint or stain finish on the piece to the construction. Isabella believed that the pieces should be of a higher standard and made changes accordingly. She wanted to change the inner workings on certain pieces, such as the dresser and the nightstand, including a better glide system on the drawers so they rolled out easily and closed smoothly. She also asked for the finish to be toned down on the antiqued silver pieces just a smidge, adding in a little more gold to make them look more antiqued. Other than that, everything else was perfect, in her opinion.

Gonzolo had lunch brought into his conference room, and the four of them sat down to discuss the progress made with the first collection. Two of his production managers joined in on the meeting to go over the changes that Isabella was requesting. When they had a clear understanding of how they needed to correct the pieces, Charles, Julian, and Isabella left for the day, agreeing to meet at the same time the next morning.

Back at the hotel, Isabella collapsed on her bed. She was tired from the hours of walking through the hot warehouse. Julian came into her room and smiled when he saw her lying there.

"Is someone tired?" he teased.

Isabella opened her eyes. "Yes, just a little. Aren't you?"

Julian curled up beside her on the bed. "Not really, but I wouldn't mind lying here with you." He kissed her nose.

"I wouldn't mind that." She smiled.

Julian touched her face tenderly and brought his lips to hers. Isabella felt her stomach flutter with excitement. His kiss was soft and sensual, so warm and intimate. It filled her with an instant desire for him, a desire she found herself wanting to give in to more and more.

"Turn over on your side," Julian whispered.

"Why? What are you up to?" She looked at him suspiciously.

He laughed. "I'm not up to anything, I promise. Just turn on your side. You'll see."

Isabella didn't believe him, but turned over anyway. She felt his hands on her shoulders, and as he began to massage her sore muscles, she let out a moan.

"Oh my God, that feels amazing."

"It should. Your shoulders are so tight. I think I found where you keep your stress."

Isabella lay there as his hands worked their magic across her shoulders, up her neck and down her back. Becoming completely relaxed, she closed her eyes and drifted off to sleep.

As she slept, Julian seized the opportunity to run down to the concierge and make dinner arrangements for the two of them. He returned to the suite an hour later to see his sleeping beauty in the same position he had left her in. He smiled. She looked so beautiful with her long, thick hair spread all around her. Her skin was so pure, her lips so red and full. She looked peaceful. He quietly crawled onto the bed and put his lips to her neck, kissing her softly over and over again.

Isabella opened her eyes and groaned. "No, I don't want to get up yet."

Julian laughed at her. "Yes, it's time to get up. It's time for you to get ready. I have a special night planned for us."

Isabella looked at him. "You do not. You're just saying that to get me up."

"No, seriously, I do. You didn't think I was going to let you lie around in the hotel all night, did you? We're in Milan—let's go out and enjoy it. Come on." Julian pulled her out of bed and pushed her in the direction of the bathroom.

"I'm going, I'm going." Isabella turned to face him and got up on her tippy toes to kiss him. "Thank you for making plans for us tonight. I would have just opted for room service."

"I know. That's why I did it."

In the shower, Isabella stood under the running water for several minutes with her eyes closed, letting it soothe her tired body. She opened her eyes to find Julian standing just outside the shower with a towel wrapped around his waist, watching her.

"What are you doing in here?"

"I was thinking, since we both need to shower, we could conserve water. May I join you?"

Isabella grinned and opened the shower door. "I wouldn't want to waste water."

Julian dropped his towel, and Isabella's eyes followed. "See something that interests you?"

"Maybe." A naughty smile appeared on her lips.

Julian stepped into the shower and pulled her to him. "Hmmm. Well, let's see if we can change that to a yes."

"Go right ahead and try."

Julian grabbed her by the back of her hair and pulled her head back, staring into her eyes. Isabella shuddered as a wave of electricity ran through her.

"I think this is going to be rather easy," he whispered. He brought his lips down on hers and found her tongue with his. Isabella pulled him more tightly to her as the warm water flowed over their bodies. Julian pushed her up against the shower wall, wrapped her legs around his waist, and teased her by rubbing his hard penis between her legs. Wanting him more than ever, Isabella moaned. He pulled his hips away and turned her face to look at him. He smiled seductively and shook his head no.

"Not yet," he said. "I want to enjoy you first."

Julian kissed her neck and made his way down to her breasts, grabbing them forcefully as his tongue lavished her nipples. He slid his hands down her wet stomach and kneeled in front of her, placed one of her legs on his shoulder, and began pleasuring her with his tongue. Isabella's breath came faster as she felt his tongue inside her. She moaned louder and louder as her sweet, warm wetness covered his mouth.

"I want you so much right now. I want to feel you inside me," Isabella begged. Her legs began to tremble; her entire body ached with desire. She grabbed his face and pulled him up to her mouth. Julian moaned as she licked his lips, causing his erection to grow.

"Oh, Bella," he breathed.

Julian pushed his weight fully against her as they passionately kissed. Their hands frantically roamed all over each other. Julian grabbed her leg again and wrapped it around his waist, and this time he plunged himself deep inside her with such force that her whole body shuddered. Overcome, Isabella screamed as Julian pushed deeper and deeper inside her.

"Yes, Julian, yes," she moaned.

He wrapped her other leg around him and, holding her up by her slender waist, thrust himself faster and deeper inside her. Isabella wrapped her arms around his shoulders, biting at his neck, she screamed out as she climaxed.

Julian kissed her hard on the mouth as he set her down. He was not done with her yet. He turned her around to face the wall and pushed her legs apart with his, then entered her again, this time from behind. With his hands on her waist, he watched as he slowly slid in and out of her.

His hand roamed between her legs, and she moaned as he teased her with his fingers. Isabella's passion for him grew. She felt his excitement throbbing inside her as his muscles tensed. He climaxed, calling out her name while she screamed in pleasure, soaking him again with her sweetness.

As his breathing slowed, Julian buried his head in her neck and kissed her shoulder. He turned her around, taking her face in his hands, and kissed her softly.

"I believe that's how you turn a maybe into a yes," he murmured.

Isabella smiled. "I have to agree. That was quite unexpected."

"You are a dirty girl, Isabella Hughes." Julian laughed wickedly.

Isabella put her finger to his lips. "Shhhh, don't tell anyone."

"Now that I know that, I want more. I want you again. I need you again."

"Don't we have plans tonight?"

"Yes, we do." He smiled slyly as he took her chin in his hand, tracing her lips with his finger. "It's called room service. I'm willing to forego the plans I made to stay here. You're all I want right now, and I intend to have you over and over again. How does that sound to you?"

His sexy voice sent tingles into all the right places. Isabella grinned. "Delicious, actually. I think I could eat you all night long." She leaned forward and bit his lower lip, tugging it with her teeth.

"Mmmmm, naughty girl, you are definitely going to get it." He reached around and smacked her on her ass.

Isabella groaned with anticipation. She knew without a doubt she wanted him again.

Julian turned off the shower and handed her a towel. He reached for his and wrapped it around his waist before scooping her up in his arms and carrying her back to the bedroom. They remained there all night long, exploring each other in ways neither had experienced before . . . over and over again.

Chapter 18

Isabella and Julian spent most of the next day with Charles and Gonzolo at the warehouse, reviewing the remaining pieces for the Classic Modern Collection, as well as a majority of pieces of the Transitional Collection. As with the Warm Modern Collection, there were minimal changes that needed to be addressed. Happy with the progress, Charles, Isabella, and Julian left the plant at a decent hour and returned to the hotel.

With their spirits high, Julian and Isabella ventured over to the famed Quadrilatero Della Moda, where they celebrated a successful trip by splurging on some designer goods. Isabella did a fair amount of damage in Valentino on several dresses, and also in Prada and Gucci, where she found a pair of must-have stilettos. To show her gratitude toward Julian for his support, she bought him a new suit and several shirts at the Armani Collection store. He tried to resist, but Isabella insisted.

After shopping, they enjoyed a delicious dinner on the outdoor patio of a small café. They couldn't have asked for a more beautiful night as they sat there for hours, talking over glasses of wine and savoring their last night in Milan.

They walked back to their hotel hand in hand, smiling and thankful to be together. Isabella couldn't remember the last time she had felt so happy and free. All she knew was that it had been a very long time.

When they arrived back at their hotel room, Isabella stepped into her bedroom and stopped at the door, letting out a small gasp. The bedroom was filled with candles that cast a beautiful glow about the room. Sprinkled all over the bed and the floor were hundreds of white rose petals. On the bedside table was a bottle of champagne, two champagne flutes, and a plate of chocolate-covered strawberries.

Isabella turned to Julian, who was standing at her side. "Did you do this?" she asked.

He smiled. "Yes, I wanted our last night in Milan to be extra special. I hope you approve."

Isabella set her bags down and kissed him softly. "I more than approve. This is so beautiful and so thoughtful. You are truly amazing, you know that?"

"Well, I try." A serious look came across his face. "You're the amazing one. I can't begin to tell you what the past few days have meant to me. I've never experienced what I feel when I'm with you. You are so sensual, and the feelings that come over me when I'm with you are so intense. I feel like in those moments, we truly are one. I never want it to end. I crave your touch, your lips—the essence of you. I want you to know that I'm so thankful for this time we've had together, and I'll never forget how I feel in this moment."

Isabella touched his face. "I'm thankful too. Never in my wildest dreams could I have imagined feeling what I do when I'm with you. I don't know how . . ." Isabella looked down as the realization set in that they would be returning to New York in the morning—returning to a world where Grayson would be waiting for her.

Julian tilted her head up and looked into her eyes. "I know things won't be easy once we return home, but I don't want to talk about that now. I want tonight to be about you and me. Forget about the world out there waiting for us and concentrate on giving into this moment completely, without thought, without hesitation. Can you do that for me? Can you do that for us?"

Her mind raced with thoughts she hadn't dared to think about in the days she had spent with him. She knew she had to push those thoughts aside, push aside the worry, just for the night. She smiled and nodded at him. "Yes, I want to give that to you, more than anything."

With that, he scooped her up and carried her to the bed. He poured them each a glass of champagne and raised his glass for a toast. "To the unforgettable time we've had here in Milan, and to our last night here, together as one. May we always remember what we're feeling in this moment, and never lose what we have come to mean to one another."

Isabella touched her glass to his, knowing she would never forget, but at the same time wondering what would become of those feelings once she returned home. He took her glass and set it aside, then kissed her lips with such passion that it took her breath away. He pulled her down on the bed and lay down on top of her, kissing her over and over again. He pulled away for a moment and gazed into her eyes for what seemed like an eternity.

"I love you," he whispered.

Isabella gazed back at him, unable to utter the words she knew he wanted to hear. She simply brought her lips to his, hoping he would know exactly how she felt.

They spent one last magical night together as one in their forbidden passion, dreading the dawn and the unknown that awaited them.

~~~

With Charles staying behind in Milan to tend to other business, Isabella and Julian hopped back on the Gulfstream early the next morning, bound for New York. They spent their last hours alone together, curled up on the sofa, enjoying being with one another.

Before stepping off the plane, Julian turned to Isabella and kissed her one last time. As he hugged her tightly, Isabella closed her eyes and held back tears. He kissed the top of her head and pulled away, looking at her for a final moment before stepping out onto the staircase of the plane. Sebastian was waiting for them with the Town Car. He loaded their bags and sped off to take each of them home.

Isabella paused at the door to her loft. She was filled with anxiety, as she had not seen Grayson since he had left for London and had not spoken to him since their fight over the phone. She was unsure what she would find when she opened the door. Her stomach sank as she thought about seeing him after being with Julian. She knew she would be wracked with guilt. At the same time, she wondered deep inside if she truly would be, and that scared her. She was stalling, and she knew it.

She took a deep breath and exhaled as she opened the metal door and peeked into the loft. It appeared to be empty. Thinking the coast was clear, she stepped in and set her bags down, then turned around to close the loft door.

"I thought I heard someone come in," Grayson said.

Startled, Isabella turned to see him standing at the top of the staircase. "You scared me. I didn't think you were home."

"I was reading up in our room. How was your trip?" he asked as he descended the staircase. He approached her and pulled her into his arms. "I feel like I haven't seen you in ages. I missed you."

Isabella stood there frozen, not returning his hug. The hairs on the back of her neck were standing straight up. "Have you? I wouldn't have guessed that, since the last time I spoke to you, you told me to fuck off." She realized as she spoke that she felt no guilt.

He pulled back from her to explain, but still held onto her arms. "Baby, I'm sorry about that. I was having a bad day. I had just gotten back from London. I was tired and cranky and looking forward to seeing you. I got a little upset when I realized you were gone, that's all."

Isabella felt anger building up inside her. She pulled her arms away from his and stepped back, looking at him with disgust and disbelief. "You were having a bad day? You were a little upset? Seriously, this is your excuse for the way you treated me? Are you kidding?"

"Why are you getting so angry with me all of a sudden?"
~~~

"It's not all of a sudden. I've been putting up with you treating me like shit for a long time now, and frankly I'm a little over it at this point."

"Isabella, please calm down. You're getting yourself all worked up over nothing." Grayson reach for her, but she jerked her arm away from him again.

"It's not nothing. You can't continue to treat me this way. I feel like your roommate instead of your wife. You come and go as you please, doing exactly what you want, without any consideration for me or my feelings. You accuse me of being insensitive to your needs, when in turn you couldn't give a rat's ass about mine. I'm tired of feeling this way, and I'm not going to put up with it anymore."

"Baby, please, come sit down." He held out his hand to her, but she just stood there with her arms folded across her chest. Grayson dropped his hand and sat down on the sofa. "Listen, I'm sorry, Izzie. You're right. I haven't been the best husband to you lately. I pulled away from you when you started this project because I knew how it was going to be—all the late hours, all the time apart. I didn't want to go through the constant disappointments with you. In a way, you could say I was protecting myself."

"How wrong is that, when you feel you have to protect yourself from me? What does that say about our relationship? Was I not trying hard enough for you this time? I was making every effort to spend time with you, but you were the one pushing me away."

Grayson sighed. "I know things haven't been the best between us, but that doesn't mean that I don't love you . . . that I don't love us. You have to believe me. I know you were trying. I'm sorry, baby. I love you, you know that."

Isabella's stomach churned. Her thoughts went to Julian and the intimate moments they had shared. The realization of the mess she had on her hands hit her all at once. She felt an enormous pressure on her chest, making it difficult for her to breathe. She knew it was the guilt that she had buried deep inside her, now surfacing. She had never thought through how conflicted she would feel. In front of her stood a man she had loved for years, but who continued to hurt and disappoint her time and time again as he pushed her away. Meanwhile, in her mind was Julian, who was constantly by her side, encouraging her and giving himself to her fully, without conflict, without turmoil. Tears filled her eyes and streamed down her face. It was too much to bear.

Grayson went to her and held her. "Baby, don't cry. I'm sorry. I didn't mean to hurt you. Please, Izzie, say you'll forgive me."

Isabella pulled away from him and wiped her tears. "You and I have a lot we have to work through. This isn't something you can fix by telling me you're sorry. We've been drifting apart for quite some time now, and if we're going to survive, we have to work through this together. You're to blame as much as I am. We created this mess of a marriage, and we both need to work at fixing it before it's too late."

"Don't say that," he pleaded. "It's not too late."

"I didn't say it was too late, I said *before* it's too late. I look at you now and see someone different than the man I've known for years. We've grown apart, and if we keep going as we are, that distance is going to keep growing, making it impossible to get back to where we were."

"Are you giving up on me . . . on us?"

"No, I'm not, but I'm not going to pretend that everything is roses, either. I've been down that road before, and it's obviously gotten us nowhere. You and I need to take some time and think about what we really want, and if we want to stay together, then we'll make it work, but if it's to be apart, then we need to figure that out now so we can stop hurting one another."

Grayson stared at her in disbelief. "I never thought I'd hear you utter those words, Isabella."

She took a deep breath and exhaled loudly. "I never thought I would utter those words either . . . and therein lies the problem."

He shook his head. "I hear you, I do. As much as it hurts right now, I know you're right. Do you want me to go? I can stay at my studio for a while if you like."

"I'm not asking you to leave. This is your home too. I'm asking you to find a reason to stay."

"Understood. And in turn, you will do the same?"

Isabella nodded. "Yes. We owe that to each other."

They stood there for a moment, wanting to find comfort in each other, but neither willing to risk the chance of being hurt.

He looked at her luggage still sitting by the door. "I can take your bags up for you if you like."

"Thank you. I would appreciate that."

"You must be hungry. I can make you something to eat."

"Thanks, but I couldn't eat right now. I'll go upstairs and get ready for bed, if you don't mind."

"No, not at all. You're probably exhausted from the flight. I'm going to grab my book and finish reading down here, if that's okay with you."

"That's fine," she said. "You don't have to sleep downstairs. Please don't think that I'm asking that of you."

Grayson nodded. "I know, baby, I know." He leaned over and kissed her cheek. "It's good to have you home."

Isabella mustered up as much of a smile as she could. "It's good to be home," she said, trying to convince herself that she believed that.

Chapter 19

The next morning, Isabella shot Gia a text, asking if they could meet at the small park near their office. She left the loft quietly, so as not to wake Grayson, who was sound asleep on the sofa. He had apparently opted not to join her upstairs after she had fallen asleep.

Isabella walked to the park and sat on a bench near the entrance, waiting for Gia. She had not slept much through the night. She kept tossing and turning, thinking about Julian, then Grayson, then Julian again. Before she went to bed, Julian had texted her to make sure she was okay and wished her a good night's sleep. He also said he missed her and wished he could be with her. She hadn't responded. Isabella became lost in thought, not noticing that Gia had walked up to her.

"Okay, what's the big emergency?" Gia asked. "I've seen that look on your face before, and I know it means mayhem and turmoil floating around inside that head of yours. What's going on?" She sat down, taking the cup of coffee Isabella handed her.

Isabella rubbed her face in frustration. "Oh my God, Gia, you have no idea what a mess I've created."

"I can only venture a guess. By the looks of you, I'd say someone is feeling guilty for getting it on with Mr. McSexy in Milan." Gia raised her eyebrow.

Isabella smacked her arm. "Can you be serious for once? I really need your help."

"So you didn't do the nasty with Julian, is that the story you're sticking to?"

"Ugh, I don't know why I bother." Isabella stood up to walk away, but Gia grabbed her arm.

"You're not going anywhere. Okay, I'm done. I've had my fun, and now I'm listening." Gia sat with her hand on her chin, waiting for Isabella to dish it out.

"Okay, yes, things got heated with Julian. It actually started before we left. Do you remember the night you came over upset?" Gia nodded. "Well, your timing was impeccable. We were about to head upstairs when you got there. I was actually thankful you came when you did, because I knew it was wrong. But then things started up again while we were in Milan. It's my fault, really. I had gotten a call from Grayson . . ."

Isabella spent the next hour filling her in on all the details of their trip together. She shared every intimate detail, as girlfriends do. When she was finished, she looked over at Gia, whose mouth was hanging open.

"Holy shit, Isabella, this type of talk is supposed to be reserved for cocktails in the evening, not coffee in the morning. I think I need to go home and take a cold shower. That has to top any of the hottest dates that I've had."

"I doubt that. Anyway, you're missing the point. What do I do?"

"Baby girl, I can't tell you what to do. It does seem to me that you and Julian have some major chemistry. I saw that from day one. You obviously have feelings for him, which I know you're having a hard time admitting. These things happen. I'm not saying that it's right, but it does happen. I'm not judging you either; you know me. This is not surprising at all. You and Grayson have been in a bad place for a while now. He's been treating you like crap for months. It was only a matter of time before he pushed you away one time too many."

Isabella sighed and put her head in her hands. "I still don't know what to do. Last night when I was looking at Grayson, all I could feel was anger, which made me want to run to Julian, which made me feel guilty looking at Grayson. I'm a mess." She rubbed her forehead.

"Listen, who says you have to make a decision now? You don't. Go back to your normal routine and see how you feel. Continue to spend time with Julian, maybe not as intimately as you did in Milan, but continue to work with him, talk with him. Keep him around to give you time to assess your feelings about him. In the meantime, work on things with Grayson and see if you can get that feeling back with him. Maybe it's too late, maybe it's not. That I can't answer for you. Only time will tell."

"You're right. How can it be fair to Grayson to keep Julian around?"

"No one said it was fair, but if you cut Julian out of your life right now, you will always wonder if you let something good slip out of your hands. That wouldn't be fair to Grayson or yourself if you're still thinking of Julian years later."

Isabella looked at her friend. "How did you get so smart?"

Gia waved her hand dismissively. "Please, I've had tons of practice in this department. It won't be easy, believe me. I don't envy you." She sighed. "Well, maybe I am a little envious about the shower sex. Holy shit, I think that visual will be permanently etched in my mind."

They both laughed.

"It was extremely hot," Isabella said wistfully. "And I did have an amazing time with him. He's so caring and thoughtful, and makes me feel wanted and loved. He seems to really enjoy my company. He makes me feel so free, like I want to sell my belongings and lay in a hammock with him on a beach, snuggling with him for the rest of my life. Not to mention the fact that he is absolutely fantastic in bed. He rocked my world. I never expected that. In a way, I feel like he knows me inside and out. It's scary sometimes."

"Just be careful with him. I know you think you know him, but be smart about it." Gia smiled at her.

Isabella gave her a hug. "I promise I will. Thank you so much for listening to me. I know that was a lot to take in and keep quiet about. That definitely goes beyond your duties as a friend."

"Oh please, considering everything you've listened to me blabber on about, this is the least I can do for you. Besides, I like having another secret to add to my collection." She winked. "Being the keeper of secrets and all."

"Great. I can only imagine what this one is going to cost me."

"I promise to go easy on you this time."

"Oh, thanks." Isabella looked at her watch. "We really should head into the office. I'm sure all hell has broken loose in our absence. James is probably running around with his spiked hair on fire."

Gia burst out laughing. "Oh my God, I can see it now." She stood up and ran around in circles with her hands flailing in the air.

Joining in the laughter, Isabella stood up and grabbed Gia's hand in hers. "Seriously, thank you for being the friend that you are to me. I don't know what I'd do without you."

"That goes both ways." Gia kissed her cheek.

Isabella hurried to her office to avoid getting bombarded with questions and problems after her absence. Now that she had completed her portion on the furniture designs and they rested in Gonzolo's hands, she could devote her attention to her other projects, mainly the building for Charles. She planned to spend the day getting caught up.

Isabella closed her office door and was headed to her desk when her chair spun around, causing her to jump. Julian sat there grinning at her.

"You scared the crap out of me," she said.

Julian grinned mischievously. "You look like you just saw a ghost."

Annoyed, Isabella shook her head. James was right; she did need to install a mirror on her window. "Not funny. It's too early for that much excitement."

"Oh really? I seem to remember you enjoying plenty of morning excitement." His smile turned seductive as he stood and approached her. Isabella felt a twinge of excitement run through her. *Damn, he is so sexy*, she thought.

"Shhh, keep your voice down," she urged. "Someone may hear you."

"Oh yeah? Do you think they can hear us talking in here with the door closed?" he teased.

She gave him a slight smile. "Now you're making fun of me again. I don't like you anymore."

Julian pulled her to him, taking her breath away. "Oh, I think you like me plenty," he whispered, and kissed her.

Isabella tensed up and pulled back from him. "Not here. Someone could come in."

"So lock the door," he said as he tightened his grip on her.

Isabella wiggled free from his grasp. "You are insatiable, you know that?"

"What can I say? I've missed you." He touched her face tenderly.

Her heart melted. He looked adorable, his eyes dancing and his smile exuding pure happiness. Isabella could see that he truly missed her, and the thought warmed her inside. It had been a long time since she had felt missed and wanted.

She placed her hand on his. "I missed you too, I did, but we need to be careful around the office. I don't need people talking. You understand that."

"Hold that thought." Julian went to the door and locked it. "I understand, and I promise to behave for the rest of the day, if you can do one thing for me."

"And that would be?" Isabella raised an eyebrow suspiciously.

Still standing by the door, he motioned with his finger for her to come to him. "Come here, and you'll find out."

Isabella rolled her eyes. He liked playing games with her. Oddly enough, she had a hard time resisting. "You kill me with these little games, you know that?"

"You love it, I know you do. Admit it." He had a devilish grin on his face.

"Maybe." Isabella shrugged.

"Interesting word choice. Do we not remember what happened the last time you gave me a *maybe*?"

Isabella remembered all too well. The memory of them in the shower flooded her mind, and excitement stirred within her as she envisioned him standing in front of her naked. She remembered the way she had wrapped her legs around him as he held her, thrusting into her while the warm water cascaded over them. Getting more than a little fired up, Isabella shook her head and smiled. She wandered over, unable to resist his charm. "What is it that you would like me to do for you, so I can get back to work?"

"Stand here and close your eyes."

She looked at him, wondering what he was up to, but did as he said. She felt his breath warm on her face and knew he had moved close to her. His lips lightly brushed hers, and his hand moved up her leg, passing under her skirt. His touch was soft and slow as he worked his way up between her legs.

She opened her eyes and met his gaze. "Julian—" she said, but he put a finger to her lips.

He moved her thong aside, finding exactly what he wanted, and began to pleasure her with his hand. Isabella shuddered as he pushed his fingers inside her. She let out a soft moan. How did he always know the right spot? With his fingers expertly exploring her, Isabella's breath quickened.

"Someone is getting excited," he whispered. "My God, you are so wet."

Julian pulled her to him and brought his lips down on hers, sending a feverish desire through her. Unable to control her urges, Isabella wrapped her arms around him and pulled him closer to her.

"That's it," he murmured.

She looked into his eyes, which pierced through her. She grabbed onto the front of his shirt and buried her face into his shoulder to silence her scream as she came. Julian pulled her head back and brought his lips down hard on hers.

Isabella stepped away from him, wondering how that had happened, while Julian smiled victoriously. He had gotten exactly what he had wanted out of her. He kissed her again and unlocked the door.

"I was craving you, Bella," he said. "All I could think about this morning was the way you taste." Julian put his finger into his mouth, savoring her sweetness. "That's all I wanted . . . for now. I'll behave myself the rest of the day, I promise. You can go back to work." He wore a mischievous smile as he left her office, bumping into Gia on his way out.

"Good morning," Gia said to him with a smirk. "Did you have a good time in Milan?"

"Good morning, Gia. Yes, I did, as a matter of fact. I had a really good time."

"So I heard," Gia said, and glanced through the doorway at Isabella.

She lowered her voice. “By the way, you have lipstick on your collar. You may want to tidy up a bit before you wander around the office.” She stepped past him and said to Isabella, “Hey, we’re ready for you in the . . .” She trailed off. “What’s wrong?”

Isabella stared into space, unable to think of a word in response.

“Hello, earth to Izzie.” Gia snapped her fingers at her.

Isabella shook her head to clear it and looked at Gia sheepishly. “I think trying not to engage with Julian is going to be a little more difficult than I thought,” she muttered.

“Control, Isabella, it’s all about control. You need to learn that you have it, and he doesn’t.”

Isabella barely heard her.

She spent the rest of the morning in the conference room with the other designers, getting caught up on all their open projects. At noon, she retreated to her office so she could return phone calls and emails. As she walked into her office, she was startled to see Grayson sitting on the sofa, waiting for her.

“What are you doing here?” she asked.

“I was in the area, so I thought I’d surprise you and see if you’d like to grab some lunch.” He stood and kissed her cheek.

“Well, that is a nice surprise. I’ll take you up on that offer. I’m starving. But I can’t do anything fancy, if you don’t mind. I have a lot of work I need to get to.”

“Understood. I’m just glad you have some time.” Grayson hugged her tightly. “I’ve missed you. You were on my mind all night and this morning. I really wanted to see you. Thank you for having the time.”

Isabella returned his squeeze. “You don’t have to thank me. I like spending time with you. You know that.”

They hugged each other for a moment in silence, trying to overcome the awkwardness that was apparent now between them. Isabella rested her head on his shoulder, trying not to focus on Julian or the turmoil of the past few months. She just wanted to enjoy the moment.

Julian’s voice came from the doorway. “Hey, Isabella, great news. I got an email from . . .” He stopped when he saw Grayson. “I’m sorry, it looks like I’m interrupting. I’ll come back later.” He lowered his head and started to leave the office.

Feeling horrible, Isabella pulled away from Grayson and reached for Julian’s arm to stop him. “Wait, what great news do you have to tell me?”

Julian turned around, looking from Isabella to Grayson. He wasn’t prepared for this run-in with Grayson. It threw him off for a moment.

But he politely extended his hand. "You must be Grayson," he said. "It's nice to finally meet you. I'm Julian. We spoke on the phone a long time ago."

Grayson's eyes hardened as he stared at Julian, and Isabella wondered if he could somehow tell that there was something between them. She flushed with anxiety and felt beads of sweat forming on her neck.

Then his expression relaxed, and he smiled politely as the two shook hands. "I've heard a lot about you, Julian. It's good to finally meet you."

"Is that so?" Julian said calmly.

Grayson cleared his throat. "Yes, I wanted to thank you. You seem to be doing a great job of keeping Izzie organized and stress free with this project. Whatever you're doing, it seems to be working, and I appreciate that."

Isabella was sure she was about to faint.

Julian smiled and looked over to Isabella, who was pale as a ghost. The devil got the best of him, and he couldn't resist. He put his arm around her shoulders, giving her a little squeeze. "Yes, well, truth be told, Isabella has made this project an absolute pleasure. I've had a lot of fun working with her. She's nothing like any other client I've worked for. Hell, it hasn't even felt like work at all."

Isabella smiled at him, but her eyes were throwing daggers. *He's going to pay for that*, she thought.

Just then, Gia appeared, but halted immediately as her eyes darted from Grayson to Julian, who still had his arm around Isabella.

"Well, now," she mumbled under her breath. As usual, she recovered quickly and did her best to defuse Isabella's anxiety. "Grayson, it's so nice to see you, babe," she said, giving him a firm hug. "It's been forever. You look hot."

Grayson's expression relaxed. "Are you trying to get on my good side, Gia?"

"As always." She winked, then turned to Julian. "Julian, I have a situation that I could use your opinion on. Would you mind helping me out?" She sweetly smiled at him.

"No problem. What is it?"

Gia flipped through the papers in her hand. "Oh shoot, I don't have it with me. Why don't we go back to my office, and we can go over it there?"

"Sure, no problem." Julian shook Grayson's hand again. "It was nice meeting you."

Grayson nodded. "Nice to finally meet you as well."

Julian turned to Isabella. "I'll catch up with you in a bit."

"Sounds good," Isabella said, relieved that Gia had executed his exit perfectly.

~~~

Isabella sat on the sofa in her office, going through some client files and making notes for the other designers. She was also making a list of the job sites that she wanted to visit with Gia the following morning. She set her papers down and stared out the window, watching the sun set in the distance. Her thoughts went to Grayson and the time they had spent together at lunch that afternoon. Although it was good, and she knew he was trying, it felt somewhat awkward and forced. The way he had looked at Julian, she wondered if he could tell something was going on between them. She also felt sad thinking of what they had lost and longed for the time when things had been easy between them. Never in a million years would she have guessed that they would be where they were now. And never in a million years could she have fathomed doing what she had done. It was moments like this, in the quietness of her mind, that darkness fell upon her, making her regret so much.

That regret made her think of Julian. Her feelings seemed clearer when she wasn't with him. Then she could rationally see what she should do, but the moment he was around, it was as if she was powerless against the pull of gravity between them. Being with him was hypnotic, in a way. Her inhibitions, her voice of reason, all went out the window. She understood what Gia meant about keeping him around until she had made her decision, but Isabella knew that as long as he was around, he would always be able to touch something inside her. The million-dollar question was, could she let that go?

"I knew I'd still find you here," Julian said as he came into her office and sat down next to her on the sofa. "What are you up to?"

"Just going through some files."

He paused. "It looked like you were preoccupied with something else. What were you thinking about?"

Isabella shrugged. "Nothing much, just work."

"I don't believe you. You looked sad. Tell me, what were you thinking?"

Isabella sighed and looked into his eyes, which were so different now than they had been that morning. "I was thinking about you."

"I make you sad then?" He frowned.

Isabella took his hand in hers. "You don't make me sad. Our situation does. It's complicated for me. I wish it wasn't, believe me, but
~~~

it is."

Julian looked down at her hand on his. "How was your lunch with Grayson today?"

"It was okay. That's not without complications either, as you know."

He nodded. "Gia feels that I should step back from you and give you some space." Julian looked up at her, searching her eyes. "Do you share her feelings? Do you want me to leave?"

She thought for a long moment. Did she want him to step back? She repeated the question over and over in her head, trying to assess how it made her feel. The thought of not seeing him sent a slight panic through her. She knew she wasn't ready for that to happen, nor could she bear losing him right then.

"Gia needs to mind her own business," she said. "I may not know what I want right now, but I know I don't want you to leave. With that said, I can't promise you anything either, so if you feel that you have to leave, I'll understand."

"I'm not going anywhere, Bella. When I said I loved you, I meant it. Even though you can't say it, I know you do too . . . in the way that you can right now. I plan to stay here and fight for that. That's what you need to understand."

"I do understand, but I don't want to hurt you, Julian."

"Then don't," Julian pleaded.

Isabella looked away as tears filled her eyes. *As if it was that easy*, she thought.

"Bella, look at me," he said, moving closer to her. "I can't stand seeing you in so much pain. Come here." Julian held her as she rested her head on his shoulder and let the tears flow.

Chapter 20

Julian headed off to the park for his usual Saturday morning run. He was thankful that the snow had been minimal that winter, allowing him to run, which helped him keep his mind clear. He had shot a text to Isabella to join him, but she hadn't responded back. Figuring she was sleeping in, he decided to venture out on his own. As he ran through the park, he wondered where her mind was at. She seemed all over the board to him, which made it very difficult. All he knew for sure was that he needed to stay in front of her.

Julian continued down the path and stopped suddenly as he came around the last curve. He saw Isabella and Grayson running in the distance. He stepped off the path before they noticed him and tucked himself behind a large tree. From there, he watched as they ran side by side. Isabella was smiling and laughing as Grayson talked to her. They stopped for a moment as Isabella drank some water and handed the bottle to Grayson. He took a long swig and handed it back to her, then leaned in and kissed her cheek. Grayson gave her a swat on the butt, and the two turned around and headed back in the direction they had come. Julian stepped out from behind the tree and watched them until they disappeared out of sight. He turned up his music and ran back in the direction he had come.

Julian returned home, showered, and headed back out for a bite to eat. He aimlessly walked the streets for a while, looking for a quiet place to sit and have lunch. He came to the café just down the street from Isabella's loft and remembered that the food was good, as he had ordered takeout for himself and Isabella before. Tired of searching, he went inside and sat down at one of the tables near the front. He checked his phone to see if Isabella had bothered to respond to him, but there was no message, which was unlike her.

Julian was eating his meal and reading emails on his Blackberry when he heard the all-too-familiar laugh. He looked up from his phone to see Isabella and Grayson standing at the hostess stand, speaking to the owner. The owner grabbed two menus, and the three of them turned, heading right in Julian's direction. It was Isabella who spotted him first. As their eyes met, her smile vanished.

Isabella felt horrible when she saw Julian sitting there alone. As they neared his table, Grayson noticed Julian as well. He stopped, figuring they should say hello.

"Julian, it's nice to see you again," Grayson said, patting him on the back. "I didn't know you lived around here."

Julian offered an awkward smile. "It's nice to see you, too. I don't, actually. I was out and about this afternoon when hunger set in. I remembered Isabella raving about the food here, so I thought I would try it." He looked at Isabella, who remained silent.

"We've been coming here for years," Grayson said as he slipped his arm around Isabella's waist. She saw Julian cringe. From the look on his face, she could tell he was upset.

"I got your text a little while ago," she said. "I'm sorry I didn't get back with you. I didn't have my phone. We were already out running this morning. Were you able to get out to the park?"

Julian nodded. "Yep. I saw you guys there, too."

Her stomach sank. "Then why didn't you come join us?"

"I didn't want to intrude. I'm sure you're sick of constantly seeing me at work."

The words stung. Her eyes pleaded that she was sorry, but Julian ignored her and looked at Grayson.

"Besides," he added, "by the time I saw you, you were running in the opposite direction."

"I could always use a running partner," Grayson said. He jabbed his thumb at Isabella. "This one is always working, so if she doesn't have you all tied up and you ever want to head out, hit me up, man, and I'll run with you."

Julian's eyes slid to Isabella, who shifted her weight nervously, uncomfortable with where the conversation was heading. He smiled at Grayson. "She hasn't had me tied up that much lately. I'll keep you in mind."

Isabella shot him a dirty look, knowing that he was intentionally making her squirm.

"Hey, do you want to join us for lunch?" Grayson asked him.

Isabella felt her eyes bug out of her head as Julian sat there thinking, as if actually considering his answer. She felt like she was going to be sick.

"Thanks for the offer, but I'm all finished here," he said. Isabella got the feeling from the tone in his voice that he wasn't talking about his meal.

"No problem, man. Another time, then. Enjoy your weekend."

Grayson turned and moved on to their table, while Isabella hung back.

"That wasn't nice," she whispered.

Julian's expression turned serious. "I told you I understood," he whispered back, "but it's hard to play nice when I'm the one who has to stand back and watch you two together. Think of how that would make you feel." He stood up, threw some money down on the table, and walked away. Isabella watched him leave, feeling awful.

Isabella struggled to let go of her anxiety over Julian as she and Grayson ate lunch and went for a stroll in their neighborhood. The conversation between them was good, and Isabella was starting to feel that there might be hope for them. They spent the entire day reconnecting with one another, trying to work past the problems of the last few months. Isabella sensed that his anger toward her was subsiding, as was hers toward him.

That night was the first night they had shared the same bed in weeks and were intimate with one another. Although it seemed to come easy for Grayson, it was Isabella who had a hard time as memories of Julian haunted her. Lying in bed beside her husband, she found herself having to push aside thoughts of Julian's kisses, his touch, and her desire for him. She tossed and turned all night, worrying about Julian.

When she woke, the first thing she did was shoot him a text, asking him to meet her at the office. When Grayson left to meet up with his friends for a pickup game of basketball at the gym, she was out the door.

Julian was waiting for her when she arrived at the office. He immediately pulled her into his arms and kissed her full on the lips. "I'm lonely. I've missed you and that naked body of yours."

Isabella tried to pull back from his grasp, but he had her in a good hold. "Julian, I don't think that . . ." Julian cut her off by bringing his lips back down to hers, kissing her over and over again, barely allowing her time to breathe.

Isabella was finally able to wiggle free and took two steps back to ensure she was out of his reach. "Julian, you need to listen to me, please," she begged. "I want to talk with you. That's why I asked you to come here."

"I don't want to talk. We've talked enough about this. You need to stop thinking and just follow what your heart desires. It really is that simple." Julian moved toward her, but she took another step back. His face hardened, as it had when Grayson had wrapped his arm around her at the restaurant.

"Please, you're not making this easy," she said. "I came here because after seeing you yesterday, I felt terrible. I knew you were upset, and that bothered me. I wanted to make sure that you were okay."

"Why? What does it matter? Why pretend you care?"

"That's not fair. I wouldn't be here if I didn't care. It's just that I need some time to figure things out. I told you that the other day. No matter how I feel, I can't let my heart get in the way of doing what's right. I simply can't be with you and think clearly. When you touch me or kiss me, I lose my senses, and I can't afford to do that right now."

"I bet you have no problem letting Grayson touch you. How fair is that? Why am I the one being punished when I've never hurt you or disrespected you? Time and time again he stabs you in the heart, while I've comforted you and held you. Please make me understand, how is that right?"

"He's my husband. What would you have me do, just up and leave without trying to work things out? I can't do that. I can't throw away ten years so easily."

He glared at her. "Did you sleep with him last night?"

"I don't see how that's relevant. I'm not going to discuss that with you, the same way that I wouldn't discuss our intimate moments with him."

"Of course you wouldn't. He wouldn't be as forgiving as I, would he?" He crossed his arms. "Answer the question, Isabella. Did you sleep with him?"

Isabella knew if she said yes, she would hurt him, but if she said no, he wouldn't believe her. It was a no-win situation. Isabella turned her gaze to the window. "Yes . . . yes, I did," she whispered.

Julian's face was expressionless, as hard as a stone. Isabella felt his green eyes burning through her. She waited for him to say something, anything, but he didn't. He simply turned away from her and walked to the window, staring blankly at the cityscape beyond. She walked over and stood next to him, watching the clouds pass in the sky. She knew she had just crushed his heart, and there was nothing she could do to recapture the words she had spoken.

"Julian, please say something." She felt the tears sting her eyes.

Julian kept his eyes on the street. "Did you think of me while you were with him?"

"Julian," Isabella pleaded.

He turned to face her. "Answer the question. Did you think of me?"

Isabella turned her gaze to the floor, unable to look at him. "Yes, I did. How could I not?"

Julian lifted her chin with his finger, bringing her eyes to his. "You thought of me because something is missing. That something is what continues to cause problems between the two of you. No matter how hard you try, it will always be there, just as I'll always be here waiting for you. Even though I feel it's completely unfair of you to push me aside, denying me your touch and your attention while giving it to someone who is undeserving, I forgive you."

Tears fell from her eyes. "You shouldn't forgive me. I don't deserve your forgiveness. I behaved in ways I shouldn't have. I gave you false expectations, and I made you believe in something that I had no right to. No, Julian, I'm not worthy of your forgiveness." Isabella bowed her head and began to sob.

He held her while she cried. "Nothing worthwhile is without struggle. I know the tears you cry are because you know in your heart how good we are together, not because my love hurts you like Grayson's love does."

"Julian, I can't do this." Isabella pulled back and looked at him, her eyes swollen from crying. Julian wiped the tears from her cheeks. "What we experienced together was amazing, there is no denying that. You touch a place in me that is beyond words. But you have to understand that no matter how great that is, I have no right to that with you. I belong to Grayson. I can't be with you, as much as it pains me to say that. I think you need to leave. We shouldn't be around each other. I can't see you, knowing that you want more from me. I feel like I'm hurting you, and it kills me."

"Bella, please don't say that. It's too soon. You still need time to figure things out. I'm sure it seems good with him now, but people don't change. He'll wind up hurting you again. I couldn't take it knowing you were hurting and I wasn't here for you. Please, don't do this. Don't push me away. I couldn't bear not seeing you."

Isabella buried her face in his chest. His words reminded her of how she had felt when her mother abandoned her, and her heart sank. In that moment, she felt she was no better than her mother—taking love from someone, then destroying them as she walked away. The thought made her sick. Why did he have to be the one who pulled at her heart? Why was he so insistent on loving her when she clearly didn't deserve it?

"Julian, how can you be around me when I'm hurting you so much? I can't even stand to be around myself right now."

"I would hurt much worse if I couldn't see you. I'd make myself sick worrying about you. Please, let me stay," he begged with tears in his eyes. "I promise I'll step back and give you your space. Just let me stay."

She thought for a moment. "I told you before all this started that I didn't want to lose what we initially had. I'd like to make that work with you—to get back to where we were before. But that means putting all this behind us. I don't know if either of us is strong enough to do that."

"We won't know until we try. I'd take that over nothing right now. I don't want to lose you completely."

"I know, but I can't give to you as I did before. You need to understand that. I don't want you to think it's easy for me, because it's not. I just know that being with you intimately will only cloud my feelings about Grayson. I need to focus on my marriage. I don't know what will happen, but I have to feel as if I tried one hundred percent before I consider walking away, if it comes to that. I need you to respect that in order for this to work. Can you do that for me?"

"I'd do anything for you. You know that. I'll do as you ask, but I will never leave your side. I respect and love you too much to let you go. And when and if the time comes, I'll be here waiting for you."

Isabella stared into the beautiful green eyes she had come to trust. She hoped for both their sakes that they would be able to work their way back from the forbidden path that they should never have ventured down.

Chapter 21

Over the next few weeks, Isabella concentrated on resuming a normal working relationship with Julian. She made an effort to put aside her feelings even though it was hard, as there were moments when she wanted to run to him and seek his comfort, but knew she couldn't. She couldn't allow herself to depend on him as she had in the past. With Grayson in her life, she could never be with Julian again.

Meanwhile, Grayson was putting forth a noticeable effort in their relationship. They were spending more time together than ever before, and it was quality time, too. Their relationship was flourishing despite the setback. They opted to spend the holidays alone, locked away in their loft, foregoing the usual holiday parties with their friends. Despite her worries, he didn't seem to suspect anything about her affair. Or if he did, he was keeping it to himself.

Returning to work after the first of the year, Isabella still sensed that Julian was having a hard time keeping his promise to her. There were moments when she found him watching her or standing closer to her than he should. He touched her hand or shoulders when he shouldn't. It was hard to be around him. She could sense his frustration growing. Even though he'd said he wanted to be around her regardless of the nature of their relationship, she worried about him. She felt her presence in his life was hurting him more than helping.

Isabella kept trying to find ways to help him along with his feelings. She tried to avoid working directly with him whenever possible. She had Gia act as a buffer between them or sent him off on other errands or projects that he could work on alone. One day, as she made her way from the conference room to her office, Julian came up behind her and grabbed her shoulder. He leaned close and whispered, "I have a surprise for you."

"Do you now?" Isabella said as she continued down the hall. She went into her office and shut the door behind them, wondering just what type of surprise Julian was ready to spring on her.

"Close your eyes," he said.

Isabella froze, remembering that nothing innocent ever followed this request.

Seeing her hesitation, Julian chuckled. "I promise I'll behave. Just close your eyes."

Isabella sighed and did as he asked. She felt her body tense and her heart speed up. She expected to feel his touch, but only heard his voice.

"Open your eyes."

Julian stood in front of her, holding open a magazine. As she focused her eyes on the pages, she realized that it was the article she had done for *Elle Decor*. Isabella let out a little shout and snatched the magazine from his hands.

"Oh my gosh, I completely forgot all about this. When did it come out?"

Julian grinned. "Just this morning. They wanted to hold the article so we could get closer to the furniture launch date. I think they did an amazing job, and you look breathtaking. What do you think?"

Isabella scanned the article, taking in all the photos. "Well, I'll have to sit down and read through it, but initially, I think everything looks great. The loft looks stunning in these photos." Isabella was beaming from ear to ear as she wrapped her arms around him in a big hug . . . completely forgetting that she shouldn't.

"I love it, Julian, I really do. Thank you so much for bringing this to me. You just made my day."

Julian pulled her to him tightly and rubbed her back. "My pleasure. Anything for you," he said softly.

The tone of his voice made her realize what she had done. She stepped back from him, and their eyes met.

"It's okay, it was just a hug," he said. "It's not like we can't hug, you know. After all, we're supposed to be friends, right?"

Isabella smiled slightly and nodded, trying to shake off the discomfort. "You're right. I'm sorry. It's just been a while, and I surprised myself, that's all."

"You have to stop worrying. I do miss you, I'm not going to lie, but I'm not so weak that I can't handle being around you."

She turned to her desk and busied herself with straightening a pile of papers. "I guess I don't know how to be around you sometimes."

His eyes searched her face. "I think that's because you still feel as strongly as I do, but unlike me, you're trying to suppress it."

Isabella knew there was truth to what he was saying, but didn't want to admit it.

Julian changed the subject before she could dart away from him like a deer dodging traffic. "Hey, what do you say to some lunch, my treat? We can celebrate the publication of the article."

"Sure, why not?" *What could lunch hurt?* she thought. She knew she had to start spending time with him to help her move past the uncomfortable feelings.

Julian moved to take her hand, but pulled back when Grayson appeared in the doorway, holding up the magazine.

"I was heading over to my studio when I passed a newsstand and saw this," Grayson said. "I was so excited, I bought every copy at the stand and raced over here." He was beaming at her. He put his arms around her and kissed her full on the mouth. Julian looked away, while Isabella cringed, knowing that was the last thing he wanted to see.

"I'm so proud of you, Izzie," Grayson rambled on. "Look at that, you're in *Elle Decor*, one of your favorite magazines. Have you seen it yet?"

Isabella smiled at him, trying to remember the last time she had seen him get excited over anything she had done. "Thank you. Yes, I just saw it. Julian brought it in to me."

"Good deal. Well, I think this is cause for celebration. Let me take you to lunch."

Julian watched her carefully, guessing which offer she would accept.

"Sure, I'd like that," she said.

Grayson looked at Julian. "Would you like to join us?"

"No, I'm good. I have some work I need to get to, but thanks anyway." He managed a small smile and moved to the doorway. At the last moment, he looked back at Isabella, and their eyes met before he walked out of the office.

Julian returned to his office, stewing. He had been waiting for over a week to surprise her with the magazine.

"Well, that's an interesting look you have on your face," Gia said as she walked in. "It's an odd mix of the cat that ate the canary and the mad scientist." She laughed.

Julian glared at her. "What do you want, Gia? I'm in no mood for your antics."

"Wow, you're crabby. Would that have anything to do with a blue-eyed, blond-haired artist I saw milling around Isabella's office a few minutes ago?" Gia taunted him. "I warned you this was going to happen. The best thing you can do is move on, Julian."

"You can leave now," he snapped.

Gia threw some papers on his desk and started to leave, but turned just before she walked out the door. "You will never come between them," she said as she left.

He sat there tapping his pen on the desk, his mind going a mile a minute. He knew that it was time to act, but what should he do? Then a light bulb went on in his head, and he raced out of his office, practically running down the hall to the elevator. He stuck his hand out just in time to stop the elevator door from closing. The door opened to reveal Isabella and Grayson standing there. Isabella looked surprised to see him. He smiled at both of them.

"I changed my mind," he said. "I'll join you for lunch after all."

"I was hoping you would," said Grayson, while Isabella remained silent, shocked and wondering what the hell he was up to.

After a strained lunch hour—at least, for Isabella—she waited until Grayson turned the corner to return to his studio. When he was out of sight, she punched Julian in the arm. "What the hell was that? Agreeing to have lunch with us? What is wrong with you? Do you know how uncomfortable that was for me?"

He merely smiled at her. "I don't see what the big deal is. There's no reason we all can't get along. I mean, Grayson and I do have a common interest, after all."

Isabella's mouth fell open. "You're insane. I don't think he would be all chummy with you if he knew you had feelings for me."

"Or that we rolled around in bed more than a few times, or that I know exactly what to do to make you blow like a volcano." Julian's laugh turned sinister as he raised his eyebrow.

Isabella slapped him again on the arm. "Stop it. You're doing this on purpose. I don't know what type of game you're playing, but I can tell you that I don't like it." Isabella glared at him.

"I'm not playing any game. I just realized that there's no reason why I always have to bow out and sit on the sidelines when Grayson is around. After all, you and I are working together. I think he would be more suspicious if I wasn't around. Besides, I'm not breaking my promise to you. I didn't say anything or touch you inappropriately in front of him, did I? I believe I've behaved myself rather nicely."

Isabella looked at him suspiciously, unconvinced. She suddenly had a feeling that he had ulterior motives. What those were, she had no idea. All she knew was that she was extremely on edge when he was around Grayson, and she didn't like it.

"You did behave . . . this time. But I don't want you to get into the habit of joining in all the time."

"Oh come on, where is your sense of adventure? What's the saying, three's company? Grayson might be down for a threesome eventually. That could be a lot of fun." Julian smirked, knowing full well he was pushing her buttons.

"Now I know you're truly insane," she said, disgusted. "That will never happen. I can assure you of that."

Julian put an arm around her shoulders. "Never say never. Who knows, one day the three of us could end up in your bedroom together. Grayson could watch; that would definitely be interesting."

"Over my dead body. I'm beginning to think you need professional help."

"You know exactly what I need, and it's not professional help." Julian winked as she pulled back from him and stalked down the street, staying three steps ahead of him the whole way.

~~~

The next day, Isabella sat in her office with Charles, discussing the progress of their project. Isabella had been waiting for the perfect opportunity to present an idea to him, and the moment had finally arrived. She hoped that everything would fall into place and that all parties would be on board, but she needed Charles's approval before she mentioned anything to Grayson.

"Now that the project is well underway," Isabella said, "I'd like to discuss with you an important part of the building's design esthetic."

"Absolutely, Isabella," said Charles. "What are your thoughts?"

"Well, the other day I was remembering how we met, and that sparked an idea."

"If my memory serves me right, it was at the gallery on West Twenty-Ninth, correct?"

"Yes, it was. Grayson had a showing there that night. And, if my memory serves me correctly, you were impressed by his paintings on display."

"That's right. He is very talented, and I was interested."

"Good, because I was thinking, with your permission, of course, that we could bring him on to create some pieces for your building." Isabella held her breath, hoping that he was open to the idea.

"What do you have in mind?"

"I'd like to have him create some large pieces for the main areas and some smaller ones for each of the floors. I thought we could show him what we've designed and let him come up with paintings that will compliment those designs. I believe that would produce the best results. I know when artists are given a blank canvas, so to speak, they're able to create freely. The pieces will be more spectacular than those that have had restrictions placed on them."

"I see." Charles nodded as he mulled over the proposal. Just then, there was a quick knock at the door, and Julian came in. He looked
~~~

surprised to see Charles there.

"Good morning, Charles, so nice to see you," Julian said as he walked over and shook Charles's hand. "I wasn't aware we were meeting today. Am I interrupting?" He looked at Isabella, who said nothing.

"Of course not. Please take a seat. Isabella and I were discussing an idea she had for the building." Charles looked back to Isabella. "Please continue."

Isabella would have preferred that Julian not be in on this meeting. She could only imagine his thoughts about having Grayson working on the project as well. But she was stuck, so she decided to continue, knowing that if all went as planned, Julian would find out sooner or later. "Charles, I want you to know that I don't recommend Grayson solely because he is my husband," she continued, avoiding Julian's stare. "I want to use him because I believe he will do an amazing job for you, and I believe the pieces he will create will only enhance what we've already done. If I thought that there was someone else out there who topped his talent in this area, I'd recommend them. Please understand that."

"I don't doubt your intentions. I know you have excellent business sense, and I trust your judgment. Is Grayson on board with this project? Have you spoken with him yet?"

"Honestly, no, I haven't. I needed to know that you were willing to proceed before I even broached the subject with him."

"How will this affect the budget? You know me—I'm a numbers man. I leave the designing to you."

Isabella smiled. "I'd need Grayson to take a look at what we're proposing and have him submit an estimate to you. Overall, in the grand scheme of the budget, I'd guess that it would be a nominal percentage."

Charles nodded. "Speak with Grayson and see if he would be willing to take this on. I want to make sure that he can devote himself to completing the pieces in a timely manner. Also, have him put together a written proposal so I know what we're looking at, and I'll go from there. How does that sound?" Charles stood.

"That sounds wonderful. Thank you, Charles. I'll speak with him tonight and get back to you on his decision." Isabella stepped around her desk to shake his hand.

He took her hand as he always did and kissed it. "It was good seeing you, Isabella, and you too, Julian." He waved as he left the office.

Isabella closed the door behind him and paused before turning around. She could already feel Julian's eyes burning a hole in the back of her head. When she turned, he was standing with his arms folded across his chest, looking pissed off.

"When were you planning on telling me?" he demanded.

She ran a hand through her hair, trying to keep calm. "Don't make a big deal over this. I just thought of it the other day when I was researching artwork for the building. I don't see what the problem is, or why you need to get yourself in a huff over it."

"It is a big deal to me. You obviously knew that I would have an issue with it, which is why you didn't mention it to me, or mention your clandestine meeting with Charles this morning."

Isabella rolled her eyes, irritated, and sat down behind her desk. "There was no clandestine meeting. I just spoke with him yesterday, and he mentioned he wanted to stop by this morning. I haven't mentioned anything to Grayson yet, either. I was just checking to see if there was any interest there before I began stirring the pot."

"So you're admitting that you knew there would be issues?"

"No, I'm not admitting anything of the kind. I merely wanted to make sure it was a viable option before I started involving everyone. That's all."

Julian nodded. "I see. Well, from what you've told me, I don't think Mr. I-Don't-Need-My-Wife's-Handouts will be too receptive once you fill him in on the details. Personally, I don't like it either. I've had to give up a lot for you, and this"—he gestured around her office—"is our time. I don't need him coming in and monopolizing your time here as well."

Isabella stood up, resting her hands on the desktop. She leaned forward, locking her eyes on his, and hissed at him, "This time in here is not *ours*, it's *mine*. The last time I checked, this was *my* office and *my* business. I don't recall needing your permission to make decisions when it comes to *my* business. If you don't like it, you can leave."

Julian stood and strode out of her office, slamming the door behind him. Isabella fell back into her chair, her body shaking. The tone she had taken with him shocked her. She closed her eyes and breathed deeply, trying to remember just why it was she continued to keep him around.

Chapter 22

When Isabella told Grayson about her idea that night, he sat up in bed, shocked. "You did what? Why on earth would you do that?"

"Don't make a big issue out of this," Isabella replied. "You'll have free reign to create the pieces you want. No one will tell you what to do or what colors to use. This will be all you. You can be as creative as you want to be."

"The big issue is that I don't want to work for the man. This is your gig, not mine. I told you from day one that I wouldn't get involved. Do you not listen to me when I talk to you? Why would you do something like this?" Grayson was beyond livid.

"You're being ridiculous. My gig is design, not art. That's your gig. This is a job, Grayson, a paying job. I thought that would make you happy. Not only will you get paid for your work, but it will be showcased in a beautiful building for hundreds, if not thousands, of people to see. Why wouldn't I do something like that for you?" She was perplexed by his stubbornness.

"I told you," he shouted, "I don't want any of your handouts, period. End of story."

Isabella was fed up with his delusions about her trying to help his career along. "It's not a handout—it's called an opportunity! I know you're smart enough to know the difference. You need to get over yourself. This whole holier-than-thou, this-job's-beneath-me bullshit is getting old."

Filled with rage, Grayson lunged to the foot of the bed, grabbed her shoulders, and shook her, causing her to scream out in fear. "You don't know shit about what I think," he spat. "How dare you speak to me like I'm beneath you."

"Stop it. You're hurting me," Isabella cried out as she tried to free herself from his grip, but the more she fought, the tighter he held on. "Let go of me, you son-of-a-bitch," she screamed.

Grayson pushed her away from him, causing her to lose her balance and fall back, hitting her head on the dresser. Stunned, she tried to get to her feet, but the pain in her head forced her back down to her knees.

When she touched the back of her head, her fingers came away covered in blood. She began to shake.

"Look what you did," she said, showing him her hand.

Grayson watched her struggle to her feet, seemingly unmoved. Isabella finally stood up, dazed and shaken by his callousness.

"I didn't do this," he said. "You did this, you stupid bitch." Grayson grabbed her purse off the dresser and shoved it into her hands. "Get out. I can't even look at you right now, let alone be in the same room with you."

Isabella's mouth fell open in shock. She tried to grasp what was happening.

"Get out," Grayson roared.

Isabella fled down the staircase and out of their loft, sobbing uncontrollably. She sat down on the front steps of her building and dug into her purse for her cell phone. Her hands trembled as she hit the speed-dial button, praying her call would be answered.

"Hello?" Julian answered.

Isabella tried to catch her breath to speak, but she was sobbing too hard.

"Bella, are you there? Baby, talk to me. What's wrong?"

"Julian," she managed to say between sobs, "I need you. Can you help me, please?"

Alarmed by her sobs, and fearing that something was seriously wrong, Julian grabbed his keys. "I'm on my way. Where are you?"

Isabella held the phone tight to her ear, her voice barely a whisper. "He hurt me, Julian. There's a lot of blood."

"Isabella, you have to tell me where you are. I can't help you if I can't get to you. Where are you, baby?"

"Outside my building," she sobbed.

"Stay right there. I'm on my way. Don't hang up the phone. I want you to stay on the line with me until I get there. Can you do that for me, Bella?"

Isabella nodded. Julian raced out of his building and jumped into his car. He took off down the street, trying to get to her as quickly as he could, listening to her cries the whole way there.

When he pulled up in front of her building, she was curled in a ball on the front step, shivering. He double parked and raced to her side. He took her cell phone, which was still clutched in her bloody hand, and carried her to his car.

Isabella opened her eyes and looked up at him. "I'm sorry," she whispered.

Julian kissed her forehead. "Shh, it's okay. You're going to be okay," he said as he placed her in the car and closed the door softly.

As he came around to the driver's side, he looked up to her loft. Grayson stood there in their bedroom window, looking down at him. Their eyes met, each holding the other's gaze. Julian did not move until Grayson finally disappeared from the window and the light from the bedroom was extinguished. Julian withdrew his eyes from the window, jumped into the car, and sped off to the hospital.

Three hours and one emergency room visit later, Julian helped Isabella out of the car in front of his apartment building.

"You don't need to fuss over me," she protested. "It's only a few stitches. You could just take me to a hotel. I would be perfectly fine there."

"A few stitches are two or three, not twelve. I'm not going to leave you at some hotel. The doctor said you shouldn't be left alone, so I'm afraid you're stuck with me for the night."

"I could stay with Gia, you know."

Julian adamantly shook his head. "There is no way I'm letting that dingbat take care of you. Stop being difficult. You're staying here tonight. I told you I would be there for you, and I will be."

She felt tears brimming in her eyes. Unable to speak, fearing she would break down again, she simply nodded and walked through the door.

In his apartment, Julian led her to the bedroom. "Let me find something for you to sleep in." He dug through his dresser drawer as she sat on the bed, exhausted mentally and physically. He handed her a T-shirt. "You can sleep in here, and I'll sleep on the sofa. If you need anything, I'll be right in the next room."

When he turned to leave, Isabella reached for his hand. "You don't have to sleep out there. I don't want to kick you out of your own bed. You can stay in here. Really, I don't mind."

"I don't want you to be uncomfortable. You need your rest."

"I'll be more comfortable knowing you're beside me, rather than out there on the sofa."

He hesitated. "Okay then, let's get you changed and into bed. The bathroom is right over there." Julian pointed down the hallway.

She stood in front of him, clutching the T-shirt. "Thank you for being here and for being so kind to me. I don't know what I would do without you. I don't deserve your kindness after the way I spoke to you today. You certainly did nothing to warrant my behavior. I'm so sorry." Isabella hung her head low, ashamed.

Julian took her into his arms and held her tight as Isabella rested her head on his chest. "I know things have been difficult for you, as they have been for me, but I'm not without fault, either. I let jealousy get the best of me at times and didn't play fair with you. There's no need to apologize."

She sighed deeply and nodded. For a long moment she stood there, swaying slightly back and forth, as if to soothe the pain.

Julian kissed the top of her head and pulled away from her. "It's late. You should get ready for bed."

Too drained to speak, Isabella retreated to the bathroom. She put her hair in a low ponytail to avoid pulling the stitches that ran across the back of her head. Standing in front of the sink, waiting for the water to warm, she caught her reflection in the mirror. Her eyes were bloodshot, and her cheeks were streaked with mascara. She hadn't realized what a mess she was. Her thoughts went back to how innocently the evening had started with Grayson. They were having a pleasant conversation until she had brought up working for Charles, a decision she now regretted. She had never seen Grayson that angry. It scared her to no end. Her mind kept returning to the rage he had expressed when he grabbed her and refused to let go. She remembered, too, the way he had watched her struggle to her feet, almost as if he were enjoying it. If she had been dying, he probably would have had no problem just standing there, watching as she slipped away. His actions were sinister and cold.

The thought nauseated her. She clutched the edge of the sink, feeling faint. She took deep breaths in and exhaled slowly, waiting for the nausea to pass.

Feeling slightly better, Isabella washed her face and changed into Julian's T-shirt. Just then, there was a soft knock on the door.

"Bella, are you okay in there? I'm starting to worry about you."

Isabella picked her clothes up off the floor and opened the door. "I'm fine. I'm just moving a little slow right now, that's all."

Julian took her clothes from her, set them on the counter, and scooped her up into his arms. "You don't look fine to me. You're as pale as a ghost." He carried her back to the bedroom, gently laid her on the bed, and pulled the covers over her. "Is there anything I can get you?"

Isabella managed a small smile. "You really need to stop fussing over me. I'm just tired, that's all."

He stared at her for a long moment, knowing she wasn't being honest. "Well, okay. If you're sure." He turned off the lights and returned to the bed, carefully lying down next to her. Isabella rested her head on his bare chest and listened to the sound of his heartbeat. Within minutes, she was fast asleep.

Julian watched her as she slept, thinking there wasn't much more she could take.

~~~

When Isabella woke the next morning, she found herself alone in bed. She was surprised to see that it was almost ten o'clock. As she sat up, her head began to throb. Her incision was no longer numb from the shot the doctor had given her before giving her stitches. She hoped Julian would have something strong she could take for the pain.

As she padded into the kitchen, she smelled coffee brewing and heard Julian fumbling around. As she rounded the corner, she was surprised to see Gia there instead.

"Well, good morning, sleepyhead. How are you feeling?" Gia reached for a mug and poured Isabella a steaming cup of coffee.

"Morning. What are you doing here?"

Gia handed her the mug, and she gladly accepted it. "Well, Julian called me and filled me in on what went down last night. He said he had a few things to take care of but didn't want to leave you alone, so he asked if I could come and stay with you." Gia sat down on the counter stool next to Isabella, her expression sympathetic. "I hear it was pretty bad last night. How are you holding up, love?"

Not ready to talk about what had happened, Isabella shook her head as tears began to flow down her face. The unbearable hurt she felt inside was too much. Gia reached out to her, and Isabella fell into her arms, sobbing.

Gia was able to get Isabella over to the sofa, where they sat for the next hour, mostly in silence, as Isabella continued to break down. She was grateful that Gia was willing to be a shoulder to cry on, rather than sharing her own thoughts about what a jackass Grayson was.

"To top off everything, I've been such a bitch to Julian lately," Isabella said. "I've been pushing him away to make things work with Grayson because it was the right thing to do. Yet here he is, once again rushing to my side when I need him." Isabella rubbed her forehead. "I don't even know why he would want to do anything for me after the way I treated him."

"Because he cares about you, Izzie. You know that. Don't worry about him, he's fine. He's been waiting for Grayson to slip up for some time now, believe me."

Isabella's lip quivered. "I don't know what to do. Everything is such a mess."
~~~

Gia took her hand. "It's still too fresh. Your mind hasn't had a chance to process what's going on, and your heart is still hurting. No one can think clearly with a broken heart." Gia patted her leg. "Time will heal all wounds. I promise it will get better."

Isabella nodded. Even though she rationally understood what Gia was saying, her heart ached so much. Every time she thought of what had happened, devastation set in.

"Can you do me a favor?" she asked.

"Anything for you, baby girl. What do you need?"

"Could you go to my loft and pack me a bag? I don't know if I'll stay here or with you, or even at a hotel, but I know I don't want to go back there."

"Absolutely. As soon as Julian gets back, I'll head over there."

"I'm not a cripple. You don't have to stay. I can take care of myself."

"Oh, no. I was given strict orders not to leave you. Julian would have my head if he came back and I was gone. Besides, I wasn't doing anything today anyway. This gives us a chance to spend some time together."

"You're such a good friend to me. I love you."

"Ditto. Now, why don't we get you into the shower, and I'll whip up something to eat."

"Hey, I thought you were my friend. I've had your cooking, remember?" Isabella made a face and laughed.

"You're funny, wise one. If you weren't hurt, I would whack you one. Come on, while you shower I'll go scrounge up something for you to wear." She smiled. "It'll give me a chance to go through Julian's underwear drawer."

Isabella rolled her eyes as she got up off the sofa and headed to the bathroom. "For your information, he wears the boy-cut shorts, but see if he has a pair of boxers in there. That would be comfy with another T-shirt until you get back with my clothes."

"You got it," Gia said, and headed to the bedroom.

After her shower, Isabella and Gia lay around in Julian's room, chatting and spending some much-needed time together. When Julian returned, Isabella smiled, in much better spirits.

"Well, don't you look cute lying there in my boxers and T-shirt." He smiled and kissed her cheek. "How are you feeling today?"

"Much better, thank you. Did you get all your stuff done?"

"I did, and I'm all yours for the rest of the day." He looked at Gia. "Thank you for coming over. I appreciate it."

Gia waved her hand, brushing him off. “Of course! It gave us some time to catch up.” She gave Isabella a hug. “Take it easy and rest today, will you? I’ll run to your place and bring your stuff back this afternoon.”

“Perfect,” Isabella said as she squeezed Gia tighter.

When Gia had left, Julian held up several DVD cases. “I stopped at the video store and picked us up some movies to watch this afternoon.” He set them on the bed for her to look through. “I also went to your office to grab these files you had sitting on your desk. I knew you were planning on working on them today. I wanted you to have them in case you feel up to it.”

His kindness touched her heart. “Come here.” Isabella patted the bed next to her, and he sat down next to her. She took his face into her hands. “You’re amazing, you know that? Thank you.”

“That is nice to hear, but you don’t have to thank me. I love being with you and taking care of you. It makes me feel good, and I rather enjoy it.”

She brought her lips to his again, and they lay down facing each other. They stayed like that for the rest of the day—actually, for the next few days—only getting up when necessary, just talking and looking into each other’s eyes. She was grateful that he didn’t push for anything more.

~~~

Julian pulled open the shade in the bedroom, allowing the morning sun to shine into the room. He crawled back into bed and hovered over Isabella, kissing her neck and cheek.

“Wake up, sleeping beauty. It’s a beautiful day out.”

Isabella peeked through her squinted eyes and groaned. “No, I don’t want to get up yet.” She rolled over, trying to pull the covers over her head, surprised that her head actually felt good.

He pulled the covers back gently. “I know it’s tempting to stay in bed, but it would be good for you to get some fresh air.”

“Fresh air is overrated.”

He laughed. “You would piss off any environmentalist if they heard you say that. Come on, we’ll go for a nice walk. The exercise will do you good.” Julian whipped the rest of the covers off her, exposing her body, clad in only his T-shirt.

Isabella reluctantly slid out of bed. “Did anyone ever tell you you’re annoying in the morning? You may want to work on that. No one likes a cheerful morning person.”
~~~

He gave her a gentle swat on the butt. "Did anyone ever tell you you're extremely grumpy in the morning? You may want to work on that."

Isabella laughed and fell back into bed, pulling him down on top of her. "I have an idea," she said. "Why don't we stay in? I'm sure we can get plenty of exercise here." She winked at him.

"I do have to say, I like the way you think, but don't think this is getting you off the hook of getting out of bed today." He kissed her nose. "You can consider this your warm-up."

Isabella smiled as he brought his lips down on hers, kissing her passionately. She could instantly feel that familiar excitement rise within her.

"I think it definitely will be more than a warm-up. It's been a while—I'm thinking it will be more like a marathon." Isabella smiled as she wrapped her legs around his waist, pushing her hips into him. "Someone is already excited." She could feel his erection pushing into her.

"You're quite the vixen! You always seem to have that effect on me," Julian said and kissed her hard on her lips, allowing his hand to caress her outer thigh. Her skin felt soft and smooth under his fingertips. He knew he would be with her again, as the certainty of Grayson's messing up was always imminent. He could feel her urgency growing with each kiss and thrust of his hips into hers.

She moaned softly, taking his face into her hands. "Make love to me, Julian." Isabella stared longingly into his eyes, as if she was searching for something. A small smile appeared on his lips, and then on hers. He pushed off of her as he came up on his knees in front of her and lowered his shorts. Isabella's eyes wandered down, and he smiled.

"See something that interests you, Bella?" He winked at her.

"Maybe." She smirked as she sat up in front of him, slowly caressing his hardness. Julian closed his eyes and began to moan. She sat up further and took him fully into her mouth. Feeling this new sensation, he instantly opened his eyes and watched her move up and down his hard shaft with her mouth, circling the tip with her tongue. He watched as she tightened her grip around his penis, just below the tip. She squeezed softly as she slowly flicked it with her tongue, and then circled around the shaft as she squeezed harder. Licking her way back up, her tongue caught a small, glistening drop of cum that dripped down the head of his penis.

Knowing that his excitement was on the verge of eruption, Julian pushed her back down to the bed. He forcefully spread her legs apart with his and plunged himself deep inside her.

Isabella gasped from the force with which he drove himself inside her. She arched her back and pushed her hips into the bed, spreading her legs further apart to take him fully inside her. Julian grabbed onto her hips, thrusting faster and faster, causing the entire bed to shake and Isabella to tremble.

"Do you have any idea how much I missed you, missed this?" Julian said, finding his voice between his panting breaths.

"I missed you too. My gosh, how I have missed you," she whispered.

She reached for his face again, bringing his eyes to hers as she tightened around him.

"No, not yet, Bella. Let me enjoy you longer," he whispered to her as he withdrew from inside her, kissing his way to drown his tongue in her sweetness. Isabella moaned, her legs shaking as his lips made contact with her already primed clit. "Mmmm, you are so wet," he said between tongue lashes. Julian groaned as he drove his tongue inside her.

She feverishly ran her fingers through his hair, holding his head tight to her. Sensing she was ready to cum, he paused, unleashing one last slow lick. Isabella grabbed onto the sheets. She felt herself start to release, but as quickly as it started, it stopped, as he withdrew his touch.

"Ah, stop teasing me!" she cried out. "Please take me now. I want to feel you inside me."

Julian flipped her over, bringing her to her tummy, and came up on his knees behind her. He grabbed her up by her waist, pulling her to her knees as well. He took his hard penis and began rubbing her swollen clit over and over again, teasing her, causing Isabella to moan in agony.

"Julian!" she panted out as she reached back, trying to guide him into her, wanting nothing more than to feel him inside her. He laughed and pulled his hips from her reach. He knew she wanted him, needed him like he was the drug she was addicted to.

In one swift moment, he drove his hardness into her. Isabella moaned as he plunged deep inside her. Moving her back and forth on his throbbing shaft, faster and faster, he pushed inside her, her sweetness soaking him completely. Isabella screamed out in pleasure as she exploded around him, causing him to cry out her name as he released inside her.

He dropped down on top of her, his body covered in sweat. They lay there for a moment, both trying to catch their breath. Julian started to laugh.

"You were right, my love. That was no warm-up!"

Isabella laughed. "No kidding. I am out of breath."

He kissed her softly on her lips. "I love you," he whispered.

Isabella gazed deep into his eyes. It was there—she could feel it. She knew she couldn't fear what she felt anymore. He needed to know how she felt, and she needed to say it.

"I love you too." She returned his soft kiss.

Julian smiled at her and hugged her body tightly into his. "I can't tell you how good it is to finally hear you say that, Bella. I've been waiting for this moment for a long time."

She touched his face. "I have loved you for a long time, Julian. I've just been fighting it. Why that is, I have no idea. You have clearly proven your love for me over and over again."

Julian beamed. "What do you say we shower, get some lunch, and go for a walk in the park?"

Isabella groaned. "Oh come on, do we have to? It's cold out. Can't we just stay here and snuggle?" She pouted out her bottom lip.

Julian laughed. "Stop being a baby. It's actually nice out today, with the sun shining. I promise we'll snuggle when we come back."

"All right," she whined, caving in as she always did with him. "Truth be told, I'm hungry."

"Wonderful."

They found a sushi place not far from his apartment and sat at a window table. A light snow was falling, but he was right—the sun was shining through breaks in the clouds, warming them even though the air was chilly. As they were finishing their sushi rolls, Isabella thought she spotted Grayson across the street, but he turned and disappeared around the corner.

"Is something wrong?" Julian asked.

She shook her head and mustered a smile. "No, I'm just seeing things." She scooted her chair back from the table and excused herself to go to the restroom. She needed a few minutes of privacy so she could shake the feeling of being watched.

~~~

While Isabella was in the restroom, Julian sat at the table, watching the passersby on the crowded sidewalks. Even though he had lived in the city for many years, he still couldn't get over the colorful array of people he saw milling about. *Strange people*, he thought. *Most of them could stand to look in the mirror before leaving the house.*
~~~

As the crowd at the corner began to cross the street, he saw Grayson. When he noticed Julian, he headed for the restaurant and stepped inside, looking like he wanted to pick a fight.

"Hello, Julian." Grayson's tone was cold.

Julian nodded. "Grayson."

"Where's *my* wife?"

Julian looked at him long and hard, contemplating just how this was going to go down. He lowered his voice. "She's here, but I think it's best if you leave her alone right now. She needs time. You need to step back."

"Are you her protector now?"

"I'm getting her to where she needs to be. That's my job, after all. I don't need you messing that up."

"Your *job*? You seem to be enjoying it a little too much."

Julian shrugged, ignoring Grayson's innuendos. "It's had its ups and downs, but now we really seem to be on the right track and off to a great finish." Julian smiled slyly.

They stared at each other, unmoving, both equally headstrong.

"Well, then," Grayson finally said, looking away. He picked up the wine glass sitting on the table across from Julian, knowing it was Isabella's, and raised it. "May you finish your job in a timely manner and be on your way."

Picking up his own glass of wine, Julian leaned across the table and said quietly, "Failure is not an option for me, but thanks for the well wishes." He chugged back the rest of his wine and stood up.

Grayson set the glass down, glared at him a moment longer, then walked away. Julian watched as he left the restaurant, crossed the street, and headed down the block.

"Was that Grayson?" Isabella asked as she returned to the table.

He sighed. "Yes, it was," he answered, hoping it wouldn't upset her.

"I thought so. I know I should have come up here to be with you, but I just couldn't. I'm sorry."

"There's no need to apologize. He's harmless, really."

"What did he want? What did he say?"

"He asked where you were, and I told him that he needed to leave you alone for a bit and that you weren't ready to see him yet." Julian left out the fact that Grayson was fishing around, trying to get a read on their relationship.

Isabella nodded. "Well, thank you for doing that for me. I know you shouldn't have to put up with dealing with him."

Julian kissed her forehead. “Anything for you, princess, anything for you.”

They paid their check and made their way into the park, finding a quiet bench by the pond. Julian used his glove to brush away the light dusting of snow, then sat down and patted his lap. She sat, resting her back on his chest as he wrapped his arms around her waist. But he sensed Isabella was as tense as he was, knowing that Grayson was lurking around, watching them.

Chapter 23

"Well, aren't you a sight for sore eyes," James said as he stepped into Isabella's office. "I've missed you. How are you feeling? Gia said you had the flu."

Isabella smiled, thankful that Gia knew enough not to reveal the real reason she had been out for a few days. She had carefully arranged her hair to hide the stitches. "I've missed you too. I'm much better, thank you."

"Well, you look fabulous. I'm jealous. If I could get the flu, I'd be able to fit back into my favorite pants." He grabbed his slight potbelly and jiggled it.

"You kill me. I could breathe on you, but I don't think it would help."

"I should have thought of that days ago." He sounded bummed.

"I hear that you've been doing a fantastic job of keeping the projects organized. Someone is in need of a raise."

"Oh my God, Isabella, don't tease me like that. I really could use one. My shopping addiction is out of control." James pointed to his loafers. "Brand new Gucci, on sale yesterday at Barney's. I couldn't pass them up. I swear I'm a shoe whore."

"You are a shoe whore, but then again, so am I. I'm upset that you didn't take me with you." She pouted.

"I know, I know, but you always snatch up the good stuff when you come along."

"That's true, but only because you're not fast enough," she teased, remembering how long it had taken him to settle on that argyle cardigan he was wearing. "So tell me, any new updates that I need to know about? I see the spa is wrapping up. Brit's grand opening is next week, right?"

"Yes, she sent over an open invitation to whoever wanted to attend. We would have wrapped up months ago if she hadn't kept changing her mind. But the spa looks fabulous. I think you're going to be happy with everything."

"Good, that's what I love to hear. I should probably pop in there today or tomorrow and give it a once-over before the grand opening."

"You may want to give your grays a once over while you're there too," James said as he looked over his glasses at the top of her head.

Isabella gasped. "Shut up. I do not have gray hairs. Those are natural highlights from the sun."

"Mm-hmm, keep telling yourself that, sister."

"You know what, you're right. You could use a bout with the flu. You're looking a little pudgy." Isabella conspicuously looked him over, head to toe.

James folded his arms over his stomach. "Oh, that was just cruel, Isabella. I have a date tonight. Now I'm going to be all self-conscious."

"You'll be fine. Just stay away from anything with a high salt content." She puffed out her cheeks.

"I can see the flu didn't rid you of your venom."

"You know I love you . . . like a cold sore." She chuckled.

"You need to give me that raise now for enduring all this abuse," James said. As he was filling her in on the other projects, Gia strolled in, carrying a tall vase bursting with gardenias.

"Someone just got a special delivery," she said as she set the vase down on Isabella's desk.

Surprised that Julian knew what her favorite flower was, Isabella pulled the card out of the center of the bouquet. But as she opened it, her smile faded.

"They're from Grayson," Isabella muttered.

"Aw. Isn't he the best," James said. "I just love him. He is so sweet."

Gia shot him a nasty look. "Don't you have some phones to answer? Oh yeah, how about updating the project board? I'll meet you there in a second."

He looked confused, wondering what was wrong, but seeing their expressions, he left well enough alone. "Yep, I'll get right on that. Great to have you back, Isabella."

When he had left, Gia asked, "What does the card say?"

"It says, 'Please forgive me. I love you with all my heart.'" Isabella groaned. "This is just like him. He does something completely off-the-wall insane, and then thinks flowers and a please-forgive-me card are going to make me forget how shitty he was. I'm tired of his games." Isabella handed her back the flowers. "Please get these out of here."

"What do you want me to do with them?"

Isabella shrugged. "Keep them in your office, throw them in the trash. I couldn't care less."

"You got it." Gia picked up the vase. "How are things going with Julian, by the way?"

"Honestly, for the first time in a long time, things are clear to me. He's amazing. I don't even know why I tried to push him away in the first place. I feel bad for doing that."

"You were trying to do the right thing, and he knows that. He never would hold that against you."

Isabella sighed. "I know. I'm thankful that he's so forgiving toward me. He really is someone I've grown to depend on. He's always there for me. It's refreshing to know I have someone there who supports me."

"Well, I'm glad you're figuring things out," Gia said.

"Not completely, but I'm headed in the right direction now."

Isabella asked her to bump up James's pay and make an appointment with Brit to see the finished spa. Gia was heading out the door with the flowers when Julian appeared, holding a vase of gardenias.

"So this is where the powwow is this morning," he said. "I didn't get the memo." He stopped when he saw Gia holding a similar vase. "Did you get her flowers, too? Great minds think alike, huh?"

Isabella looked at Gia and shook her head, not wanting Grayson's flowers left in her office.

Gia smiled at him. "No, these are actually from a guy I've been seeing."

He looked at her strangely. "You and Isabella like the same flowers?"

"Um . . . yeah. We've been friends for so long that we like the same things. We've morphed into one another. We're like twins."

Isabella was thankful for Gia's ability to produce a convincing lie faster than anyone she knew.

"It's a good thing I'm seeing the sane twin, then," Julian quipped.

"Ha ha, very funny." Gia left, closing the door behind her to give them some privacy.

Isabella sweetly smiled at Julian. "You got me flowers?"

"Yes, because I love you." He set the vase down and came around her desk. Spinning her chair so she faced him, he bent down and rested his hand on the chair so that they were face-to-face. Her stomach was filled with butterflies as he kissed her.

"You are beyond amazing," she whispered, returning his kiss. "I love you too." Isabella felt the happiest she had felt in a long time. "It's good to be back at work. My mind is clear, and I'm ready to dive back into it. And that's because of you. Thank you."

He put his hand over hers. "It was my pleasure. It's all worth it to see you smiling again, my love." He stood. "Have you heard from Gonzolo on the progress of the last pieces yet?"

Isabella took a swig of coffee and nodded. "Yes, in fact, I had an email from him this morning. He sent me some photos and wants me to go through them. I think he's trying to avoid my having to go back to Milan. I'm having James print out the photos for us to look at."

"Damn, I was hoping that we would be going back to Milan soon. That was amazing." Julian grinned, causing Isabella to blush.

"It's not off the table. First we'll see what we can decipher from the photos."

"What photos?" He smiled mischievously at her.

Isabella laughed. "You are bad. I think the last few days have proven we don't need Milan."

"True, but I enjoyed being alone with you far away from here, wandering around the streets with my arm around you, and kissing you without worrying about someone seeing us. Why is it that all I can think about right now is putting you up on your desk and having my way with you?"

Standing there before her with his hands in his pockets and a glint in his eye, he looked incredibly sexy. "Because you're a man with a one-track mind, and it keeps veering off work. You need to focus—otherwise I'll call for James and have him sit in here with us all day."

"Please don't torture me like that."

"Who's torturing who?" James said as he opened the door.

Isabella giggled. "No one's torturing anybody. Julian is just being difficult. Are those the photos Gonzolo sent over?" Isabella pointed to the large envelope tucked under James's arm.

"Yes, and might I add, they look fabulous, Izzie, absolutely fabulous." He handed her the envelope.

Isabella and Julian sat on her sofa and pored over the pictures. James was right: the pieces looked fabulous. Gonzolo had made notes on each one for Isabella to review. After going through the warehouse with her, he had a good sense of the things she was looking for. The items he felt wouldn't meet her standards had been pulled and reconstructed. Anything that he felt was worth noting, he did, asking her to pay close attention to that specific detail.

Isabella and Julian were about halfway done looking through the photos when there was a knock at the door.

"Come in," she said, turning back to the dining table photo. "I don't know if I like the finish. Does the stain look a little too cherry to you? I don't want any hint of red in the stain."

"I can't tell from the photo. It could be from the camera flash."

"Am I interrupting?"

Isabella's breath caught. She looked up to see Grayson standing before them. "What are you doing here?" she demanded. She couldn't believe he had the nerve to come to her office after what he'd done.

"I wanted to speak with you," he said. "Do you think you could spare me a few minutes?"

The tension in the room could have been cut with a knife as Isabella stared at him coldly. She felt her blood pressure rising with each passing moment. "I really don't have time right now. I know it's a foreign concept to you, but I'm working here." She felt Julian's leg move against hers, as if to remind her that he was there for her.

Grayson's jaw clenched, and his eyes narrowed. "I didn't come here to argue, so there's no need to be a bitch. All I'm asking for is five minutes of your time. I think as my wife, you can spare that for me."

She knew she didn't owe him anything, but she heard herself saying, "Fine. You have five minutes, starting now."

"I want to speak to you alone," he said.

"There's no reason Julian has to leave. Whatever you need to say to me, you can say in front of him."

Grayson ignored her and looked at Julian. "I'd like to speak to *my* wife alone, in private. Would you be so kind to give us a moment, please?"

Julian glared at Grayson, wondering what the hell he was up to. He knew he had to make a split-second decision. He turned to Isabella, whose eyes were pleading with him not to leave her alone with him. Knowing it was best to leave, he patted her leg and stood up. "I'll find Gia so we can finish going through these photos when you're done talking. I'll be right outside if you need anything."

Isabella nodded, although she was a little surprised that he would leave her alone with Grayson.

"You two have become close," Grayson said when Julian had left.

"Of course we're close. We work together all the time. Julian is a good friend and a good person."

"He's just a friend? Really? Well, I see him as a problem."

"Julian is not the problem. You are." She looked at her watch. "Now you're down to four minutes. Are you going to spend them talking about Julian, or are you going to tell me what the hell it is you came here to talk to me about?"

Grayson moved closer to her, causing alarm bells to go off in her head. Fear flooded through her. Then he pulled a wad of folded paper from his back pocket and threw it down on the table in front of her. "After you left, I spent a lot of time thinking about what you said, and I realized you were right." He pointed to the papers. "Those are copies of the estimates for Mr. Vanderbeck. I thought you should have them. I already met with him this morning and agreed to take on his project. He has approved my fees and will be sending over the contracts for me to sign this afternoon. So it looks like you and I will be working together after all."

Isabella was stunned. The room started to spin around her, and she felt like she was about to pass out. She knew he hadn't taken the job because he really wanted to do it. No, he had done it so he could be around her, making her life miserable.

"Why on earth would you think I'd want to work with you after what you did to me?" Her voice rose. "You're delusional if you think for one moment that I want anything to do with you right now."

"'Right now' being the key words. We've been together too long for you to just walk away from me, from us. I overreacted, but I'm sorry. In time, I know you'll forgive me."

"You're smoking some serious crack if you think I'll forgive you after what you did. You hurt me, Grayson, physically hurt me. And the worst part was how you stood over me as I struggled. You couldn't have cared less that I was hurt. You never even offered to help me—instead you threw me out onto the street like a piece of garbage. Yes, believe me, for the first time in all the years we've been together, I see just how much you love me."

He closed his eyes and rubbed his hand over his face. "You have to believe me when I say I'm sorry," he said, looking back at her. "I had a bad day. I'd been drinking and was already in a foul mood before you came home. I'm sorry things got so out of hand. I would never intentionally hurt you. In all these years, I've never laid so much as a finger on you in anger. After you left, I felt horrible for what happened. I tried to find you, but you were already gone."

Isabella held up her hand. "Stop, Grayson. Stop with all the lies. I can't take it anymore. I don't know how you can stand there and look me in the eye while you flat-out lie to me. You make me sick . . . literally sick. I'm done, do you hear me? Done with your lies, done with your excuses, done with letting you think you can do whatever the hell you want. Yes, I'm done." Isabella picked up the papers and threw them at him. "Get out of here, and get out of my life, you son-of-a-bitch."

Isabella was screaming so loudly that Julian burst into her office, alarmed. She was shaking, wild-eyed, raging with vengeance.

"Julian, could you please make sure this piece of shit finds his way out of our office?" she asked. "And tell security that he is no longer allowed access onto our floor."

Grayson tried to reach for her, but Isabella pulled away from him. "Don't touch me," she said through clenched teeth, ready to explode.

"Isabella, don't do this," Grayson pleaded. "Baby, calm down. You're getting yourself all worked up over nothing."

"Nothing? Nothing?" she screamed. "Do you call twelve stitches nothing? Did you not hear me the first time, or are you really that stupid? Get out!"

Julian walked over to Grayson, who hadn't budged an inch. "She's asked you twice now. You need to leave."

Grayson ignored him. "I'm not giving up on you or us. I don't care how long it takes, you will have to come home, and when you do, I'll be waiting for you."

Isabella glared at him. The hatred she felt for him consumed her. "You'll be waiting a long time, then, because I'm not coming back. By the way, if I remember correctly, the loft is mine. I found it, I paid for it. You've just had the privilege of living there. I want you out by tomorrow."

Grayson sneered at her. He turned to Julian. "Enjoy it while it lasts, because before you know it, she'll be gone."

Ignoring his comment, Julian walked over and opened the door. Grayson followed, but paused right in front of him before leaving. He smiled and leaned into Julian's ear. "That won't be long either," he whispered. Again, Julian said nothing as Grayson left the office.

Julian closed the door and rushed to Isabella, who had fallen down to the sofa, crying. He cradled her in his arms. "I'm so sorry. I should have stayed with you. I should have never left you alone with him." He held her tighter as she buried her face in his chest. "Shhh, baby, please don't cry. You're going to be okay. I'll never let him hurt you again, I promise."

"Can you believe he met with Charles today and agreed to work on the project? Charles accepted his bid, and now the bastard will be working with us. How messed up is that? How can I work with him when I can't even stand looking at him?"

"Why don't you just call Charles and tell him that after careful consideration, you don't want Grayson on the project due to a conflict of interest? I'm sure he'll have no problem backing out of the agreement for you."

"I can't do that. I'm the one who recommended him to begin with. I can't go to Charles now and say I've changed my mind. He trusted my judgment. I'd lose credibility with him. I'm royally screwed." Isabella put her face in her hands and rubbed her forehead. “And Grayson knew that. I just got played. He’s such a bastard.”

Julian turned her to face him. “Who says you have to give him the upper hand? If you think he took this project just to be around you, assign someone else to work with him—Gia, or me, for that matter. All we have to do is meet up with him to go over the designs and send him on his merry way to paint.” He pulled her to him. “Everything will work out for the best, you’ll see. I know you’re hurt, but try not to let him mess with your head. Who knows, maybe he’ll back out when he realizes he won’t get what he wants.”

“I hope so, Julian, I really do.”

Chapter 24

In the weeks that followed, Isabella kept to herself—well, herself and Julian, that is. Rumors spread around the office faster than a forest wildfire regarding her throwing Grayson out of the office. Even though Gia and Julian were the only people who knew what went down, that didn't stop other employees who were in close proximity at the time of the argument from concocting their own sordid versions.

Isabella spent most of her time in her own office, locked away from the unwelcome stares and whispering. She knew that she should have addressed the issue instead of hiding away, but she was too emotionally spent to deal with the nonsense of office gossip. She wisely used the time to visit her project sites, again partly to avoid the office, where she felt she now lived under a microscope. Her world seemed to be slowly falling apart, piece by piece. Once confident and secure, she was now shaken to the core and felt unsure and vulnerable. She tried to put up a good front, but those closest to her sensed the change.

On several occasions, James, who was still a fan of Grayson's, had attempted to talk with her, but she wasn't interested in anyone singing Grayson's praises. Gia pulled out all the stops trying to distract her from her worries, but her attempts were also futile, as Isabella remained closed off and unwilling to partake in some of her favorite activities. Not knowing what they could do to help, her friends chose to tiptoe around the elephant in the room.

Julian was the only one Isabella was willing to engage with, which didn't bother him any. He knew the time she spent with him only secured his place in her heart. If she wasn't at her office, she was with him. She chose to stay at his apartment for a few weeks, allowing Grayson plenty of time to clear out of the loft. She had no desire to run into him, especially there.

With Julian off at a meeting one evening, Isabella decided it was time and headed over to the loft. She needed to decide if she was going to stay there, or just grab a few things and return to Julian's. She was waiting to see how she felt once she was there.

Isabella pulled back the door to the loft and paused, not crossing the threshold. Her eyes scanned the room, looking for signs that Grayson might still be around. Finally she stepped in and closed the door behind her. The silence gave her an eerie feeling. She kept replaying the night she had left, bleeding profusely from her head. She shook the memory from her mind as she ascended the stairs.

In the bedroom, Isabella noticed the room was tidy and their bed showed no signs of being slept in. It was perfectly made, which she knew Grayson would never have done. Breathing a sigh of relief, she went to her closet for a few outfits she wanted to take over to Julian's. Being alone in the loft made her realize that she wasn't comfortable staying there on her own yet.

She turned on the light and gasped when she saw Grayson's clothes still hanging next to hers. A wave of panic came over her as she realized that he had obviously not vacated as she had asked. Isabella fumbled to turn off the light and backed out of the closet. She turned around and let out a small scream as she came face-to-face with Grayson.

"You scared the shit out of me," she exclaimed, her voice shaking with fear. "What are you still doing here?"

"I live here, Isabella. Why wouldn't I be here?"

She glared at him. "If I remember correctly, I told you to leave."

Grayson let out a big sigh. "You did, but I know that was just the anger talking, so I stayed."

Isabella sneered and tried to push past him, but he grabbed her arms. "Let go of me," she demanded. "I'm done with you. I don't want to be here."

"You need to stop and listen to me. I'm not going to hurt you. I love you."

Not interested in anything he had to say, she tried getting away from him again, but he tightened his grip.

"Stop it. You're hurting me."

"I wouldn't be hurting you if you would just stop. Why are you so unwilling to hear me out? Has Julian gotten so far into your head that you won't even listen to me now?"

Isabella stopped fighting him when she heard Julian's name. "Julian has nothing to do with our problems," she spat.

He let out a condescending laugh. "I beg to differ. How stupid do you think I am? I saw you two in the park. I'm not blind to the way he looks at you, and you at him. Are you going to stand there and lie to my face, telling me nothing is going on between the two of you?"

So he did suspect. Isabella didn't know what to say as her anger was abruptly replaced by guilt. She looked away to avoid his eyes. No matter what Grayson had done to her, no matter how badly he had hurt her, she knew that she was the one who had betrayed him first.

Grayson released his grip on her and ran his hand through his hair. "Your silence speaks volumes. I know we've had our differences lately and things haven't been the greatest between us, but never in a million years would I have guessed you'd betray me like that."

As the insurmountable shame built inside her, a wave of nausea came over her. She felt flushed, and her heart pumped furiously in her chest. Somewhere along the way, her anger toward her husband had overshadowed any concern she had for his feelings, or her willingness to do what was right.

"Did you sleep with him?" he asked, his eyes boring into hers. "Please tell me that you didn't."

She closed her eyes, trying to push back the tears. Visions of her and Julian making love flashed through her head. His touch, his kiss, his desire for her, her desire for him, all seemed tainted now. She inhaled and exhaled deeply, trying to calm herself as she opened her eyes.

Grayson threw his head back, running both hands through his hair now as he let out a growl of frustration. He drew back his arm, and Isabella cringed, certain he was going to hit her. His arm flew past her shoulder and made a booming sound as it made contact with the wall behind her.

He came nose-to-nose with her, getting right up in her face. She stilled, not sure what he was going to do next. She felt his hot breath pouring onto her face. He looked like a raging bull ready to explode out of his pen. "That's what you did," he yelled, pointing at the gaping hole in the wall. "That's exactly what you did. You crushed me and our marriage." Grayson grabbed her jaw, forcing her to face his devastation. "How could you do that? How could you allow him to come between us?"

Isabella was shaking. Frightened by his sudden burst of anger, she feared for her safety. She needed to leave. She glanced to the door, but knew she couldn't make it out without him fast on her heels.

Grayson grabbed her shoulders, startling her, and shook her back and forth. "Answer me, damn it!" he shouted. "Answer me. How could you do this?"

"I'm sorry," was all she could muster, as tears streamed down her face.

His hands fell away from her, almost as if he was repulsed to touch her. "You're sorry? You're sorry? The thought of you two together makes me sick. You're mine, Isabella Hughes. *My* wife. How could you let him touch you? Do you have any idea, any fucking idea at all what

I've been doing for you, for us, while you've been rolling around in bed with him?"

Confused, Isabella shook her head. Her mind was reeling. Given the way he'd been treating her, she wouldn't have guess he'd been doing anything for her, let alone for their relationship.

"Come here." Grayson grabbed her by the wrist and pulled her down the hallway to the vacant room at the end of the hall. He stopped at the door and took the key out of his pocket. Isabella struggled to free her wrist from his hold, wondering what he was planning to do to her once he got her inside.

Grayson shoved the key into the lock, the loud click of the deadbolt resounding into the hallway. Isabella clawed at his hand, trying to break his hold, but he ignored her attempts. He pushed open the door and shoved her inside. Isabella stumbled across the threshold and gasped as the room came into focus.

The once barren room had been transformed into a nursery. Not just any nursery, but the one she had sketched out years ago. It was exactly as she had envisioned it. The walls were painted a vibrant kelly green, which contrasted beautifully against the stark white crown and base moldings that he had added to the room. The flooring was the same ebony hardwood in the rest of the loft. Anchoring the room was a large, black-and-white, geometric area rug. To the left of the door sat a modern, high-gloss black crib. The bedding was simple and white, double piped with black and kelly-green cording. Past the crib on the left was a rocking horse, a small black table and chair set, and behind them three tall, white bookcases filled with toys and books. Adjacent to the crib was a hand-painted armoire in a distressed gold finish, softly brushed with silver, with knobs that resembled crystal sunbursts. Beside it stood a white dresser with gold drawer pulls. The top of the dresser served as a diaper changing station. Above it hung a large, round mirror with a zebra-hide frame. Facing the windows, angled to create a sitting area, was a cozy rocking chair and ottoman upholstered in a black-and-white houndstooth fabric, with an antiqued gold side table beside them. Directly under the warehouse windows, which had been cleaned of all the dirt and flaking rust, sat a modern gray sofa decorated with a combination of toss pillows in black, kelly green, and a black-and-white floral print. In front of the sofa sat a square, tufted cocktail ottoman in an adorable paisley green fabric, piped in gold. The windows were dressed in cream silk drapery panels trimmed out with a black fabric that puddled on the floor.

"This is what I've been doing while you've been out betraying me.

All of this is for you, for us, for the family you wanted to start. Tell me again how much I do not love you. You're the one who lost faith in our love, Isabella, not me." Grayson's voice broke, and tears fell from his eyes.

Isabella stumbled to her knees and began to sob. There were no words to convey the guilt and sorrow that coursed through her. It was then that she understood the full magnitude of what she had done. She now knew that the consequences for her actions would wind up costing her everything she had ever wanted.

Still on her knees, she looked up at him. "I don't understand. Why . . . why would you do this?"

"I did this for you. This is what you said you wanted."

Isabella shook her head. "That's not what I meant. I don't understand why you would do this after the way you've treated me. You've been so cruel and cold. Why would you go and do something like this, feeling the way you do? I don't understand."

He lowered his voice in shame. "I know I've hurt you. But it hasn't been you that I've been angry with. It's me. Since my show, I've tried to search deep within myself, and honestly, I haven't liked what I've found. I knew I needed to make some changes, but I struggled with those changes—changes like this." Grayson pointed to the room. "Everything that you've ever said to me, you were right about. I was just unwilling to see it. I've been fighting within myself."

Isabella stood up in front of him, searching his eyes. "Then why didn't you tell me that, instead of pushing me away like you did? Why wouldn't you let me help you?"

Grayson sighed. "This was something I needed to figure out on my own. You couldn't have helped me. I needed to do it alone so I could be sure it was what I truly wanted. I couldn't take the chance of being clouded with your thoughts and feelings, which already are so strong inside me."

Isabella shook her head again. "But, you were so . . . so angry with me. It felt like you hated me. You hurt me beyond words." She began to cry. "I wanted to die. That's how much you hurt me. How can you say you loved me? I would never hurt you like that."

"But you did hurt me. You hurt me when you decided to sleep with Julian. Do you have any idea how that feels? I'm literally sick to my stomach thinking that another man has touched you the way I do. I'm sick thinking you gave to him what was mine, what was ours. There's no getting that back. There's a part of me, of us, you completely destroyed."

Isabella bowed her head as her tears poured from her eyes. There was nothing she could say that would take back the betrayal he felt—nothing she could do to ease his pain. “I’m sorry. I know I can’t even begin to make up for what I’ve done, but you have to believe me when I say that I’m truly sorry. I thought I had lost you. I thought you didn’t love me anymore. It was there in your eyes, the hatred—I saw it. I was scared.” She knew what she had to ask him, but the words caught in her throat. “Do you want me to leave?” she whispered.

Grayson stared at her long and hard. “Do you want to leave?”

“I don’t see how I could stay. I think we both know that the damage has been done. There’s nothing left to salvage. We’ll only end up hurting each other more, and I don’t want to do that to you.”

He sighed, and the anger seemed to leave him. “I don’t want to hurt you, either. I guess there is something to be said for the fact that we both care about not hurting the other further. Could that be enough of a reason to stay and fight for us . . . for our marriage?”

“I don’t know. I honestly don’t know.”

“Do you think we owe it to ourselves, after all this time, to find out?”

Isabella remained silent, unsure of how she felt. There had been so much hurt and betrayal between them, she wasn’t sure they could ever survive, let alone reconcile their marriage. The thought saddened her, and more tears dampened her face.

Seeing tears on his face as well, Isabella wiped his cheeks. He put his hand on hers and pulled her into his arms, where they cried together for the love they’d had, the love they’d lost, and the uncertainty of ever finding love with one another again.

Chapter 25

Isabella glanced at her phone as it rang for the eighth time in an hour. Grayson looked at her and then back at her phone.

"He's persistent, I will give him that," he said. "You should answer it. Otherwise he won't leave you alone."

Isabella reached over and hit the button to ignore the call. "I know. He's just worried, that's all. There's no way I can talk to him right now. I wouldn't know what to say. Do you mind if I send him a text, at least, to let him know I'm okay so he'll stop calling?"

He hesitated, but said, "Sure, go ahead. Maybe then we can have some peace and quiet."

She sent a text saying that she was staying at the loft with Gia for the night and that she would see him in the morning. Then she shot Gia a text asking her to tell Julian they were together at the loft if he asked. She promised to explain everything later, and not to worry. Then she turned her phone off.

"I'm sorry. It's off now." Isabella showed him the phone and threw it back on the tufted ottoman. Then his phone vibrated, alerting him to a text. Isabella couldn't see who it was from, but she saw him type the word *Yes*, hit send, and turn if off.

"Mine is off too, so we shouldn't have any further distractions."

Isabella nodded and looked around the room again. She still couldn't believe he had actually turned his old studio into a nursery.

"I don't know how you did this," she mused. "It couldn't have been easy. You had to have help."

"You don't believe I could have done this myself?"

"Not in a million years."

Grayson pretended to be offended, then smiled. "You're right, as usual. I found the sketches in a drawer downstairs and gave them to James. I threatened to burn every single pair of loafers he owned, along with every cardigan, if he breathed one word of it to you. He agreed and worked on it with another designer at your firm. I gave him a key to get in when they needed to, but I did do a lot of the work. All the moldings and painting I'll take the credit for. They did all the fluffy stuff."

Isabella was shocked. "That little shit actually kept a secret from me the whole time? Oh, he is going to pay for that one." She shook her head. "No wonder."

"No wonder, what?"

"He kept trying to convince me to give you another chance. I kept shutting him down every time your name flew out of his mouth." Isabella smiled ruefully. "It all makes sense now. He knew what you were doing, but he couldn't tell me."

"He kept trying to talk to me, too. Although I think I scare him a little more than you do, so he didn't try too often. He's a good kid."

"He is a good kid. He's been doing a great job for me, and apparently for you as well. I love this room. It's exactly what I always wanted."

Grayson smiled at her. "You know this room is not complete, though."

Isabella looked around, trying to identify what was missing. Everything looked perfect. "I give up. What's missing?"

Grayson pointed to the crib. "A baby. The room is missing a baby."

Isabella took his hand in hers. "I think it's going to be a while before we can finish the room. We have a lot to work through, and I don't think the answer to our problems is a baby. As much as I'd love to be a mother, that would be wrong right now."

Disappointment showed all over his face as he looked down at her hand and nodded. "I know, you're right. Even though I've struggled with the idea of being a father all this time, unsure whether I wanted to take that step, now that it's done, I'm actually looking forward to it."

Isabella smiled, happy to finally hear him say that after all these years. "I'm glad you feel that way. When the time is right, when we are right, it will happen. I promise."

He looked up, searching her eyes, and touched her cheek. "I'm sorry that I ever made you doubt my love. I know what happened is just as much my fault as it is yours. We will get through this, Izzie. I promise I'll find a way to forgive you, and I'll also find a way to make you believe in me again."

"I needed to hear that, Grayson. Thank you for saying that."

He watched her intently. He saw a deep sadness in her eyes. He just wasn't sure if it was truly all for him, or if it was for Julian as well. He had to know. He had to ask. "Do you love him?" His voice was barely a whisper.

Isabella looked down at her lap, as if the answer would be there. Had she fallen in love with Julian? She could hear herself professing her love for him, but had she really felt it? Was it love, or lust? Flashbacks flooded her mind, her heart, her soul. It was then that she knew. Isabella brought her eyes back to his. He had asked, but she knew in her heart that he didn't really want to hear the truth.

Her heart sank into the darkest depths. She had done the unthinkable: she had fallen in love with another man. Isabella felt her chest tighten, and her throat began to close. She felt as if she couldn't breathe. Inside, she was suffocating. She would have to let her love for Julian go. She knew the pain and heartache she felt in that moment would soon be delivered upon Julian. The thought overwhelmed her. She took a deep breath and smiled at Grayson, trying to keep her composure, trying to hide her true feelings.

"No, Grayson, I do not love Julian," she lied.

He kissed a tear as it rolled down her cheek. He pulled back, and their eyes met before he leaned in again. This time he brought his lips to hers and pulled her down on the sofa. Unable to control her emotions, Isabella released her tears. She cried for herself, for Grayson, for Julian, and for the damage and heartbreak she had ultimately delivered upon all of them. Grayson held her tight. They remained that way the rest of the night.

~~~

When Isabella woke the next morning, Grayson was gone from the nursery. She got up and walked out into the hall. Out of habit, she reached back to shut the door, but realized she no longer had to keep it closed. The room that had once served as a haunting reminder of the life she so desperately wanted now offered a promise of the life that was yet to be. Smiling, she took one last look at the room and bounded down the stairs, where she heard Grayson in the kitchen.

"Good morning, beautiful." Grayson smiled as he looked up from the pan on the stove.

"Good morning. You're up early."

"I wanted to make you breakfast and start your day off good. I know it will be a hard day for you." Grayson carefully watched her.

Isabella nodded and looked away. They had talked a lot about Julian. Grayson had told her that in order for them to move on, she needed to remove Julian from her life. He also expected her to let Julian go from her office. He knew that seeing him every day would be a constant reminder for her, and he didn't feel comfortable with her continuing to see her lover. She had promised that she would talk to Julian, but she knew that was not going to be an easy task. She'd barely had enough time to process her own feelings, let alone deal with the way Julian would handle her asking him to leave.

As it stood, she was still trying to convince herself that she was
~~~

making the right decision in trying to work things out with Grayson. She had wondered several times that night if she would have been inclined to stay without the promise of starting a family. Perhaps it was like the Hope Diamond being dangled in front of her, drawing her in. These thoughts clouded her mind and her heart. Letting Julian go was not going to be without heartache and pain.

"Isabella? Are you okay?"

"Yeah . . . yeah, I'm fine. I was just thinking of everything I have going on today."

"You're in agreement that you have to let him go, right? You do want that, don't you?" Grayson pushed.

Isabella let out a deep sigh. Truth was, she wasn't one hundred percent sure. "I do, but it's a difficult, sticky situation. I know it's the right thing to do, it's just that . . . that . . ." Isabella looked away again as a strong wave of sadness came over her.

Grayson pushed her further. "It's just what, Isabella? That you would rather be with him instead of me?"

Isabella shook her head. "No. I keep thinking that he has never done anything wrong. He has always been there for me, helping me when I needed someone. When I was hurting, when . . . when I had to go to the hospital after our fight, he was the one who stood by me and got me through it. That's all."

Grayson's expression seemed to waver between guilt and anger. "I see," he said as he went back to making breakfast.

"I don't say these things to upset you. I'm just trying to be honest about how I feel. If you want this to work between us, I need—we need—to be honest with each other. I feel bad knowing I'm going to walk in there today and hurt him more than he deserves to be hurt. That's where my head is at right now." She watched him as he continued to vigorously stir the eggs in the pan.

"And in my head, all I can think about is killing the son-of-a-bitch for touching you," Grayson said coldly, never taking his eyes off the stove. "The thought of his hands on you, pleasing you, makes me sick."

"I see. Maybe I should have kept my thoughts to myself, then," Isabella whispered. She turned away and started up the stairs to get ready for work.

Grayson dropped the spoon on the counter and ran after her, reaching for her arm to stop her. She turned and looked at him. His eyes were filled with tears. "I'm sorry I ever hurt you. I never wanted that. But this is also hard for me. I understand that you have feelings for him, and that he helped you when I drove you away. But I also feel betrayed. Please try to consider my feelings. I love you."

Isabella mustered a small smile for him and then disappeared into the bedroom, making a beeline for the bathroom. Once inside, she locked the door, slid down to the floor, pulled her knees to her chest, and buried her face into her legs to muffle her sobs.

~~~

Isabella had spent the entire ride into work trying to figure out what she would say to Julian. She was having a hard time. The problem was that she wasn't convinced in her heart that she wanted to let him go. Isabella knew he would see that, which made it harder. She was trying to make her heart believe that she wasn't in love with him and that she belonged with Grayson. Her heart was not cooperating with her mind. She knew her convictions needed to be strong—otherwise he would know she was conflicted and would use that to talk his way into staying. Isabella could not afford to let that happen, as she had made a promise to Grayson that she would rid Julian from her life.

Feeling like she was caught in a bad dream that she couldn't wake from, Isabella made her way into her office. As she expected, Julian was already there waiting for her.

"There you are," he said as he came over to her and pulled her into his arms. "I missed you last night and this morning. The bed was lonely without you. I was lonely without you."

Isabella closed her eyes, feeling the warmth in his embrace, trying to burn it into her memory, knowing it would be the last time she would ever feel his arms around her. She felt like she was dying inside, faced with the reality that within minutes she would deliver the blow that would end their love. Isabella clung to him, holding on to every last moment as she pushed back tears. She prayed she had the strength to make it through.

Julian kissed the top of her head. "Wow, someone must have missed me too. I can't say I mind. I could stand here holding you forever, my love. You make me feel so good."

Isabella's heart sank. His words made her feel worse than she already did. She wanted to run far away to a place where she didn't have to hurt the ones she loved—a place where her heart and mind were at peace.

Julian pulled back and looked at her. "Something is wrong, I can feel it. Bella, tell me, what's wrong?"

"Julian, I . . . I can't . . . we can't." Isabella struggled to find the words. She paused, shaking her head no. "I'm sorry," she whispered.

"Isabella, you're scaring me. What's wrong, baby?"

Her voice quivered. "I can't see you anymore. You have to leave. We
~~~

can't be together anymore. I'm sorry."

"I don't understand. Everything was fine . . . we were fine. Why would you want me to leave? Did I do something to hurt you?"

"No, you didn't. It's me. I just can't do this anymore. It's not right." Her guilt forced her to look away from him.

Julian grabbed her chin, forcing her eyes back to his. "I don't believe you. Something else is going on. Talk to me. What has gotten you so upset?"

Isabella couldn't bring herself to give voice to the reason they couldn't be together.

"I don't understand. You were fine when I left you yesterday before you went to your . . ." Julian paused, tilting his head as he searched her eyes for the truth. He took a step back, his face contorted in disbelief, making Isabella cringe.

"Julian, please, let me explain," she pleaded.

"How could you possibly go back to him, after everything he has done to you? I'm shocked that you would even consider giving him another chance."

"Please understand that I didn't mean to . . ."

"Didn't mean to what? Use me the way you did?" he spat.

Isabella gasped. "Don't say that. I didn't use you. I would never do that to you."

"Really? Because that's exactly what it feels like to me." He glared at her. "And I actually believed you when you said you loved me. How stupid was I? How could you do that to me, knowing that I truly loved you?"

"I did . . . I did care about you . . ."

"No, that's not what you said. *Love*, that's what you said. You said you loved me. There's a big difference between caring for someone and loving someone. You have obviously been in a bad relationship for too long to know the difference."

"I know what love is," she said calmly.

"That's right. You do know what love is, because of me. I showed you what love is. I showed you how amazing love can feel. Grayson sure as hell didn't show you that, and believe me, he never will." He grew more agitated. "I can't believe how naive you are, thinking that he would ever love you the way I do. You're making a huge mistake, Isabella."

"What do you want me to do? He's my husband. He wants us to work things out. I think I owe that to him, after all these years together. We've both done things to drive a wedge into our relationship. I'm as much to blame as he is."

"Unbelievable. You did try to work it out with him, remember? That ended well for you, didn't it? Have you so quickly forgotten how his love drove you to the front steps of your building, broken and bleeding as you called me to come and rescue you?"

"I haven't forgotten. He was struggling then, going through things I didn't understand at the time, and now I do. I shouldn't have pushed him the way I did."

Julian smirked. "And that's your fault? It's your fault he treated you like garbage, lost his temper, and hurt you in the process? Come on. Can't you see what he's doing? He's turning this around on you. What type of man stands over his wife as she's bleeding profusely and does nothing?"

"He knows," she said, raising her voice. "He knows about us. He had every right to blame me. I'm the one who betrayed him."

Julian shook his head in disbelief. "Only after he consistently treated you like shit over and over again did you betray him. Think, Isabella. He's playing off your guilt. He knows you would never come back on your own. He knows you too well and is making you feel guilty so you'll overlook what he's done to you. Why would you let him do that?"

Hearing his words, Isabella's stomach turned. She wondered if he was right. "It's not like that."

"It is exactly like that." Julian paused, thinking. "But I know you. You wouldn't go back without a reason. What did he tell you he was going to do for you this time?"

Isabella didn't respond.

"Answer me," he yelled, startling her.

"He didn't promise me anything. He just made some decisions recently, which lead me to believe that he's willing to move forward, that's all." Isabella didn't feel it was necessary that he knew about Grayson's willingness to start a family with her.

"Well, I made decisions too—months ago. I decided that I loved you and I would stand by you. I decided to comfort you when you needed comforting, to make you laugh when you were crying, to hold you when you were conflicted, to love you unconditionally. That's what I decided."

"I know you did, and believe me, I've appreciated everything you've done for me—"

"I don't want your appreciation, Isabella. Our relationship was not a business arrangement. I want your love—the love that you were ready to give me, the love that I know you still have in your heart for me. I can see it in your eyes. You can't deny it."

Julian was right—she did love him. But that love could never amount to anything as long as Grayson was there, she realized now. She knew Julian wasn't going to give up. She had been fearful that he would be unwilling to let her go.

She looked into Julian's green eyes, seeing the love he had for her one last time before she destroyed it, destroyed him. Trying to keep her voice from shaking, she steadied herself by letting out a heavy sigh.

"You're right, Julian, I did use you," she lied. "I needed someone to be there for me, and you were the easiest choice. I took Gia's advice and used you to release my stress, keeping you around mainly for the sex. I took advantage of you and the feelings you had for me, and like a fool you completely fell for it. I had you wrapped around my finger so tight that you thought I actually loved you."

He narrowed his eyes. "You're lying. I don't believe you for one minute."

"Julian, why do you think I keep going back to him? Why am I always so willing to give him chance after chance, even though he has hurt me, and at the same time give you up when you haven't? I love him more than anything." Isabella knew that she had already stuck the knife in his heart. It was time to deliver the final twist. "I could never love you the way I love Grayson, not in a million years. You could never have my heart like he does, and you never did."

He abruptly backhanded her across her face. Isabella shrieked and raised a hand to her stinging cheek, grimacing in horror.

Julian's eyes glowed with anger. "You cold-hearted bitch. I gave you everything I had inside. I loved you, and this is how you treat me? I don't deserve this." His voice boomed through her office.

Shocked and infuriated, Isabella struggled to keep her voice low. "You got exactly what you deserved, and you got paid handsomely for it, too. Your services are no longer needed in this office or my bed. We can do this one of two ways. You can quietly leave the office on your own, or I can call security and have you escorted out. The choice is yours." She hoped Julian would leave on his own; the last thing she needed was yet another scene for the staff to gossip about. Although it was probably already too late for that.

The veins in his forehead were pulsing. His expression hardened. He stepped forward, their faces inches apart. "One day, Isabella Hughes, you will regret what you've done, and when that time comes, I'll be watching, smiling, as your world comes crashing down around you."

His sinister stare sent chills up her spine. Isabella stepped back from him, saying nothing. Julian turned, choosing to leave the office on his own. He hesitated at the doorway.

"Mark my words," he said. "You just made a big mistake. You will regret this."

"Is that a threat?" Isabella defensively folded her arms across her chest.

"I'd watch myself if I were you," he warned, and left her office.

Shaking, Isabella stumbled to her desk, came down hard on her knees in front of the wastebasket, and vomited.

Chapter 26

It was almost dusk as Isabella came around the last bend in the park and finished her run. She despised running after work. She had more energy in the morning, but had given up her morning runs when she kept seeing Julian at the park. Whether the encounters were intentional or accidental, she didn't know, but she had altered her schedule to avoid him altogether. Seeing him now made the hairs on the back of her neck stand up. Only on the weekends, when Grayson joined her, did she run in the morning.

She had never realized how unstable Julian was until after she'd kicked him out of her office that day. Maybe she had been blinded by her feelings for him. Maybe he was a master at manipulating her, or maybe he simply couldn't get over her choosing Grayson. Whatever it was, his odd behavior was now apparent, and it made it easier for her to get over him.

The day after he had left, Isabella arrived at work to find her office covered in bouquets of gardenias from him. She had counted more than twenty-five arrangements. Her office smelled like a funeral home, which creeped her out. She asked Gia to remove every arrangement and throw them in the trash, along with every card that professed his love to her, begging her to take him back.

After that attempt failed, the endless calls began. Sometimes he hung up. Other times he left long-winded messages about how he missed her and how much he loved her. Then there were the times when he screamed, telling her what a horrible person she was for hurting him. He was all over the board. Isabella couldn't take it; she had finally stopped listening to the messages.

When his phone messages went unanswered, he began texting her. Her phone was chiming or vibrating all day long with the arrival of each text. Isabella began turning it off so she wouldn't have to hear the alerts. She deleted them all at the end of the day.

What angered her the most was when she received a call from Charles Vanderbeck's office. With the reveal of the furniture line drawing near, plans were in full swing for the launch party. Evette had contacted her about a message that Julian had left requesting press release materials and passes for media personnel. She had heard that he was no longer working for Isabella and wanted clarification on whether she could release that to him or not. Isabella was livid that he would attempt to gain access to the event. She immediately sent an email to everyone on Vanderbeck's staff, informing them that Julian no longer worked for her company and that under no circumstances should he be privileged to any further information regarding the project or the furniture launch. She alerted her own staff as well. She was careful in her wording, simply stating that with the project near completion, Julian had decided to move on to a current project with another company. The last thing she needed was more rumors flying around the office.

The most worrisome behavior, months after letting him go, were the constant run-ins that she had with him. Almost everywhere she went, he was there. At first he approached her. Sometimes he seemed friendly, as if trying to win her back, being overly sweet and complimentary. Other times, he made threatening comments, but always at a whisper so no one around them would hear. Those were the times Isabella feared for her safety. It was during one of those run-ins that Isabella became fed up and finally exploded at him. After that, he stopped approaching her, and instead began watching her from a distance.

One afternoon, Gia and Isabella were out having lunch when Isabella spotted him sitting on a bench, observing her from across the street.

"Ugh, seriously, Gia, this has to stop. I don't know what to do anymore. He's obsessed with the idea of us getting back together. He's making me crazy. I don't know what more I can say or do to make him go away."

"What does Grayson say?" Gia asked. "You have told him, haven't you?"

"Not about everything, but he knows Julian is still hanging around. He keeps telling me to ignore him, and he'll go away. That's easy for him to say. He's not the one being stalked."

"You really think he's stalking you? Come on, Izzie, you got to know him pretty well. Do you think he would hurt you?"

Isabella sighed. "If you had asked me that months ago, I would have said you were crazy to even think it, but now . . . I don't know. He's making me wonder. The other day, I was running in the park after work, and I could have sworn someone was following me. I had forgotten my iPod at home, so I wasn't listening to music. I kept hearing footsteps behind me, but every time I turned around, no one was there. When I left the park, I crossed the street and looked back at the entrance, and I swear I saw him standing there watching me. I never ran so fast the rest of the way home."

"Have you thought about going to the police?"

"And say what? I think the man I had an affair with may or may not be stalking me, but I don't have any proof? How crazy does that sound?" Isabella was growing frustrated.

"Well, maybe you need to start getting proof. If he sends you a text, save it. If he calls you, don't delete the message. Maybe you'll get enough evidence over time, and you can go to the police." Gia glanced in Julian's direction. "Or you can send in your best friend to knock some sense into his pea brain." Gia stood up and threw her napkin on the table. "Excuse me. This won't take long."

Before Isabella could stop her, Gia was gone. She tore out of the restaurant like a bat out of hell, dodging cars as she ran across the street, and landed in front of Julian within seconds.

"This has got to stop," Gia yelled at him, her hands on her hips.

"What has to stop, Gia?" he asked nonchalantly.

"You, stalking Isabella. You need to leave her alone. She has made her choice, and oh, so sorry, it wasn't you. Take it like a man and move on."

"I have no idea what you're talking about. I was simply out walking, enjoying the day, when I saw this empty bench and decided to have a seat and take in some fresh air."

"We live in New York. There's no such thing as fresh air here."

He laughed at her. "I, and many other New Yorkers, would beg to differ with you."

"I'm going to make this really simple for you. If you don't leave her alone and stop following her, I'm going to make life extremely difficult for you. I don't think I need to remind you that I'm the only one who knows everything that has gone down between the two of you. I have no problems twisting details in her favor, making the police stick a scope so far up your ass, you'll actually taste it."

"Are you threatening me?"

"You bet your ass I am," she hissed. "You don't want to mess with me, Julian. I'll take you down."

Julian stood up and tried staring her down, but Gia held her ground, not budging an inch.

"You just made a big mistake threatening me," he said before walking away.

Gia returned to their table with a satisfied expression.

"He looked like he was pissed," said Isabella. "I don't want you getting in the middle of this."

"I'm fine, Izzie. Trust me, I can take care of myself. He was just mad because I called him out, that's all. I don't think you need to worry about him bothering you anymore. If he's smart, he'll stay away from you."

Isabella nodded, but Gia's face showed a twinge of concern as she turned to look down the street, making sure he was gone. Isabella hoped her friend was right.

~~~

A few days later, Isabella was walking home from the gym when she heard her friend Anastashia calling her name from the door of her children's boutique.

"Come in, Isabella. I have a package for you," she yelled from across the street.

Isabella turned. "Something for me? I don't remember ordering anything."

"Grayson did, for the nursery. It just came in."

Isabella jaywalked across the street through the passing traffic and greeted Anastashia with a hug. "Hello, my friend. I hear you and my husband have been busy little bees."

She laughed. "Yes, he was so excited." She patted Isabella's tummy. "Soon, no?"

"Soon," Isabella said, not wanting to burst her bubble with the fact that she and Grayson had decided to work on their marriage first before they began to try for a baby.

"I'm so excited for the two of you. You loved the nursery, no? He did a beautiful job, Isabella. He brought me over to see it. Your design was exquisite."

"It's my favorite room now. I love to sit in there and read. It's so quiet and calming."

Anastashia pushed opened the door further, stepping out of the way for Isabella. "Come inside, and I will grab the package for you."

Isabella wound up staying for over an hour as she caught up with her old friend. Anastashia was so excited, showing off the new products that she knew Isabella would want.

Anastashia loaded up two large bags for her to take, including extra bedding for the crib that Grayson had purchased, and Isabella headed home. As she turned the corner, she came face-to-face with Julian.

Isabella stopped, and their eyes met. His expression told her he was disturbed. To avoid another argument with him, Isabella turned to retreat back to Anastasia's store, where she knew she would be safe, but Julian grabbed her arm.
~~~

"Do you have something to tell me?" he demanded.

"No, why would you ask me that?"

"Are you pregnant?"

"No, Julian, I'm not pregnant." She tried to pull her arm from his grasp. "Could you let go of me, please?"

"I don't believe you. If you're not pregnant, why would you have a nursery? Why would Anastashia have a package for you?"

"See, I knew you were following me. You need to stop this. I don't know what else to say to make you understand that what we had is over. I can never go back to you." Isabella watched him carefully, not wanting to upset him further. She tried to calm her voice. "Julian, please, could you let go of my arm?"

His eyes weren't quite right, she noticed, as if he was on some kind of drug. "I think you are pregnant, and that would make that baby mine. I'm telling you right now, Grayson will not raise my child."

"Let go. You're hurting me." She tugged her arm away, but he only held on tighter.

"I don't mean to hurt you, but I'm not letting go until you tell me the truth."

Isabella sighed. "Grayson turned his old studio into a nursery to surprise me, but that's it. There is no baby, and there will be no baby for a while. I need to fix the damage that I did first—that we did—before I can bring a child into this world."

Julian looked at her stomach, and then back up to her face. "I'm disappointed. I wish you were pregnant. I'd take you and our baby far away from here, where we could be a family. We could be happy like we were before. You and I don't have to fix any damage. You know I love you, and I know that deep down you love me too."

She remained silent. The more he spoke, the more his delusion became obvious. But she also needed to keep him calm and avoid angering him. Isabella set down her packages and placed her left hand on his, which was still clamped around her right wrist.

"Julian, you know that if things were different, I would." She rubbed his hand. "If our situation was different, I would . . . but it's not. What we had was wonderful, but it wasn't right. I was wrong to be with you when I was already with someone else."

Julian bowed his head, letting his gaze rest on her hand. Isabella felt his grip starting to loosen on her wrist. She relaxed slightly, knowing that he was finally hearing her. Out of nowhere, he flew backward and landed flat on his ass. Stunned, Isabella turned to see Gia standing beside her.

"Was I not crystal clear enough for you?" Gia yelled at him. "I thought I told you to stay the hell away from her. What more do I have to do or say to get it through that head of yours? She doesn't love you. She never loved you, you moron."

Julian scrambled to his feet and got right up in her face, pushing her with his body. Gia pushed back with her chest. Isabella thought that he was literally going to beat the shit out of her.

He jabbed a finger in her chest. "If you ever fucking touch me like that again, whore, I swear it will be the last thing you do."

"Is that right, tough guy?"

"You can count on it, bitch."

Gia wiggled her fingers in front of his face. "Ooooh, I'm so afraid."

His face was filled with vengeance. "You should be."

He looked at Isabella, who watched, horrified by their exchange. His demeanor changed when he saw her face. "I'm sorry, Bella," he whispered before scurrying away with his head hung low.

Isabella knew he was in pain, and regardless of what he had done, she knew she was the cause of that pain. She looked at Gia. "Are you out of your mind? What the hell is wrong with you?"

"Calm down, Izzie. He needs to be taught a lesson. He can't come up to you whenever he pleases, grabbing you and taking you hostage."

"I had it under control. I was getting through to him, until you flew in here like a crazy nut, knocking him over. Do you know the saying, 'Don't poke a sleeping bear'?"

"Yes, but—"

"But nothing. Don't poke the bear. He's not right, and I don't need you pissing him off further."

"You're being overdramatic. He's just a lovesick, wounded puppy, wandering around looking for your attention. He's harmless."

"Regardless, don't poke the bear, don't talk to the bear, and for the love of God don't go near the bear again. Is that clear?"

Gia blew her breath out in a huff. "You got it. Whatever makes you happy."

"What makes me happy is peace. I want everything to be peaceful again. I hate feeling this way. I can take care of myself. Understood?"

"I know you can. You're right. I can get overprotective sometimes. I'm sorry, Izzie."

The two friends hugged, and Isabella ventured home, where she knew Grayson was waiting for her.

When Isabella got off the elevator on her floor, she noticed a trail of rose petals that went from the elevator doors, down the hallway, and around the corner. Isabella smiled, wondering what surprise Grayson had in store for her. On the front door of the loft was a note telling her to shower first, then to come back down and follow the petals. First she took her bags to the nursery and placed the new bedding in a drawer. She was about to crinkle up the bag when she felt something inside and pulled it out. It was a beautiful, scrolled black picture frame that Anastashia must have placed in the bag. Isabella smiled at her friend's thoughtfulness. She set the empty frame on the bookcase and headed to the bedroom to shower.

Isabella hurried through her shower, kept her makeup light and simple, put her hair up into a high ponytail, and threw on a pair of jeans and white tank top with a black cardigan, keeping it casual.

Isabella raced back down the steps and out into the hallway, back to her trail of roses. She shut the loft door and ventured down the hallway, following the trail around the corner and down another short hallway that ended at the fire escape. She pushed opened the door, revealing more rose petals on the stairs that led up to the roof. She smiled, knowing exactly where Grayson was now.

At the top of the stairwell, she pushed open the door to the roof and peeked out. There, in the corner of the rooftop, stood Grayson, surrounded by rose petals and hundreds of candles. He had set up a small bistro table covered in white linens, and he had dinner ready and waiting for her. Isabella smiled as she walked over to him.

"This is amazingly romantic. I'm speechless."

He walked around the table, took her into his arms, and kissed her. "I'm glad you approve. I wanted tonight to be special for you. Happy birthday, Izzie." He smiled.

"I'd hoped we were forgetting birthdays this year."

He laughed. "Absolutely not. This is your day, and we're celebrating."

"Well, can we at least call it something else? You know how much I adore birthdays." She frowned.

Grayson thought for a moment. "How about we celebrate the past two months of being together? Is that better?"

"Wow, has it been two months already?"

"It has. I can't believe it either. I guess time flies when you're having fun and things are going great. I lucked out on the weather today too, so we can also celebrate that if you like."

"You sure did." The warm temperature reminded her that summer was coming soon. "I'm glad we opted to work things out. I can't imagine spending my life without you." She kissed him. "I'm so happy right now."

Grayson took her face in his hands. "I love you more than anything, Isabella. Thank you for having enough faith in me, in us, to stay." He kissed her again, slowly at first, then with more urgency. Isabella reached for him, pulling him closer to her. They stood on the rooftop, holding each other tight, simply enjoying their love for one another. All of a sudden, Grayson gasped and spun her around, pointing at the sky.

"Look, a shooting star. Quick, make a wish."

Isabella closed her eyes, as he did, and they both made a wish. Still looking up to the sky, Isabella rested her head back on his shoulder.

"It's such a beautiful night. The sky is so clear. Look at all those stars."

"Mmmm, yes it is, a perfect night for your birthday—I mean, our romantic rooftop dinner." Grayson winked at her.

She let her gaze wander to the street six stories below. After a moment, she moved away from him and rested her hand on the railing, leaning over.

"What is it, baby?" he asked.

"I thought I saw something," Isabella mumbled, searching the darkness between the streetlights.

He peeked over the railing. "I don't see anything down there."

Isabella shook her head. "Maybe I was seeing things. I could have sworn someone was down there under the streetlight, watching us."

"You and your overactive imagination," Grayson teased her. "Whoever it was, they were probably just envying us for our romantic dinner up here." Grayson pulled her by the hand, leading her away from the railing. "Come, sit down. Let's enjoy our dinner."

She gave him a small smile, but glanced back to the street below, silently praying that the "someone" he was referring to was not Julian.

Despite her uneasiness, Isabella and Grayson had a wonderful dinner. As the breezes began to pick up, they ventured back down to their loft, seeking warmth. Grayson pulled the door open, and they felt the warm air upon them.

"It was getting chilly up there. I didn't realize how cold I was until I came in." Isabella shivered as she wrapped her arms around herself.

"Come here and let me warm you up." He wrapped his arms around her as they walked to the living room.

"Mmmm, that feels so good. Thank you." Something caught her eye on the sofa, and she pulled away. "Grayson, did you take out that blanket?"

"Do you want a blanket?"

"No, I'm asking if you took it out of the closet." Isabella pointed to the blanket on the arm of the sofa.

"Nope. You must have put it there."

"No . . . no, I didn't."

"Izzie, you must have. I don't even know where you keep those blankets."

"I keep them in that front closet by the door. The point is, I did not pull that blanket out. I'm telling you, I didn't do it." She suddenly felt flushed.

"What are you getting yourself so worked up about? Big deal, there's a blanket on the sofa." He laughed.

"You're not getting it. If you or I didn't pull it out, who did?"

"No one was in here. I think you're allowing your mind to play tricks on you. First you think you see someone outside, and now you think someone was in here. What's going on with you?"

"I think it's Julian," she whispered.

Grayson's body stiffened. "Why would you think that? Are you talking to him again?"

"No, I swear I'm not. But I keep seeing him around. I feel like he's watching me. I'm telling you, he's not right."

"I think you're being paranoid. He does live around here, does he not?"

"I'm not being paranoid." She was starting to get annoyed.

"What reason would he have for coming into our home? That's absurd, Izzie."

"Because he's obsessed with me. I'm telling you, I don't feel right about him."

"But why would he pull a blanket out if he came here? That doesn't make sense."

"Because . . . we used to take that blanket to the park." Isabella lowered her eyes to the floor. "We would go there together and have lunch. He knew where it was. He's been in here before. He knew where I kept it." Isabella was having difficulty catching her breath, thinking he had been in her home. She felt violated.

Grayson grabbed her arms and sat her down on the sofa. "Calm down before you pass out. Maybe I pulled out the blanket looking for something and I don't remember. There's no way Julian could have gotten in here. That's insane."

Isabella kept shaking her head, her eyes wild with fear. "No, no, no. You said you didn't do it."

As she began to cry, Grayson took her face between his hands and forced her to look at him.

"Baby, stop. No one was in here. If you want, I'll go through the entire loft, checking every nook and cranny. Will that make you feel better?"

Isabella nodded. "Please. I won't be able to sleep unless you do."

He sighed and kissed her forehead. "Okay, stay here."

"No way. I'm coming with you."

"Honestly, Isabella, what has gotten into you?" He laughed weakly.

"Don't laugh at me. You haven't seen the things I've seen lately."

"Come on." Grayson pulled her off the sofa. "You've watched too many scary movies."

Isabella glared at him, frustrated that he was not taking her seriously. They spent the next twenty minutes walking through the loft room by room, checking every closet, behind every door, and even under their bed. Although Isabella was satisfied that the loft was clear, she still made him double-check the front door before coming to bed.

~~~

Over the next week, Isabella felt like she was constantly looking over her shoulder. Even though she hadn't seen Julian since that day in front of Anastashia's boutique, something felt off. It was making her crazy. She started to think Grayson was right, that her imagination was getting the best of her. She decided to try relaxing, and started treating herself to massages. She even began taking a yoga class, trying to find some inner balance.

One evening, while Grayson was at his studio creating the paintings for the Vanderbeck project, Isabella was sitting in the nursery going through some papers she had brought home from work. She loved being in there. The room relaxed and comforted her. Sometimes she just rocked in the rocking chair, daydreaming about the baby she and Grayson would have one day. She knew that their relationship was stronger, which allowed her mind to wander to the little bundle that she knew would bring them so much joy.

She reached for her steaming cup of green tea on the ottoman and brought it to her lips. As she blew on it to cool it off, she glanced at the bookcase and noticed the frame Anastashia had given her, remembering that she still hadn't thanked her for it. She did a double-take and gasped. She shot off the sofa, spilling her entire cup of tea on the floor, and snatched the frame off the shelf.

Isabella covered her mouth and shrieked in horror. A picture of her and Julian now sat in the frame. The room spun around her, and she lowered herself to the floor. With her back against the bookcase, she
~~~

clutched the frame, trying to slow her breathing. She fell forward as she began to sob.

"Why? Why are you doing this to me?" she screamed. "Please stop, please stop . . ." she rambled on and on.

That was how Grayson found her, huddled in a ball, sobbing hysterically and yelling at someone who wasn't even there.

"Izzie, what the hell is going on?"

She pushed the frame into his face. "Look, look at this. Tell me I'm just being paranoid now. How did this get in here?"

Grayson took the frame from her, focusing on the picture of her and Julian. He looked back at her. "I don't know, Isabella. Are you sure you didn't put it in there?"

Isabella's mouth fell open. "Are you seriously asking me that? Why would I ever do such a thing? I don't even have a photo of Julian and me together. I'm telling you that when I put that frame on the bookcase, it was empty. He was in here, Grayson, I know it." She started to cry louder and pulled at his shirt. "It was that night, the other night when the blanket was out. I knew he was in here, and you didn't believe me. I told you, Grayson, I told you."

"Isabella, you need to calm down. Baby, please calm down." He pulled her to her feet and started to pace back and forth. "Who took this picture?"

"The waitress did. We were in Milan, having dinner. Julian asked her to take a photo of us. Do you believe me now? I didn't put that picture in that frame, and unless you did, Julian was in here. He was in this house."

Grayson looked at her, exhaling deeply. "Okay, I believe you. What do you want me to do about it? How do you want me to deal with your problem, Isabella?"

"My problem?" she yelled. "How is this just my problem? He's coming into *our* home now."

"Well, I certainly didn't sleep with him or bring him into our home. It's obvious that I'm not the one he's after," he snapped.

"What the hell is wrong with you? I'm your wife, damn it. You should be concerned for my safety. You should be willing to take care of the situation. Don't you care?" She was shocked.

"I think that I've shown you over the past few months that I care plenty. Do you have any idea how hard this has been for me? Do you think I enjoy thinking about him or even hearing his name? I don't. I try to avoid the thought of him and his existence at all costs, but time and time again, you keep bringing him up, making him present in our relationship."

"Unbelievable." Isabella snatched the frame from his hands. "Don't worry, Grayson, I won't bother you anymore. I'll take care of my own problem." She stormed out of the nursery.

Grayson heard their bathroom door slam shut. He sat down on the sofa, running his hands through his hair. He leaned his head back, closed his eyes, and exhaled loudly. This had to end. He knew she was quickly coming unglued.

~~~

The next morning Isabella headed straight over to Julian's apartment with the picture frame in hand. She stood at his door, pounding so hard the whole wall shook. With no answer, she banged harder, calling his name. After ten minutes of pounding and two nasty looks from a neighbor, Isabella gave up. As she stepped outside, a taxi cab pulled up in front of the building. She froze when she saw Julian get out of the back of the cab. As he turned back to pay the driver, she raced down the steps, knocking into him from behind and slamming him into the cab. He turned around with his arms raised, ready to retaliate, but stopped, seeing that it was Isabella.

"Are you insane?" he said. "What the hell is wrong with you? I almost hit you."

Isabella jabbed the frame into his chest. "Am *I* insane? I was going to ask you the same thing. What the hell is this, Julian?"

Perplexed, he looked down. "It looks like a picture frame. I'm sure you've seen one before."

"Don't be a smartass. I'm talking about the picture inside the frame. How did that get there?"

"Well, I'm assuming you opened the back and put it inside. Isn't that how it usually works?"

Isabella punched him in the arm. "You know what I mean. Why would you break into my home and do that?"

"I have no idea what you're talking about," he snapped.

"Don't deny it. I know you were in my house, went into my nursery, and put that picture in the frame."

"I'm telling you, I did no such thing. First of all, I would never do something like that to you, or to anyone for that matter. Second, I've been out of town." Julian pointed to the cab. "I'm just getting back from the airport. Ask the driver yourself. He just picked me up. My luggage is in the trunk. There's no way I could have been at your house."

Isabella's mind was going a mile a minute. She went to the back of the cab and threw open the trunk. Just as Julian had said, his luggage
~~~

was in there. Dazed, Isabella backed away from the cab.

"But . . . but I just saw you the other day."

Julian cautiously walked toward her. "Yes, you did. I left after that. Gia got me so angry that I had to get out of here. When I saw the look on your face, how horrified you were by my behavior, it killed me. I knew I needed to get away and clear my mind. I packed a bag, headed to the airport, and jumped on the first plane out of here."

Isabella shook her head. "No . . . no, I know it was you. It had to be you." She started to cry.

"Bella, please don't cry. I never like to see you cry." Julian reached for her, but she took another step back, wrapping her arms around herself to block his touch.

Julian sighed and dropped his hand. "Bella, are you okay?"

Isabella looked up, her eyes glazed over. "No, I'm not okay. How could I be okay? I don't know what to think right now. I don't know what to do, and it's your fault. You've completely destroyed me."

"Don't say that. I didn't do this to you. What purpose would it serve me? I love you too much."

"I don't know, Julian. What purpose *does* it serve you?" she echoed.

"It doesn't. It only makes you angry and afraid of me. What you need to be asking yourself is, who gains from that? Who gains from you being angry with me? Who could possibly want to punish you?" Julian raised an eyebrow.

Knowing just what he was implying, Isabella continued to shake her head as she backed away from him. Julian tried reaching out to her again, but she turned and ran off down the street.

Chapter 27

Isabella did her best to muddle through the workweek. She mentioned nothing to Grayson of her confrontation with Julian. Unable to process what had happened and unwilling to deal with the turmoil in her mind, she buried it deeper inside.

Wanting to get a start on the weekend after a stressful week, Isabella left the office earlier than her usual 8:00 p.m. First she popped into Gia's office and reminded her of the promise she had made to go to yoga with her the following morning. Gia groaned in protest, saying she had plans that night, which she was sure would turn into morning breakfast.

"I don't care. You promised me, Gia. I really need this."

"Why do I have to go with you?" Gia whined.

"Oh, stop your bitching and be a good friend and go with me. A little yoga is not going to kill you."

"If I'm tied up like a pretzel the night before, I'd say it very well could."

Isabella sighed loudly. "Who are we granting the privilege to this time?"

Gia shrugged her shoulders. "Whoever I deem worthy at the bar tonight." She smiled.

"How wonderful," Isabella said sarcastically. "Don't you think it's time to find some nice guy and settle down?"

Gia grabbed her wastebasket and acted like she was throwing up. "Yeah, I'm thinking no on that. I see how well that's working for you, but thanks for the suggestion." Gia gave her a thumbs-up.

"I seriously have no idea why I'm friends with you."

Gia laughed. "Because your life would be boring without me, and you know it."

There's been more than enough excitement in my life lately, Isabella thought.

Isabella had Sebastian drop her off at Grayson's studio. She couldn't remember the last time she had even been there—a year ago, at least. She was looking forward to getting a sneak peek at the artwork for the Vanderbeck project—if Grayson would allow her one, that is.

Once inside, Isabella remembered why it was she didn't come there. The studio was in a small, rundown industrial building that needed to be knocked down. The corridors were dark and musty, with exposed, rusty pipes and broken concrete. Every unit had a gray metal door with badly peeling paint. There was not one speck of flooring in the entire building. The concrete showed years of scuffs, spills, and what Isabella hoped were not remnants of a crime scene stain.

Isabella made her way up to Grayson's studio on the second floor, trying to breathe only through her mouth to avoid smelling the stench that permeated the hallway. As she opened the door to the studio, she saw Grayson standing next to his old sofa, folding a sheet. Isabella smiled, remembering the hundreds of movie nights and makeout sessions they'd had on that sofa in his apartment many years ago. It was on its last leg then, and she couldn't believe it was still standing.

"I can't believe you still have that smelly old sofa."

Startled, Grayson turned. "Izzie, what are you doing here?"

"I thought I would come by and surprise you." Isabella smiled as she walked over to him. "Looks like I did," she said as she kissed him on his lips.

"Well, I'm surprised. You never come here. I believe the last time you were here you mumbled something like, 'I'm never coming back to this pisshole.'"

Isabella laughed. "Very good memory you have. I see nothing has changed. It was a pisshole then, and it's still a pisshole today. What is that God-awful stench in the hallway?"

"What stench?"

Isabella crinkled up her nose. "You obviously spend way too much time here, if you don't smell that. I think something or someone is rotting away behind one of those doors."

"It's an old building, Izzie. They smell." He shrugged his shoulders. "Not everything can smell like Fifth Avenue. You should probably get going so the smell doesn't seep into your Gucci dress."

"Ha ha, very funny. It's Prada, by the way. You really need to learn your designers."

"I'll pass. Why is it that you're here again?"

"No real reason. I just wanted to see you."

"Mm-hm," Grayson mumbled, as if he didn't believe her. "I know you better than that. Are you sure it has nothing to do with you checking up on my work for Mr. Vanderbeck?"

Isabella's mouth fell open. "I'm shocked that you would even imply that."

"You know how I feel about being checked up on."

"I wasn't—" Isabella paused as the bathroom door opened.

"Hey doll, you know what I was thinking?" Evette Vanderbeck said as she emerged from the bathroom, fastening the belt on her jeans.

"Evette?" Isabella questioned, surprised to see her there.

Evette looked up. "Oh, hey Isabella. How are you?"

"I'm good, thanks. What are you doing here?"

"I came by to check up on the progress of the art pieces. Daddy made it clear that he wanted me to stay on top of it . . . being in charge of the creative end and all." Evette smiled. "I've been working with Grayson to make sure the pieces are exactly what Daddy wants."

Isabella shot Grayson a nasty look, then turned back to Evette. "I didn't know you guys were working together."

"Yeah, for a while now. Being an artist myself, I know how great it is to be able to bounce ideas off of another artist. I think the pieces are coming along fabulously."

Isabella felt her skin crawl, irritated that Grayson never allowed her any input in his art, or even let her see it, for that matter.

"Well, isn't that nice," she said sarcastically, smiling at Evette. "I'm sure Grayson has appreciated you sharing your ideas with him. Haven't you, Grayson?" Isabella glared at him.

Grayson smiled slightly. "Yes, but Evette already knows what a big help she's been."

Isabella clapped her hands together. "Well now, on that note, I think I'm going to leave and let you two get back to your work. It was great seeing you, Evette. Please tell your father I said hello." She turned to Grayson. "I'll see you later, *doll.*"

Her stilettos clicked harshly on the concrete as she stalked to the door. She paused at the doorway and turned back. "Evette, if I were you, I'd have your father renegotiate the contracts for the art, seeing as how you've had a lot of input in the pieces. There's no reason why Grayson should reap all the benefits." Not waiting for a response, Isabella winked at Grayson and left.

Isabella hailed a cab and headed for home. Still fuming, she called Gia. Before she could say a word, Gia cut her off.

"Izzie, I'm sorry, I can't talk right now. I'm running late. I still have to jump in the shower. Can I call you in a bit?"

Isabella let out a sigh. "Sure. Please call me back, though. I need to talk to you."

"I will, I promise. I love you. Bye." Gia ended the call before hearing Isabella's "Love you too."

Back at the loft, Isabella spent the remainder of the night drowning her anger in several tall glasses of vodka and soda—mainly vodka with a splash of soda. With no return call from Gia, Isabella tried reaching her at least a dozen times, getting more annoyed each time her voicemail picked up. What annoyed her further was the fact that Grayson still hadn't bothered to come home. Where the hell was he? She finally stumbled up to her bedroom around one in the morning and passed out.

~~~

Isabella woke the next morning to the sound of her alarm going off. She reached over and slammed her hand down on the snooze button. Her head was pounding from the previous night's drinking binge. She closed her eyes and massaged her temples, wondering why she had done that to herself. Then she remembered. She opened her eyes and looked at the other side of the bed. Grayson lay next to her, snoring away. She wondered what time he had crawled in.

Rolling over on her side, she reached for her phone on the nightstand to see if Gia had called or texted. Nothing. She whipped the covers off and went to the bathroom, where she doused her face with cold water over and over again, trying to calm the fire in her cheeks. She couldn't remember the last time she had felt that bad from drinking. *How much did I have?* she wondered. Isabella swallowed some aspirin, threw her hair up in a ponytail, did a fast, two-minute make-up job, and dressed in a pair of sweats and a T-shirt. She grabbed a zip-up sweatshirt off the hook behind her door and went downstairs to make some coffee—strong coffee.

With her travel mug in hand, she hailed a cab, jumped inside, and took off to Gia's apartment. With any luck, she could stop her from going to the yoga studio. There would be no downward dog position for Isabella that morning. The only down position she was willing to engage in involved her entire body on a sofa with a pillow.

She took the stairs up to the third floor and found Gia's apartment at the end of the hallway. As she was about to knock, she noticed Gia's keys dangling from the door handle. She rolled her eyes, envisioning Gia and some guy feverishly lip-locked, trying to make their way into her apartment as they groped each other. *Not a smart move leaving the keys in the lock, especially in New York*, Isabella thought.

There was no answer after several vigorous knocks. Isabella wasn't sure if she should use the keys and go inside; she wasn't interested in seeing some naked man sprawled out in the apartment. She contemplated what to do. *Screw it*, she thought, and turned the key to
~~~

unlock the door, but it was already unlocked. Pulling the key out, she stepped inside.

The apartment was dark and had a funky smell. Knowing Gia wasn't the best housekeeper, Isabella carefully maneuvered through the living room, stepping over clothes and empty food containers. She was trying to avoid stepping on anything squishy or that was furry and squeaked.

Making her way down the short hallway to the bedroom, Isabella called Gia's name, but there was no answer. Isabella sighed, knowing she would find her passed out on the bathroom floor or hanging off the side of the bed. She hoped Gia was alone and not with some stranger, creating an awkward moment.

"I promise I'll call you back," Isabella mumbled, remembering Gia's words. *Some friend*, she thought.

"Gia?" she whispered as she peeked into the dark bedroom. She thought she saw Gia lying on the bed, but couldn't tell for sure. Isabella whispered her name again; still nothing. Irritated, she felt for the light switch she knew was to the right of the door. She switched on the light and gasped.

Gia's naked body lay sprawled on the bed, bound with rope by her hands and feet to the bed posts. Her open eyes stared blankly ahead. Over her mouth was a single piece of duct tape, and across her throat was a large gash. Blood soaked the bed beneath her. On the wall behind the bed, the word *WHORE* had been written in blood.

Isabella screamed and fell back into the hallway, covering her eyes, shielding them from the horror before her. Her throat convulsed, and she ran to the front door with her hand over her mouth. Just as she reached the threshold, she leaned over and violently threw up. Sweating and shaking, she pulled out her cell phone and dialed 911.

The operator kept telling her to calm down so she could get the address, but Isabella could barely speak through her hysterical sobbing. Within minutes, she heard sirens. She hung up and dialed Grayson.

"Hello," he said, still groggy.

"Grayson, I need you!" she screamed.

"Izzie, what the hell is going on? Are you okay?"

"She's dead. She's dead." She broke down crying.

"Who is dead? What are you talking about?"

She tried to catch her breath, but she couldn't.

"Isabella, calm down and talk to me. Who is dead?"

"It was him," she cried out. "I know he did this to her."

"You are not making any sense. Who is dead?"

Isabella felt her stomach start to churn. She swallowed hard. "Gia's dead . . . I know Julian killed her."

There was a long pause. "Listen to me, Izzie, listen to me carefully. Don't say a word to anyone. Do you hear me?"

"She's dead," Isabella sobbed, barely hearing him.

"Do you understand, Isabella? Don't talk to anyone. I'm on my way, okay?"

Unable to answer, she pulled her knees to her chest, rocking herself back and forth as she cried.

"Answer me. Do you hear me?"

"Yes," she whispered.

"Good. I mean it, Isabella, not a word. I'm on my way."

Chapter 28

Pushing through the crowd that had gathered in front of Gia's apartment building, Grayson was able to find a police officer who allowed him permission to enter the building. Once inside, he took off up the stairs, taking two, sometimes three steps at a time. When he arrived on the third floor, he found a group of police officers gathered in front of Gia's apartment and Isabella sitting in the corner of the hallway with a blanket wrapped around her shoulders, knees pulled to her chest, shaking as she rocked back and forth. She was as pale as a ghost. Her dark brown eyes were lifeless and blankly focused on the air in front of her. She looked disturbed—maybe eerie was more like it, he thought. He bent down in front of her, his face directly in front of hers, and stared into her eyes, which now looked through him. Even though she was looking at him, nothing registered with her.

"Isabella, it's me, baby," he whispered. "I'm here to take you home."

She stared ahead blankly, unable to respond.

Grayson took her chin in his hand. "Isabella, look at me. It's me. I'm here to take you home. Isabella, can you look at me?"

Grayson watched her eyes carefully. It took a moment, but he could see she was beginning to process his presence in front of her. He kept speaking to her. "Isabella, I'm here for you, baby. I'm going to take you home. I know you must want to go home. Isabella, do you hear me?"

She blinked her eyes, bringing them into focus. "Gia's dead," she whispered as a single tear ran down her face.

Grayson wiped away the tear. "I know, baby. It's going to be okay. You're going to be okay."

Isabella shook her head. "No, it's not okay. It's my fault."

"Shhh, don't say that. We don't know what happened."

"I do. I know exactly what happened."

Grayson looked around, making sure no one had overheard her. Relieved that everyone seemed to be busy, he turned his attention back to her. "Isabella, you need to stop talking. You don't want any problems for yourself right now. Don't utter another word. Do you understand what I'm saying?"

She stared into his eyes. "Gia's dead. It's my fault."

Grayson exhaled loudly in frustration. He knew he needed to get her out of there fast. He stood up and approached one of the detectives standing just outside the apartment.

He introduced himself and pointed to Isabella. "That's Isabella, my wife. As you can see, she's in no condition to speak right now. Could I get your permission to take her home for the time being?"

The detective extended his hand. "Mr. Hughes, I'm Detective Patterson, and this is Detective Stone." He pointed to the man standing next to him. "We've been assigned to work on this case. Can you tell me when it was that you think your wife last had contact with Ms. Hausen?"

"I'm just guessing, but I'd say that was yesterday around seven. Isabella left work and came to my studio just after that. They work together, and I assume Gia would have been at the office. You can verify that with James, Isabella's assistant."

Detective Stone jotted down notes on his notepad. "Is there anyone you can think of who would want to harm Ms. Hausen?"

Grayson shook his head. "Gia didn't have enemies. She was somewhat of a free spirit. She marched to the beat of her own drum. What she did have, though, were a lot of male friends. She was . . ." Grayson paused, searching for the appropriate word. "Not traditional when it came to dating, if you get my drift."

"So there was no steady boyfriend then?" Patterson asked.

"No, the only thing that was steady in Gia's life besides her job was the constant traffic of men in and out of her place. That's the way she liked it, and she made no apologies for it. I believe Isabella once told me that Gia was married and had gotten hurt really bad, so settling down for her wasn't an option."

The detectives nodded. "We got you," Detective Patterson said. "We'll need to speak to your wife sooner rather than later. We're hoping she can shed some light as to where Ms. Hausen was and who she was with last night."

"Of course. For now, I'd like to get her home and call her doctor, if you don't mind."

Detective Stone looked at Isabella, who still sat in the hallway, rocking back and forth. "I think that's a good idea. I recommend that she be taken to the hospital, though. They can admit her and administer sedatives." Detective Stone looked Grayson in the eye. "What she witnessed was extremely gruesome. She'll have a hard time dealing with that."

"Thank you, Detective. I'll make sure she gets what she needs."

"If you like, we can have the ambulance take her over."

"That's not necessary. I have my car. I'll get her over there myself."

Grayson gave the detectives his contact information and returned to Isabella. He scooped her up from the floor, cradling her in his arms like a baby. She rested her head on his shoulder, tightly squeezing her eyes closed as if she were a child, willing away a bogeyman in front of her. Grayson sighed, knowing she would never fully recover from Gia's death.

He carried her down three flights of steps and out to the street. He carefully placed her in the passenger seat of his car, which was parked around the corner, buckled her in, and took off to the hospital.

An hour later, Grayson stood in the corner of the hospital room, watching as the IV fluid dripped down the long tube into her arm. She looked broken as she lay in the hospital bed, covered by several warming blankets, with an oxygen tube resting just inside her nose. Her face was even paler than usual, and her cheeks looked sunken. Grayson knew she had most likely taken her last emotional blow. There was no doubt in his mind that she would be a mental mess. The doctor had given her a sedative to help ease her suffering and aid her sleep. She had not uttered a word except to repeat over and over that Gia was dead.

"Mr. Hughes, I'm Dr. Clifton. I came to check on your wife's progress."

Grayson looked up to see an older gentleman standing in the doorway. He was tall with blue eyes, a friendly smile, and salt-and-pepper hair—probably a big hit with the nurses who worked for him. Grayson just nodded as Dr. Clifton entered the room and began looking over Isabella's chart.

"I'm assuming that Dr. Radcliff spoke to you this morning on Isabella's condition and what things you need to watch for when you take her home?"

"Honestly, if he did, I wasn't paying attention. Things were a little crazy when we got here. Could you possibly refresh my memory?"

Dr. Clifton gave Grayson a disapproving look. "Your wife is suffering from traumatic shock, Mr. Hughes. While it is common for people to go into shock after witnessing a horrific event and recover fully, we are more concerned about the lasting effects for those who cannot. Your wife will most likely experience insomnia and nightmares, agitation, fatigue, and difficulty concentrating. She may be easily startled. You may notice her becoming irritable and having mood swings. She could seem confused and anxious. She may even start to withdraw from you and her colleagues due to grief and guilt. It's a condition known as PTSD."

"Post traumatic stress disorder?" Grayson chuckled. "With all due respect, Dr. Clifton, she wasn't in combat."

The doctor frowned. "Mr. Hughes, I don't think you understand the severity of her condition. Your wife has suffered a traumatic experience. From what Detective Patterson and Stone have told me, the scene was disturbing. She may require much more than a sedative to sleep it off."

"Like?"

Dr. Clifton seemed irritated by Grayson's nonchalant attitude. "Like someone who cares about her and will look out for signs that she is suffering from PTSD."

"I can assure you, Dr. Clifton, she's in good hands." Grayson smiled.

"If you say so, Mr. Hughes. But understand that if her condition worsens, or you notice any of these symptoms, it's important that you seek out professional help for her. It's also imperative that she remain calm and avoid situations or persons that could agitate her. I'll have the nurse go over some information with you before you leave."

Grayson looked over at Isabella, who was sleeping soundly. "And when would that be? I'm not a big fan of hospitals."

"I'll be keeping her overnight so we can monitor her closely. You can take her home in the morning."

Grayson sighed. "Morning, as in first thing?"

"You are more than welcome to leave. Isabella will be sleeping the remainder of the night, and if she does wake, she will be comfortable here."

"I just might do that. I'd rather get a good night's sleep and be fresh for her tomorrow."

Dr. Clifton nodded. "Very well, I'll let the nurses know. Please leave your cell phone number at the desk, just in case they need to reach you during the night."

"I will do that, thank you."

After the doctor left, Grayson stood by the bed watching Isabella for a few more minutes. Her breathing was slow, and she seemed very calm and peaceful.

"Sleep tight," Grayson said as he left.

~~~

Isabella's eyes fluttered open. She felt dazed, as if she had been drugged. Her eyelids were heavy, so heavy that she had to fight to keep them open. Squinting, she made out a large clock that hung on the wall across from her, which read 2:25 a.m. As she rubbed her eyes to clear away the fuzziness, she noticed a long tube attached to her hand.
~~~

An IV bag filled with clear fluid hung from a post attached to the bed. It was then that she remembered. Tears filled her eyes.

"You're okay," said a voice. "You're in the hospital. Everything is going to be okay."

Isabella's breath caught. She searched the darkness of her room. "Grayson, is that you?" Someone was sitting in the chair in the corner of her room. "Grayson?"

The figure stood up and walked over to her. Isabella's head bobbed back as her eyes closed. She forced them open again, and they grew wide as the figure came into focus.

Julian smiled. "You're going to be okay. Everything is going to be okay."

Frozen with fear, Isabella felt the blood drain from her face. She broke out in a sweat, and a wave of nausea came over her.

"Bella, Bella." Julian wiped the beads of sweat from her forehead. "You look as pale as a ghost. What's wrong, baby? I'm worried about you."

Isabella started to shake from his touch. "It was you. I know it was you."

"Yes, Bella, it's me. I'm here with you. I came as soon as I heard. I told you I would always be here for you, my love."

Isabella shook her head. "No, no, no. You killed her," she said weakly. "I know you did it."

Julian grabbed the IV bag and read the label. "What kind of drugs do they have you on, baby? You're not making any sense. I didn't kill anyone." Julian reached for her forehead again, but Isabella jerked away.

"I heard the way you spoke to her, and I saw the look in your eyes. I know it was you."

His laugh was sinister. "You think I'd take the chance of ruining my life to kill that whore? Considering the number of strange men she took back to her place, someone was bound to kill her sooner or later."

"It wasn't like that, and you know it. Don't talk about her like that."

"It was exactly like that. She obviously didn't share with you the details of the time she invited me over to her apartment." Julian rubbed his chin. "Let me see, I can't remember if that was before we left for Milan or after."

"Stop it. Gia would never have done that."

"You must not have known her as well as you think you did." Julian snapped his fingers. "Ah, right. It was after we got back from Milan. Yes, I remember it well. She was comforting me when you decided to wander back to that loser husband of yours."

Isabella covered her ears. "You're evil. I'm not listening to you." She started to cry. "She was my friend. How could you do that to me? She was innocent in all this. She was just protecting me. Why? Why would you do that?"

Julian grabbed her chin, forcing her face to his. She felt his breath on her cheek. "Gia wasn't as innocent as you think. It's not right to accuse someone of a crime when you have no proof. For the second time, I'm telling you I did not do it." Julian pushed her face away with his hand.

Filled with fear, Isabella felt around the bed for the nurse's call button she knew had to be there. Julian chuckled. Isabella looked up at him to see the call button dangling from his hand.

"Looking for this?" He smiled wickedly.

Isabella glared at him. "Get out of here before I scream. I don't think it would take long before someone came bursting in here to help me, do you?"

Isabella's body convulsed as Julian leaned over her. He grabbed the back of her hair, bringing her face within inches of his. "I'd be very careful how you proceed. Gia wasn't so careful, and look what happened to her."

He stared at her for a moment, then brought his lips down hard on hers, forcing his tongue into her mouth. Isabella fought to push him away, but her weakened state was no match for his strength. She took a breath to scream, but he put his hand over her mouth. Tears spilled from her eyes as she stared up at him, horrified at what he had become and more certain than ever that he had killed her friend.

Julian brought his finger to his lips. "Shhh." Smiling again, he released his hand from her mouth and bolted out the door.

Isabella squeezed her eyes shut and turned over on her side. She curled into a ball and began rocking herself back and forth.

Chapter 29

"I'm telling you, Izzie, you can't go to the police," Grayson argued.

"I don't understand why not. I know he killed her. Why don't you believe me?"

Grayson had arrived the next morning to bring her home. They still sat in her hospital room, waiting for the doctor's final okay for her to be discharged.

"First of all, you have no proof," Grayson was saying. "Just because he had an argument with her doesn't mean he killed her. Second, I know you loved her and you want there to be justice, but if you go to the police, they'll start digging around, and your dirty little affair with him will be exposed. I don't think that's the kind of publicity you need when you're getting ready to launch a furniture line. The media will have a field day. I also don't think Mr. Vanderbeck will be pleased when you're pegged as the adulterous whore he hired to design his furniture line. Not to mention the suggestion that your lover possibly killed your business partner." He stood and began pacing in the narrow space next to her bed. "Personally, I'd like to keep your affair quiet and not have it blasted all over the news where my friends will find out, making me a laughingstock. Both of us could be destroyed."

Isabella sat up in her hospital bed. "I'm not a whore. That was really cruel."

He raised his voice. "Are you kidding? That's what you picked up from everything I just said to you? Are you on some good drugs right now, or are you just stupid? Did you not hear a word I said?"

"Stop yelling at me. Please stop yelling." She started to cry.

"You need to listen—" Startled by the door opening, Grayson stopped and turned.

It was Dr. Clifton. His eyes moved back and forth between them with a look of concern. "I'm sorry to interrupt. I just came by to check on Isabella this morning before I release her." He went to Isabella, who was rocking back and forth in the bed. "Isabella, how are you doing today?"

"I'm fine," she whispered, looking down at her lap.

"You don't look fine to me. You seem upset. What is upsetting you this morning?" Dr. Clifton glanced at Grayson again.

"Gia's dead. I just want to go home, please."

Dr. Clifton nodded. "I know, but I need to make sure you're stable before I send you home."

Isabella rubbed her face with both hands. "My best friend was murdered. I found her with her feet and hands bound by rope to her bed. She was naked, and there were bruises and scratches all over her body, like someone had beaten and raped her. Her mouth was taped shut to silence her screams, and her throat was slashed open, ensuring she would never speak again." Isabella's voiced cracked, while tears poured down her face. "There was blood everywhere. Her eyes . . . her perfect blue eyes were open. She lay there looking at me, almost begging me to help her, but . . . but I couldn't, I couldn't help her." Her voice rose until she was screaming, and her fists pounded into the bed. "I couldn't help her because she was already dead. So to answer your question, I'm not okay! Would you be okay if you found your friend like that? Would you?"

"Izzie!" Grayson yelled, shocked by her temper.

Dr. Clifton raised his hand to Grayson, motioning for him to stop. "I warned you about agitating her further," he whispered, then turned his attention back to Isabella. "Isabella, I know what you've been through has been very difficult. It would be difficult for anyone. No one is saying that this is going to be easy. It will take some time to recover."

Isabella glared at him. "Don't try to psychoanalyze me. My friend was gruesomely murdered. I have every right to be upset, end of story. I want to go home . . . I want to go home now."

Dr. Clifton sighed. "I think it's best if I have someone come in and talk to you before—"

Isabella cut him off. "Before what? Before I kill myself? I'm not delusional, Doctor . . ." Isabella searched his coat for his nametag. "Clifton. I'm grieving the loss of my friend. Correct me if I'm wrong, but I think tears and anger are part of the grieving process."

Dr. Clifton nodded. "You are correct. I'm just concerned about you. Would you at least humor me and talk to Dr. Lewis before I send you home? It will only take a few minutes."

Her anger deflated, and she fell back against the pillow. "All right, but no matter what, I want to go home. I don't feel safe here."

At that, his eyebrows rose. "Why don't you feel safe? Did something happen to make you feel that way?"

Isabella's mind filled with images of Julian standing over her bed, grinning at her as he grabbed her by her hair. She looked at Grayson who, with a disapproving look, cautioned her to watch what she said.

Isabella shook her head. "No. There's just no privacy here and no locks on the doors. Not knowing what happened to Gia, I'd feel safer at home."

"Okay, let me get Dr. Lewis in here, and we can get you released." Dr. Clifton smiled at her and left, but not before subtly motioning for Grayson to follow him out.

"Baby, I'll be right back," Grayson told her. "I'm going to see if I can get some paperwork started at the front desk so we can get you out of here faster." Grayson kissed her forehead and hurried after the doctor.

Dr. Clifton was standing outside Isabella's room, his arms folded across his chest. As soon as Grayson came out, the doctor laid into him. "What part of 'you need to keep her calm and not agitate her' did you not understand, Mr. Hughes?"

"She was babbling and talking crazy when I got here this morning. I was just trying to talk with her."

"It sounded more like yelling to me. You have to understand that her mind is in a very fragile state right now. Did you see her demeanor completely change in there? One minute she's rocking back and forth, and the next, she's arguing her condition to me like a lawyer would a case. I'm telling you, she is not mentally stable. I will be recommending to Dr. Lewis that she set up outpatient sessions so Isabella can come in and speak to her to work through her feelings. That way we can closely monitor her."

"If you feel that's necessary," Grayson said.

Dr. Clifton stared at him for a long moment. "What concerns me, Mr. Hughes, is you, honestly."

"Me? Why would I concern you?" Grayson asked, showing his irritation.

"Not you, per se, but your attitude toward her. You don't seem like someone who would be very attentive to her, or who cares about how she feels."

"Not that it's any of your business, but Isabella and I have been working through a rough patch lately. That may be what you sense, but I can assure you I will take good care of her. I appreciate your concern, but she will get exactly what she needs. You can count on that."

"I hope you mean that, Mr. Hughes, because she will need you now more than ever." Dr. Clifton looked at Grayson, questioning his sincerity.

"I know my wife, and I know what she needs. I also know my patience is wearing thin with this hospital, so if you could just do your job and get her released, I can take her home, where she wants to be. I know her well, and Isabella wants to be in her own home, surrounded by her own things, resting in her own bed. The sooner you make that happen, the sooner she'll be happy." Grayson glared at him.

Dr. Clifton nodded, not willing to engage in an argument with him. "Very well, Mr. Hughes. I will go get Dr. Lewis."

Within a few hours, Isabella was released with a script for an anti-anxiety medication and had an appointment scheduled to meet with Dr. Lewis two days later.

As Grayson was helping Isabella into his car in front of the hospital, she glanced across the street. Julian stood leaning against a light post, watching her. Panicking, Isabella jumped inside the car and slammed the door behind her.

"Izzie, what's wrong?" Grayson asked as he slid into the driver's seat. "You look like you've seen a ghost."

"It's Julian," she said, ducking down in her seat. "Do you see him? He's by the light post."

"No, Izzie. No one's there."

Isabella took a second look, but he was gone. "I swear, Grayson, he was right there. He was watching me."

Grayson sighed loudly. "You're seeing things again," he muttered as he started the car.

"I know what I saw. I'm not crazy."

Grayson just shook his head and drove off.

Isabella rode the rest of the way home in silence, staring out the window. She tried not to think of Gia, but there were too many reminders along the way: the sushi restaurant where they often ate lunch; the café where they drank coffee and people watched; the boutique with the fabulous purses where they liked to shop; the housewares store where they bought the best accessories for clients; the bar where Gia had busted her heel while trying to hit on some hot guy. There were simply too many memories of Gia all around her. She couldn't believe that she would never see her friend again—the friend who had always been there for her, the friend she had laughed and cried with, the friend she had shared her innermost feelings with, the friend she could never tell goodbye. She kept thinking of things she wished she had said when Gia was still around. Had Gia known that she loved her more than anything? If only she had never hired Julian, none of this would have happened. If she could go back, she would. Things would be different, and Gia would still be alive.

Isabella bowed her head and wept silently, asking forgiveness for the sins that had cost her friend her life.

At home, Grayson prepared some crackers and ginger ale to help settle her stomach. As she nibbled on a cracker, she asked, "Have you talked to James today?"

"I did. He said he was going to stop by and see you later."

"How is he?"

"Upset, but he's okay. I think he's more concerned about you. He wasn't really that close with Gia, you know."

"I know, but they had a brother/sister type of relationship. I know they cared about each other, deep down."

Grayson nodded. "James said that he sent an email out to everyone. He figured it was best the news came from you, so he drafted it from your email. He kept it simple, informing them what had happened and that details regarding Gia's funeral would be forwarded when they became available."

Just hearing the word "funeral" caused her eyes to sting with tears. It made it all too real.

"I'm sure the police have contacted her sister, who lives here. I should touch base with her tomorrow and find out what they're doing. She has no other family . . . *had* no other family."

Grayson rubbed her leg. "It may take some time, but eventually you'll be okay. Everything is fresh in your mind right now. You have to give yourself time."

Isabella shook her head. "I don't think time can ever erase the pain I feel. I can't imagine being okay with this. How could I, when it was my fault?"

"You need to stop saying that. It was not your fault. You can't be one hundred percent sure that Julian killed her. It could have been random. It could have been some guy she screwed over. You really have no idea."

"No, I know. Julian showed up at the hospital. He's not right. I've been telling you that for months now, but you didn't listen to me, and now she's dead."

"Again, where's the proof? You were ranting and raving. It was crazy talk. I think you're looking for someone to blame, and he's an easy target."

"Why are you defending him?" she demanded, her voice rising.

"I'm not defending him, Isabella, but I'm not going to accuse the man of murdering someone just because I detest him for sleeping with my wife. Believe me, if anyone was going to kill someone around here, it would have been me. Think about it. Even with all the anger I feel and how much I despise him, I wouldn't just go out and kill him."

Isabella looked away. “I’m just scared. I don’t want you or me to be next.”

Grayson laughed. “Now you’re being ridiculous. Nothing is going to happen. You’ve become so paranoid.”

Upset that he was not taking her seriously, she turned and pushed her hands into his chest, knocking him back on the sofa. “Don’t laugh at me! This is serious. I’m telling you I’m frightened because I know he’s coming. I don’t want to have to go through this pain again if he does something to you. I can’t, Grayson . . . I just can’t.” Her eyes were wild and full of fear.

His anger quickly rose. He was fed up. He stood and looked down at her. “If that’s what you believe, then I hope it was worth it.”

She stared at him. “I can’t believe you just said that, you asshole!” she yelled.

“What would you have me say? I’m tired of this mess you created. Just when I think we’ve moved past it, *boom*—there’s something else pulling us back. It never seems to go away—or is it that you never let it go away? Why can’t you let it go? Why can’t you let *him* go?” His voice echoed through the loft.

Isabella put her hands over her ears. “Leave me alone!”

“As you wish.” He stormed to the door. “You need to figure this out, and fast. I can’t take it anymore.” He stepped into the hall and slammed the door behind him.

Isabella bowed her head, his words stinging in her ears. She broke down as the reality of it all sank in. She cried for the friend she loved, the beautiful life she had lost, and the heart-wrenching guilt she would forever carry inside her. She lay down on the sofa, her body and mind no longer suppressing the sorrow inside. Suddenly nauseated, she ran to the bathroom and hunched over the toilet as her body violently tried to rid itself of all the medication that had been pumped into her in an effort to numb her pain.

Assured that she had voided everything that could possibly be in her stomach, Isabella steadied herself against the bathroom counter. She turned on the faucet and splashed her face with the icy water. Just as she was returning to the sofa, the intercom buzzed.

She pressed the button. “Yes?”

“Mrs. Hughes, it’s Detective Stone and Detective Patterson. May we come up? We have a few questions for you.”

Isabella sighed. She really wasn’t in the mood for questions. Without responding, she buzzed them in anyway. She opened the loft door just a bit so she wouldn’t have to get back up when they arrived, and curled up on the sofa with a throw blanket wrapped around her.

Within minutes, the loft door opened further as the two detectives made their way inside.

"Mrs. Hughes," said the taller, dark-haired man, "I'm Detective Stone, and this is Detective Patterson. We met the other day at Ms. Hausen's apartment."

Isabella had no recollection of meeting either of them. Detective Stone was at least six feet tall and had a five o'clock shadow that accentuated his high cheekbones. He looked more like a model than a police detective, she thought.

"I'm sorry, but I don't remember you," she said. "You'll have to forgive me."

"No apologies are necessary. I completely understand." Detective Stone smiled. "How are you doing?"

"I'm fine," she lied.

Looking as if he knew better, Detective Stone nodded. "We wanted to ask you a few questions about Ms. Hausen's whereabouts the night she was killed."

Isabella shuddered as her mind flashed back to the scene at Gia's apartment. She knew she couldn't escape the conversation. "Please have a seat."

As the detectives sat down in chairs opposite the sofa, Isabella looked at Detective Patterson. She didn't get a warm, fuzzy feeling from him, and unlike his partner, his appearance screamed *police officer*. He wore his hair in a short military crewcut, and his face was hard. The lines on his face showed years of stress from working in the New York City justice system. Feeling uncomfortable under the stare of his piercing blue eyes, she turned her attention back to Detective Stone.

"Isabella, when was the last time you had contact with Ms. Hausen?" he asked.

"Her name is Gia . . . was Gia," Isabella said.

"I'm sorry, Gia—when was the last time you had contact with Gia?"

"The last time I saw her was Friday afternoon at our office, just after seven." She remembered standing in Gia's office, trying to con her into going to yoga. "The last time I spoke with her was later that evening."

"What did you talk about?"

"We didn't really talk. I had called her to talk, but she cut me off, saying she was running late and needed to shower. She said she would call me a little later, but she never did."

"What time was that?"

"I'm not sure, honestly. I would say maybe after eight thirty or nine.

I was on my way back from my husband's studio."

"Did she say where she was going or who she was going out with?"

"No, but I don't think she was meeting anyone in particular."

Detective Stone tilted his head, squinting his eyes in question. "What would make you say that?"

"Gia would have said something, like, 'I'm going out with that guy I met last week,' or 'So-and-so is in town and I'm seeing him tonight,' something like that, but she didn't."

"What did she say?"

"Just that she was heading out. She never mentioned where, though. I walked away from our conversation with the feeling that she had no intention of seeing anyone she knew."

Detective Stone nodded. "According to your husband, we understand that Gia wasn't interested in traditional relationships. He said she didn't have a steady boyfriend. Would you say that's a fair assessment of Ms. . . . er, Gia's lifestyle?"

Just then, the loft door pulled back, and Grayson stepped inside. He looked surprised to see the detectives sitting there with Isabella.

Before he could utter a word, Isabella spoke. "My husband has no business discussing Gia's lifestyle with you, nor does he have any room to pass judgment on anyone."

Detective Stone looked at Grayson, then back to Isabella. He seemed to sense the tension there. "I can't speak for your husband, but I don't think he was passing judgment. We're simply looking for any information that would lead us to a possible suspect. It's more common than not that the suspect is someone close to the victim."

Isabella's face flushed as Detective Stone's words hit her like a ton of bricks. Her mind turned to Julian and the sinister look on his face as he stood over her hospital bed. She looked to Grayson, who stood there watching her, realizing she was like a pressure cooker ready to explode. He knew he quickly needed to derail the conversation and get the detectives out of the loft before she started running her mouth about Julian.

Detective Patterson opened his mouth to speak just as Grayson said, "I'm sorry to interrupt the interview here, but it's time for me to get Isabella upstairs so I can give her some medication. She needs to rest, gentlemen."

The detectives looked at each other, then back to Isabella. "We'll let you get some rest," said Detective Patterson, "but before we leave, one more question. We need you to think, Isabella. Think very hard. Is there anyone who might have wanted to harm Gia? Anyone at all, no matter how insignificant you may think it is? Sometimes an innocent threat or a small argument will lead us in a direction, even if that individual didn't commit the crime."

She tore her gaze from Detective Patterson and looked back at Grayson, who was staring at her with wide eyes. After a long pause, she swallowed the words she eagerly wanted to voice and shook her head no. She was certain that if she opened her mouth, something about Julian would spill out.

The detectives glanced at Grayson and reluctantly stood up. "Very well, then," said Detective Stone, reaching into his jacket pocket. He pulled out a business card and laid it on the cocktail table. "If there is anything else you can think of or remember, please don't hesitate to give us a call."

Grayson took the card and slipped it into his pocket. "Thank you, Detective. We'll let you know if anything comes to mind."

Isabella felt the detectives' eyes on her as she sat picking at a thread on the blanket wrapped around her.

"Thank you." The detectives shook Grayson's hand, then Detective Stone turned to Isabella again. He leaned over and patted her leg, causing her to raise her eyes to him. "I know this is a difficult time for you," he said. "Finding your friend like that is something nobody wants to go through. I can tell you from my experience that it does get better over time. I can't promise that you will ever forget, but you will find a way to go on and live your life the way she would have wanted you to."

She fought back tears. *If it were only that simple*, she thought. She wondered what his years of experience would say about the guilt she felt for putting Gia in danger—danger delivered by a man she once loved.

"I don't see how that's possible, but thank you, Detective."

"Don't underestimate the power of time." He patted her leg again. "If there is anything you need or want to talk about, you can call me anytime." He smiled at her.

"Thank you. I'll keep that in mind." She managed a half smile.

"I'll show you out," Grayson said, and swiftly escorted them to the door. He stepped aside to let them pass by.

When they were gone, he returned to her side. "That was good, don't you think?" he asked.

Isabella stared blankly into his eyes. "No, that was not good. You heard what he said. More often than not, the killer is someone the victim knows. It's wrong of me to hide what I know to save my reputation. Gia's dead, and that's my fault. I owe it to her to make that bastard pay for what he did."

"Now you're worried about right and wrong? You didn't seem to have any problem choosing wrong when it felt good."

"You're a bastard," Isabella hissed at him.

"Listen to me, and listen to me good. It's not just your reputation on the line, it's mine as well. I'll be damned if I'll let you ruin me because of your mistake."

"How many times can I say I'm sorry? How many times are you going to keep throwing it in my face? It's a horrible thing to do when you know how sick I feel over what has happened."

"What is horrible is the fact that I have to go through all this, when you're the one who created this mess. I just want to get on with our lives and put this behind us. You need to let it go. No good will ever come from exposing your involvement with Julian or your suspicions about Gia's death. You'll drag yourself down a dark hole, and I'll do whatever it takes to make sure I won't be pulled down with you."

Isabella stared at him. "It's amazing how something like this opens your eyes. When I look at you now, all I see is ugliness. You don't care about me. All you care about is yourself."

"That's not true, and you know it. If I didn't care, I wouldn't have fought to get you back."

"Maybe, but now I question just why you care. Is it me, or is it the convenience of being with me?"

Grayson laughed bitterly. "Being with you is not easy, Isabella. You have proven that time and time again."

"It should be. Love should be easy, that I know."

"Why, because he showed you that? Well then, maybe you should have stayed with him," Grayson snapped.

Isabella knew there was no use arguing with him. She swung her legs around him to get up from the sofa.

"Maybe I should have stayed with him," she said furiously. "Things didn't start going wrong until I took your ass back. At least Gia would still be here." Before he could respond, she stormed up the stairs to find peace and quiet in the nursery.

Chapter 30

Isabella sat silently in the back seat of the Town Car with Grayson beside her. She wore a simple black Prada dress with black peep-toe pumps. Having no desire to fuss with her hair, she had pulled it back in a low knot on her neck. Even though clouds loomed in the sky, she had donned a pair of oversized sunglasses to hide the dark circles under her eyes.

Gia's death had taken its toll on her, mentally and physically. She had begun to have nightmares, which made it difficult to sleep. She was constantly awakened during the night in a state of panic, sweating profusely. The medication the doctors had her on, and which Grayson insisted she take, made her nauseated constantly, and all the vomiting sapped her energy. She couldn't remember the last time she had kept any food down. If she wasn't curled up in her bed from the exhaustion, she was in the bathroom getting sick. It was a miracle that she had actually made it out of the house that morning. She credited that to flushing the pill Grayson had given her, rather than swallowing it. She wasn't sure if that was the smartest thing to do, given the sorrow the day would bring, but she knew she had to do whatever it took to be present.

Isabella raised her head as Sebastian pulled the car slowly through the gates of the cemetery. A shiver ran through her. She had never liked cemeteries. Maybe it was the spooky movies she had watched as a child, or her strong belief in spirits. Isabella had been relieved when her grandparents requested to have their ashes spread on their farm instead of being buried. She knew she could never bring herself to visit a gravesite, so she was grateful for their request.

Gravesite, Isabella thought. Gia would now have a gravesite. She would now have to come and visit her here. Isabella realized she was holding her breath and exhaled, still barely believing that Gia was dead. Her life felt surreal. She kept hoping that it was all a bad dream, just like her nightmares.

Sebastian pulled the Town Car to the curb. Isabella looked out the window at the large crowd that had gathered near an old oak in the distance. Isabella watched her employees huddled together in conversation. It had been almost a week since she'd last seen them, something she now regretted. She had stayed away simply because she knew she was unable to console them the way they needed to be consoled. She knew they would be looking to her to guide them through the difficult loss of someone who was an integral part of the company, but she had nothing to give. Now she felt like a nervous kindergartener walking into school for the first time.

Grayson's hand touched her leg. "Isabella, it's time," he said.

She looked down at his hand, and then into his eyes. "I can't," she whispered.

"You can, and you will. You've been hiding for too long. It's time you got out there and interacted with everyone again. They need you as much as you need them. It's not healthy for you to stay locked away in that mind of yours, replaying what happened." Grayson took her hands in his. "Gia wouldn't have wanted that for you. She would have wanted you to go on living. Unfortunately, in order for that to happen, you have to let her go. You need to put her to rest so you can move on."

Isabella nodded, wondering why he was being so nice, and opened her door. The damp, cool breeze felt good on her face. *Why is the weather always gloomy at funerals?* she wondered as Sebastian helped her out of the car.

"Thank you, Sebastian," she said.

"Anytime, Mrs. Hughes. I'll be right here whenever you're ready to leave." He squeezed her hand.

Isabella mustered a smile and moved forward, taking Grayson's hand as they joined the crowd of mourners. Still unwilling to engage, Isabella kept her eyes on the ground.

"Isabella," Grayson whispered.

She let out a sigh and lifted her head. The majority of the crowd had turned in her direction. Isabella felt everyone's eyes on her, and a hush came over the group. A few of her designers leaned into each other, whispering as she drew closer. It was James who broke from the group and rushed to her side. Isabella stopped just shy of the rows of chairs set in front of the casket, which she was avoiding like the plague.

James wrapped his arms around her, squeezing her tight. "Oh, how I've missed you. I came by the other day, but Grayson said you were sleeping, so I didn't want to wake you. How are you holding up?"

Isabella squeezed him back. "I'm getting there," she said, holding back tears. "I've missed you too, very much." She kissed his cheek. "I really need to thank you for all you've done while I was away. Your emails have been appreciated. I've been able to keep up with what's been happening. You're doing a fabulous job. Thank you."

"It's the least I can do after everything you've done for me." He smiled and pushed up his glasses with his finger. "I have to tell you, Izzie, you look amazingly vogue right now. A little thin, but vogue nonetheless."

"Well, that's what meds and nausea will do to you. Pretty soon I'll be sporting a size double zero." She smiled, realizing that it had been a long time since she had done so.

James rolled his eyes. "Please, we all know your size. Besides, the whole anorexic-model look would never work for you. Even Gia would have rolled her eyes at that."

Isabella laughed. She did miss him. James always had a way of cheering her, even in the most difficult circumstances. His playful nature brought out a less serious side of her. Grayson was right; she had spent too much time on her own. She realized in that moment that she did need to be around her friends and coworkers. It was the first time in over a week that she hadn't cried at the sound of Gia's name.

She turned to Grayson. "Will you excuse me for a moment?"

"Absolutely, go and talk with them. I'll get us a seat."

"We have two reserved for you and Isabella in the front row," James said. He took her hand and walked her over to her designers.

Isabella started to feel more comfortable as each of her employees and friends came up to her, offering their condolences. Some just shook her hand; others went for an embrace with that extra squeeze, letting her know they were there for her. She was actually starting to feel as if she could get through the day. Eventually she made her way to Gia's sister, Lydia. They hugged each other tightly, bonding over their loss. Isabella invited her to come to the office the following week. She wanted to set up a fund from Gia's portion of the business for her sister's family, believing that Gia would have wanted it that way.

As the priest approached the casket, the mourners found their seats. Isabella took her seat at the front next to Grayson. She still could not bring herself to look at Gia's casket, which sat directly in front of her. Pushing away the images that had been etched in her mind from that fateful day, she envisioned Gia lying inside the beautiful, champagne-colored casket. She imagined her in a couture dress with her fiery red hair in soft curls, cascading around her. Isabella smiled, remembering the effort it had taken for Gia to tame her unruly locks, and how she repeatedly used that as an excuse when she arrived at work looking like she had been attacked by a crazed pigeon.

Hearing the priest utter Gia's name, Isabella raised her eyes, finally allowing herself to take in what lay before her. On top of the casket was a gorgeous spray of red roses with a white silk sash running through it that simply said, *Loving Sister and Aunt.* On either end of the casket, white pillars held two floral arrangements. The arrangement on the right, a bouquet of white roses, was from the office. To the left was a stunning arrangement of white gardenias in a crystal vase. Tied around the vase was a large red bow with gold lettering that simply said, *Dearest Friend.* Tears filled Isabella's eyes as she let out the smallest whimper, trying to hold back her emotions. Grayson's arm wrapped around her shoulders, pulling her closer to him, and she rested her head on his shoulder as she let the tears come. She remained that way through the rest of the service.

With the conclusion of the last prayer, the mourners filed past the casket, paying their final respects. Isabella remained seated in the front row as each friend, coworker, and acquaintance passed by. Her mind raced back through all the wonderful memories she had shared with Gia, and the many years she was blessed to have such a special friend in her life. She felt frantic, knowing the final moment was approaching much too soon. She wanted to run, to scream, to be anywhere but there, saying goodbye to someone she loved more than anything. She wanted Gia back. She wanted to hear her laugh, to hear her sing, to hear her argue and complain. She wanted to hug her and feel Gia hug her back, to tell her everything was going to be okay like she always did. Isabella wanted her friend to make it better, to take all the pain way, but knew she never could. She would never hear Gia laugh or cry or complain again. She would never hear her crazy words of wisdom, or be able to lean her head on Gia's shoulder as she had so many times that she'd lost count. She would never again find comfort in the friend she had grown to trust and love and depend on. Her heart ached more than she ever thought possible. She wanted to die, and in that moment she would have gladly given anything to take Gia's place.

"Isabella, they're waiting on you," Grayson said to her as he rubbed her shoulder.

Isabella broke down, shaking uncontrollably. She kept trying to speak, but each time she did, a sob caught her breath.

"Shh, it's okay. You can do this," he whispered.

"I don't want to do this. I don't want to say goodbye." She grabbed onto his suit coat. "I want her back. Don't you understand? This isn't right. She was a good person. She didn't deserve this. She didn't deserve to die like she did, frightened and alone. I wasn't even there to help her when she needed me the most. I want more time—more time to tell her how sorry I am, to tell her how much I love her. Do you think she knows? Please tell me she knows."

Her friends and employees had all stopped dead in their tracks when they heard her cry out. They huddled together, watching as Isabella became unglued.

Grayson took her face in his hands. "She knows, baby. She knows how much you loved her, and how you wish you could have been there. She also knows that it's time for you to let her go and move on. There isn't anything more you can do for her. It's time for you to say goodbye." He wrapped his arms around her and pulled her close to him to whisper in her ear. "Isabella, you're making a scene. Everyone is watching you, including Detective Stone. We don't need to raise any suspicions. I understand this is hard for you, but please pull yourself together long enough to make it back to the car. Can you do that for me?"

"I don't care," she cried out. "I don't care what anyone else thinks anymore."

"You need to care." Grayson spoke through his teeth in a low, angry whisper. "She is dead, Isabella. There's nothing you can do for her now. You're alive, and you're destroying your reputation and mine with your behavior. Now get your ass up off the chair, say goodbye, and let's get out of here. I have work to do." Grayson pulled away from her so she could see how angry he was and that he meant what he had said.

It was inconceivable to her how cold and callous he was. As she'd suspected, he didn't care about what she was going through; he was only concerned about himself. Isabella leaned toward him, wrapping her arms around his shoulders, and whispered in his ear. "You're an insensitive bastard. You're the one who should be lying in that casket right now, not her." She pulled back, smiled wickedly at him, and stood up.

Standing before the casket, Isabella bowed her head and interlocked her fingers to pray.

After a few minutes of silence, she lifted her head and made the sign of the cross. She placed her hand on the top of the casket and said softly, "I love you more than anything in this world, Gia. It kills me this has happened to you. I don't know how I'll ever be able to survive without you by my side. You meant the world to me, and I feel that I never showed you how much I appreciated and loved you. Please know that if I could go back, I would. I'd give everything to have you here with me, to go back and cherish every moment we had together . . . to do things differently." Isabella bowed her head, trying to find the strength to continue. "There won't be a day, a moment that I won't think of you . . .

that I won't miss you." Her voice quivered. "You will always be with me in death, as you were in life. I know one day we will meet again, and when we do, I can only pray that you will forgive me." Isabella leaned forward and placed her lips on the casket. "I love you, my sweet Gia." She broke down as she walked away, wrapping her arms tightly around herself.

Grayson jumped up and followed her. When he caught up to her, he went to put his arm around her shoulders, but Isabella jerked her shoulder back and knocked his arm away from her.

"Don't touch me, you son-of-a-bitch," she said under her breath.

"Isabella, people are watching," he whispered back.

"I don't give a shit what people think. From the looks of it, they'll think you're an asshole, which is fine by me." She moved toward the Town Car, nodding to Sebastian to open the door.

As she was about to step into the car, she heard Detective Stone calling her name. She stopped and turned.

"Careful now," Grayson whispered.

"Isabella, I wanted to come over and offer you my condolences," said Detective Stone as he approached them. "I know how upset you've been, and I wanted to see how you're holding up."

"I'm holding up as best as I can right now. Thank you for your concern. How is the case coming along? Are there any new leads?"

Detective Stone shook his head. "I'm afraid not at this time. The building Gia lived in didn't have a working security system, so we have nothing on film and no hard evidence to lead us in any particular direction. We're counting on witnesses who may have seen her that night to come forward and help us fill in the details."

"That's not very encouraging," Isabella said.

"Lack of evidence is something that has never discouraged us, Isabella. We will find the person responsible, I promise you that." Detective Stone looked at Grayson.

"I certainly hope so," she said. "If you will excuse me, Detective, it's been a trying day."

Isabella and Grayson were silent during the long drive back to the loft through heavy traffic. Finally, Grayson spoke. "Isabella—"

She cut him off. "I don't want to talk to you. I don't want to hear your voice. Please."

He fell quiet for a moment. "I only said those things for your benefit. For our benefit. You were upset and didn't know what you were saying."

Isabella pushed the button to raise the privacy glass, hoping to spare

Sebastian the argument she knew was coming. "I knew exactly what I was saying. I'm not as irrational as you think."

"You see, I have a hard time with that, because you're still holding onto this notion that Julian is a killer. But he looks normal to me, not like a man who just murdered someone. At the funeral, he was quiet and polite."

She finally turned to look at him, her mouth open in shock. "What? He was there today, at the cemetery?"

"Yes, he was standing in the back."

"I didn't see him. Why didn't you tell me he was there?"

"Why would I? You were a wreck and could barely control your emotions. I didn't need you going off on him and making a scene, especially with the detective there."

"Unbelievable. I can't believe he would actually show his face at the funeral."

"Think about it. If he killed her, do you honestly believe he would show up at her funeral to pay respects?"

"Yes, yes I do. That's exactly the type of thing a sick, sadistic bastard would do. He had no right to be there. You should have said something, if not to me, then to someone else who could have dragged his ass out of there."

Grayson grabbed her by the shoulders. "This is exactly what I was talking about. You've become obsessed with him. I'll say this for the hundredth time: you have no proof. Hell, you even heard Detective Stone say they have no evidence."

She raised her voice. "That's because they don't know about him, because you won't let me say anything."

He gave her a good shake to get her attention. "Keep it down." He glanced at the privacy glass to see if Sebastian appeared to be listening.

Isabella pushed him away from her. "He can't hear anything. The glass is soundproof."

"The police have no fingerprints, no photos, no physical evidence," he continued, "so even if they knew about Julian, they would have nothing to link him to the crime. The damage you will do to yourself and to me will be for nothing. How do you not understand that?"

"I think—" she started to say, but he cut her off.

"No, you don't think. That's the problem. You haven't been thinking clearly for weeks now. It's time you drop all this nonsense and move on. You need to concentrate on your business and the furniture launch instead of trying to pin your ex-lover for murdering your best friend. You also need to concentrate on our marriage before you destroy that, too."

"Stop talking. Please, stop talking." Isabella covered her ears.

Grayson pulled her hands away so she could hear him. "You want me to stop talking because you know I'm right and the truth hurts, doesn't it? You alone are destroying us and yourself. Stop blaming me for our problems, when you're the one who is sabotaging us."

Isabella pleaded with him. "Please stop. I can't do this anymore, Grayson, not today."

Isabella felt the car come to a stop. She looked out the window and saw that they were in front of the loft. Without a word, Grayson got out and proceeded up the stairs to the entrance. Isabella watched him disappear inside. Sebastian came around and opened the door for her.

"Would you mind driving me over to the park?" she asked. "I'd like to go for a walk. I need some fresh air."

"No problem, Mrs. Hughes." He smiled and shut the door.

Isabella sank down in the back seat, closed her eyes, and just breathed.

Chapter 31

Detective Ian Stone hadn't been able to get Isabella off his mind since he had met her. There was something there that intrigued him. Yes, she was beautiful and he found himself attracted to her, but he knew it was something entirely different. At first he thought it was the compassion he had felt when he found her huddled in the corner outside Gia's apartment, but after seeing her since then, he knew that wasn't it. The look in her eyes haunted his thoughts; her words constantly replayed in his mind. He had a strong suspicion that there was more she wanted to express, but that she was being coerced into keeping quiet. Even though he hadn't met her before Gia's death, he assumed she was a strong woman. The company she owned was reputable and successful. But now she bore no resemblance to an independent businesswoman. In his eyes, Isabella Hughes seemed tormented and disturbed, nervous and fragile. The detective inside him wanted to know just what she was holding back, while the man inside wanted to protect her.

"Hey, I don't have all day here. Are you going to order something or not?" the street vendor said rudely as Ian stood there, lost in his thoughts.

"Yeah, I'm sorry, just a coffee please." He pulled a five-dollar bill out of his pocket and handed it to the vendor. "Keep the change," he said as he took his coffee, hoping that would cheer the man up.

"Hey, thanks man." The vendor smiled.

Ian started to take a sip from the coffee but stopped as his attention gravitated across the street to the park entrance, where Isabella Hughes was stepping out of a Town Car, still wearing the dress she'd worn to the funeral. She was alone. Her hair hung loose around her shoulders, blowing in the breeze. She pulled a black wrap tightly around her shoulders as she disappeared into the park. Feeling drawn to her, he crossed the street and carefully trailed behind her.

~~~

Isabella's thoughts were scattered as she walked through the park but finally settled on Julian. It was hard to believe how badly everything had turned out. It seemed like yesterday when she had spotted him during a run through the park. She sighed at the memory.
~~~

Everything was so innocent then. She remembered the way he smiled and teased her, giving her a renewed sense of freedom. He had felt like a breath of fresh air, a sedative that calmed her, but now his presence triggered a storm within her and left her gasping for air. How could one person change so drastically? Or was it she who had changed? Maybe he had always been that way, and her perception of him was skewed. But how could her judgment have been so off?

Isabella wandered to a bench and sat down. Oddly enough, it was the same bench where she and Julian had snuggled together only months before. How quickly things had changed. For the first time in a long time, she allowed herself to reminisce about when things had been good, when she had walked through her days smiling and laughing, feeling on top of the world and filled with an amazing and unexpected love.

She even permitted herself to reminisce about the intimate times she and Julian had shared, which were buried inside her. Their strong desire for each other at the beginning . . . the way she had fought her feelings . . . the way she had given into them in Milan. Tears filled her eyes as she remembered his touch, his kiss, his tenderness. She missed that Julian. That was the Julian she loved deep in her heart, the Julian she had been forced to let go. Was that it? Was that the reason she kept bringing him into their lives now, because she had never wanted to let him go in the first place? She remembered that day in her office when she had forced herself to say goodbye to him, how intensely her heart had ached as she crushed his love for her, all the while wanting to reach out and take comfort in his arms as she had done so many times. She remembered the feeling of his embrace before she delivered the blow to his heart, and how she tried frantically to hold onto the last moment of something so pure and beautiful.

Isabella closed her eyes, recalling how quickly things had gone awry in her life after that final goodbye. The warmth of the memories escaped her, leaving her lonely and depressed.

Her thoughts turned to her marriage. "Grayson," she whispered through a sigh. She had known he was struggling professionally, and now it was apparent that he was struggling personally as well. There were times when she looked at him that she could still see the love there, but more often than not, all she could see was coldness. It was as if he felt a disdain for her that he didn't voice, but wanted her to know, to feel. She had made a mistake that she wasn't proud of. She had accepted her wrongdoing and constantly tried to let him know how sorry she was. What she wouldn't and couldn't accept was that she was the one solely responsible for fixing the problems they faced. He was no saint. Emotionally, he had not been there for her in a long time, and his distance grew more and more every day. She had felt the strain for quite some time. And his cruelty to her at the funeral and in the car afterward still stung.

A voice startled her. "This is a great place to come and clear your mind. I come here often myself."

Isabella looked up to see Detective Stone standing in front of her.

"I'm sorry," he said. "I didn't mean to scare you. That was quite rude of me. Please accept my apology."

"No apology needed. I was lost in my thoughts, and you caught me off guard. I should have been paying more attention to my surroundings."

"As a detective, I'd say yes, you should." He smiled ruefully. "But I understand getting lost in your thoughts. I do it all the time." He pointed to the bench. "May I?"

"Oh yes, please sit down." Isabella forced a smile.

"I have to admit, I saw you come into the park, and I was drawn to follow you."

Isabella looked at him suspiciously, pulling her wrap more tightly around her shoulders. "Why is that, Detective?"

"Please call me Ian."

"Okay, Ian. Why is it that you're following me?"

"I'm not following you. I just saw you coming into the park. You looked upset. I thought maybe I could help somehow."

"Well, I do appreciate your concern, but there is really nothing you can do for me."

"I know this is a trying time. I know how hard it is finding someone you love like that." He paused and let his gaze drift across the pond. A duck was waddling onto shore. "Three years ago, I was working late on a case at the station. I came home early the next morning to find that my house had been broken into. My wife was killed that night. I found her in our bedroom horribly beaten and bound." He let out a heavy sigh and looked at Isabella again. "She had been raped and stabbed repeatedly."

Isabella gasped. "Oh my gosh, that is awful. I'm so sorry. I . . . I had no idea."

"Thank you, but I'm not telling you this to make you feel bad for me." Ian put his hand on hers. "I'm telling you this to let you know I understand what you're going through better than anyone. When I told you before that it does get better, I was speaking from my own personal experience. I spent too much time wallowing in my grief. I shut out everyone close to me and sought comfort in whatever bottle of hard liquor I could find. It was a dark time, one I almost didn't escape. I don't want the same thing to happen to you. I know what you're feeling, but you will find the strength to continue on. You will push through the grief and anger and find your way again."

She saw the sincerity in his eyes and almost felt a bond with him. But she wasn't ready to hear the "You can make it through this" speech. She asked, "Did you ever catch the person who was responsible?"

Ian nodded. "Eventually, it wasn't easy. There wasn't much physical evidence, but I never gave up, and in time, piece by piece, everything came together. As I said to you before, more often than not, the perpetrator is someone the victim knew. In my wife's case, it was someone I knew. A criminal, out for vengeance, you could say. For that, I carry around a lot of guilt. I felt like I should have protected her more than I did."

Isabella felt a churning in the pit of her stomach. She was all too familiar with the feeling of putting a loved one in harm's way. Unable to offer words of comfort, she sat quietly while his words raced through her mind. Finally she offered, "I'm sorry. I don't know what to say."

"Words aren't necessary. I've made peace with my mistakes, and I know in time you will too." Ian watched her.

"You're right. I do feel guilty . . . guilty for not being there to protect her. That is one thing that hurts me the most."

"And the other things are?"

Isabella knew their conversation was bordering on a confessional. Even though she felt comfortable with him, she hadn't forgotten Grayson's warnings. She knew she should leave the conversation where it was before she said too much.

Ian seemed to sense she was withdrawing. "Isabella, I'm speaking to you off the record here. I have a feeling that you want to say more than you've told me about Gia. By no means do I think you're involved in her death or even know what happened. I do, however, sense that you have a strong feeling about what may have happened, and I'd like you to share that with me. I can help you, Isabella. I can make it better for you, but you need to trust me enough to let me do that for you."

The desire to speak her mind was becoming stronger. She had been forced to keep her feelings and thoughts bottled up inside, and she knew Detective Stone was the match that could ignite them, possibly creating even more chaos in her life—as Grayson had repeatedly reminded her. Tears welled in her eyes and dripped down her face.

Ian spoke again. "Isabella, I don't know what has you so frightened that you feel you need to keep this inside. You don't have to take this on all by yourself. I want you to trust me. I need you to trust me so I can help you."

Isabella shook her head and stood up, trying to get away from him. Ian grabbed her hand to stop her.

"Isabella, please don't go. Talk to me . . . tell me what's on your mind."

She avoided his gaze. "There is nothing to tell. I just can't do this right now. I've been through too much today, and I don't want to talk anymore."

"I understand exactly where you're coming from, but don't you want to find the person responsible for Gia's death?"

Isabella pulled her hand away from his. "That's unfair, Detective. Of course I do. I want nothing more than to see Gia's killer behind bars, and for you to imply that I want anything less than that is offensive." Isabella folded her arms across her chest and pulled her wrap tighter.

"I'm sorry. It was not my intent to offend you," he said as he stood up.

Isabella stared into his dark brown eyes for a long moment. She could see that he truly cared. He wasn't just being a probing detective. "I do appreciate your concern. I know you mean well, but right now nothing makes sense. In time, when things become clearer, I know where to find you. Rest assured, I will seek you out."

"And in the meantime?" he pressed her further.

Her lip quivered. "In the meantime, I hope that you will continue to look for the son-of-a-bitch who took my beautiful friend from me, shredding my heart into a million pieces."

Ian touched her hand again. "I promise, Isabella, I won't stop until I do."

"Thank you." She squeezed his hand and walked down the path to the park exit.

Isabella found herself wandering the streets with no real purpose or direction. Ian's words resonated in her mind. She couldn't fathom what he must have gone through finding his wife the way he did. She knew how devastating it had been to find Gia in a similar manner—she couldn't even fathom the feeling if it was a spouse. Isabella shuddered at the thought of finding Grayson that way, murdered at the hands of someone she had brought into their lives. Ian was right: she was frightened—frightened that she or Grayson would suffer from Julian's wrath; frightened to speak up, fearing Grayson's warning about how it would destroy them. But he had not seen what she had. A sixth sense told her that something bad was to come, and it would be much worse than what they had already experienced. She felt like a sitting duck in open waters with a hunter looming in the reeds. But she knew Grayson would never share her desire to go to the police.

Isabella stopped walking as nausea churned in her stomach. She closed her eyes, trying to take comfort in Detective Stone's words that he would not stop until he brought Gia's killer to justice. She just hoped he would be able to do so before it was too late.

When she opened her eyes, she realized she was standing in front of the coffee shop where she and Gia had become friends many years ago. Isabella peered inside, remembering that it was the table in the back corner where they had spent hours chatting and creating an unbreakable bond. *Unbreakable until now*, she thought. Feeling the despair welling up inside her again, Isabella went to turn away but stopped when she caught sight of her reflection in the window. A small gasp escaped her. Who was this person? The stress and anxiety had taken its toll on her. She looked withdrawn and pale, fragile and thin, almost like a drug addict in need of a fix. She could understand why Grayson had thought she was crazy. *How did this happen?* she thought. *How could I have sunk so low?* It was disturbing to realize she was no longer the pillar of strength she had prided herself on being. She looked pathetic, defeated, and broken.

As she stared at her reflection, Ian's words pulsed in her ears: *It was a dark time for me, one I almost didn't escape. I don't want that to happen to you.*

This was why he had said what he did. He saw it. He knew where she was at—in a dark cavern, an abyss of despair. The realization hit her hard. Each blow she had suffered had pushed her further into this pit, leaving her unstable and taking her further from the person she had worked so hard to become. Isabella felt overwhelmed. How could she get that back? It seemed impossible. She didn't have the energy or the drive she once did. Everything had changed drastically. It was inconceivable to think that she could put the recent events behind her, to walk through life as she had before, as if nothing had happened.

Isabella backed away from the window and turned her gaze to the street behind her, watching the passing pedestrians who looked as if they didn't have a care in the world. A couple strolled by holding hands, laughing and enjoying each other's company. A mother was tickling the baby she held in her arms. Two friends with their arms loaded with shopping bags discussed which new dress they were going to wear that evening. Isabella realized life was moving all around her, while she stood still, unmotivated to engage. Life was passing her by.

She focused her attention on a small restaurant across the street, where a familiar face caught her eye. Grayson was sitting there alone at a window seat, sipping a glass of wine. Isabella watched as he finished off the remaining wine in his glass and reached for the bottle, helping himself to more. Finally she talked herself into going over and making an effort to communicate with him. Life was happening with or without her; that was abundantly clear to her now. She needed to try to rid her mind of the demons that had claimed her thoughts, her words, and her actions. She may have felt it was impossible to get back what she had, what she was, but she had to at least try. That was what the old Isabella would have done.

She started to cross the street, but froze when she saw Evette Vanderbeck slide into the seat across from Grayson. She leaned over and whispered something in his ear, and Grayson erupted in laughter. He poured her a glass of wine. Isabella felt her heart pumping hard in her chest, and her cheeks felt flushed. She couldn't remember the last time Grayson had laughed like that around her. To be honest, she couldn't remember the last time she had seen him smile. Her heart sank. She remembered a time when he had smiled at her the way he was smiling at Evette now. Never before a jealous person, Isabella suddenly felt irritated by their obviously close relationship. *When did this happen?* she wondered. *How close have they become?*

Knowing it was best that she not join them, since it would only erupt into another argument, Isabella turned away and briskly walked down the street. Confident she was out of their view, she stepped into the street and hailed a taxi for home.

Chapter 32

Isabella woke from her nap to the sound of her cell phone ringing. She grabbed it from the nightstand and answered the call before the final ring.

"Hello," Isabella said groggily.

"Isabella, Charles Vanderbeck here. Did I catch you at a bad time?"

"No, not at all, Charles," she said, trying not to sound disoriented. "How can I help you?"

"First I want to extend my deepest condolences for your loss. I know how close you were to Gia, and I can only imagine what you must be going through right now."

"I appreciate that. It has been difficult."

"I'm sure it has. Losing someone you care about is never easy, especially when that person was an important part of your business, as well. Living as long as I have, I can certainly attest to that. I assume you're receiving good support from that wonderful husband of yours?"

Isabella looked at the empty space in the bed next to her, knowing that her wonderful husband was probably shacked up with Evette at his studio.

"Yes, thank you. Grayson has been amazing." Isabella swallowed hard, hoping he hadn't detected her sarcasm.

"Wonderful. I really have enjoyed having him on the project. My daughter Evette is enthralled with him, and between you and me, seeing Evette excited and engaged in any of my projects has me thrilled to death." Charles laughed. "I've been trying to get that one involved in our business for years. Who knew all it would take to get her motivated was to bring an artist on board? I would have done it years ago."

Isabella swallowed again as bile rose in her throat. *I bet he's motivating her, all right*, she thought. "I'm so glad things are working out for you with Evette. Grayson can be very inspiring. I'm thrilled to hear you're so happy with the progress."

"I am, Isabella, which brings me to my reason for calling. As I stated before, I know things have been difficult for you lately, and I understand. This is why I've allowed you your time to grieve the loss of your friend."

Isabella pushed herself into an upright position on her bed, wondering where he was going with the conversation. "Again, Charles, I have really appreciated your patience. Please go on."

"Well, I'm sure you're aware that we are within a few weeks of launching Vanderbeck Home, and while I've been happy with James and his competence to fill in for you in your absence, I need you to step back in the game, so to speak. Your presence in these final meetings is of the utmost importance. Gonzolo will be arriving this week, and we've set up several meetings with him and his team for final concerns, questions, and last-minute changes."

"I completely understand."

"We also have the launch party right around the corner. We've set up a series of interviews with various media sources, and since you're the face of this line, my dear, you will need to partake in these interviews and photo shoots."

Isabella winced, remembering the image of herself reflected in the window that afternoon. She knew it would take the makeup artist of all makeup artists to make her look anywhere near presentable. She also remembered her anxiety about the last interview. If it hadn't been for Julian, she would have fallen apart. Memories of that day whizzed through her mind, pausing on the image of Julian standing next to her sofa, shirtless, as he unzipped her dress. Everything was so simple then.

"Isabella? Are you there? Did I lose you?"

Isabella snapped her attention away from the memory. "Yes, Charles, I'm here. I was just calculating the time chart in my head." Isabella began to panic. Who would help her through this? She no longer had Gia or Julian, and Grayson surely hadn't been someone she could lean on. She bit her lip. She would have to rely on herself to pull through the launch. That was how she had begun her business anyway—by herself. She would somehow have to draw on that strength, God willing it was still there.

She assured Charles that she would be returning to her place at the helm and would be at the office the next morning. "I also want you to know that in my absence I've kept a close eye on the project through James and am aware of every aspect. I don't want you to think I just handed him the reigns and let him run solo."

"I understand. He let us know that he was only substituting as your voice. We knew he was running everything by you, and the decisions that were being made were coming from you, not him."

Isabella breathed a sigh of relief, glad that she had not upset Charles. They agreed to meet the next day at their usual Italian restaurant to discuss the completion of the project.

When she hung up, she noticed it was after eight o'clock. How long had she been sleeping? She had never bothered to look after her walk. Apparently she had needed the nap.

As she was changing out of her dress, she heard the loft door open. Isabella held her breath, listening to the footsteps as they made their way through the loft. She heard a set of keys clanging on the counter and the refrigerator door being opened. Isabella exhaled and relaxed, knowing it was only Grayson. She slipped into comfortable black boy shorts and a white tank top, went through her nightly beauty routine, and climbed into bed.

She had just closed her eyes when Grayson spoke. "I see you're back. Where did you vanish to earlier?"

Isabella opened her eyes to see Grayson standing at the foot of their bed. "I could ask you the same question."

"I didn't vanish. I came in when we got back from the funeral. I assumed you were following behind me."

"You assumed wrong," she snapped.

"There's no need to be a bitch, Isabella. I was concerned about you. You had me worried."

"Yeah, you really looked worried as you were enjoying your wine and lunch with Evette." Isabella glared at him. "I didn't realize the two of you had gotten so close. Is there anything you need to tell me, Grayson?"

He watched as she sat up and crossed her arms across her chest. "Yes, in fact, I do need to tell you something," he said.

Isabella's heart skipped a beat, and she braced herself for the words she was no longer sure she wanted to hear.

"Evette and I have been working together on an art project for her father—you may have heard about it," he said condescendingly. "He's turning a building he purchased into a high-end luxury complex."

Anger replaced her anxiety. "Don't be a smartass. I know what I saw, and from my viewpoint, it didn't look like any Picassos were being created over the wine you two were enjoying."

"Wow, jealous much?" He smirked. "I've never known you to be jealous. It's not a very attractive quality, by the way. Maybe your own guilt is finally starting to get to you."

"Don't try to change the subject. I saw the connection between you and Evette today. It made me sad, because we used to have that connection. We used to go out and have fun. We used to laugh and enjoying being together. Today I was wishing it was me you laughed with, me you smiled at, me you loved with all your heart. But it's not me anymore, is it? It's her."

"You're being ridiculous. She's a friend. She helps me with my work. Of course I'm close to her, but not like you're implying. Please don't compare me to you and Julian. I would never hurt you the way you hurt me."

"That's just it. You hurt me every day. You accuse me of constantly bringing Julian back into our lives, when you're the one who has been unable to let him go. You have a grudge against me, and whether or not you admit it, you lash out at me all the time in one way or another."

Grayson let out a frustrated sigh and ran his hand through his thick hair. He sat down at the foot of the bed and bowed his head in thought. Finally he said, "You're right. Every time I look at you, I see the two of you together. The thought of him touching you makes me sick. I don't know how to make that stop. I want it to, but I don't know how."

Isabella sighed. How many times were they going to have this same conversation? She wasn't sure either of them had the strength to continue fighting this fight in order to stay together.

"Maybe we should . . ." Her voice quivered, and she paused. She took a deep breath before continuing. "Maybe we should separate for a while until we can figure this out. We need to find out if we even love each other enough to stay together."

Grayson couldn't let her walk away and leave him. He lifted his head, bringing his eyes to meet hers. "Is that what you really want?"

She shook her head. "No, it's not want I want, but I don't think we have another choice."

"But I love you and don't want to lose you . . . I don't want to lose us."

"I love you too, but in all honesty, I think we already lost *us* a long time ago. You haven't been happy for some time now, and God knows I'm a train wreck. I think too much has happened for us to ever get back to the way we were. Please don't think for one moment that this is not killing me inside. You were my everything. I never imagined my life without you in it. I'm just sick when I think of what a mess we've become."

Grayson scooted closer to her on the bed and took her hands in his. "Please don't say that. I know things have been bad, but we can do this. We can fight to stay together. I know we can."

Isabella squeezed his hand. "I have no more fight left in me. Between what transpired with Julian, our troubled relationship, Gia's death, and Charles Vanderbeck's project, I'm spent. I don't have the energy to fix things as I did before. I can barely make it through the day. I'm tired, and it's time for me to throw in the towel."

"I've never known you to be a quitter," he said, searching her eyes. "That's not the person you are."

"Well, unfortunately, that's the person I've become. There is only so much a person can take, and I've reached my limit." Isabella bowed her head. "I have nothing left to give you. I'm so tired. Every breath I take is a chore for me." Isabella buried her face into her hands and began to cry.

He pulled her into his arms. "Shhh, it's going to be okay." He kissed the top of her head as she nuzzled into his chest.

"I'm not going anywhere," he said. "I know I haven't been the best husband to you, but I will get better. I'll get us through this."

Desperately wanting to believe him, Isabella wrapped her arms around his chest and squeezed him as hard as her fragile arms could. She wanted to think that this time would be different, that the love they had left would get them through this.

It was then, for the first time since he had entered the room, that it hit her. Isabella breathed in again to assure herself. She closed her eyes, now more certain than ever that it was Evette's perfume she smelled on him.

"I love you," she said as she buried her face further into his chest, unwilling to acknowledge what she silently feared. For the first time in a long time, she fell asleep in his arms.

Chapter 33

Transitioning back into her daily work routine was not an easy feat for Isabella. The first week back in the office was difficult, to say the least. She found it hard to be in the place where she and Gia had spent countless hours together. There were reminders at every turn, and she felt as if her days were now spent living in the memories of the past, as well as the nightmare of the present.

Before she returned, James had cleared out Gia's office. He knew Isabella well enough to know that if the office remained as it was, she would wander in more than she should. He did everything in his power to give her a fresh start. He had even made sure he scheduled her time away from the office so she could get in to see her therapist, something she constantly put up a fight about. Isabella hated going. She complained that she always felt worse afterward. She felt that the memories were best kept buried and not dug up and reanalyzed every few days. She didn't understand how it was helping her, but James reassured her that in time she would understand.

Even though she was present in the office and attending to her duties, James knew she was struggling. More than ever, he remained by her side throughout the day, keeping her on track and on schedule. He kept trying to pump her full of super foods that promoted energy and had a steady supply of caffeine readily available, but she always felt sick and nauseated. On more than one occasion, he had tried to get her to see the doctor, but she had refused. Her stubbornness was the one thing not affected by her depression.

Near the end of her first week, when Isabella returned to her office after another meeting for Vanderbeck Home, James came in carrying a covered tray.

"Hey, girly, how did the meeting go?" he asked as he set the tray on her desk.

"It was good. We went over the media schedule and details for the launch party. Everything seems to be on target—" She took her eyes off the papers on her desk. "What is that God-awful smell?"

James lifted the silver cover off the tray. "Sushi. Your favorite, I might add."

Isabella put her hand over her mouth and nose. "Not anymore. Please get that out of here before I get sick." Isabella moved away from the tray, but she wasn't quick enough. "Oh my God," she cried out as she grabbed for the wastebasket and began to vomit.

"Isabella, what the hell has come over you? You love sushi. I even went out of my way to go to your favorite place." James replaced the cover on the tray.

Isabella rose from the wastebasket. "I don't know, but please get that out of here. Maybe it's bad. The smell is absolutely revolting."

James lifted the cover again and took a long sniff of the sushi rolls. "It smells fine to me." He took a roll off the plate and popped it into his mouth as Isabella watched. "Tastes fine, too," he said between chews.

"Oh my gosh." Isabella puffed out her cheeks and turned her head back to the wastebasket as another wave of nausea overcame her.

"Oh, for Pete's sake. I'll take the tray out of here. But don't think this is getting you off the hook. I'll be back with something else . . . I can guarantee you that."

Isabella stood up as he took the tray away. "Thank you, James. I'm sorry for being so difficult. Do you think you could find me some soup?"

James replied, but she only stared at him blankly. She sensed that he had asked her something, but she couldn't remember what. She felt beads of sweat forming on the back of her neck, and her ears started to ring. The room spun.

"Izzie, you're as pale as a ghost. Are you okay? I think you need to sit down."

Before he could reach her, she hit the floor. He let out a shriek and raced over to her, kneeling down beside her. He shook her shoulders and called her name, but she didn't respond. He felt for her pulse, which was low, and her breath seemed shallow. Panicked, he called 911.

It wasn't long before the paramedics had Isabella strapped to a gurney and were wheeling her down the hallway, with James following behind. The entire staff had gathered in the front lobby of the office, trying to figure out what all the commotion was about. As the gurney whizzed by them, they stood back in shock when they realized it was Isabella.

At the hospital, Isabella was given a bed and an IV with fluids. She was surprised to see Dr. Clifton, the physician who had treated her before. After he had given her the test results, James was invited into the room.

"Isabella is going to be just fine," Dr. Clifton explained. "Having seen her previously, I was concerned about how she has been feeling. We've run some tests, and everything has come back fine."

James had a puzzled look on his face. "I don't understand. She's been so sick, and she literally passed out today. That cannot be fine."

"The nausea has been partly caused by the medications. Isabella became dehydrated and somewhat malnourished from all the vomiting. That's why she passed out."

James looked at the doctor over his glasses. "You said *partly* caused by the medication. What's the other part?"

Dr. Clifton looked to Isabella. "Do you want to tell him?"

Confused, James's eyes darted to Isabella. "Izzie, what did they find? Oh my God, is it cancer? Please tell me you don't have cancer." James began to fan himself with his hand. "My legs feel weak; I think I need to sit down." He frantically began searching the room for a chair.

Isabella laughed at him. "You're such a drama queen. Calm down, I don't have cancer." Isabella smiled. "I'm pregnant."

James whipped his head around so fast, Isabella thought it was going to fly off his body. "Come again? You're what?" He looked over his glasses at her.

"Pregnant, silly. I'm pregnant."

His mouth dropped open. "Shut the front door. You are not."

"I am." Isabella giggled. "Two and a half months pregnant, in fact. That's why I've been so sick."

"Oh my God, Izzie. This is crazy. I can't believe it. I'm in shock."

"You're in shock? How do you think I feel?"

James leaned close to her. "It is Grayson's, right?" he whispered.

Isabella swatted his arm. "Of course it's Grayson's." She had already done that calculation in her head, and there was no way the baby could be Julian's. She shot James a shut-your-yap look, then smiled at Dr. Clifton. "Besides being overdramatic, he thinks he's a comedian, too."

Dr. Clifton laughed. "Well, I'll let you two enjoy the good news. I'm just waiting on a few more blood tests to come back. I want to make sure your levels are good and that your iron is not too low. I'm going to keep you here for a few hours and let that IV perk you up a bit, if you don't mind."

After the doctor left, James sagged onto the edge of the bed. "I'm in awe, Isabella. You're preggers. Who would have ever thought? This is a holy-shit moment." He gasped loudly. "Oh my God, Izzie, you're going to need maternity clothes. I'll start looking now, 'cause honey, have you seen what's out there?" James stuck his finger down his throat, pretending to gag.

Isabella chuckled. "Just slow down, sister. Who says I'm going to need maternity clothes? I'm almost through my first trimester, and my clothes are literally falling off me because I've been so sick. There may be a good chance I can get by with just a bigger size."

James guffawed. "Oh sure, a *fat* chance." He pointed to her belly. "Do you have any idea how fast those things grow in there? You'll be packing a five-pound watermelon in no time."

"Stop it. My baby is not a watermelon."

James took her hand. "So all kidding aside, this baby, you're sure it's Grayson's?"

"I'm one hundred percent sure. Why would you ask me that?"

"Well, you never said anything, but I'm not stupid. I know you too well not to see that something was going on. There was also office talk about you having an affair with Julian. I never asked because I figured if you wanted to tell me, you would have. I assumed it ended when he left."

Isabella stared at him for a long while. He was right; she had never said anything to him. Even though she felt close to him, and he was literally her only true friend in the world now, she felt it best not to fill him in on all the sordid details. The less he knew, the better.

"There's no possibility that the father is anyone but Grayson, and that's all I'm going to say." She raised her eyebrow, letting him know the conversation was over.

"Fair enough. I respect you and your wishes and will never utter another word about it."

Isabella rubbed his hand. "Thank you. You really are a good friend."

"Speaking of the baby's daddy, though, I called Grayson several times and he didn't pick up. I left him a message to come here, but I haven't seen him yet. Do you know where I could reach him?"

Isabella pulled out her phone and began looking through her contacts. "Here, try Evette Vanderbeck's number. I'm sure she knows his whereabouts." She handed her phone to him so he could see the number. "And James, not a word about me being pregnant, please. I want to tell Grayson myself when the time is right, and right now is not the time, if you understand what I'm saying."

She could see the questions flying through his mind, but he simply nodded and dialed Evette. Isabella held her breath, praying she was wrong and that Grayson was not with her. Evette picked up on the second ring. James explained who he was, and within two seconds, Grayson was on the line. When he learned what had happened, he said he would be at the hospital as soon as possible.

After hanging up, James looked at Isabella, who sat in bed with her head down. "Isabella?" he whispered.

"Please, I don't want to talk right now."

"Very well, we don't have to talk. We can just sit here and hold hands if you like." He reached for her hand.

Isabella raised her head, smiling, and gave him her hand. "You're so good to me. I would like that very much, love."

The two friends sat there hand in hand, lost in their own thoughts. Isabella tried to comprehend just what this news would mean for her and Grayson and their rocky relationship. They were just beginning to reestablish being with one another and were still having a tough time managing that. She couldn't imagine what bringing a child into their lives would do to their marriage. She knew without a doubt that she wanted this baby, but did she want it with Grayson? Did he even want it with her? How did Evette play into all of that? There were too many questions running rapidly through her mind.

Isabella didn't want to tell Grayson right away, but she also knew she didn't have much time. It wouldn't take long for her bump to start showing on her small frame. Grayson would quickly figure out what was going on. She had to do some soul searching and understand just what she wanted, but more importantly, what would be best for her baby.

It was crazy how two little words—*you're pregnant*—had changed her mindset completely. In that moment, she wasn't thinking of the friend she had lost or how devastated she was. She wasn't thinking of Julian and his insanity. All she could think about was the life that was now being created inside her. Isabella looked down at her tummy and slowly rubbed her hand over it. Would she have a boy or a girl? Would her baby take after her, with her dark hair and dark eyes, or Grayson, with his light hair and light eyes? Maybe it would be a combination of both, with dark hair and light eyes or light hair and dark eyes. It brought a smile to her face knowing that in six months she would get to hold her precious gift, her ray of light that shone through the dark cloud hovering above her.

"Someone is having a happy thought," James said as he watched her.

Isabella was beaming. "It's all so surreal, you know? I still can't believe it. You have no idea how much I've wanted this. I never thought it would happen, and for it to happen right now is insane. My life has been so messed up. I've been so messed up. The thought of having a baby never crossed my mind."

"Maybe this is a blessing in disguise. Maybe your little angel friend up there knew this was exactly what you needed." James lowered his glasses and looked at her. "You know that just killed me to call her an angel."

"Stop it. Don't be mean to my Gia." Isabella pinched his hand, and he let out a yelp. "You know she's an angel. Regardless of how she led her life, she was a good person. She had a heart of gold and would do anything for the people around her."

"I do know that. But the thought of her up there sporting a pair of wings is laughable." James rolled his eyes.

Isabella couldn't help but smile. "Think of them as Victoria's Secret Angel wings. That's more appropriate."

James busted out laughing. "Oh my God, yes. Bet you she's sporting some blingy rhinestone bra, too."

"With matching panties."

"Because, you never know," they said in unison.

Isabella and James sat there laughing together as they imagined it. It had been so long since she had laughed like that. It felt good, and she only hoped that it meant there were more of those times to come.

"What is so funny in here?" Grayson asked as he pulled back the curtain. "You know you guys are in a hospital, right?"

"We were just reminiscing about Gia and her lingerie," James said to Grayson, who wore a disapproving look. "Inside joke, never mind. Well, since you're here, I'm going to get back to the office and try to salvage the rest of the day." James leaned over to give Isabella a kiss. "Take care of yourself, and I'll forward you any emails you may need to keep you in the office loop."

After James had left, Grayson sat down on the bed. "What happened to you today? How did you end up here?"

Isabella explained the incident at the office. "Dr. Clifton said that my medications were making me sick and that I was dehydrated from all the vomiting. He doesn't want me taking anything right now. He wants to give my body a chance to heal on its own before introducing any new medications."

Grayson looked irritated. "Is he aware of what a mess you've been lately? Do you really think it's best to stop taking your medication?"

"Honestly, yes I do. Don't be mad at me, but I haven't been one hundred percent faithful in taking it. I don't like the way it makes me feel. I think I'll be fine without it." Isabella needed him to believe her. There was no way she was going to take any type of medication now that she was pregnant. Dr. Clifton had reassured her that what she had taken would have no effect on her baby's health, but he agreed that it was in the best interests of her baby the she discontinue it.

"I'm glad you think you'll be fine, but baby, I live with you. I know how bad you get. I really don't think this is a good idea."

"You have to trust me on this. The pills are the reason I've been so sick. I hate feeling that way. Imagine going through your days feeling like you're moving in slow motion, and on top of that, you're nauseated all day long. It's awful. I promise you I'll be fine. Can you at least let me try?"

Grayson sighed. "Okay, but the moment I feel you're not doing well, you'll need to go see Dr. Lewis for a script of something else. I don't want you to relapse so far that we lose what we've already gained."

Isabella smiled, knowing she had won the battle for now. As long as she could hold it together, she was in the clear. "Thank you for hearing me. That means a lot."

Grayson caressed her face. "I'm just looking out for you, baby. I want what's best for you, and if you feel that this is what it is, then I'm good with that. I just want you better. I want my wife back."

She brought her hand to his. "I want that too."

"I was so worried when James called. All I kept thinking about the whole way over was what I would do if I lost you. It made me sick to think you could have been taken from me. I never want that to happen. I'm so relieved you're okay." Grayson took her face into his hands and stared into her eyes. "I love you, Izzie."

"I love you too," she whispered, wishing she could believe him.

Grayson brought his lips to hers. His kiss was warm and comforting.

Isabella felt something stir within her. It was a small ember, but at least there was an ember, she thought. Grayson climbed into the bed next to her and put his arms around her as she rested her head on his shoulder. They lay there in silence while he stroked her hair. In that moment, Isabella felt a sense of peace and serenity wash over her. She closed her eyes, and for the first time in a long time, dreamed happy dreams.

Chapter 34

"Come on, Izzie, it's amazing outside. I want to go for a run," Grayson said as he ripped the covers off her.

Isabella groaned and tried to snuggle into the bed. "No, I'm still sleepy." She reached for the covers, but Grayson was kneeling on them so she couldn't move them. She opted to put her pillow over her head instead.

"Oh, no you don't." Grayson laughed and tried to pull the pillow off. Isabella had a tight hold of it, though—until he started tickling her. "Get up, sleepy one. I want to enjoy the day with you."

Isabella giggled as she thrashed around on the bed. "All right, all right, stop tickling me." It was then that an odd sense of déjà vu came over her. She tried to focus on the feeling. She closed her eyes, trying to recall the memory, but let it go, remembering that it wasn't of her and Grayson. She was remembering a morning with Julian. Isabella pushed him out of her mind and smiled at her husband.

Grayson climbed on top of her and grabbed her wrists, pinning her to the bed. Hovering over her, he brought his nose to hers. "I'll stop tickling you if you promise you'll get out of bed."

Isabella kissed his perfect lips. "I'll make you a deal."

"Oh, this I have to hear." Grayson grinned suspiciously.

"I'll get out of bed if you massage my shoulders first," she said, trying to look innocent.

"Hmmm . . ." Grayson rubbed his chin, as if pondering the offer. "So let me get this straight. If I massage your shoulders, you'll get out of bed so we can head out and spend the day together, but if I don't, you'll stay in bed all day and let me enjoy this beautiful day on my own?"

"Yep, that's right." Isabella mischievously smiled at him.

Grayson let go of her wrist and jumped off the bed. "Okay then, sleep the day away."

"Hey, that wasn't nice." Isabella chucked her pillow at him.

Grayson smiled. "Neither is bribing your husband for a massage."

"As if that has ever been an issue. Since when do you not want to give me a massage?"

"I'm saving my hands for my paintings tomorrow."

"Oh really?"

Grayson smiled and nodded.

Isabella got up on her knees, tilted her head seductively, and pouted out her lip. "Please, I've been so stressed. It's the least you could do before you torture me with a run today."

Grayson smiled at her. She looked amazingly adorable, enticing him as she always did. He charged the bed, grabbed her by the waist, and threw her back onto the bed.

"Careful," Isabella shouted, fearing that his rough play would hurt the baby.

"Careful? Since when? You always like it when I play rough with you."

"I do, but I just got out of the hospital the other day. I'm still trying to recoup, hence the massage."

Grayson kissed her hard on the lips and rolled over, pulling her on top of him. "Okay, how about I propose another deal?"

"Which is?"

"I will massage your shoulders now, then we will go for our run, but when we return, I would like to spend some time with you back in this bed, minus the tank top and shorts you have on. What do you say to that deal?"

Isabella smiled. "Yes, I would like that."

"Really?" Grayson asked, surprised that she had agreed so quickly.

"Yes, really. I haven't been feeling well. You know that, and I'm sorry. Today is the first day since, well . . . since I can remember that I feel human again. I mean, I still have a little nausea, but the doctor said that would subside soon. I think I feel better mentally."

"That is so good to hear. I'm glad you finally seem to be turning that corner. What changed, though?"

Isabella shrugged her shoulders. "Maybe it was getting back to work this week, or maybe it was our talk and recognizing your efforts to get us back on track. Maybe it was the fact that I passed out and was rushed to the hospital. That would scare anyone straight. Or maybe it was the meds. I really don't know." She knew it was the life that she was now carrying that had given her a new purpose.

Grayson squeezed her hand. "Well, whatever it was, I'm not complaining." He grinned and kissed her forehead. "I'm just happy to have my wife back. We have too much history to give up so easily. Too many sacrifices have been made for us to just walk away."

Isabella wondered if he was referring to both of them, or just him in particular. Although she would be devastated to lose his love, she knew her life in general would not be affected. His, on the other hand, would be greatly affected. Was that it? Was he fighting so hard to stay because of circumstances, or did he really love her? She knew she could never voice that without hurting him, so she pushed the thought aside.

"What are you thinking?" Grayson asked.

She paused, searching for something to say. To her relief, her stomach answered for her, letting out a loud growl. "I was thinking of how hungry I am. What do you say to some breakfast?"

"I would say that is the first time in weeks I've heard you ask for food. How about you jump in the shower, and I'll head down and rustle something up for us?"

She wrinkled her nose. "There's food down there?"

He laughed. "Yes. Unlike you, I do go grocery shopping once in a while."

After her shower, Isabella left the bedroom and could smell the breakfast aromas floating up the staircase. Enticing as they were, she paused at the landing and looked down the hall to the nursery. She turned away from the staircase, smiling, and wandered to the room. She was beaming from ear to ear as she stood at the doorway, looking in. It had been a while since she had come into the nursery. Everything looked so different to her now, in a good way. She no longer had to daydream of the baby she longed for. Now she actually envisioned being in there, holding her little bundle of joy. She couldn't believe that in six short months, her dream would come true. Isabella walked to the crib and felt the soft linens that lined the inside. Unbelievable warmth came over her. She felt as if she were in heaven.

"Here you are. Didn't you hear me calling you?" Grayson said as he came into the nursery, startling her. "What are you doing in here?"

"I'm sorry, I didn't hear you. I was on my way downstairs, but I came in here instead. I've just missed it, that's all." Isabella hoped she hadn't raised any suspicion with him. She wasn't ready to tell him about the baby just yet.

"I come in here a lot myself," he said. He stood behind her and wrapped his arms around her shoulders. "I'm hoping with us being back on track now, we can finally give this room an occupant." His hand wandered down and began to rub her belly.

Isabella stiffened. She didn't know anything about being pregnant, so she wasn't sure if he would be able to notice something different. She turned to face him, causing his hand to fall from her stomach. "I'm sure when the time is right for us, we will. But for now, let's enjoy us." Isabella winked at him.

"You're not going to put this off again, are you?"

"No, not at all. I do want a baby, but we're just getting back on our feet. That's all I'm saying. Let's focus on that first." Just then, her stomach growled again.

"I think you need to focus on food first. Come on, love, your breakfast is ready."

After breakfast, Isabella and Grayson stepped outside to enjoy the day. The weather was perfect. The sun was shining bright, and there was not a cloud in the sky. Summer was in full force, and the streets showed it. Crowds of people were out and about, soaking up the warm weather and enjoying the fresh air. As Isabella and Grayson strolled in the park, their conversation was nice and easy. They chatted about everything and nothing in particular. It reminded her of how their relationship used to be, before all their troubles started. They laughed and joked with such ease. It felt so good.

Grayson wound up running into a group of his friends who were playing a pick-up game of basketball. Isabella told him she was fine watching him play and encouraged him to join in. She found a spot on a hill near the basketball court and settled in to watch the testosterone fly on the court. Isabella was laughing as she watched them play. They were all acting like a bunch of hyped-up college boys, horsing around with each other so much that Isabella wasn't sure just how much basketball was being played. She wondered when it was that men actually grew up.

"It's been a long time since I've seen you smile like that. I do miss that smile."

Isabella's smile faded as she recognized the voice. She turned to see that Julian had managed to sneak up beside her. Fear filled her as she scrambled to her feet.

"Bella, don't be frightened. I just wanted to say hello to you."

"Get away from me," she hissed.

Julian smiled. "I don't know why you're getting so upset. You know I would never hurt you."

"Really? Putting your hand over my mouth so I couldn't scream while I lay in my hospital bed is not hurting me? You're crazy."

"I did no such thing, my Bella. I never came to see you at the hospital."

"Stop calling me that. I'm not your Bella. I know what happened that night."

"Correct me if I'm wrong, but didn't you go a little crazy after Gia's tragic demise? Maybe that's why you thought I was there, but I can assure you I wasn't."

Isabella glared at him. "I know you were there, just like I know you killed her."

Julian rolled his eyes. "Are you still hung up on that? Really, you need to let that go already. I've told you many times, I did not kill your precious little whore."

Isabella slapped him across his face so hard, pain shot through her own hand. "You bastard. I'm revolted to think that I ever had feelings for you. Get away from me."

Julian stood there rubbing his cheek and grinning. "There's my girl. You found your feistiness again. Bravo. I'm so proud of you."

"What's going on here?" Grayson said as he came running up the hill. He looked at Isabella. "Are you okay?" She was shaking and unable to answer. Grayson turned to Julian. "What the hell did you say to her?"

"Nothing. I came over because I saw her sitting here smiling and looking so happy. I simply said how proud I was that she seemed to be back to herself again." Julian glanced at Isabella, who was staring through him with eyes that could kill. "All of a sudden, she just wigged out on me. Honestly, I'm sorry if my praise caused her any distress. That was not my intention."

Grayson looked at Isabella again, but she said nothing. He sighed and turned back to Julian. "Listen, man, maybe that was not your intent, but it's obvious that your presence upsets her. I think it's best if you leave right now."

Julian nodded. He turned and started to walk away, but stopped and looked back. "Look, I'm sorry. But I still worry about her."

"She's not your concern," Grayson replied. "She's mine. She made her choice, and it wasn't you. It's time that you cut your ties to her."

"I understand, but there's no need to be cruel about it. I still love her very much, you know. That doesn't just go away."

"She doesn't love you, and she never will. She loves me, and the sooner you realize that and leave her alone, the sooner we all can get our lives back."

"We'll see." Julian smirked and walked away.

Grayson exhaled loudly and turned to Isabella. "Are you okay?"

"I'm sorry," she whispered. "We were having such a great day."

"You have nothing to be sorry about, Izzie. I know he pushes your buttons. That's why I rushed over here when I saw him."

"He's never going to go away, you know," she said sadly with tears in her eyes.

"I'll make sure he does. Don't you worry, baby. I promise, everything will get better . . . real soon." Grayson pulled her into his arms and stared at Julian, who stood watching them from a distance.

Chapter 35

Notwithstanding the run-in with Julian, Isabella and Grayson spent a wonderful weekend together, reconnecting and renewing their faith in one another. Isabella felt like their relationship was back on track. She knew without a doubt that she had made the right choice in staying, and she felt she was close to telling Grayson she was expecting his baby. She had wanted to share it with him so many times that weekend, but the moment never seemed quite right. She wanted it to be special, and while they had shared many intimate moments, something had always stopped her.

Isabella started her work week with a renewed spirit. She felt that her head was clear and she was ready to focus on launching the furniture line. That clarity and sense of determination to push for the project completion couldn't have come at a better time. Her week was filled with media interviews and photo shoots, followed by last-minute meetings to go over details for the launch party that weekend.

Charles Vanderbeck had spared no expense on the venue for the party, and the details were planned to perfection. It was going to be the must-attend party of the year, as far as Isabella was concerned. She felt this was finally her moment to shine, and she was ready to bask in the spotlight. She had made peace with the demons that had haunted her as best as she could, knowing that in order for her to regain any sort of normalcy, she needed to put her grief behind her.

What she found most difficult was ridding her mind of the fear that Julian was lurking out there, plotting his next move. She knew her fears were largely due to the special cargo she was now carrying. She prayed that she could keep her pregnancy hidden as long as possible. The last thing she needed was him getting wind that she and Grayson were having a baby. Memories of how crazed he was when he thought she was pregnant before still sent chills up her spine. It helped to have Grayson on board with her. After the run-in at the park, he had seemed more receptive to her concerns over Julian's odd behavior. To ease her anxiety, he had hired extra security to work the entrance of the party.

Isabella and James spent the better part of Monday putting together outfits for her interviews. She had a variety of looks to choose from depending on the magazine or news outlet doing the interviewing. In addition to the interview outfits, they had found an amazing Gucci gown for her to wear to the party. The strapless dress was the epitome of modern elegance, with just the right amount of bling. The bodice was adorned with rectangular gold and black sequins set in a modern geometrical pattern. The dress was cinched at the waist with a wide black belt that accentuated her tiny frame. The skirt flowed to the floor, with thousands of black sequins that subtly shimmered in the light. A sexy slit up the side showed off just the right amount of leg.

James gasped when she came out of the dressing room. He suggested that she should wear her hair in a high, sleek ponytail, making the ensemble chic. Isabella agreed as she looked in the mirror, thinking she was the spitting image of retro Barbie—with dark hair, of course.

To ensure she looked her best for the interviews, James had scheduled a makeup artist and hairstylist for the week. In her office hung a long list of all the interview and prep times that preceded each interview. Next to that was a rack filled with her wardrobe options. He had done a fabulous job of organizing everything for her. She would have been lost without him. James had known that she wouldn't be up to overseeing any aspect of the interviews herself, and although he didn't say it, he was hoping the makeup artist could help her look less pale and withdrawn.

As the week progressed, Isabella gained more confidence with each interview. She learned to calm her nerves by trying to forget about the cameras in the room and focus on the interviewer. She reminded herself not to babble on, answering the questions in the quickest and most efficient way possible. By far, her easiest interviews were the ones that included Charles. She allowed him to take the lead as she nodded, answering only when directly addressed.

Isabella was amazed at the stability she had regained in such a short time. She was proud of herself when she thought about how far she had come since her first interview, when she had been a nervous wreck and required Julian to calm her down. Through these interviews though, she was calm, cool, and collected. James, too, was pleasantly surprised by the ease with which she breezed through them.

By Friday, everyone in the office was buzzing around, preparing for the anticipated event. The launch of the furniture line was not only a major deal for Isabella, but for her entire company. The media push that was in full force had taken Hughes & Associates to another level, presenting them as the must-have design firm of the greater New York area. The designers had been fielding calls all week in regard to their services and the new furniture line, not only from clients, but from other designers as well. The work schedule was quickly filling up with prospective projects and new clients. Isabella couldn't have been more ecstatic.

Isabella had always strived for the status of an elite design firm, but she secretly feared that she wouldn't be able to handle the fame and the massive workload, combined with the responsibilities of a baby. It was certainly not a good time to be a new mother, and she was still struggling inside. She wasn't the strong businesswoman she had once been. She hoped Grayson would be able to offer some suggestions or wisdom about how all of that was going to work . . . that is, when she finally told him. Isabella planned to surprise him with the news after they got home from the party. It was the perfect occasion. She wanted to be able to make it *their* night, not just hers. She saw it as a new beginning of sorts, with the launch of her furniture line and the completion of his artwork for Vanderbeck's building. What could be better than mixing in the excitement that they were expecting a baby? Isabella felt that she and Grayson were back on the right path, one that would lead them into a lifetime of happiness. The ominous black cloud that had hovered over her was slowly starting to lift and dissipate. There was hope on the horizon.

Isabella's alarm went off far too early for a Saturday. She hit the snooze button and rolled onto her side, closing her eyes, but as she did so, she remembered . . . today was the day. Isabella smiled and lay on her back, staring up at the metal beams on the ceiling, envisioning just what the day would bring. Her day was scheduled out precisely to the hour. She had planned to grab a quick breakfast before heading to the spa, where she would indulge in a manicure, pedicure, and deep-cleansing body scrub so her skin would look immaculate. James had planned to join her. They were going to spend the morning together getting pampered, then have lunch and return to Isabella's to get ready. James had arranged for her makeup artist and hairstylist to meet them at the loft. After the "villagers," as James called them, worked their magic on her, Sebastian would pick them up, and they would be off to the party. At first James had felt a little awkward about tagging along with Grayson and Isabella, but she had refused to have him drive alone and had insisted that he join them.

Isabella actually had butterflies in her stomach. She looked at Grayson, who was sleeping soundly beside her. She caressed his hair as she snuggled up close to him, kissing his neck.

"Good morning," she whispered in his ear before kissing him again.

"Are you up?"

Grayson let out a soft moan and rolled over onto his side. Isabella moved closer and wrapped her arms around his shoulders. "I'm so excited about today. It's time to get up. We have a lot to do before all the fun can begin."

"*You* have a lot to do," he mumbled. "I only need fifteen minutes, thirty tops. Besides, I'm not feeling well, baby. I need more sleep."

"What's wrong?"

"I don't know. I have a pounding headache and just don't feel well."

"Oh no, please tell me you're not getting sick." Isabella felt his forehead. She couldn't tell if he felt warm from being under the covers or if he had a slight fever. "Can I get you anything?"

"I could use some aspirin, babe."

"You got it." Isabella brought him a couple of aspirin and a glass of water and watched as he popped the pills into his mouth and took a long swig of the water. He handed the glass back to her and fell into his pillow.

"I hope you're going to be okay," she said worriedly. "Today is a really big day. I really want you there with me."

Grayson looked up at her sad face and touched her cheek. "I'll be fine, love. It's just a headache—please don't worry. Wild horses couldn't keep me away from your side tonight. I just need a little more sleep, I think. Go and relax with James at the spa, and I'll see you when you get back."

Isabella leaned over and kissed his forehead. "Okay. I'll have my cell phone if you need anything. You can call me anytime, and I'll come right back."

Grayson smiled. "You're sweet, but I'll be fine. Now go and have fun with your girlfriend."

~~~

"Seriously, Izzie, what do you think of this pomegranate martini red?" James said as he grabbed the nail polish bottle off the shelf and slid into the pedicure chair next to her.

Isabella rolled her eyes. "You are *not* doing color on your nails."

"Oh, stop." James waved her off. "This is too trashy for me. I would never do red. I was thinking for you." He smiled innocently.

Isabella let out a high-pitched gasp. "Are you implying I'm trashy?"

James looked over his glasses at her. "If the pleather boot fits." He smirked.

She threw her hand towel at him. "That's a lot of sassy talk for someone who's looking for another raise." She smirked back at him.
~~~

"I love how you always threaten me with money."

"It's your weakness, this I know."

"Yes, sadly it is." James sighed and reached for a small white box on the table next to his chair. "And I know that your weakness is chocolate." James opened the box and turned it around, revealing four large, perfectly dipped chocolate-covered strawberries.

Wide-eyed, Isabella tried to snatch the box from his hands, but he was too quick for her. Isabella glared at him. "Oh, that is so mean. You do know that you're not supposed to tease a pregnant woman with food, right?"

James kissed her cheek and handed her the box. "I didn't, but after seeing that look in your eyes and knowing how much I value my life, they're all yours, honey."

Isabella chose one of the confections and took a huge bite. She closed her eyes, savoring each chew. "James, these are amazing. Where did you get them?"

"You know I don't kiss and tell." He winked at her.

"Oh yeah, that's right, your lips are never loose." She licked the chocolate off her fingers.

James waved her off again. "Okay, whatever. Think of it as a bargaining tool."

"*Bribery* is more like it. Fine, don't tell me, but I expect a box of these every Friday on my desk while I'm pregnant."

"What do I get in return?"

"You get to keep your job."

"I hate that you always have the upper hand," he huffed.

"One day you'll be the boss, and then you can have the upper hand." She grinned. "Thank you for coming with me today. You always make me laugh and forget about whatever worries are flying through my head."

"What are you worried about? Everything will go smoothly tonight, you'll see."

"It's just a big night, and I want everything to be perfect."

"I'm sure it will be fine. Mr. Vanderbeck and his staff have had countless meetings about the party, you know that. Everything is precisely planned. The night will be seamless. I guarantee you there will be no problems."

Isabella looked down at her feet as the warm water bubbled around them. She secretly feared that her special day would be the perfect breeding ground for Julian's mayhem and revenge. She didn't trust him in the slightest, and wouldn't put it past him to wait for an opportunity like this to bring her down. She couldn't help but think that during some important moment, he would make his grand entrance and cause a scene. The last thing she needed was to be embarrassed in front of the press and Charles.

"Hello, earth to Izzie." James snapped his fingers to get her attention. "Where did you drift off to?"

"I'm sorry. I was just thinking."

"You know I don't like to pry into your personal life. I always left that for Gia, but since she's not here, I feel I need to step in for her. Is everything okay with you and Grayson?"

Isabella realized that even though she was close to him, she hadn't shared much of her personal life with him. "Yes, everything is good with Grayson. It wasn't for a long time, but now we're doing great."

"If it's not Grayson, what is it? What's really bothering you?"

Isabella sighed again. "It's complicated."

"You know I do complicated very well." James smiled and reached for her hand. "Talk to me."

Isabella searched his eyes, wondering if he really could handle her thoughts and feelings, and more so, if she should even express them. Without waiting for her mind to process an answer, the words fell from her mouth. "It's Julian. I worry that he's . . . well, that he's not right with the way things ended. I keep thinking that he'll somehow disturb the event tonight." Isabella held her breath, waiting for her words to sink in.

He gave her a puzzled look. "I don't understand. Why would Julian cause you issues? I thought he left rather amicably."

"There's a lot you don't know. I'll tell you everything eventually, but for now, that's all I can really say." Isabella squeezed his hand. "I hope you understand."

James nodded. "I know you've never been someone who likes to air her dirty laundry in public, so I get it. I want you to know, though, that no matter what has happened, I'll always have your back."

"I appreciate that, I really do."

"As far as tonight is concerned, I'll make sure that he won't step one foot inside that ballroom or come anywhere near you. That is a solid promise. I know you have a lot riding on this; we all do."

Isabella leaned over the side of her chair and kissed his cheek. "Thank you. You're an amazing friend. Gia would be proud of you."

James patted her hand. "Stop, you're making me blush."

"Please, I know you love compliments."

James winked at her. "Well, of course, but I have to at least pretend to be humble, you know."

Isabella shook her head and laughed. She was thankful he was there with her and that she had found the courage to voice her fears. It was hard to keep everything inside all the time.

James picked up their glasses of sparkling water and handed one to Isabella. "Let's make a toast," he said, holding his glass out to her. "Here's to you, Isabella Hughes, and everything you've done to bring this moment to fruition. May the celebration tonight be everything you desire it to be, and may your fears be replaced by happy thoughts and joyous memories."

Isabella touched her glass to his. "From your lips to God's ears." She smiled half-heartedly, hoping that someone out there heard that.

After their pedicures, Isabella wandered back down the hallway, looking for the women's locker room. She got herself turned around and somehow wound up in the meditation room instead. She peeked in and noticed a snack bar, including a pitcher of watermelon water and other healthy snacks. Isabella quietly closed the door and poured herself a glass of water, then took a handful of trail mix from a bowl next to some delicious-looking muffins.

"It's addictive. Once you start eating, you can't stop."

Isabella spun around. Her glass slipped out of her hand and hit the counter as the trail mix scattered on the floor. Julian sat in a chair near the fireplace at the other end of the room.

"What are you doing here?" she demanded. "Are you following me?"

Julian laughed and stood up, loosening the tie on his white terrycloth robe. Isabella backed up as he approached her, but realized there was nowhere to go when she bumped into the counter behind her. She glared at him with her arms crossed over her chest. He moved toward her liked a jungle cat ready to strike its prey, his eyes piercing through her as he licked his lips. She knew no pure thoughts were running through his mind. Julian reached out to touch her arm, but she flinched away.

"Someone is jumpy." He grinned. "I didn't follow you. I'm here for my weekly massage. I had no idea you would be here, but this is a delightful surprise."

"I have to go." Isabella tried to push past him, but he stepped in front of her and grabbed her arm to block her escape. Isabella slapped his hand away and stepped back. She was shaking and could hear her heart pounding in her ears. "Don't touch me."

"Bella, I don't know why you're so frightened by me or my touch. I'm surprised that you've already forgotten how much you loved it when I touched you, how you always craved to be in my arms. You remember how good it felt, don't you?" He smiled as he let his robe fall open, exposing his naked body to her. "You remember how much you liked this." He reached down and stroked his shaft.

"Stop it," she hissed. "I don't have any feelings for you. In fact, you need to get it through your head that I despise you."

"*Despise* is a hefty word. I know you couldn't possibly feel that way. Not after all we shared."

"Yes, Julian, that is exactly how I feel. You made me feel that way."

Julian shook his head as his smile faded. "No. I know you don't feel that way. It's Grayson. He's putting those thoughts in your head. He's always getting in the way, injecting his venom into your mind, making you think these ugly, untruthful things about me. He has to go away so you and I can be together." Julian grabbed her by the wrists, pulling her against him. "We belong together. You know we do."

Isabella's face contorted in fear. She realized she wasn't the one in danger . . . Grayson was. But resisting Julian now would only fuel his vendetta. She needed to find a way to calm him long enough to buy her and Grayson some time.

"Julian, you need to listen to me. So much has happened between us. I'm sorry that things have gotten this bad. Maybe I went about it wrong, I don't know, but I think we need to step back and take some time to figure things out. I hear you, I do, but you need to give me time to sort through my feelings. Can you do that?" Isabella held her breath, praying he believed her act.

"I've waited long enough. I miss you. I don't want to go another day without you near me."

"I know, but I can't make everything right in a day. Please, I beg you."

Julian carefully searched her eyes. "You're lying. You don't want to fix this. You want to stay with him. Don't lie to me." His nostrils flared.

"Julian, please lower your voice. This is not the time or the place to be having this discussion. All I'm asking for is time. If you love me like you say you do, why can't you give that to me?"

"How much time do you want?" he questioned, still suspicious.

"I don't know. I just know that the problems we have are not going to go away overnight. You have to understand that."

He stared at her for a long moment. "Do you love me, Bella?"

Isabella's gaze fell to the floor as she considered what she should say, but there was only one thing she could say. She swallowed, knowing she had to lie. She raised her eyes to his, only to shudder from the evil that she saw there. "You know the answer to that."

"I want to hear you say it," he whispered.

"With all that we've been through, of course I do. I'm not a hard and callous person. I can't shut off my feelings so readily." Her voice was barely audible.

Julian pulled her into his arms and held her tight. Isabella froze as every hair on her body stood at attention and every nerve ending fired warning signals. The feel of his naked body against hers repulsed her. She swallowed back the need to gag. Her heart sank as she realized that she had just made a deal with the devil himself.

Julian kissed the top of her head. "I knew you did. I've always known you loved me. I'll give you what you asked for, but I won't wait long."

Isabella pulled away from his grasp, forcing a smile. "I know, and I appreciate that."

"Mr. Grossaint?" a woman called out as she opened the door. "Are you ready for your massage now?"

"Yes, thank you. I'm coming." He stayed facing Isabella as he fastened his robe. "I'll see you soon, then."

Relieved that the massage therapist had come in when she had, Isabella smiled slightly as Julian kissed her cheek before heading off to his massage. As soon as the door closed, she fell to her knees in tears. He was crazy, this she knew. She also knew that Grayson was in more danger than she had realized. She would not allow Julian to hurt him. She couldn't endure the pain and heartache of losing someone she loved ever again because of him. She would stop him at all costs. He would not win this time. Yes, that she was certain of.

Chapter 36

"You're worrying again, aren't you?" James asked as they left the café.

"I'm fine."

"Please, you are not fine. You barely said two words at lunch, and you kept pushing your food around your plate. Correct me if I'm wrong, but I believe you said you were starving."

Isabella sighed. She had not told him about her run-in with Julian. Still shaken and confused, she wanted to call Detective Stone but feared that would only cause more issues. She knew in her heart the only person she could confide in was Grayson. All she kept focusing on was that she needed to get through the evening, and then she could deal with the whole situation in the morning. She was pretty confident that he would not show his face at the party, but after that, she wasn't so confident that he would stay away from her, or Grayson, for that matter.

"Okay, you got me. I snuck into the meditation room and grabbed a few snacks before we left. I knew I couldn't make it," Isabella lied, trying to throw him off the track.

"You know there's a problem when you're closet snacking, missy. You're eating your way up to those pants with the hideous stretchy panel in the front." James wrinkled his nose.

"Shut up. I am not." Isabella laughed and rolled her eyes, wishing that she could live a day in his naive mind. She was, however, grateful that he was easy to distract. He would never make a good detective—or hunting dog, for that matter.

James looked at his watch. "We need to pick up the pace. Your villagers will be at your loft in less than twenty-five minutes. You still have to shower, you know."

"I'm pregnant. Don't rush me."

"Yeah, like only three months. You can't use that excuse already." James swatted her behind. "Move it, sister. We have the daunting task of taking you from frumpy stepsister to beautiful princess. We're going to need all the time we can get."

"Hey, that wasn't nice."

"Neither are dark circles or bad hair. Move it."

Isabella punched him in the arm.

"Ouch. What was that for?" He rubbed his arm.

"Consider it a love tap." She smirked and hurried down the street ahead of him, leaving thoughts of Julian behind her.

When they reached her loft, Isabella noticed that everything looked as it had when she left that morning. She immediately ran up the stairs to check on Grayson and let out a loud, disappointed huff when she saw him still lying in bed.

"Are you still not feeling good, babe?" she asked worriedly as she sat down on the edge of the bed next to him.

Grayson barely opened his eyes as he looked up at her. "I'm so sick. I can't remember feeling this crappy. I think I must have the flu or something. My head is pounding and my stomach is queasy."

Isabella felt his forehead. He didn't feel feverish, but he didn't look well. "Is there anything I can get you?"

"No, I'll be okay," he said as he closed his eyes.

"How about I get you some soup or something? Have you eaten at all?"

"No, babe. I don't feel like eating anything. I don't think I could keep it down if I did."

"Ginger ale . . . I'll get you some ginger ale. That will help your stomach." Isabella started to get up, but Grayson reached for her arm.

"Babe, I'm fine. Don't worry about me. You have to get ready."

"I think I can afford the few minutes it would take to get you something to drink. In fact, I have a better idea." Isabella went out into the hall and called down to James, asking him to bring up some ginger ale and crackers for Grayson.

"Now you have your employees waiting on me?" He chuckled.

"Please, he likes to feel needed. He's a little ADD and is better if he keeps busy."

"How was the spa?"

Isabella sat down on the end of the bed with her back to him and started to take off her shoes. She knew he would be able to tell she was lying, so she didn't want to look at him. "It was good. Nice and relaxing. I had a great time with James."

"That's good. I'm glad you two are getting closer." Grayson started rubbing his temples. "If you don't mind, I'm going to lie here for a little bit longer, and then I'll get up and out of your way so your crew can come in."

"Absolutely not. You don't have to leave your own bed. I'll just have them set up downstairs or in the nursery. Don't even worry about it. I want you to rest."

"It's not a big deal. I can go lie on the sofa in the nursery. I have to get up soon anyway to get ready myself."

Isabella sat down next to him. "Babe, how are you going to do that? Look at you. You look miserable."

"I'm not missing your special night."

"You're sick, Grayson," she said, trying not to sound bummed.

"You go to work sick. Why can't I go to your event sick?"

"That's different. This is a huge social party. You can't just sit in a corner somewhere. You'll have to mingle and talk with people. You'll be miserable."

"I'll be fine." He tried to sound convincing.

Isabella glared at him, knowing he was only being his stubborn self.

"Okay, stop giving me the evil eye. Let me rest some more, and we'll see. If I'm not better an hour before you have to leave, I'll stay home. But if I feel well enough to get up, you need to zip your lip and let me go." Grayson smiled at her. "Deal?"

"Of course it's a deal. I would like nothing more than to have you there."

Grayson touched her cheek. "You're sweet. Do you know how much I love you?"

"I think I do. Too bad you're not feeling better, because then you could really show me." Isabella winked at him and kissed his forehead.

"Your sexual appetite is insane."

"Well, look at you. Who could resist this?" Isabella pointed at his handsome face.

"OH MY GOSH, you're not even in the shower yet," James shouted as he came in with Grayson's ginger ale and crackers. "Isabella Hughes, get your ass moving, please."

"I'm going, I'm going. I just wanted to see how he was doing."

James pulled her off the bed and shooed her toward the bathroom. "Get in there. I'll take care of him."

"Try to get him to eat something," she said over her shoulder.

"I've got this. Now go." James gave her one last shove and shut the bathroom door. He turned around and shook his head. "I swear, how do you put up with her?"

"It's not easy, believe me," Grayson said, shaking his head.

Over the next two hours, the make-up artist and hair stylist worked their magic on Isabella. Instead of the high ponytail, they opted to do large, soft waves throughout her long hair. They kept it more tousled than perfectly styled for a subtle edge. To compliment the edge in the hairstyle, the makeup artist created a sophisticated smoky eye with a nude lip. She was amazed when she looked in the mirror and saw her hair falling nicely down her back, with a small portion seductively cascading over her shoulder. It had a shine normally reserved for models gracing the pages of Vogue. Her makeup was stunning, making her skin look flawless. It wasn't until she slipped into her dress that everyone in the room stood back in awe. James swore she looked like a runway model—only shorter and older, he teased.

As she gazed at her reflection, she felt tears well up in her eyes. This was a far cry from the person she had seen in the café window not too long ago. She had come a long way in a short time, but she still had a long way to go. Tonight, though, she only wished that she felt the confidence her outward appearance exuded. Thoughts of Julian kept creeping back into her mind, tormenting her. It revolted her that she'd had to tell him that she loved him. The very thought made her stomach turn. Worse, he was out there now believing that she still did. She had no idea how she was going to rectify that or how she could ensure that Grayson was safe once Julian knew the truth.

Before leaving for the party, Isabella tiptoed in to see Grayson. She'd had James check on him an hour before she was ready to go, and he'd reported that Grayson was out cold. Isabella knew there was no way he would make it to the party. She kissed her finger and placed it on his lips before turning to leave.

"Izzie?" he said. "Are you leaving already?"

She turned back to him. "Yes, Sebastian is waiting for me downstairs. How are you feeling?"

"Like a shitty husband for not being there for you tonight."

"You're sick, babe. You can't control that. I know you would be there if you could. Am I bummed? Sure, but these things can't be helped."

"I know. I just wish it hadn't happened tonight. I hate disappointing you."

Isabella sat down next to him and took his hand in hers. "You didn't disappoint me. I don't blame you. I blame the damn flu bug."

"Thanks, babe. You look amazing." He kissed her hand. "I'm so proud of you, not only for what you've accomplished with the furniture line, but with how far you've come since Gia died. I know it's been a tough road for you, but looking at you now, no one would guess the struggles you've been through. I hope this means that better things are to come for you—for us."

Isabella smiled. He had no idea how right he was. There *was* something better to come. *Well, someone*, she thought. It made her even more excited to come back and spring the news on him.

Ten minutes later, Isabella was in the limo as it proceeded down Fifth Avenue. She could see the Plaza Hotel in the distance. Charles Vanderbeck had selected the venue for its prestigious name and location. Located in the heart of Manhattan, it was the most luxurious, iconic hotel in the world. With its fantastic architectural details and rich history, it was the perfect location for the launch party. Charles had secured the massive 4,800-square-foot Grand Ballroom for the party. Crews had been working for days setting up vignettes of furniture throughout the ballroom, while still allowing for a good amount of traffic in the room.

Using his impeccable culinary skills, the executive chef for the Plaza had created a spectacular menu of petite plates and appetizers. The strolling buffet concept was perfect, as it allowed for the guests to nibble as they moved around the room and took in the vignettes. The party was also to be staffed with an army of servers, waitstaff, and bartenders. Vanderbeck was adamant that each guest be catered to from the moment they stepped through the door.

Isabella looked out the window of the limousine as they pulled up to the entrance. She smiled as she noticed the Pulitzer Fountain of Abundance, thinking how perfect that was. She hoped that it was a good sign, signifying what was to come for her.

"Here we go. Are you excited?" James squeezed her hand as they pulled up to the front of the Plaza.

"I literally have bats in my stomach. I'm so nervous."

"Don't worry, Izzie. There is nothing to be nervous about. The furniture is spectacular. Everyone will love it. Just go in there and be yourself. Work the party as you usually would, and try to enjoy yourself."

"You'll stay close by?" she nervously asked.

"I'll be your shadow all night. Wherever you go, I'll be there, except for the ladies' room. I've been in ladies' rooms before; you guys are pigs." James made a disapproving face.

Isabella laughed. "I love the bowtie, by the way. You look extremely handsome."

"Oh good, because I'm hoping to meet some hot guy tonight. Well, I'd better meet some hot guy tonight. How could I not, with the caliber of people invited?" He winked at her. "You ready to do this?"

"Yes, go ahead and open the door." She took a deep breath and exhaled slowly.

James reached for the door handle, but she grabbed his arm, stopping him.

"I thought you were ready," he said.

"One more thing, James . . . I love you so much. Thank you for everything you've done for me." Isabella hugged him tight.

"Not as much as I adore you."

James opened the door, and they were blinded by a sea of camera flashes.

Chapter 37

Four hours later, Isabella sat in the back seat of the limo, beaming from ear to ear. The launch had been a complete success for her, as well as for Charles Vanderbeck. There was already a buzz about the Vanderbeck Home collection, and offers had poured in from prominent retailers and high-end designers wanting to carry the furniture line. All their hard work over the last year had finally paid off. The room buzzed with high praise for the pieces Isabella had designed. With James in tow the entire night, she had worked the room like a pro. She was introduced to several influential people and made some serious contacts that could potentially bring her even more business opportunities. It had been an amazing night overall. Isabella was excited to get home and share the good news with Grayson.

As the limousine pulled up in front of her loft, Isabella looked up to the dimly lit bedroom window. Sebastian opened the door for her.

"I just wanted to tell you, Mrs. Hughes, you absolutely shined tonight. Being your driver for all these years, I can honestly say that I'm more proud of you than I ever was before."

Isabella put her arms around him. "Aw, you're going to make me cry," she said as she hugged him. "I appreciate that, Sebastian. Thank you."

He gave her a squeeze back. "You're welcome, Mrs. Hughes. You go in and get some rest now. I'll be back for you Monday morning at nine."

"I'll see you then. Good night, Sebastian."

Sebastian waved as he got back into the limo, and Isabella bounded up the stairs. She was excited to finally be able to tell Grayson their good news. As she approached the loft door, she noticed that it was slightly ajar. She paused, trying to remember who had gone out the door last when she left, but then figured Grayson had ordered some takeout and forgot to close the door all the way.

"Grayson?" Isabella called out as she stepped inside, wondering if he was awake. She stood there listening for a response, but the apartment was quiet.

Isabella kicked off her stilettos and threw her purse on the console near the door. In the kitchen, she reached for a bottle of wine out of habit, but instead poured herself a glass of water. She turned off the lights and headed up the stairs.

"Grayson?" she called out again as she hit the upstairs landing. "Grayson, baby, I'm home, and I have some amazing news," she said as she walked into their bedroom. Isabella stopped at the doorway, letting her glass fall from her hand and shatter on the floor.

"Grayson! Oh my God!" she screamed as she rushed to the bed. His hands and feet were bound, and his mouth had been taped shut. Isabella's hands shook as she started to gently pull the tape from his mouth. "Oh my God . . . oh my God. Who did this to you?" When she was almost done removing the tape, she noticed his eyes looking beyond her. Sensing that someone was there, she spun around to see Julian standing there, watching.

Filled with rage, she charged at him, screaming as her arms lashed out and hit him over and over again. "*You!* You bastard. Why are you doing this?"

Julian snickered as he grabbed Isabella's wrists, trying to restrain her. She fought to free herself while he laughed, but her attempts were futile. She stopped fighting and began to sob, realizing she was getting nowhere.

"Bella, my love, where is all this anger coming from?" he asked.

Isabella glared at him. "You make me sick." She sobbed harder. "Why, why would you do this? What do you want from me?"

Julian touched her face, but Isabella flinched away from him, averting her gaze. "Oh Bella, you know how much I love you. I didn't do anything, sweetheart. You did this." He ducked down, bringing his face to within inches of hers. "It all could have been so simple, but you lied." Isabella felt his breath on her face. "Tsk, tsk, tsk, someone's been a very bad girl, telling someone they love them when they don't. Did you think I actually fell for your little act this afternoon?"

Isabella pulled her head back from his, her eyes no longer taking solace in the floor.

"We could have had a wonderful life together, you and me. The love we had was amazing. It was so passionate, so intense, but you ruined that by crawling back to your no-good loser husband. He doesn't deserve you. He doesn't appreciate you, and he certainly doesn't love you like I do."

Isabella looked at Grayson. The sight of him bound was more than she could bear. It reminded her of Gia. Isabella lowered her head and began to sob again.

With the tape no longer silencing him, Grayson shouted, "Let go of her, Julian. Izzie, don't listen to him. He's crazy."

"I don't remember anyone talking to you," Julian yelled. "I suggest you keep quiet before I do something you'll regret."

"Julian, please," she pleaded. "Please, please, I beg you, let him go. He's never done anything to you." Isabella cried louder as the realization sank in that Grayson's life was in danger.

"Oh, but you see, Isabella, that's where you're wrong. He has gotten in the way. He's taken away the one thing I love the most in this world—you. Now I'm going to take back what is mine and let him feel the pain I've felt all these months." Julian pulled her to him and slammed his lips down on hers, forcing his tongue into her mouth.

Isabella pulled away and spit in his face. "I'm not yours, and I never will be. You disgust me," she screamed, her voice shaking.

Julian backhanded her, cutting her face with his ring. Blood trickled down her cheek, and her face throbbed.

"You son-of-a-bitch," Grayson yelled, trying to break free from his restraints.

"Shut up," Julian ordered, then turned his attention to Isabella. He lifted her head and touched her reddened cheek. He wiped away the blood and licked it from his finger. "Why do you make me do this?" he asked. "You're always so difficult. It doesn't have to be this hard. Come here." He put his arms around her and kissed her forehead, then rested his head on hers. "Don't you get it? I love you. I've always loved you. From the moment I walked into your office, I knew I loved you, and I knew you felt the same way. Don't you want that love again? Don't you want to feel as you did before? Remember the endless nights of exploring each other, making love over and over again as we became one? I know deep down that you love me. How could you not? We can have all that again. We can be together. I know you want us to be together."

Isabella shook her head as she cried, pushing away from him. "I don't love you, Julian. I never loved you. You were just someone who was there, someone who saw my vulnerability, and like a snake you slithered your way into my life, into my bed. I could never love someone like you, someone who could do this. I will *never* love you!" she screamed.

Raged filled his eyes. He grabbed her by the throat and pushed her back until she slammed into the wall behind her. Isabella was stunned. She tried to struggle free from his grasp, but his grip was too tight. She started to choke.

"No," Grayson shouted, "leave her alone!"

Julian ignored him and continued squeezing the life from her. His eyes were wide and wild. “I think someone needs to be reminded of what we had,” he hissed through his teeth.

Julian whipped her around, pushed her face into the wall, and unzipped her dress, causing it to fall to the floor. He kicked the dress out of the way and yanked her back around to face him. Isabella stood there in her black bra and thong, shaking like a leaf, gasping for air.

“Julian, stop,” she begged, trying to push him off of her. “Let go of me. You don’t want to do this.”

Ignoring her, he rubbed the inside of her leg harshly, his fingers clawing into her skin. He tugged at her thong until it ripped in two. No matter how Isabella fought, he pushed his full weight against her, making it impossible for her to get away. He grabbed both of her wrists in one hand and held them above her head.

“Do you remember how much you loved me touching you? Touching you like this?” Julian plunged his fingers inside her.

“No! Stop! Please, Stop. Don’t do this,” she screamed. “You’re hurting me.”

As he forcefully violated her with his hand, he kissed and bit at her neck and breasts. His breathing increased as his arousal grew.

Isabella screamed louder. “Please help me. God no, please help me.”

Grayson watched in horror as Julian tormented her. “Don’t do this to her. Julian, please, I beg you, don’t do this.”

Julian looked back at him with a grin so sinister, so evil, Grayson knew he could not be stopped. He would take her, prove to her she was his for the taking, inflicting upon her a physical pain so horrific Isabella would not survive.

“No!” Grayson cried out.

Julian unzipped his pants. He pushed her legs apart with his, took his swelling penis out of his jeans, and rubbed her clit with his hard, wet tip. Isabella whimpered. Her legs trembled uncontrollably as he taunted her.

“Please, Julian,” she whispered as tears rolled down her face. “Please don’t do this, I beg of you. If you ever loved me, please don’t do this to me.”

Julian stilled for moment, searching her pleading eyes. He kissed her tears. “Shhh,” he whispered. A small smile formed on his lips as he slammed himself inside her without warning, thrusting and pushing her into the wall with such force she screamed. Isabella thrashed about, trying to free herself from his hold, but the pain crippled her attempts.

Julian brought his lips down hard on hers to quiet her screams. His tongue violated her mouth over and over again. Isabella couldn’t breathe. She was gasping for air, but he showed her no mercy as his mouth continued to cover hers. Finally he bit her lip as he pulled away and glared into her eyes.

"You remember, don't you?" he demanded. "You loved feeling me inside you, didn't you? Tell him—tell him how much you liked it. Tell him how we made love in Milan over and over again, in your bed, in your shower. You remember, don't you? You couldn't get enough."

"Shut up," Isabella screamed as she brought her knee up, trying to push him off of her.

Julian just laughed. "Tell him," he shouted at the top of his lungs.

Isabella violently shook as he continued thrusting himself inside her.

"It can always be like this, baby, just me and you. We can always be together." He retracted his hard cock from inside her for a moment, then plunged it back into her. Isabella screamed in agony as the force of his thrusts sent pain radiating through her pelvis. "You'll see. It will be perfect, just like you wanted it to be. We'll have the perfect love, the perfect marriage, the perfect life." He pulled her head back by her hair and stared into her eyes. "And one day, my love, we can finally have that family you always wanted—the one he would never give you." He began to pump faster and deeper inside her. Her thrashing and screaming only ignited his sick desire further. He was ready to claim her as Grayson watched.

Isabella tried to catch her breath in between sobs. "Julian, please, you're hurting me. Please stop . . . I'm pregnant," she blurted out.

In that moment of revelation, everything stopped. Julian stared at her as he tried to comprehend what she had said. Grayson's face went from terror to shock, as he realized that it was not only her life being threatened, but his baby's as well.

Julian grabbed her chin. "What did you say?"

"I'm pregnant," she whispered, knowing that her words would likely send him further off the deep end, but she held out hope that he would be encouraged to stop.

"Izzie," Grayson cried out. "Get off of her, Julian, or I swear to God I will kill you."

Julian paused to look at Grayson, then turned back to Isabella. He pushed himself off of her and slapped her across her face. "How could you do that? How could you let him do that to you, to us?" Julian grabbed her shoulders and shook her. "Bella, what have you done?"

"Julian, please let me go. I promise I won't say anything to anyone. You can go and be free. I promise."

He slapped her again, then rammed her head into the wall, causing her to fall to her knees. “You bitch. You ruined everything. How could you do this to us?” His voice boomed through the room as he stood over her, berating her like a child.

Julian started to pace back and forth while Isabella sobbed, still on her knees. He stopped in front of her, pulled a gun from under his shirt, and pointed it at her head.

“No,” Grayson pleaded. “Enough. This is over. Don’t hurt her, do you hear me? I’ll give you whatever you want, just please don’t hurt her.”

Julian raced to the bed and pushed the gun against Grayson’s forehead. “Whatever I want? Whatever I want?” he yelled. “I don’t want your money—or should I say *her* money. I want her. What part of that do you not understand? Once again, you’re getting in the way. Why won’t you just go away?” Julian smacked him in the temple with the gun.

He walked backed to Isabella, grabbed her hair, and dragged her to her feet in front of him. He put his arm around her shoulders to steady her against his chest. Isabella felt his panicked breaths on her neck.

He brought his lips to her ear and whispered, “Why did you do this? This was not the way it was supposed to be. This is your fault.” Julian released his grasp and began pacing again, while tapping his head with the gun and mumbling to himself. “How are we going to do this? How?”

Naked and shaking, Isabella looked at Grayson, who stared back at her, helpless, his eyes filled with horror. Isabella jumped when she felt Julian’s arm come back around her. He nuzzled his head into hers. Her stomach sank as she wondered what was next.

“It will take some time, but I’ll forgive you,” Julian said, kissing her neck, “just as in time you will love me. We’ll go far away from here and start over, the three of us—you, me, and our baby. I know I’ll grow to love our baby one day. It’ll just take some time.”

“No,” Grayson yelled. “Julian, enough is enough. I said let her go. It’s over.”

Julian pointed the gun at him. “Shut up before I permanently shut you up.”

“Please, don’t hurt him,” Isabella begged. “This is not his fault.”

Julian began to stroke her hair. “You’ll see, Bella my love. It will be fine. We will all be fine.” Julian kissed her head. “But before we can leave here, you need to take care of your mistake. We can’t have any loose ends running around.”

Julian placed the gun in her hands. Isabella refused to take it, but he wrapped her hands around it and placed his hands over hers.

"No," she protested. "I won't. I won't do this. Please, God, no."

"This is your mistake. You were right—all this is your fault. You made this mess and destroyed our lives. You chose this, Bella, and now you must take care of what you did."

"This has gone too far," Grayson said. "Leave now, and we won't go to the police. I promise. You can walk out of here a free man."

Julian ignored him and yelled at Isabella. "Do it! Do it now!"

Isabella's arms shook as she raised the gun. She looked tearfully into Grayson's eyes.

"Isabella, don't listen to him. He's crazy," Grayson pleaded.

Isabella shook her head. "He's right. This is my fault. All of this is my fault. I'm the one who did this." She sobbed and tried to catch her breath. "I'm the one who was weak and let him in. I'm the one who let him destroy everything that was good in my life, in our life. I'm responsible for Gia's death. I'm responsible for hurting you. It's my fault, Grayson, all of it is."

"Isabella, no, it's not your fault. You're letting him get into your head like he always does. This is not your fault. It's his fault. Think, Isabella—this is what he wants. He wants me out of the picture so he can have you to himself. That's all he wants."

Julian smiled and whispered in her ear, "That's my girl. Do it. Get rid of him." Julian dropped his hands from hers and stepped back. "Do it."

Shaking, Isabella pointed the gun at Grayson. A sob caught her breath as she looked into his beautiful blue eyes.

"I'm so sorry," she whispered.

"No!" Grayson screamed.

The gun went off, and the world went black.

Chapter 38

Isabella stood at the foot of the bronze casket and placed her hand on top. The feel of the cool metal made her shudder. She placed her other hand on Grayson's shoulder as he kneeled in front of the casket, praying.

"I'm sorry," she whispered, even though she knew he couldn't hear her or feel her touch.

She had taken her own life that day and the life of her unborn child because she knew in her heart that Julian was right. It was her fault—all of it. She had known that she and Grayson would never be free to continue on as they had before. Julian would always be there in one way or another, terrorizing them, and the only way she could give Grayson any chance of a normal life, any chance of happiness, was to leave.

The devastation he must have been feeling was undoubtedly great, but as hard as things might seem right now, time would pass, and he would be able to move on to a better place without her. Leaving this world was her final gift to him. He would go on to live and love another without the hurt and betrayal. *I owed that to him for all the pain and hurt I caused*, she thought sadly.

"Mr. Hughes, we are ready to proceed when you are," the priest said.

Grayson looked up to him. "Thank you, Father. I'm ready." He stood and bowed his head one last time in prayer, then reached into the casket, placing his hand on hers. "I love you. I wish things were different and you were here. I'll never forget you. Please take care of our little one for me until I can be with you two again." He leaned into the casket and kissed her cheek.

Grayson walked to his friends, who sat nearby, and took a seat between his friends Andre and Aidan, who put his arm around Grayson as he sat down. James sat nearby, looking devastated, his eyes red and swollen from the countless tears he had shed. The priest directed everyone else to take their seats as the funeral director closed the casket. Everyone bowed their heads, and the priest began one last prayer before Isabella was taken to her final resting place.

Isabella's friends filed out of the room and lined the hallway of the funeral home. A moment later, the casket was rolled past them. Grayson stood near the hearse, watching as his friends guided her casket into the back.

The morning air was cool and dewy as dark clouds covered the morning sun. A light fog hovered over the ground, making the grass wet. Isabella and Grayson's friends gathered around her casket at the gravesite. Those who had been here for Gia's funeral felt they had returned much too soon. Isabella would be laid to rest next to her beloved friend.

Isabella stood in the distance, watching Grayson and wondering what was going through his mind. It was a while after the last friend had passed that Grayson finally stood up to say his last goodbye. He knelt down and placed his head on the casket as he cried quietly. Feeling like she needed to be close to him, Isabella wandered over and knelt behind him, resting her head on his back as her own tears flowed.

I wish he could know how sorry I am for what I've done, sorry for betraying him the way I did, sorry for losing faith in our love. I wish he could know how deeply I regret taking away his opportunity to know his son and be the father he always wanted to be. The cross I carry is that of burden and undeniable regret.

Grayson stood and placed his hand on the casket one last time. "Goodbye, Izzie," he whispered, and walked away.

With her head bowed, Isabella walked in the opposite direction, glancing back at him one last time as she left him to continue his life without her.

Detective Ian Stone was waiting for Grayson near his car. "Mr. Hughes, I want you to know how sorry I am for your loss," he said.

"Thank you, Detective."

"Isabella's death came as a shock. The last time I saw her, I sensed she was troubled. I knew she wanted to tell me something, but I couldn't get her to open up to me. I wish there was something more I could have done to help her."

Grayson stared at Detective Stone. He had never really liked the man, and now it appeared that Stone had an odd obsession with his wife. "Well, seeing that she was my wife, I share your feelings."

Detective Stone felt a strange vibe run through him. Maybe it was Grayson's cold tone, or maybe it was his sense that Grayson was the reason Isabella had been afraid to open up. He wasn't sure, but his radar kept telling him something was off. "I want you to know that we're still working Gia's case, as I promised Isabella we would."

"I'm sure she would appreciate that, Detective, as I do. Now, if you'll excuse me, it would be in poor taste if I was late to her luncheon."

"Oh, sure, I'm sorry for taking up your time." Detective Stone pulled a card from his wallet and handed it to Grayson. "If there's anything you need, please don't hesitate to call me."

Grayson held up his hand. "Thank you, but I have your number from the last time you gave it to me. If I need you, I'll call." He slid into the back seat of the Town Car and shut the door.

Detective Stone felt uneasy as he watched the Town Car pull away.

~~~

After the funeral luncheon, James wandered around town like a lost puppy. He had no particular place to go, nothing he wanted to do, and certainly no one he wanted to see. He needed time alone. He found himself drawn to the office. He had a strong desire to feel close to Isabella and knew he could take comfort in her surroundings.

After learning of her death, he had shut the entire office down for a few days. He thought it was best to allow the employees a chance to grieve and come to terms with the tragic loss of yet another friend and colleague. James himself was having a hard time understanding how all this had happened. It was only a short time ago that Isabella had seemed on top of the world. He remembered how excited she was when she learned she was pregnant, how she had shone on the night of the launch party. He remembered her smiling and laughing. Nothing made sense.

James flicked on the light as he entered her office. His eyes filled with tears as he realized she would never be there again. Oh, how he missed her. He missed her endlessly poking fun at him and teasing him about his sweaters and his hair. He even missed her bossing him around the way she did when she was crabby. He missed all of it. They had grown so close after Gia's death. It wasn't fair that she wasn't with him now. He loved her with everything he had inside, and he knew he would forever miss having her in his life.

James wiped away his tears as he fell into her desk chair with a loud huff. *What now?* he thought as he looked around the room. What would happen to the company? He wondered what Grayson would do with Hughes & Associates. He knew Isabella would be devastated to see her business sold off and ripped apart. He wondered if there was any way he could keep things going for her. They still had the talent of the other designers, and with the name recognition the furniture line had brought, he was confident it would be successful. He would have to talk to Grayson when the time was right. There were too many thoughts running through his head to make sense of anything right then.

Hoping to organize his thoughts, James opened the top drawer of the
~~~

desk to look for a notepad. He was digging through the drawer when he discovered an envelope with his name on it. His heart raced as he recognized the handwriting. He tore the envelope open, his eyes frantically reading Isabella's words.

> *My Dearest James:*
>
> *I pray that you will never have to read this letter. If you are reading this, that means my worst fears have come true and something tragic has happened to me. There are so many things that you don't know, things I haven't told you for good reason. Please believe me when I say that I wasn't keeping this hidden from you because I didn't trust you. I do trust you, James. I was trying to protect you. I realize now that if I'm no longer here, I can't do that. You need to know the truth so you can protect yourself . . .*

James gasped and covered his mouth. He started to tremble and felt as if he was going to be physically ill.

"Oh my God," he whispered. How on earth had she kept this bottled up inside her? Now he understood everything. He realized why she was so shaken by Gia's death. It was her guilt, the feeling that she was in some way responsible for what had happened. "Oh, Izzie."

James looked in the envelope and found the card Isabella spoke of in her letter. He reached for the phone, his hands shaking.

A male voice answered. "This is Detective Stone."

"Detective Stone, my name is James Spencer," he said nervously. "I am—excuse me, I was Isabella Hughes's assistant. I remember speaking to you after Gia Hausen's death."

"Yes, James, I remember you. How can I help you?"

"I was wondering if I could come down to the station. I found something that I think you should see." James prayed he was doing the right thing, as Isabella had left it solely up to his discretion.

"May I ask what this is regarding?" Detective Stone asked.

"I found a disturbing letter that Isabella left for me, and I think you need to see it."

There was a pause. "How quickly can you get here?"

"I'm on my way now," James said.

"I'll be waiting."

~~~

Grayson arrived home at the loft, taking comfort in the quiet that greeted him. It had been a long day, and he was looking forward to
~~~

kicking back and relaxing with a large glass of scotch.

He tossed his keys on the counter, took a glass from the kitchen cabinet, and opened the freezer. As he threw some ice in his glass, he paused, looking at the food inside, and debated whether he was hungry. Choosing to stick with a liquid dinner, he shut the door and jumped as he came face-to-face with Julian.

The two stared at each other.

"I thought I told you never to come here," Grayson hissed through his teeth. "What if someone sees us together?"

Julian didn't blink. "I got a visit from Detective Stone today . . . we have a problem."

THE DECEPTION CONTINUES WITH...

NIGHT MINDS

COMING FALL 2014

22270133R00174

Made in the USA
Charleston, SC
13 September 2013